PRAISE FOR THE NOVELS OF DONNA THORLAND

Mistress Firebrand

"I loved this book from the first page and raced through it. The plot is seamless, the characters (all of them) compelling, and the romance just lovely. The two main characters are a perfect balance of equals. I consider this author a major find. . . . I am adding Donna Thorland to my list of favorite authors."

—Mary Balogh, *New York Times* bestselling author of
Beyond the Sunrise and *Longing*

"Donna Thorland is an author I adore, and I loved *Mistress Firebrand* every bit as much as her first two books, *The Turncoat* and *The Rebel Pirate*. Her unique mix of history, romance, and adventure all add up to create stunning, sensual stories you cannot put down. For readers who yearn for historical fiction with a distinctive edge, Thorland's Revolutionary War–set novels deliver."

—Jennifer McQuiston, *New York Times* and *USA Today*
bestselling author of *What Happens in Scotland*

The Rebel Pirate

"Donna Thorland has started her own revolution in American historical romance and placed her original stamp on an era. Authentic detail, amazing characters, and a dazzlingly broad sweep of action make this a richly romantic adventure that's hard to put down. Truly brilliant. Prepare to be blown away."

—Susanna Kearsley, *New York Times* bestselling author of
Season of Storms

"A fast-paced, soundly researched historical intrigue with vivid characters and sharp writing, *The Rebel Pirate* is a compelling read."

—Madeline Hunter, *New York Times* bestselling author of
His Wicked Reputation

continued . . .

"A stay-up-all-night, swashbuckling, breath-holding adventure of a novel . . . an extraordinary book about an extraordinary heroine."
—Lauren Willig, *New York Times* bestselling author of the Pink Carnation series

"Kept me up far too late . . . an absolutely gripping read."
—Meredith Duran, bestselling author of *Fool Me Twice*

"It's a trip into the dangerous past from the comfort of your reading chair, filled with romance, authenticity, and great storytelling—the very best of what historical fiction can be."
—Simone St. James, author of *Silence for the Dead*

"Thorland takes you on an incredible adventure through a wonderfully realized depiction of Colonial America. I was so taken by the story, I finished the novel in a single sitting. Highly recommended to anyone with a love of adventure, intrigue, and romance!"
—Corey May, writer of video game Assassin's Creed 3

"An exhilarating, intelligent, and superbly intricate spy thriller that keeps its tension vibrating and surprises crackling until the very last page. Heroine Kate is a strong, resourceful, and memorable character."
—*RT Book Reviews*

"A strong debut . . . provides a strong historical background for readers, with plenty of action in the field of battle to balance out the society and bedroom scenes."
—Historical Novel Society

"One high-stakes adventure, crossing historical fiction with romance, danger, and sex. . . . Thorland's believable dialogue steals each scene."
—New Jersey Monthly

OTHER NOVELS BY DONNA THORLAND

Renegades of the American Revolution Series

The Turncoat
The Rebel Pirate

Mistress Firebrand

RENEGADES OF THE AMERICAN REVOLUTION

DONNA THORLAND

NEW AMERICAN LIBRARY

New American Library
Published by the Penguin Group
Penguin Group (USA) LLC, 375 Hudson Street,
New York, New York 10014

USA I Canada I UK I Ireland I Australia I New Zealand I India I South Africa I China
penguin.com
A Penguin Random House Company

First published by New American Library,
a division of Penguin Group (USA) LLC

First Printing, March 2015

 REGISTERED TRADEMARK—MARCA REGISTRADA

LIBRARY OF CONGRESS CATALOGING-IN-PUBLICATION DATA:

Thorland, Donna.
  Mistress Firebrand: renegades of the American Revolution / Donna Thorland.
    pages cm
  ISBN 978-0-451-47101-7 (pbk.)
  1. Actresses—Fiction. 2. Manhattan (New York, N.Y.)—History—18th century—
Fiction. 3. United States—History—Revolution, 1775–1783—Fiction. I. Title.
II. Title: Renegades of the American Revolution.
  PS3620.H766M57 2015
  813'.6—dc23 2014036540

Printed in the United States of America
10 9 8 7 6 5 4 3 2 1

Set in Janson Text
Designed by Spring Hoteling

For Ellen,
whose story sense is invaluable

Mistress Firebrand

One

Manhattan Island
December 1775

John Burgoyne was in New York.

Jenny overheard the wine merchant telling the tavern keeper in hushed tones. She knew better than to look up when she felt their eyes on her. Two years in a city buffeted by mob violence and political intrigue had honed her instinct for self-preservation. She kept her head down and studied her mother's letter from home.

Seated beside one of the tall windows in the elegant taproom at the Fraunces Tavern, with its lofty ceilings and fine painted paneling, she nursed her single cup of chocolate and tried to concentrate on the words on the page, but her mind kept returning to Burgoyne. For the wine seller and the publican, Burgoyne's presence meant a business opportunity, and one that must be kept secret from the Liberty Boys, who had abducted a loyalist judge, an Anglican clergyman, and a British physician from their homes only the week before. Politics, the two merchants agreed, were terrible for trade.

They were also murder on the Muses. Isaac Sears and his rabble had stormed the theater, broken all the benches in the pit, and would have beaten the players as well if the company had been performing. Congress had closed all the other theaters in the colonies. Only New York's John Street remained open, performing without a license, and at the mercy of the Rebel mob, which saw it as a British institution and an instrument of tyranny.

There was no future for a playwright in North America.

Jenny's mother tried to tell her as much in her weekly reports from New Brunswick. The newsy letters arrived every Tuesday like clockwork, carried by the dishearteningly efficient Rebel post, threaded with the subtle message that, in such trying times, Jenny would be wise to come home.

But even her mother could not claim that New Brunswick was untouched by the current troubles. It had taken eight men a whole day, she wrote, to raise the new church bell, which had been cast in Holland from six hundred pounds of silver donated by the first families of the parish, into the steeple. It had been rung only once before word reached the town that the British were abroad—hunting for caches of weapons and confiscating church bells along the way so that the Rebels could not raise the countryside with their alarms.

Whatever their individual political leanings, the faithful of New Brunswick had denuded their tables and donated their plate for the glory of God, not King George. The church consistory voted unanimously, her mother wrote with obvious satisfaction, to take the bell down and bury it in the orchard across the lane.

If Jenny did not do something about it, she would end up like the bell, buried in New Brunswick until the Rebels were routed. Teased and tormented by four loving brothers who had followed her father into the brick-making trade and could not understand why a pretty girl bothered herself with scribbling for players.

There was no future for a playwright . . . in North America. That was why Jenny wanted, needed, to meet Burgoyne.

The general was said to be a personal friend of David Garrick. Burgoyne's plays had been performed at Drury Lane in London.

"The *Boyne* will be a week at least refitting," murmured Andries Van Dam, who was arranging to send a crate of his best Madeira aboard the ship. "The general also asks for six quarts of Spanish olives, twelve pounds of Jordan almonds"—the tavern keeper began writing it all down, eyes alight—"two dozen doilies, one box of citron, six jars of pickles, and one Parmesan cheese."

Jenny waited until they disappeared into the storeroom—all furtive glances and quiet whispers—before dashing out of the tavern. Samuel Fraunces, publican—Black Sam, to his friends—was a notorious Rebel, but evidently not a man to let that get in the way of trade. Jenny had never cared for politics. She liked them even less now that the royal governor and the garrison had retreated to their gun ships in the harbor and left ordinary New Yorkers like herself to the pity of the rabble, who had none.

She wanted nothing better than to dash directly home to John Street and Aunt Frances with her news, but she still had errands to run for the theater's manager: costumes to pick up from the mantua maker, canvas to fetch for repairing the scenery, playbills waiting at the printer. This, though, gave her the opportunity to make discreet inquiries about the *Boyne* with the sailmakers and victuallers. By the time Jenny reached the little blue house next door to the theater, wrapped in her plain wool cloak and laden with packages, she had acquired a box of oranges and knew that the *Boyne* was anchored off the Battery, undergoing repairs.

Aunt Frances was upstairs, at her desk in the little parlor, working on a manuscript. She looked effortlessly stylish—as always—in a simple blue silk gown with her hair teased and tinted to match. Her arrival in New Brunswick, after fleeing her London creditors, had changed Jenny's life. Aunt Frances was old enough— just—to be her mother, but unlike the matrons of Jenny's acquaintance she had not rushed headlong into the trappings of domesticity or middle age. She wore no frumpy caps or homely aprons. She neither baked nor sewed. She wrote a little, acted a great deal, and charmed the patrons in the greenroom, always.

Without raising her head, she said, "How is your mother and everyone in New Bumpkin?"

"New Brunswick," Jenny corrected. "They are fine. And Burgoyne is in New York."

Aunt Frances stopped writing and looked up. "On what business?"

Jenny had not thought to find out. "Does it matter?"

She put her pen down. "Yes, actually. Very much so. He was in Boston a week ago, staging amateur theatricals and lamenting his lack of seniority over Clinton and Howe. If he is being recalled to England, it might signal a change in the government's policy toward America."

Jenny did not care about seniority or policies. "If he saw one of my plays, if he thought it was any good, would he be able to introduce me to David Garrick?" she asked.

Her aunt considered. "Yes. He knows Garrick. More importantly, his plays have made money for Garrick. But you have no experience handling a man like John Burgoyne."

The playwright general known for his heroic cavalry charges was said to be the bastard of a lord and had eloped with the daughter of an earl. Jenny knew she was out of her depth. "That is why I hoped you would help me get aboard the *Boyne*."

Her aunt shook her head. "No. Go to Caesar like Cleopatra, rolled in a rug? *That* is what you absolutely must not do."

"What, then?" asked Jenny, feeling keenly her lack of sophistication.

"You do not want this man entranced by your person," said Frances Leighton. "All *that* will get you at Drury Lane is a place as an opera dancer. You want Burgoyne enthralled by your writing, enough to sponsor a London production of your work—or convince Garrick to do so. Nothing less will serve." She swept her manuscript aside, pulled a clean letter sheet out of the drawer, dipped her pen, and offered it to Jenny. "To that end, we must lure the general here, to John Street."

Severin Devere was standing on deck when the case of Madeira was hoisted aboard the *Boyne*. He considered sending the crate back to shore, but that would only attract more notice, and drawing further attention to the crippled man-of-war in New York Harbor was the last thing he wanted to do.

He had been sent to America for the purpose— among other things—of fetching John Burgoyne home quietly and discreetly. The King and Lord Germain, the secretary of state for America, had read Burgoyne's letters from Boston describing the fiasco of Bunker Hill—for which he had been present but not in command—and his proposals for pacifying the colonies. They had found these observations full of good sense. Now they wished to hear more, preferably without alerting the Rebels to their intentions.

Unfortunately, John Burgoyne did nothing quietly or discreetly.

Severin's faint hope that the general had exercised a modicum of good judgment in his transaction with the wine merchant was dashed when he broke the seal on the receipt that accompanied the crate.

Burgoyne had bought the Madeira under his own name, which meant his departure from Boston was no longer secret.

The other letter that had come aboard with the wine was also addressed to Burgoyne. It was sealed with cheap wax, written in a round, girlish hand, and scented with a whiff of scandal. *Marvelous.* Severin pocketed the missive and descended belowdecks to the general's cabin.

Four lieutenants had been displaced to create Burgoyne's apartment, and part of the wardroom had been cannibalized. Captain Hartwell had balked at removing any of the guns, though, so Burgoyne had draped the thirty-two-pounders with thick furs and Indian-tanned hides and brightly beaded garments he had bought as souvenirs.

The general sat at his breakfast table wearing a striped silk banyan and an embroidered turban. His slippered feet rested upon a Turkey carpet. On the table alongside the serving dishes was spread a map with a carefully penciled line running from Quebec to Albany.

This was the contradiction in Burgoyne's character that fascinated Severin. The man had an appetite for luxury, and a tendency toward egotism and bombast, but he wasn't lazy. A few years past fifty, he had the vigor and ambition of a man half his age, evident in his still-black hair and avid, heavy-lidded eyes.

"Your wine has come aboard," said Severin. He dropped the two letters on the table beside Burgoyne's notes and gestured for the servant to leave. The man scurried from the room.

"Excellent," said Burgoyne, slicing into a chop.

"Lord Germain had hoped that your departure from Boston might go unnoticed by the Rebels. You gave the wine merchant your name and direction."

Burgoyne shook his head. "Secrecy is impossible. Everyone will know I have gone when I am not present at *The Blockade of Boston*. If you had wanted my departure to go unnoticed, we should have delayed it until after the performance."

He meant his farce, being rehearsed for a benefit night at Faneuil Hall, though Severin had never known the proceeds of such events to reach any of the advertised widows and orphans.

"Give me leave to doubt the noteworthiness of a

general missing the odd theatrical event when his country is at war," said Severin.

"War *is* theater," said Burgoyne. "I should have thought that a man with your . . . *expertise* . . . regarding the savages of North America would know that. Do the Mohawk not paint their faces before going into battle?"

Severin's Mohawk ancestry was one of the reasons he had been chosen to fetch Burgoyne, so he might advise the general, who desired to employ native allies in his proposed campaign next year. The difficulty was that Burgoyne had proved disposed to respect the opinion of an Englishman—*any* Englishman—on native questions more than that of a man who had lived among the Mohawk, especially one the general believed was tainted by Indian blood, like Severin.

"Think of our visit to New York as a mummer's play, then," advised Severin, "and perform the role accordingly. Lord Germain does not wish the Rebels informed of your movements, sir. There must be no more transactions with Van Dam, or anyone else in New York."

Burgoyne sighed. "I do not need your advice on dealing with shopkeepers, Devere. If I had not used my name, Van Dam would have sent me an inferior vintage at double the price."

"And now he will make up his loss on the wine by peddling the news that you are in New York. For those alert to affairs of consequence, your recall to London will tell them all they need to know about the character of the next campaign." Generals Gage and Howe had always treated the colonials like brothers, because they were decent men and they had ties to America. They were doing everything within their power to avoid bloodshed and bring about a peaceful resolution to the conflict. "Gentleman Johnny" Burgoyne would not.

The general made a little show of setting down his fork and leaned back in his chair. "Have you considered that such news might serve to scare sense into these people?"

It was a widely held opinion that the Americans were spoiled children, that a show of force was all that was needed to bring them into line.

"Lexington Green and Bunker Hill," said Severin, "argue otherwise."

Burgoyne waved away the two biggest British military disasters in recent memory. Evidently he not only preferred an Englishman's understanding of Indians, but gave little weight to an *Indian's* views on the English. "Poor planning and poorer leadership."

Severin drew the other letter from his pocket. In the close quarters of the cabin he discovered that it was scented with more than scandal. It had a hint of orange about it. Not the sophisticated tincture of neroli, but the bright perfume of freshly peeled fruit.

It made Devere long for uncomplicated pleasures, for warm summer afternoons far from war and intrigue. For a moment, Severin did not want to part with the smooth, scented envelope.

But he had a point to make. "We have already been the target of sabotage." The spoiled beef in the *Boyne's* stores had almost undoubtedly been poisoned, and the ship's spar had been intentionally damaged. "Now that the Americans know you are here, they will try again."

"Let them," said Burgoyne, breaking the seal and scanning the letter. For a moment the bouquet of orange intensified, then faded. Then Burgoyne barked with laughter and tossed the letter, along with a slender booklet, to Severin.

"An actress," he crowed. "One enterprising harlot knows I am in New York. So much for your 'consequences.' *One* rather provincial invitation to sin."

Severin picked the letter up off the table. He noted the round feminine hand once more. It was the product of a thorough education in penmanship, every character neat and well formed. There were no showy flourishes, which indicated restraint and taste. Scarcely the hallmarks of a harlot. But the contents, calculated to elicit Burgoyne's interest, roused Severin's suspicions.

The missive opened with effusive praise for Burgoyne's skills as a playwright and closed with an invitation to occupy the royal box at the John Street Theater. This was accompanied by a printed pamphlet-bound play, *The American Prodigal*, by Miss Jennifer Leighton.

Burgoyne shed his banyan and reached for his coat.

"You are not going to accept her invitation," said Severin.

"Of course I am. It's the last opportunity I'll have for a gallop until we reach Portsmouth."

"Possibly at the cost of your life."

"Not unless the little rustic is well and truly poxed."

That was the far more common contradiction of their age. That an English gentleman could be as devoted to his wife as Burgoyne was to Lady Charlotte, but cavalierly betray her when opportunity presented. Fidelity, for men like Burgoyne, meant not *keeping* a mistress. It did not mean forgoing convenient "gallops."

That still didn't make it safe. "New York is not

London, General, and the John Street Theater is not Drury Lane. In 'sixty-six, after the business with the stamps, a mob of Liberty Boys tore down the theater on Chapel Street and whipped the players from the Battery to the palisade. This could be an innocent"—if somewhat gauche, he thought to himself—"invitation, or it might be a plot to lure you into the city and capture or kill you under the cover of a riot. I cannot allow you to go."

Burgoyne tied his neck cloth and rummaged through a jewel case. "I genuinely don't see how you can prevent me."

"I can take measures."

Burgoyne stiffened. For a moment all was stillness in the cabin and the cries of the sailors at work above could clearly be heard. Then Burgoyne set the diamond pin he had just selected on the table with a click and looked Severin over. "That," he said coldly, "is why your kind make such good informers and spies. Honor offers you no impediment."

"So I have been given to understand," said Severin smoothly. That, he knew, was how the government saw him: as a ruthless savage who made a useful tool. It was not how he saw himself. Until recently he had not cared much what others thought of him. Lately, since Boston, that had begun to change.

He pocketed Jennifer Leighton's orange-scented letter.

"Very well," said Burgoyne. "We are both men of the world. You desire that I should stay aboard the *Boyne*, and I desire to bed a pretty actress before we sail."

"You don't even know that she's pretty. Or that she exists at all." The oranges, though, were real enough.

"Then find out for me," said Burgoyne, retaking his seat. "And if she's pretty, bundle her back to the *Boyne*."

"I am not a procurer."

"Of course not."

Burgoyne left the words unspoken. *What you are is scarcely more honorable.*

And he was right, because men like Severin gave him the luxury of being right, of being *honorable*. Severin did what was necessary, and carried it on his conscience, so that others did not have to.

"Give me your word, as a gentleman," said Severin, "that you will remain aboard the *Boyne* and write no more letters to shore, and I will go fetch you your actress."

Two

Jenny stood in the wings waiting for her cue. She could feel the tidelike pull of the stage, the lure of the flickering footlights. She played only the small roles, the maids and messengers and next-door neighbors with few lines. Acting was not her talent, but that did not diminish the thrill of being part of the performance.

Aunt Frances, of course, was the real star. The sweetheart of Drury Lane. A name that sold tickets, even if sometimes she was not entirely herself.

Like tonight. The Divine Fanny was wandering. Jenny knew the signs, could read volumes in the dreamy look on her aunt's lovely, distracted face. Frances might be standing at the center of the raked stage, framed by pastoral scenery meant to evoke Arcadia, but her usually sharp mind was somewhere else.

The audience had not yet noticed, but Bobby Hallam,

John Street's manager and leading man, had. He put himself right in her line of sight to deliver his speech, demanding her attention.

"My greatest fear, madam," he declaimed in a rich tenor that carried to the back of the house, "is not that I should lose this duel, but that I should acquit myself in such a manner as to disgrace my ancestors."

Jenny mouthed the words along with him. She knew every line, because she had written them. She waited for Aunt Frances' response, but the silence lengthened, and the audience grew restless.

Far, far too late, she replied: "I cannot speak to *disgrace*, sir, but I fancy they might find your intemperate haste to join them a little . . . *disappointing*."

Her delivery saved the joke. Almost. The audience, catching the conceit like a bouquet, tittered. Not the gale of laughter that usually swept the gallery, but it was something.

That made twice this week. Frances' spells were getting more frequent, harder to hide from Bobby Hallam and the ticket-buying public.

Jenny couldn't help but look up at the royal box where she hoped Burgoyne sat. Her heart sank when she heard it. The beginnings of the speech that had made Aunt Frances' career. The lines that had brought her to the attention of David Garrick, the role that had caught the eye of her first titled lover.

She had gone off book entirely.

"How hard is the condition of our sex?" asked Frances Leighton, turning to the audience. "Through every stage of life the slave of man?"

"How now?" asked Bobby Hallam, who didn't know

Nicholas Rowe's play at all, because it wasn't in the company's repertoire. "It's to be pistols at dawn," Bobby asserted, trying to draw Aunt Frances back into the scene. "Will you pray for me?"

Apparently she would not. Aunt Frances ignored Bobby completely. She was no longer playing Mistress Spartan in Jenny's *American Prodigal*, but was reciting Calista's speech from *The Fair Penitent*.

"In all the dear delightful days of youth, a rigid father dictates to our wills—"

"Surely not so rigid," Bobby coaxed, taking her arm.

Frances shook him off and walked downstage to the footlights, her leonine grace and bold striped polonaise drawing every eye in the house. "And deals out pleasure with a scanty hand."

The stage manager, Mr. Dearborn, touched Jenny's shoulder and spoke in her ear. "It's a fine speech. But it's not in the play. Shall I lower the curtain?"

It was how Bobby had dealt with Frances' little spells in the past. If the Divine Fanny couldn't be coaxed back to book, Bobby ordered the curtain lowered and rushed Miss Richards, who sang prettily, out onto the apron.

It would save the show and safeguard their box office, but the humiliation would crush Aunt Frances. Jenny had seen it happen, and she could not do that to Fanny again.

She had to get her aunt off the apron, gently, so she could come back to herself in private. Jenny doubted any of this would impress John Burgoyne, but she couldn't worry about that right now.

Upstage, Bobby Hallam nodded his powdered head,

an unmistakable signal for the curtain to close—unless Jenny could stop it.

Devere made his way on foot north from the Battery. New York was a tiny city, barely a mile from Fort George to the palisade. The town resembled less an English port and more a Garden of Eden. Every lane was shaded by towering elms and beeches: a verdant roof in summer, now an autumn canopy of fiery gold.

Severin followed Broad Street, lined with the painted-brick mansions of the rich, to the intersection of Nassau and Wall streets, where a subtle change took place. The paint on the houses was not as bright here, the pigments cheaper, the coats thinner. The dwellings grew smaller, then began to jostle with shops and taverns. One thing remained constant, though: the presence of slaves. New York was the Sparta of the new world, a quarter of her population in chains, all of them obliged to carry a lantern after dark, a legacy of the slave plot to burn New York in '41.

Slavery gave the lie to all the Liberty Boys' cries for freedom, but that didn't make the rabble any less dangerous, so Severin wore a more than ornamental sword at his hip and kept a close eye on the alleys that opened between houses.

He turned left onto John Street and found the theater on his right. It looked like most provincial British playhouses—long, narrow, and featureless—but at home it would have been constructed of brick or local stone. Here it was clapboard painted a deep, dark red that appeared almost black in the failing light, save where lanterns brought the color to life.

Severin would not have paused in the bare, cold lobby save for the playbill pinned to the chipped white paneling. It was the name, printed in bold capitals above the list of comedies, that caught his eye: Frances Leighton.

The sweetheart of Drury Lane, who had spurned a titled lover for a merely rich and talented one. An accomplished woman, to be sure. Severin recalled she had a volume of well-received poems and a novel to her name, but scandal, in the form of a dead lover and the man's vengeful wife, dogged her.

"I didn't know you were in New York, Devere."

The voice was familiar to Severin. Though it had been many years since he had heard it, the effect was like listening to an orchestra strike up a favorite air. It filled him with sudden nostalgia and threw his isolation and loneliness into high relief.

"And I thought the garrison had withdrawn to the safety of the *Asia* after the Liberty Boys stormed the Battery," Severin replied, turning to face Courtney Fairchild. His old classmate was not wearing his usual red army regimentals but a suit of fine worsted like Severin.

"Just so," agreed Courtney, "but the officers are tolerated in the town so long as we dress in mufti."

Severin was glad to hear it. After two weeks of Burgoyne's company, seeing Fairchild, who had been more brotherly to him than his own brother when they were at school, was a balm for the soul. "I have tickets for the royal box," said Severin. "Would you care to join me? Unless you have other plans."

"I'd like that very much." Courtney beamed and projected the same manly bonhomie that had seemed oversized for his scrawny frame at school but suited the bluff soldier he had become. "The Divine Fanny is performing tonight and everything but the gallery is sold out."

Inside, the actual theater was warm and surprisingly pretty in a provincial way. The galleries were painted in a classical scheme of swags and garlands, all pale green and rosy pink, with the names of the great English dramatists—Marlowe, Shakespeare, Dryden, Rowe—inscribed in cartouches above the stage. Including the pit and the gallery, the theater probably seated seven or eight hundred, though barely half that number were in attendance. The "royal" box was just a small enclosure overhanging the apron above the proscenium doors.

The play was surprisingly enjoyable. Severin forgot entirely about spotting Burgoyne's harlot and became caught up in the drama. The characters might have been stock, but they were well drawn and had been cleverly tweaked for an American setting. The country bumpkin in homespun was fresh from a Massachusetts farm, the charming rake in silk was a Dutch patroon, and the Divine Fanny played an aristocratic Philadelphia lady of fashion and prodigious carnal appetite. It was a knowing slant on Frances Leighton's offstage persona, an inside joke for the sophisticated theatergoer.

"They say she has no protector in New York, though Van Dam has offered a fortune and Stanwyck is known to be paying her bills in hopes of future gratitude," whispered Courtney.

"Are you in the running?" Severin asked with amusement. Frances Leighton was slender, graceful, and impossible to look away from. Only her leading man was able to hold his own onstage with her. The other players came and went leaving little impression— save for the somewhat mousy girl acting the part of the maid, the younger brother, and the gossipy neighbor, in a series of equally unattractive costume changes. Severin noticed her only because of the distinctive way she darted on and offstage.

Yet for all of the Divine Fanny's obvious appeal, Severin did not find her greatly attractive. She was a little too like a certain lady he had met in Boston, a very dangerous lady. His ribs still ached from that encounter.

"I don't have the depth of pocket," said Courtney Fairchild, with a sigh, "to support the Divine Fanny. She is a damnably expensive trollop. But I attend her salon, and I plan on visiting the greenroom after the play to see if anything else tempts my eye. Will you be joining me?"

Severin hadn't spotted Burgoyne's harlot yet, so he would be obliged to attend. He was about to say so when Frances Leighton cocked her head and began to declaim a speech utterly at odds with the action of the scene. Severin could not place it, though he was certain he had heard it before.

"In all the dear delightful days of youth," spoke Frances Leighton, as though from heart and not from memory, "a rigid father dictates to our wills, and deals out pleasure with a scanty hand."

Whatever Frances Leighton was doing, it was not part of the planned entertainment. A frisson of real tension, not playacted, electrified the stage and Severin found himself sitting forward in his chair, knees pressed to the kicking board.

"To his, the tyrant husband's reign succeeds, proud with opinion of superior reason. He holds domestic business and devotion all we are capable to know, and shuts us, like cloistered idiots, from the world's acquaintance, and all the joys of freedom. Wherefore are we born with high souls, but to assert our selves, shake off this vile obedience they exact, and claim an equal empire over the world?"

She froze there in front of the footlights, her lithe body outlined by the bold lavender stripes of her polonaise, and waited for someone—the audience, her leading man, the voice of God perhaps—to answer.

Wherefore indeed, Severin thought, his mind teasing potential meanings and messages out of the appeal.

There came a groan and then a catcall from the gallery. Severin reached for the sword at his hip and glanced quickly over at Courtney Fairchild, who was also readying his weapon. If this was the prelude to a plot, a planned incitement intended to start a riot, then Severin was lucky to have encountered this stalwart friend of his youth. Say what you like about Courtney—he'd always had a cool head.

An apple core landed on the stage at Frances Leighton's feet, and beside him Fairchild made a noise that sounded awfully like a snarl. An empty bottle struck one of the flats beside the Divine Fanny's head and clattered to the ground. Nothing broke in upon her perfect composure.

The mood of the crowd was balanced on a knife's edge. Their attention was focused on Frances Leighton, but it would be easy—all too easy—to turn it

elsewhere, to focus it on the royal box and the repre-
sentatives of the Crown within. Severin readied for an
attack.

It didn't come.

Instead, a girl entered stage right. She was barefoot
and her slender curves were outlined in buff breeches
and silk stays. Her copper hair tumbled free over her
back. Severin judged her to be in her middle twenties.
Her body was so graceful that she appeared to glide to
Frances Leighton.

With a start Severin realized that she was the same
actress who had played the mousy maid and the younger
son and the trilling neighbor, transformed—or, more
accurately, revealed.

"Forgive me, fair Calista," she said, dropping to
one knee, "if I presume, on privilege of friendship, to
join my grief to yours, and mourn the evils that hurt
your peace, and quench those eyes in tears."

She went on in her low, mellow voice, entreating
Frances Leighton to share her burdens. The rabble in
the gallery quieted, and listened, rapt, to this girl.

Severin watched her coax the Divine Fanny off the
stage. A lump rose in his throat. His world had been
sharp edges and hard corners for too long. He wished he
had been in Frances Leighton's place, wished that the
girl had been addressing him. Stripped bare by catharsis,
Severin could not deny what he felt. He craved that kind
of understanding and solicitude.

Especially since Boston.

The play resumed, without the Divine Fanny. Another actress of similar height appeared in her striped
gown, or one very like it, and assumed the role.

As for the fascinating girl: she returned to the

stage three more times. Before, she had been unremarkable, almost invisible. Now Severin couldn't help but notice her.

And want to meet her.

He was not the sort of man to court actresses. He knew fantasy from reality. It didn't matter. He was tired of sparring verbally with Burgoyne and his ribs still ached from sparring physically with the Widow in Boston and he wanted, just once, something for himself, even if it was an illusion.

The players lined up for their curtain call, and the object of his desire stepped forward, hand in hand with the leading man, to curtsy, her long copper hair almost kissing the boards. He wanted to feel it against his bare skin. Severin had come on an errand for Burgoyne, of course, but there was no reason he shouldn't find some entertainment for himself.

"Who is she?" asked Severin.

"Jenny? She's the Divine Fanny's niece and dresser. Bit of a scribbler. Writes the comedies. Never made much of an impression before. I'd no idea she was so pretty."

The Divine Fanny's niece. Jenny. Bit of a scribbler.

Jennifer Leighton, Burgoyne's harlot.

Severin felt an intense flare of resentment, of the kind he had not experienced in years, not since his parents had brought him to England as a boy and he had discovered that the circumstances of his childhood had created an invisible but nearly tangible barrier between himself and the other youths at school—except for the rare *Fairchilds* of the world, who embraced both the letter and the spirit of their status as gentlemen.

"Van Dam was willing to take her in lieu of her

aunt, although on more modest terms, but she turned him down," added Courtney. "I could make an introduction, if you would like."

"Yes," said Devere, though the word tasted bitter on his lips, because he had made a gentleman's agreement, ungentlemanly though it was, and Miss Jennifer Leighton was not for him.

Three

Jenny slipped inside her aunt's tiny dressing room. The Divine Fanny was seated at a little table, surrounded by heaps of costumes, writing furiously, her pen scratching briskly over the paper.

Frances Leighton put her quill down and looked up from her pages. "I wandered off book again tonight, didn't I?" she said.

"Yes, you did."

"I am sorry. And on tonight of all nights. Was Burgoyne in the box?"

"I don't know. Aunt Frances, you must see a doctor." She wished her words didn't sound so curt in her own ears.

"Nonsense. Ancients like myself are known to wander now and then."

"You're barely forty."

"That is *venerable* for an actress. We age in dog years."

Jenny knew that some New Yorkers speculated that Aunt Frances drank. Jenny was fairly sure she did not. She never found bottles in their dressing room or hidden about the theater, nor did Aunt Frances smell of spirits. She dabbled occasionally in drafts from her personal medicine chest to combat megrims, but never before a performance.

Jenny did not want to put into words the other explanation she had heard whispered in the wings: madness. She had never known a madwoman, so had no example by which to judge her aunt, save poor Ophelia from Shakespeare's play, and Frances Leighton had long since weathered more loss than the affections of a melancholy Dane.

"Perhaps a holiday in the country, some rest," Jenny suggested. They had no shortage of invitations, though Frances never accepted them.

"Holidays are for the rich, and we players must labor for our bread," Fanny replied brightly, dropping her closely written manuscript—her memoirs—into the iron-bound chest that held her fine London-made paints and glamorous tinted wigs, as though nothing unusual had happened. "Let us go next door and find out if Burgoyne accepted your invitation. If he *was* in attendance tonight, he'll surely be there. Johnny never could resist the pleasures of the greenroom. Major general or not, he has changed little over the years, I'll warrant."

She closed the lid on her chest and with it further talk of doctors and holidays.

"I should put on a better gown," said Jenny, swallowing the lump in her throat that rose every time she failed to get Aunt Frances to see a doctor.

"Best not," said Frances Leighton. "You want Burgoyne's *patronage*, not his *protection*. If you dress the part of the actress, you'll be cast firmly in the role."

The John Street's greenroom was on the ground floor of the little house next door, where Jenny and Aunt Frances had their apartments, and, quite unusually, the double parlor where the city's elite gathered after the performance to eat, drink, and speak with the players was actually green—verdigris, to be exact, with that slight coppery iridescence that shimmered in candlelight and lent a special glamour to powdered skin and silk damask.

The greenroom was thronged, the theater's patrons spilling out onto the granite steps in front, fortified against the chill December air by strong punch and Madeira wine. The scents of beeswax tapers, expensive perfume, rum punch, and ginger cakes mingled in the humid air.

From her vantage point beside the hearth, Jenny surveyed the crowd. All the usual patrons were present tonight, along with a contingent from the *Asia*, the officers in civilian dress so they could move about the town unmolested, including the irrepressible Major Fairchild—who had taken Aunt Fanny's rebuff last March with such good grace, and continued to visit and make regular appearances in her salon.

Beside him stood a tall stranger in fine dove gray wool. The color was subdued, but the cut was remarkably stylish. London made, most likely, or by an American tailor with access to the latest English designs. The sleeves were so tightly fitted and ended in such narrow cuffs that Jenny would not have been surprised to learn that the wearer had been sewn into them. The body of the coat was trim, the breeches equally neat. The gentleman himself was lean but compactly muscular, well-formed calves on display in white silk stockings, biceps outlined by meticulously sculpted sleeves.

His face was long and lean, with high, wide-set cheekbones that would have shaded toward the pretty if the man's jawline had not been so masculine. His complexion was unfashionably dark, and he wore no powder. His eyes were so deep a brown as to appear almost black, and his hair was like unrelieved jet braided neatly at the back of his neck. She did not think him handsome exactly, but he was quite the most striking man she had ever seen. *Extraordinary.*

And he moved like an actor. Not like the elder generation of Hallams. He took care to move in such a way that did *not* attract notice.

He was very good at it. Despite the fine figure he cut, absolutely no one was looking at him except Jenny.

But he was looking straight at her.

And she was staring.

She blushed, which was ludicrous, because for the past two years she had been privy to the secrets of one of the most notorious women of the age, and though she was personally inexperienced with men, she had received a thorough practical education on the subject of congress between the sexes.

It made no difference. When she looked at the man in dove gray wool, she flushed like a naive virgin fresh off the hay wain from the country. Upon consideration, she realized he was indeed handsome.

"Is that him?" she asked Aunt Frances, trying to regain her composure and willing herself to look away.

Aunt Frances' smile faded, and she lowered the glass of Madeira that had only just touched her lips.

"No, dear. That is not Burgoyne. The playwright is a fair bit older. *That* is a man with a very different calling. And one best avoided, if possible."

Aunt Fanny placed a slender hand, sleeves dripping with lace *engageants*, upon Jenny's arm and started to rise, but Major Fairchild and the man in gray were already crossing the room. Jenny found herself transfixed by his eyes, which looked nearly black in the candlelight. *Glistening, almost like pools of molten pitch.*

"Madam Leighton." Fairchild bowed and reached for Aunt Fanny's hand.

They were caught. There was no escaping without insulting a well-liked British officer in full sight of all of New York society, and without the support of loyalists, the John Street would not survive.

Aunt Frances regained her aplomb and acknowledged the major with a regal nod of her head.

"It is lovely to see you and your niece again," Fairchild said.

The man in gray had still not spoken. He was studying Jenny, his face a mask of polite interest, but his eyes more intent than good manners allowed.

"We are honored to have the garrison's patronage," said Aunt Frances smoothly.

"May I present my old friend Severin Devere?"

The man in gray bowed.

This elicited another regal nod from Aunt Fanny, a touch colder and more formal.

Devere bowed to Aunt Fanny, but it was Jenny this

striking creature in gray addressed when he rose. "I have come to apologize on a certain officer's behalf. He was immensely flattered by your invitation, but pressing matters prevented him from attending. He has hopes you will consent to dine with him tonight aboard his ship so that he might express his admiration for your work in person."

He meant Burgoyne. Jenny was so surprised that all she fixed on was "dine" and "admiration."

"Really?" asked Aunt Frances, in her best Lady Highstep voice. It was one of the reasons actors could mingle so freely with their "betters," because they could mimic their accents and ape their manners, and when it came to pure nerve, they often surpassed them.

"I fail to see how 'the officer' can so admire Jenny's play when he has not even seen it," said Bobby Hallam, who appeared at her side with two frosted glasses of sangaree.

Her employer had changed from the showy blue silk and silver lace of his stage costume to understated coffee velvet that set off his chestnut hair. He'd brushed the powder out and tied his shiny locks loosely back with a ribbon. He handed a glass to Jenny with a studied casualness. It was meant to suggest an intimacy, a long and close acquaintance, and he was trying to protect her.

Devere noted Hallam's gesture with his night dark eyes, and she decided that this was a man who missed very little. A dangerous man, Aunt Frances had intimated, and Jenny did not want Bobby Hallam putting himself in harm's way for her.

"Mr. Hallam has a point," said Jenny, reining in her excitement. She did not need a dinner invitation from a

rake. She needed Burgoyne to come here. "The officer"—
and here she bowed to Devere's obvious preference not to
name Burgoyne—"has not seen the play. Bobby's voice
has been known to echo off the Battery on occasion, but I
doubt it could carry all the way to the *Boyne*."

Severin was supposed to bring her back to Burgoyne,
but he did not know how to do that. He did not even
know what to make of Jennifer Leighton. She was staring up at him now, a study in contradictions and a
woman entirely outside his experience.

Burgoyne had charged him with fetching a harlot.
But Jennifer Leighton was no light skirt. He'd watched
her progress just now through the greenroom. She
didn't flirt with the theater's patrons, and despite what
Robert Hallam was trying to intimate with his body
language, she was not his mistress.

She was a decided wit. But she was no wellborn
bluestocking.

And then there was the gown. To wear it onstage
was one thing. Some roles required frumpery. To wear
it outside the theater, to a center of fashion like a
greenroom, was a statement. It said, *I advertise nothing.
I am not for sale.*

Jennifer Leighton was making no effort to seduce
anyone.

Except that there was the letter. An intelligent woman
could not write such a letter to a known rake like Burgoyne without realizing the implications. Beautiful, ambitious women traded their bodies for wealth, fame, and
position all the time. There was nothing wrong with such
a transaction as long as the woman was willing and under

no coercion. Severin's conscience in acting in such a matter should, by the standards of English society, be entirely clear.

And yet something about it rubbed him the wrong way. It was more than the *undeniable* fact that he desired her himself. It was the matter of coercion, or rather, of *genuine choice* that—quite unexpectedly—struck him as problematic. Jennifer Leighton was an original. She possessed genuine talent as a playwright, but she just as obviously lived in a country without scope for it.

If the girl had been born into wealth and had no need to sell her work to support herself, she might have been able to write—assuming she had indulgent parents or husband—from a position of relative safety, but men habitually assumed that a woman who sold the products of her mind sold other parts of her person as well. And there were always those waiting to take advantage of that market.

For a woman without fortune, Miss Leighton's options were extraordinarily limited, and no route to production for her plays was more direct than through the public patronage of a wealthy man. There were few such who would expect nothing in return.

And suddenly the prospect of delivering this creature up to John Burgoyne, even if she was *willing*, did not seem so harmless.

"You are right," Devere conceded. "The officer of whom we speak has not seen the play acted, and while its wit was plain on the printed page, paper has only two dimensions, and cannot fully engage the senses."

Severin observed Robert Hallam smile in triumph. Of course he would. Any savvy theater manager would want to keep Jenny to himself. If nothing else, her limited prospects meant he could have her excellent original plays on the cheap. And if Severin read the man right, he wanted her body into the bargain. That she was not already taking advantage of Hallam's obvious fixation—the man was handsome, charming, and influential—to improve her lot made Jennifer Leighton a very unusual woman indeed.

"But did it engage his mind?" asked Miss Leighton, the tentative hope in her voice genuine and affecting.

Severin hesitated. His business was lies, but he did not want to lie to her. And he did not want to act as a procurer. Yet if he failed to bring Miss Jennifer Leighton to John Burgoyne, the general would likely blunder ashore in search of entertainment, and that, with the Liberty Boys roaming the streets, Severin could not risk. It was the sort of calculus he was required to make all the time, and in his calling the virtue of one provincial actress did not weigh as much as the safety of Britain's best hope for holding on to her colonies.

That did not mean he liked it. Not one bit.

"I can reassure you that the officer in question read your words and that they moved him to immediate action. Only the demands of duty prevented his attendance tonight."

That was not *exactly* a lie. After all, Burgoyne *had* read Jennifer Leighton's letter and on the instant decided to seek the young woman out for a gallop. And Severin, the government's representative on the spot, *had* prevented him from coming to collect his prize in person.

"Which passages, *specifically*, moved him?" she asked. Jennifer Leighton wanted to believe him. That much was plain on her face. But she wasn't stupid, or gullible.

"Yes, do tell us," Robert Hallam said, hardly bothering now to cloak his challenge in politeness. "We provincials are always flattered to hear that our rustic entertainments have the power to charm our English masters, at least with their simplicity."

Hallam, Severin decided, was shrewd but hot-tempered, and probably in love with Jennifer Leighton. "For that," Severin replied, addressing Jenny and not her enamored manager, "you would have to come to the *Boyne*."

"Out of the question," said Robert Hallam coldly. "We play again on Wednesday. If *General Burgoyne* wishes to speak with Jenny, he can come to John Street."

That, thought Severin, nodding to be polite, was *not* going to happen.

Hallam bowed, stiffly, and offered his arm to Jennifer Leighton, but she did not accept it. He was an actor, and a good one. Only his eyes betrayed his displeasure. He turned smoothly to Frances Leighton, who was a veteran player and, fortunately for Hallam, inclined to save the scene. They disappeared together into the crowd, leaving Severin alone with Jennifer Leighton.

She watched them go, then turned to Devere. "And what did *you* think of Aunt Frances' monologue?"

Another surprise. A more artful woman would not have brought the topic up at all, would have blithely pretended that the whole incident had not happened. Severin should not have felt so pleased that Jennifer Leighton cared to know his thoughts. Or so unhappy that he could not say, *Your rescue of your aunt was the most moving thing I have ever seen upon the stage.*

But he could say none of that.

"*The Fair Penitent*," he said, "is perhaps not the most politic choice in New York at the moment. Talk of tyrants tends to be divisive. Americans are ready to see one in any man who disagrees with them."

"I might just have to use that line in one of my plays. Are you a regular theatergoer, Mr. Devere?"

It had been a world of wonders, the first time his mother had taken him, a boy plucked from the forests of New York and thrust into confining clothes and pinching shoes and sick for a month on an ocean voyage he could barely remember. Nothing in London had impressed him, but that cathedral to emotion, the shared trance of the audience, the way his eyes had watered at the end for the hero's fate . . . *Catharsis*, he later learned the Greeks called it. He had shed all of his months of grief in the darkness that night. And gone back every chance he got.

"Yes," he said. "It is one of the consolations of urban life. A beguiling contradiction: that a narrow wooden box can open on a myriad of wide vistas, tonight Arcadia, tomorrow Rome."

"Denmark on Wednesdays, when Bobby is in the mood to soliloquize," she replied. "Rome, alas, is contested territory. The Whigs cry 'Cassius from bondage will deliver Cassius,' and the Sons of Liberty sign their letters to the *Gazette* 'Brutus' while the Tories 'Cry havoc and let slip the dogs of war.'"

"And whose part do you take?"

"If the Rebels have their way, I will be forced to play Cleopatra, and turn to Rome to keep my throne. Congress has banned the theater here. There is no future for a playwright in America. I need a patron with influence in London."

Something Severin did not have, but Burgoyne did. He should not feel so bitter about it. He had only just met her. He scarcely knew her. He should not even be in New York. The Widow had warned him to leave America and not come back. But for the sabotage of the *Boyne*, which kept them in the harbor refitting, he would be en route to London now.

If he pressed her, she would come with him to-night, but he found he did not have the stomach for it and he told himself there was always tomorrow. "If you wish to meet Burgoyne aboard his ship, you can send word to me through the London Coffee House." He handed her his card.

She turned it over in her small, neat hands. Jennifer Leighton wore no rings or bracelets. Her nails were smooth, clean ovals but the pads of her fingers on her right hand were smudged with ink, and he found that more charming than sapphires.

"*Se-ve-rin*," she sounded out.

"Pronounced *Sev-ren*," he replied. It should not give him so much pleasure to hear his name trip off her tongue.

"No doubt Congress would tell you that the extra written syllable was a British extravagance, like the theater," she said.

"And Englishmen tell me it is a *French* extravagance, even at two syllables. 'Severin' smacks a deal too much of the Gaul. 'Severus'—Latin and learned—might be better received by the English and your Congress alike."

"Congress," replied Jenny, "forgets that the ancient republics they admire so much venerated the theater."

"They might admit the virtue of tragedy," suggested Severin.

"But not of Plautus or Terence."

"The *servus callidus* makes them nervous," he said, and was gratified at the way her face lit up at the allusion. "To be fair, I am given to understand that the Virginian who leads the army besieging Boston is quite fond of the theater." This was hardly an item of closely held military intelligence, but it was one of the pieces of minutiae he collected, and he found he wanted to gift it to her.

"With a taste for the dour and edifying, no doubt," said Jenny.

"*Cato the Censor*," conceded Severin, "is his favorite play."

She shuddered in mock horror; then her clear brow furrowed and mischief lit her eyes. "How do you happen to know such a thing?"

"Gossip," he said, lightly. But Frances Leighton's cold, appraising eye earlier had indicated that *she* understood exactly how he knew the sort of things he knew. And so would the lovely Miss Leighton, as soon as the Divine Fanny told her. And then she wouldn't curtsy prettily, as she was doing now, and banter about the theater and Whigs and Tories as she had done tonight.

She would fear him.

Four

Jenny watched Severin Devere leave and felt a surprising pang of disappointment. She wished he had been Burgoyne. She had enjoyed their conversation and had never once, she realized with surprise, felt out of her depth with him, though their talk had ranged from the comfortable and familiar confines of the theater to the thorny and dangerous arena of politics. He had addressed her throughout as an equal.

She was still examining his card when Bobby Hallam plucked it from her hands and tossed it onto the fire.

For a second the fine paper rested atop the coals, the firelight glowing orange through the linen weave. Then the edges browned and curled and flames licked across the printed surface until it was wholly consumed.

"A fine performance," Jenny said, turning to her employer, "but I memorize hundreds of lines a week.

I'm not likely to forget Devere's name or the direction he left."

"No, unfortunately not," replied Bobby. "A paltry act, satisfying nonetheless. You don't need him or Burgoyne, Jenny. You don't need London. I'll produce anything you care to write, and I won't expect anything in return for the privilege."

For as long as the John Street remained open, which would not be long at all if the Rebels brought their army to New York.

"There is no harm in dining with the general," she said.

"Generals do not dine with actresses to hear their opinions on Aristophanes."

"Neither do theater managers," she said.

"Do not compare me to a known rake like Burgoyne."

"Now, children," said Frances Leighton, approaching warily.

"Tell me there is a better way," Jenny said, turning to her aunt. "Tell me that the *patronage* of men like Burgoyne did not open doors for you."

"If I could tell my younger self anything," Frances Leighton said carefully, "it would be not to rush headlong through such doors."

Jenny knew that her aunt loved her and wanted to protect her, but so had her parents, and if she had listened to them, she would still be in New Bumpkin, far from the footlights of even the provincial John Street Theater. "And how would you characterize my prospects as a playwright in America, under the present circumstances?"

Frances Leighton had the honesty to look Jenny in the eye and say, "Poor, at best."

Jenny turned triumphantly to Bobby, whose expression was grim.

"Will you force me to play the tyrant?" he asked.

"You can't forbid me from going."

"No, I can't forbid you, but I can protect you from yourself. I can make you choose. Burgoyne or John Street, Jenny. You can't have both. Make an assignation with him, and you're out of the company."

Severin was grateful for Courtney Fairchild's presence on the walk back to the waterfront. He did not want to be alone with his thoughts about Jennifer Leighton just yet. It was rare that his conscience troubled him, but it did tonight.

The amiable Fairchild accompanied him south to the docks, and Severin used the opportunity to gather more intelligence about the situation in New York, which was, in a word, delicate. He had schooled himself to learn a great deal from little things: body language, tones of voice, an overheard word or phrase. By the time they'd reached the quay and Fairchild spoke a boat for him, he knew he had been right to keep Burgoyne aboard the ship.

"We had two companies of the Royal Irish, my own regiment," explained Fairchild, "in the garrison, but the men were withdrawn to the *Asia* after the Provincial Congress threatened to arrest them. The governor still meets with his council daily aboard the *Duchess of Gordon*, although how long that will continue is difficult to say. The Rebels have threatened to put a stop to it, which will mean the end of any pretense of royal government in New York."

The major paused as a small group of mechanics slouched past, making their way, Severin expected, to some nearby tavern. Then Courtney went on more quietly: "Last month Isaac Sears and his Liberty Boys—or the Spawn of Liberty and his Inquisition, as Montresor likes to call them—set fire to the sloop that provisions the *Asia*, which is why you will have no aid from Captain Vandeput. The next day they rode into New York in broad daylight and confiscated all the type used to print Mr. Rivington's Tory *Gazetteer*, leaving us with no newspaper. So much for the free and open encounter of ideas. And the best part? The very best part is that the people we are supposedly here to protect cheered them as they marched out of town playing 'Yankee Doodle.'

"You never know who or what their next target will be," Fairchild continued. "They'll say it is government and taxes if it suits them, but sometimes it is pure mischief. Looting and outright brigandry. They rampaged through town and arrested a town mayor, a clergyman, and a judge, and I do not doubt it was for the sake of confiscating their property. And there is nothing—*nothing*—we can do about it until Howe breaks out of Boston and brings his army here."

Severin knew better than to say that Howe had no chance of breaking out of Boston. He had infiltrated the Rebel lines in Cambridge for the general himself, walked their ranks in his old battered coat, falling into American speech patterns and using their idioms and being welcomed, warmly, as a brother, along with the other thousands who had flocked to the occupied city's aid. It was not a professional army. It was a mob, but an angry mob leavened with men who had spent their adult lives fighting the French and the Indians and trained their children up to do the same.

Courtney, unlike Burgoyne, might actually listen to his opinion on the subject, but of course he could not share it, because it was information he had obtained while spying. His work put him on intimate terms with men like Burgoyne and distanced him from friends like Courtney. Tonight he felt keenly his isolation. He wished he could talk frankly with his friend, share his misgivings about Jennifer Leighton, his disquiet over what had happened in Boston.

Instead they exchanged family news from home in England, and Fairchild congratulated Severin on his brother's success in Parliament. Severin thanked him politely. He did his best not to resent his older brother, but some wounds never really healed. It was not Julian's fault that Lord Devere preferred him, but it had been Julian's choice to distance himself from his younger brother at school, to make it clear that he believed what the world believed: that Severin was not Lord Devere's true son.

Then the boat was ready, and Severin was being rowed out to the *Boyne*. The water was choppy, mirroring his turbulent thoughts, which swirled around the enigma that was the attractive little playwright.

He did not want her to meet with Burgoyne.

She lived, according to Fairchild, with Frances Leighton, so she could not be naive. Innocent, perhaps, though even that was doubtful for a grown woman—approaching her middle twenties, he'd suppose—connected with the theater. Even if she had written the letter to Burgoyne without the insight of her worldly aunt or the shrewd Robert Hallam, they would have acquainted her with its practical implications by now. If she came aboard the *Boyne* to dine with the general, it would be with a full understanding of Burgoyne's expectations.

It was no concern of Severin's at all.

He could not get it out of his head.

He did not report to Burgoyne on his night's reconnaissance when he reached the *Boyne*. He was not certain, just yet, what he wanted to do about Jennifer Leighton.

He could not sleep, so he busied himself making notes on his personal observations in New York and recording details he had learned from Fairchild. When light began filtering through the gun port in his cramped quarters, he locked his papers in his chest and went in search of Captain Hartwell.

They agreed in the main that the *Boyne* must be made ready to sail to England as quickly as possible and that work, once supplies came aboard, must be carried out round the clock. They differed on how easily this might be accomplished.

"What Captain Vandeput possesses in his stores," said Hartwell with asperity, "he is loath to part with. He must keep the *Asia* in good repair or he will lose all semblance of control over the city. His sloop is burnt and he knows that the town may turn on him at any time, and he cannot rely on the locals for reprovisioning if we exhaust his warehouse. That leaves us bargaining directly with the merchants of New York, Devere, who know we have no other choice, and *that* means that we have no bargaining position at all. They gouge us, plain and simple. They want hard specie, and the *Boyne* does not carry sufficient gold to pay them for *your* necessaries. If General Burgoyne wishes to be under way, he is welcome to make up the shortfall out of his own pocket, because I—quite bluntly—am not in a position to do so."

"Then what, exactly, *are* you doing?" Severin asked.

"I've dispatched a request to the admiral in Boston for funds."

That would take a week—*if* the admiral had funds available to release to them. A week before serious repairs could begin, pushing them deeper into December and rough sailing weather, which might mean further delays.

"We cannot wait a week," said Severin.

There were several reasons they could not wait a week that had absolutely nothing to do with keeping Jennifer Leighton out of Burgoyne's bed. A week was sufficient time for news of his presence to reach the Widow in Boston. She had spared his life in their last encounter, but he knew better than to count on her mercy a second time, because he knew what she looked like now.

Sentiment, Severin assured himself, played no part in his calculations. It was self-preservation, plain and simple, and had nothing to do with the fate of a pretty actress.

Hartwell only shrugged. "Conditions do not favor a speedy departure," he said, as though that explained everything.

Naval men, in Severin's experience, blamed a great deal on conditions: on weather and supply and forces beyond their control. Whereas, in the army, no one was ever allowed to say, *Sorry we couldn't have a battle that day because the wind wasn't right and we were short a cask of salt beef.*

"That won't answer," said Severin.

"Then fix it, Devere. That's what you *do*, isn't it?"

It *was* what he did. Sometimes with ruthless violence. Never before had he questioned the necessity of . . . doing whatever was *necessary*. Now was not the time to start.

Jenny had not been able to sleep after her quarrel with Bobby Hallam. She had left the greenroom as soon as she could slip away, hoping her aunt would follow. But Frances Leighton had remained downstairs, in her element: drinking brandy, gambling, and keeping the patrons of the John Street Theater guessing as to who among them would be the one to enjoy her much acclaimed favors. Such speculation kept the boxes full at night, which was why Bobby covered the Divine Fanny's modest losses at cards—Jenny suspected that her aunt lost exactly what she chose to lose—and let them their rooms above so cheaply. And it was also why he made no mention of Aunt Frances' bad spells.

For hours Jenny lay awake in bed tossing and turning. She desperately wanted to talk to Fanny. As the night wore on, the stuffy garret chamber she so loved—that had represented freedom and possibility to her when they'd first arrived in New York—started to feel like a cage.

So she freed herself the way she had always done at home in New Brunswick: by opening a book. After an hour with *The Adventures of Unca Eliza Winkfield*, she was even less sleepy than before, so she sharpened her pen and opened her desk and resumed work on the new play she was writing. She found a place to insert Severin Devere's perceptive line about tyrants, which was good, but she discovered that she did not know how to resolve the subplot about the farmer's daughter, which was frustrating.

Finally, as dawn approached, and the carters and drovers began to rumble by in the street below, she wrapped herself in her shawl and went downstairs in search of Frances Leighton.

Fanny had the great drafty second-floor room on the west side of the house with the modern fireplace. This morning her door was closed. Jenny had never known her aunt to entertain gentlemen. In fact, for a woman so famous for her love affairs, she had been re-markably chaste since coming to America. She had taken no lovers that Jenny knew of, and she and her aunt were apart only rarely in New York.

But Jenny had learned from experience that after a night spent gambling and drinking in the greenroom, Frances Leighton was no good to anyone before noon.

Jenny decided against going back to her bed and curled up on the daybed in the parlor. She must have dozed, because the next thing she knew she was open-ing her eyes and the room was already warm, and the maid who cooked and cleaned for them was kneeling in front of the hearth toasting cakes and boiling water for tea.

A maid like Margaret was a luxury they could scarcely afford, but Aunt Fanny had always insisted upon it. "If you make up the fires and cook and clean and bake and wash, you will never have any time for anything else. That is the real advantage men have over women. Even in the meanest of households a man is free from domestic work to pursue his aspirations, and so must we be."

As Jenny *had* become, the day her aunt had turned up in New Brunswick with six boxes of gowns, wigs, costumes, paints, and papers and a nearly exhausted purse, on the run from her creditors in London—with an unexplained tragedy in her past and a plan to remake her fortune in America.

Jenny stretched—her neck was sore from falling asleep on the daybed—and surveyed the room, discovering her aunt seated at the table in front of the window, looking sleek and stylish in a simple chocolate silk gown with a jaunty black faille belt and paste buckle. Her hair was gathered loosely around her face and powdered a chic gray that set off her striking eyes.

She was writing, as usual, her pen scratching briskly across the paper. Jenny struggled to shake off sleep as Frances signed, folded, and sealed a letter and handed it off to Margaret with a coin. "Take this to Black Sam Fraunces' tavern and put it into Davey's hands, and no other's."

That struck Jenny as odd. Fanny didn't write letters. She was always working on poems or a novel or her memoirs—her diligence inspired Jenny—but she carried on no regular correspondence. Jenny waited until the maid had gone and asked, "Who did you write to?"

"A friend in Boston."

"I didn't know you had any friends in Boston."

"I don't," Frances admitted. "She's only visiting."

It would have been rude to ask what she had written about, ruder still to say: *But you never write to anyone*. Fanny had once told her, "Every woman has her secrets. The richness of her life can be accurately measured by how dangerous those secrets are." Aunt Frances' secrets had to be kept in a locked box.

Jenny had never kept secrets. Not about anything important, anyway. Her invitation to Burgoyne had been the first. She had hidden that from Bobby, and it had gotten her into an argument with him, rewarded her with a sleepless night and an aggravating crick in the neck.

She did not think she wanted a particularly rich life in that sense.

"I needed to talk to you last night," said Jenny.

"Yes, I gathered," said Frances Leighton. "For an actress, you're awfully transparent offstage."

"I'm not much of an actress," Jenny said. There was no way she would have earned a place in the company fresh from New Brunswick if she had not been Frances Leighton's niece. Her skills had improved some since then, but she was not the veteran her aunt was, and she had not been raised up in the theater like Bobby Hallam.

"Comedy is not your strong suit, though you write it well enough, and might yet develop such skills. But you have real promise at tragic roles, or so I was reliably informed by several gentlemen last night."

"So you don't remember what happened, do you?"

"It was not my best exit—I remember that much."

"Your episodes are getting worse," said Jenny. They were growing more frequent, and longer.

Aunt Frances shrugged. "Sic transit gloria mundi,"

she said. "If my memory fails entirely, I will have my memoirs." She indicated the manuscript before her. "And you can read the scandalous bits back to me and I can enjoy them all over again."

"I do not think you would make light of these spells if they were not serious," said Jenny.

Aunt Fanny sighed. "Perception is a blessing and curse. Like talent. Your life might be simpler if you didn't have either, or if you had never discovered them. Contentment is difficult to come by for the perceptive and the talented."

She was so good at turning the conversation away from herself that Jenny gave up again. "I was hardly content in New Brunswick," she said.

"But until New York you did not know of John Street and until John Street you did not know of Drury Lane. If you think you can go back, if you think you can be happy doing *anything* else, then you should give up the stage and go home, because the theater is a hard life and it never gets any easier, no matter how high you rise."

"Do you think Burgoyne will accept Bobby's invitation to attend on Wednesday?"

"I think it unlikely that Devere will allow him to set foot onshore. And if you accept *his* invitation to dine on the *Boyne*, while you may secure his patronage, it will not be without a cost. You must be honest with yourself about what Burgoyne will expect of you."

"I understand what Burgoyne will expect." She was not totally unsophisticated. And she did not think herself better than all the actresses who had been forced to tread this path before her.

"No, you don't. Not really. You only think you do,"

said her aunt. "That is because you have not yet met a man to tempt you. You will, eventually, and you will regret Burgoyne, but that is one of the privileges so often denied our sex: the right to make—and erase—our own mistakes."

"Does that mean you will help me?"

"If I can't dissuade you, then yes."

"If Bobby finds out, it's back to New Brunswick for me."

"New Brunswick should be the least of your fears. To reach Burgoyne you must go through Severin Devere."

The intriguing dark-eyed man who had introduced himself as Burgoyne's emissary last night. Who had not at first impressed her as handsome, but whose powerful appeal had then struck her with force. Who she had wished, truth be told, *had* been Burgoyne.

"Who is he?"

"The Honorable Severin Devere is—I understand— the half-breed son of a belted earl, the natural child of a frontier encounter with an Indian. His elder *brother* is a member of Parliament.

"As for Severin Devere—he is, at the moment, attached to Lord Germain's government in some manner. On occasions he holds rank in the army—as a colonel, I am told—although he is rarely seen in uniform. He is a spy, certainly, but he is more than that. As far as I've heard he has no fixed political beliefs. He serves whoever holds the reins of power. Devere acts sometimes as confidential secretary to great men, sometimes as negotiator for the government."

True to her craft, Aunt Frances paused for effect. "I am told Devere's methods can be quite . . . *direct*. On occasion, he kills. Whatever else he has been tasked with, protecting Burgoyne from peril and disgrace will be his first care, and he is a *very* dangerous man."

Jenny felt the color drain from her face. She'd enjoyed bantering with Severin Devere, but she'd mistaken a wolf for a hound. "I'll take care not to cross him, then," she said.

"You must also deceive Bobby, and that will be difficult. He's a fellow actor. If you counterfeit illness, he *will* know."

"Then it is impossible," said Jenny.

"Not impossible," said Aunt Frances, "but difficult. And entirely dependent on how much you are willing to risk."

Five

Severin was able to avoid Burgoyne and any decision about Jennifer Leighton for much of Tuesday. He spent the morning applying leverage aboard the *Asia*, where he met with Captain Vandeput, a capable officer of Huguenot descent who was the acknowledged but illegitimate son of a baronet. Vandeput had no legal issue himself, but was extraordinarily fond of his wife's niece, one Miss Sarah Wells, who was being courted by a spendthrift lieutenant who had thus far managed to conceal—but not from Severin's excellent sources—that he was three thousand pounds in debt.

Information, of course, was currency, and Severin spent that particular coin to buy thirty casks of salted beef and twelve barrels of portable soup to replace the suspect victuals from the *Boyne*.

Because Severin understood how such matters worked, he'd already had the tainted casks of beef from the *Boyne* split and thrown overboard—as soon as they'd dropped anchor, in fact. Had he not, the provisions would have ended up traded or sold in some shady transaction. The navy was rife with such underhanded business—and ordinarily Severin would not have interfered, but he had examined the sailors who had fallen ill from the beef and he was almost certain they had been poisoned. Only the cook's scanty hand with the meat had saved the crew—all but two unlucky souls whose bodies had already been committed to the sea.

Severin had watched as the *Boyne*'s sailors tipped their dead fellows, sewn up in sailcloth, over the side, but he would never grow used to burial at sea. Perhaps it was the Mohawk in him—used to burial in the earth—or the landsman at any rate. Discomfort or no, he watched.

Burgoyne had not stirred from his cabin.

The deaths proved that the danger to the *Boyne* and her illustrious passenger was real and, as Severin knew from experience, impossible to entirely eliminate. Unfortunately, the threat of assassination had only roused Burgoyne's worst impulses toward bravado and bombast, and as Severin returned to the *Boyne* he discovered the general preparing to go ashore in a boat.

He could not blame Hartwell, who had not wanted this duty and who had already borne more than his share of slighting remarks from the playwright general who expected to be entertained in style when he traveled and did not care for the captain's dour frugality.

"Where is it you planned to go?" Devere asked his charge.

"To stretch my legs in Vauxhall Gardens," said Burgoyne irritably.

"The deck is sufficiently long for that," replied Severin coolly. "And Vauxhall is closed for the season."

"The Holy Ground, then," said Burgoyne, meaning the neighborhood between St. Peter's and the college where *companionship* could be purchased. "We will be at sea a month, Devere. You come and go freely. There is no reason that I should not do the same."

"There is *every* reason that you should not. The Liberty Boys make daylight raids on the city and kidnap loyalists from their own homes." And lovely young actresses with too much to lose might admit you to their parlors and their beds.

"And yet you walk the city streets with impunity."

"I am not a major general," answered Devere.

"And of course, you were born here," added Burgoyne.

"So were the loyalists who are now at the bottom of a copper mine in Connecticut."

"And did the Liberty Boys also spirit away my actress?" asked Burgoyne. "Or did she resist your effort to capture her?"

The word choice, Severin knew, was intentional.

"She was tired," said Devere. "And her manager is very protective." His choice of words was intentional as well. Severin knew that Jennifer Leighton was not Robert Hallam's mistress, but he would not mind if John Burgoyne thought so, and was discouraged accordingly.

Burgoyne, though, was not discouraged. "One of the Douglasses or the Hallams, no doubt. They would not be good enough to tread the boards in Bath or Bristol, yet in America they are celebrated as serious thespians. Was she pretty?"

Original. Clever. Engaging. That was not what Burgoyne asked. "Pretty enough," admitted Severin.

"Then fetch her here."

I am not your dog. But he was. He had made himself so, cultivating a reputation for reliability, effectiveness, discretion, *calm.* Distinctly unsavage qualities. Such discipline had earned him a place beside great men, the place his father and brother would not make for him, but he was as much at the beck and call of such men as a faithful hound, and like a dog that has been pushed too far, he now wanted to bite. He stifled the impulse to snap at Burgoyne, because that would only play to the man's expectations.

"She has our direction," Severin said at last.

"She does indeed," said Burgoyne, producing a folded missive from his coat.

The letter, if it could be called that, was written in a decent approximation of Jennifer Leighton's round, clear hand, but it was not good enough to fool Severin. Even if the script had been a closer match, Devere would have recognized it for a forgery. The contents were what he had expected the day before, a very explicit invitation from a harlot. It promised Burgoyne the pleasures of the "royal box" for Wednesday evening. That, and a plethora of similar double entendre cribbed from the bawdy novels of Cleland. Even if Jennifer Leighton meant to barter herself to John Burgoyne, Severin did not think she would put matters so crudely.

Severin tucked the letter in his pocket, in case he encountered that forging hand again. "A ruse," he said to Burgoyne.

"That is what you said about the first invitation, which turned out to be genuine."

"It is not written in the same hand."

Burgoyne shrugged. "Then perhaps it was dictated."

The letter was not from the pretty playwright. Severin knew that. He would never convince Burgoyne of it, though, because the man wanted to believe in his appeal to the fair sex, and no doubt lovely young actresses did vie for his attention in London. He had not met Jennifer Leighton, so he did not know that she was something more than a pretty young actress. Long experience had taught Severin that the truth was irrelevant to most people. They believed the version of events that most closely matched their prejudices and preferences, and blithely ignored any inconvenient evidence to the contrary.

Severin then met with Hartwell and made it clear that Burgoyne was not to be allowed to leave the ship and that any letters he asked to have sent to shore should be held for Severin. Hartwell knew him well enough not to take his instructions lightly.

The following morning Severin visited the yards along the waterfront where spars, cordage, caulk, and sail were sold, and he began applying leverage to induce the merchants to deal with the *Boyne*.

In this he was not as successful as he would have liked. Even merchants he knew to be quietly loyal were wary. They did not want to be seen dealing with the navy, lest Isaac Sears and the Liberty Boys descend on their homes and spirit them off to Connecticut. Apparently, the Provincial Congress had condemned Sears' November raid but had no problem holding the judge and the others who had been abducted at the bottom of their grim mine indefinitely.

That, at least, was the fear that the merchants confided to Severin over rum, over brandy, over Madeira wine, over sangaree, over steaming flip, each according to his taste and circumstances. New Yorkers, Devere discovered, tippled all day, and to do business with them was a test of a man's constitution.

Severin drank as little at each stop as he could without giving offense and listened to what the merchants did *not* say, observing, while they talked, the disposition of their premises and goods.

Real riots, Severin knew, were impossible to predict. The right conditions could simmer for days, weeks, months, until the pot of anger simply boiled dry.

Or a single heated exchange between the butcher's boy and a surly merchant could ignite a conflagration.

New York had been a cauldron over the fire for a decade. That was nothing new. Most of the inhabitants going about their daily business on Wednesday sensed no change in atmosphere, but Severin could read the signs. There were provocateurs at work. He knew because he had carried out such designs himself.

Everywhere he went he saw men taking silent precautions. Shop doors stood open, but awnings were rolled tight; goods were on display, but pulled safely back from windows; fire buckets hung in entryways, and water barrels were full to the brim. Someone expected a mob—whether because rumor whispered it on the wind or the word had been passed from friend to friend, Severin did not yet know.

He could feel it in his bones, like an approaching storm. The whole of New York vibrated with quiet fear.

It was not, in point of fact, his problem. His problem

was John Burgoyne, and the sabotaged *Boyne* and the recalcitrant merchants of New York. But trouble on the docks, a burnt warehouse or destroyed stores, could dash the *Boyne*'s fragile hope of sailing this week, so Severin continued to make his way along the docks, bartering for provisions and naval stores and keeping one ear to the ground.

When his business took him as far north as John Street, he found himself straying from the docks toward the theater. The Divine Fanny kept a well-regarded salon in her chambers over the greenroom. He could present himself and listen to the gossip of the loyalists, discover if they were aware of the trouble brewing on their streets.

And he could speak with Jennifer Leighton again, who would banter with him on equal terms. He had spent all day listening to differing assessments of the governor and the leading men of New York, some feeble and some astute, and he found he wanted to know what *she* thought of Tryon and DeLancey and the presence of the *Asia* in the harbor. He wanted to hear, filtered through the same wit that had written *The American Prodigal*, a canny opinion on the situation in New York to compare with his own.

More, he wanted to talk theater and comedy and argue the merits of the *Mostellaria* and save her from an evening with the Miles Gloriosus he was charged with protecting.

That was drink talking, too many glasses of beer and sangaree with the merchants of New York loosening his reason and tempting him to give in to his desires. And those desires made him no better than Burgoyne. Except that he had actually seen her play and admired its wit, and been moved by her impromptu performance. And he did not despise Americans, as Burgoyne did, as a race of clods and peasants, or view the first citizens of her thriving cities as somehow *lesser* than their counterparts in London or Bath or Bristol. The English had a peculiar notion that success in America was easier, that to carve wealth out of a wilderness was without toil, and indeed that the colonial atmosphere bred indolence and ingratitude.

He knew, from experience, that it did not. His very first memories were of learning to hunt for his dinner. He did not think often of that time, those ten years in the wilderness, when he had been the favored son. Ashur Rice had taught both Devere boys to kill with the blade and the bow, how to line up a shot, gauge wind and distance with a rifle and wait for the right moment to fire. In England it had all seemed a remote dream, an Arcadian idyll long past recovering, but in America it seemed real once more, though still just out of reach.

Like Jennifer Leighton.

As with so many colonists, the girl very obviously felt the pinch of her status as a provincial, and admired all things English and "sophisticated." It would be so easy to play on that, to manipulate her into his bed by preying on her insecurities. As he had been maneuvered, he fully realized, into his role as spy and provocateur to counter the stigma of his Indian blood. He had never been bitter about it before. Not until this trip to America. Not until Boston.

He was not even certain it would be so very wrong to use his hard-earned status as an Englishman to attract her, because Jennifer Leighton's American character was a decided part of her appeal for Severin—but he was not in New York to indulge himself.

And the girl was not for him. He fixed things for powerful men. Reordered some bothersome aspect of the world to their requirements or advantage. A part of him wanted to fix things for Jennifer Leighton, to warn her that Burgoyne was a brilliant soldier and a talented playwright, and a selfish ass with no intention of advancing her career in the theater—except, perhaps, at a price that she should not have to pay—but his duty was to get the man home in one piece, not to safeguard the virtue of a woman who might be willing to part with it cheaply anyway.

He bypassed John Street and the charms of Jennifer Leighton in favor of duty, following the telltale signs of conspiracy to Beekman's Slip, where Jasper Drake's tavern stood opposite the quay.

Drake's was not a grand public house like Mr. Fraunces' or the King's Arms or Smith's in Philadelphia, all handsome brick structures with lofty ceilings and large windows. This was a workingman's tavern, an old squat clapboard dwelling with a saltbox roof that sloped so low the shingles nearly kissed the ground at the back and the whole thing was more lean-to than gable. And it was a notorious gathering place for Liberty Boys and the dregs of the New York docks.

In his battered leather coat and old buckskin breeches Severin blended in with the sailors and stevedores and laborers who frequented the place. It was easy to do because the smoky taproom with its yawning hearth was packed and the patrons were full of the particular sort of good cheer engendered by free pints of steaming flip.

There was no obvious occasion for this merrymaking, no identifiable source of this unlooked-for generosity. It was an absence, Severin reflected, as a pretty barmaid pressed a foaming pot into his hands with a smile that told him there was more than spiked beer on offer, which told its own story.

That, along with the two mechanics slumming in homespun and passing through the crowd like proud parents at a wedding, with a warm word for every man there.

It was an art, this kind of provocation, stirring up trouble and convincing otherwise law-abiding men to rob their neighbors, and these two were very, very good at it. Dressed like common workingmen but with suspiciously clean fingernails and soft hands, one was tall and blond but too lean faced to be handsome and the other was a small, dark, bandy-legged fellow with greasy hair who spoke in a nasal New England twang.

It did not take long for the two mechanics, who had the rhetorical skills of revival preachers, to stir up trouble, calling to each other, song and response, across the crowded room, decrying the decadence of the rich loyalists who supported the corrupt governor by provisioning the *Duchess of Gordon*, his floating office in exile in New York Harbor, and Vandeput's *Asia*, whose guns were trained, even now, on the town.

These were legitimate complaints, not just the dogma of the church of liberty. No Englishman should have to live under the threat of English guns. Severin had found it difficult to maintain his detachment when he had infiltrated the Rebel lines outside of Boston. He felt the same tonight, even though he knew that someone was definitely fanning the flames of American outrage.

The *Asia*, though, and the *Duchess of Gordon* were unattainable targets of impotent rage. The trick was focusing that anger on an object within reach. A vessel anchored at the wharf, a warehouse filled with British goods, a prominent loyalist whose thrashing, humiliation, or imprisonment would intimidate others.

A pot of black grease paint and a bag of feathers appeared, passed from hand to hand, and that was when Severin knew it was more than a show. The Rebels had done the same in Boston when they had destroyed the tea, disguised, in a manner that might obscure identity but fooled absolutely no one, as Mohawks.

Severin accepted the grease paint when it reached him, and pressed his hand over his face. He stayed his practiced fingers, remembered to smear the paint so that it did not look too convincing. The feathers were sad things plucked from domestic fowl, and he would not have been caught dead in them under any other circumstances.

Devere edged toward the door so that he could slip away as soon as he was certain of the mob's direction. If their object was naval stores needed by the *Boyne*, he would have to compel Governor Tryon to call out his regulars, and devil take the consequences.

The short mechanic began preaching the sins of *decadence* and *dissipation* and *idolatry*, while the tall one unrolled his sheaf of broadsides with a flourish worthy of Garrick, and set them alight.

The flames licked at a familiar name picked out in bold type and Severin felt a queer fluttering in his stomach. The mob's object was not the wharf or the warehouses. The governor would not call out the troops because the place was operating with no official license, and with Burgoyne safely aboard the *Boyne*, the matter touched on Severin's professional affairs not at all.

The broadsides were playbills for the John Street and *The American Prodigal*, the same ones Severin had seen in the lobby Monday night. The mob was being stirred up to pull down the theater, drag the players through the streets, and whip them to the palisade. Had Severin not intercepted Burgoyne, the general would be there right now, directly in the path of the angry mob, as no doubt the writer of the innuendo-filled letter had intended.

Burgoyne, of course, was safe, but Jennifer Leighton was not.

Burgoyne was not coming. For two days Jenny had held out hope that the general might put in an appearance at their next performance. She turned Frances Leighton's risky plan over and over in her mind, but could not commit to it if there was even a slender chance that her potential patron might come to John Street. A professional visit would set the tone for all their future dealings. A personal one would put Jenny's foot squarely upon the path that Frances Leighton had trod.

Her aunt's regrets had been palpable, and Jenny knew she must not make the decision to pursue the more personal variety of patronage lightly. It would change, forever, how the world viewed her, and she was wise enough—in this at least—to know that it might change how she saw herself.

She stood in the wings, stage right, listening to Bobby give the prologue and trying to discern if there were deeper shadows within the enclosure of the royal box, but it was too dark to see. Jenny turned to find Mr. Dearborn watching her, and when he shook his head she finally knew for certain that Burgoyne had not come.

There was always Friday, two nights hence, their last performance for the week, that the general might attend. Perhaps she could send another invitation by way of Devere. For tonight, though, the play had to go on.

Aunt Frances was moving stiffly tonight. The aches that plagued her in the damp weather had started early this year. Otherwise, though, she was in fine form, her charm so potent Jenny could almost see the spell she cast over the house, like a gossamer net. Jenny knew she herself didn't have the talent as an actress to enter directly into that kind of emotional communion with the audience, but her words could be the catechism, and if she found a patron to champion her, they might be heard by tens, even hundreds, of thousands of people in London.

They were acting the duel at the end when it started. Jenny did not recognize the sounds for what they were at first. Her sword clashing with Bobby's was loud in her ears, the war whoops in the street just a distant ruckus, not unusual at night in this neighborhood.

The doors at the back of the house burst open. The audience murmured and turned. Men with feathers in their hair and paint on their faces streamed into the pit, shouting, "Liberty!" and overturning the stands and knocking down anyone who stood in their way. More than a few brandished weapons—cudgels or balks of wood, even a few cutlasses and knives.

The boxes emptied, both tiers, in a stampede of silk

and lace. The audience in the pit fled in a more plebeian exodus of linen and leather. The rabble up in the gallery cheered and threw fruit at the mob, because they were high above the fray and, for them, a riot was just another form of theater.

Jenny dropped her blade and teetered frozen on the apron as the mob surged toward the stage. She did not know what to do.

The Mohawks reached the footlights, and Bobby cursed. "Mr. Dearborn," he shouted. "The lights, if you please!"

Jenny saw the danger at once. If the mob ransacked John Street, the company could rebuild, but it would take only one candle toppled, one sconce unseated, one curtain touched by flames, to destroy the playhouse utterly, and the company's future with it, provided they didn't all burn to death.

Jenny ran to the great torchère on the left side of the stage. Matthew Dearborn was already lowering the footlights, safe in their deep trough of water, into the cellar, while Bobby vaulted into the gallery and began extinguishing lights. The high chandeliers above the stage, the pit, and the gallery would be securely out of reach so long as no one lowered—or cut—the ropes.

Jenny put out the torchère and turned to cross the stage, but the apron was seething with Mohawks smashing props and furniture and hacking at the painted scenery. She was buffeted by their bodies and by the smells of salt fish and wet wool and cooking oil and spilled beer and sweat.

A burly mechanic in a dirty mustard shirt and leather apron took great handfuls of the main curtain and heaved until the rod started to groan high over-head. It was, after the scenery, perhaps the most essential fitting in the building.

Jenny acted out of instinct, grasping the curtain herself and trying to pull it out of his grip. For a moment they were engaged in something like a tug-of-rope contest, with Jenny throwing all her weight onto her heels. Then the rogue let go without warning, and something—*someone*—struck her a blow that slammed her back into the proscenium door hard enough to knock the air from her lungs.

Pain exploded in her chest. She couldn't hear. Her vision swam. Her knees crumpled and she slid to the floor. A booted foot trampled her fingers but she could not draw breath to scream. Wind ruffled her hair and buffeted her face, taunting her because she could feel it on her cheeks and over her eyelids but could not get it inside her chest, and something—the curtain, she registered, through her haze, on its heavy bar, hundreds of muffling yards of velvet on an iron rod—hurtled down toward her.

Another Mohawk, all grease paint and feathers and hard biting hands, gripped her by the armpits and threw her through the proscenium door into the cool darkness of the slot.

Her back hit the flimsy canvas wall. The stage shook violently and the flats trembled as the curtain struck the stage. Her Mohawk cursed, pulled the door shut, and shot the bolt home, trapping her alone with him in the enclosure.

She tried to cry out but her lungs would not fill with air and hot tears coursed down her face. Hands grasped her waist, hauling her up and propping her against the wall. They ran over her arms and legs and took hold of her stays and cut through the laces with a knife. Her rib cage expanded enough to make a strangled noise, more a whimper than a scream.

"Easy," said a cultured voice in the dark. "It is Devere. You are safe, and not, that I can detect, badly injured. No broken bones, in any case. You've just gotten the wind knocked out of you."

It was a narrow enclosure, just enough room for a single actor to wait his cue, but the second door, the one that led to the boxes, told its other function: a vestige of the "traditions" of the English stage, when such slots were a trysting spot for actresses and their patrons. Devere's every move in the tiny room brought his body into contact with hers. There was no avoiding touching him as she clawed involuntarily through the dark while she gasped for air.

He caught her hands in his and held them. "You're going to be fine," he said. "You'll be able to breathe normally again in a moment."

It didn't feel like it. It felt like she was going to die. She was locked, voiceless, in a body that could barely perform its most basic function. Devere's touch was her only tether to the world. And then her lungs began to work again. Only a little at first, and it was pure, undiluted agony, and sweet, joyous relief.

She breathed at first in ragged, ugly gasps, like an old bellows. Each expansion, each contraction made her chest ache. Her eyes watered and she was only glad that in the pitch blackness of the slot Devere could not see how horrible she must look, like a hooked fish, mouth open, flopping on deck.

Finally, when she was breathing normally, she became aware of the sounds of destruction, of splintering wood and tearing cloth, muffled by the thin walls. She gathered herself together and tried to push past Devere.

"Where do you think you are going?" he asked, without moving.

"To stop them, or there will be nothing left."

"They'll stop when the rum runs its course, and not before. Until then, there is nothing practical one can do to deter a drunken mob."

"So John Street is ransacked while trembling Governor Tryon sleeps snug on the *Duchess of Gordon* tonight," she said bitterly.

"Some would say it is the price you pay for trying to play both sides. You can't stage plays catering to loyalists and appease the radicals at the same time."

"We were managing until tonight."

"You were managing until you invited Burgoyne to the theater and someone in the Rebel faction found out about it."

"I was discreet," she said.

"But someone else wasn't," replied Devere. "And *The American Prodigal* is an easy target for Whig ire."

"A play—or a person—that expresses no point of view might as well not exist at all."

"Then may I suggest choosing a less divisive one?"

"It is impossible to stage anything in New York at the moment without giving offense to someone."

"Have you considered that there are safer ways to earn your bread?"

"That is what my parents say."

"*Is* there a mother and a father Leighton?"

"My birth was not the stuff of miracles. Quite the opposite, or so my mother and the midwife like to remind me. Usually in company. It is exceedingly embarrassing."

"Forgive me, but I can't be the first man to have wondered if you are a natural daughter of Frances Leighton."

The idea had certainly never occurred to Jenny. "I am twenty-five. Aunt Frances is barely forty."

"She was fifteen when she made her debut on the stage, and it is not so very uncommon for women in such circumstances to invent origins for their bastards that allow them to be kept close to hand," Devere said.

Jenny hadn't known that. Aunt Frances, she was coming to think, practiced a decidedly selective form of candor. "Then she did a very poor job of it. I met Aunt Fanny once when I was eleven and didn't see her again until she turned up on our doorstep two years ago. In between she sent me a subscription to the circulating library and boxes of plays. And my parents are very real. You cannot get much more prosaic than being a bricklayer in New Brunswick."

"Have you considered going home to them?"

"Have you ever been to New Brunswick? My aunt calls it New Bumpkin, and with good reason."

"It may be dull, but I'll wager it's a good deal safer than New York at the moment."

"So is London. And yet here you are, dressed—if the blow did not disorder my mind—as a Mohawk." She thought of Aunt Frances' remarks about the man's parentage.

"It was the easiest way to infiltrate the mob, but the several ironies of the costume are not lost on me," he said.

"Are those *chicken* feathers?" she asked, reaching up to pluck them free. His hair was silkier than she'd expected, and touching it was far more intimate than she'd intended.

"Unfortunately, yes."

They were knee to knee, thigh to thigh in the narrow enclosure and it would be impossible now to lower her arms without touching him.

"If it is any consolation," she said, feeling a flush rise up her neck to heat her face, "I am dressed in my bumpkin's costume, though I would not be caught dead in it even in New Brunswick."

"But it is what the audience expects," he said.

"Yes."

She did not mean for it to come out quite so breathless.

His lips, unexpectedly soft, covered hers. It was the lightest of touches—a question, not an answer—but when his mouth urged hers open, she responded. The wetness of it startled her. The slick penetration of his tongue suggested another kind of joining.

Her hips tilted to meet his. She grasped his shoulders for balance. He placed his palm at the small of her back and pressed her closer still, where she needed him. Her chest ached from the blow earlier, but she didn't care because this was too good to stop.

Her fingers met the silk rope of his braided hair at the back of his neck, thick and heavy atop the collar of his coat. She wanted more. She tugged at the ribbon until the bow opened and she could comb through his hair in greedy handfuls.

He groaned, and shocked her by gathering her petticoats, the rough linen and old threadbare cotton rustling in the dark. Surprise gave way to delight as she felt his knuckles dance over her calves, her knees, the ribbons that tied her stockings, her bare thighs, and then—

The startled cry that bubbled up to her lips was muffled by his mouth, but he stopped just then, fingers stroking slick fire between her legs, to whisper in her ear, "Let me do this for you."

She had been doing *this* for herself for so long that the idea of having someone else do it to her had become a remote fantasy. When she opened her mouth the word that tumbled out was, "Yes." And, *Yes*. And, *Yes*. Over and over again.

It was building, spiraling, climbing, the thing she had decided she could live without if she had to, or at least abide without sharing with someone else. How wrong she had been. She wanted to be open, wider, for him, but there was no room in the close confines of the slot so she lifted her knee and placed her foot on his lean hip, and he licked her ear and whispered, "Good girl," into the shell of it.

A tentative invasion followed, the tip of his finger, hovering at her entrance, until her throaty groan encouraged him onward.

"Jenny!"

She heard Bobby's voice calling for her and realized that the shouting, the sounds of destruction, had at some point stopped.

Devere froze, one hand pressed to the small of her back, the other between her legs. "Stay with me, Jenny," he said. His finger slid home.

She felt like crying. And screaming. And dying, preferably to Devere's tender ministrations, but the desperation in Robert Hallam's voice recalled her to reason and she thrust Devere's hand away and smoothed her petticoats down and tried to get her breathing under control.

"I must go," she said.

"Is he your lover?"

"No, but he is my employer and my landlord and, until I can find another, my patron." That was the reality. She was not free to explore passion with men like Severin Devere. "He won't come now, to John Street, will he?"

She meant Burgoyne, of course.

"No," said Devere. "I could not allow him."

"Then tell him," she said, accepting that one path was now closed to her, "tell him that I shall be delighted to dine with him, Friday, on the *Boyne*."

Six

Severin had forgotten how much rejection hurt. The frustration of thwarted desire—which he was certain had been mutual—didn't help either.

He knew better than to blame Jennifer Leighton, though. He waited in the darkened slot listening to her and Hallam talking. She might not be the theater manager's lover, but she was right about her predicament. The man was her patron. Her plays were performed only through his good graces.

That did not change how Devere felt. He was a professional eavesdropper. It was a skill, as mechanical, usually, as picking a lock or deciphering a code. Not so now. Instead of fixing on key words or promising leads in their conversation—and there were many—he was consumed by irrational jealousy. Of course, Jennifer Leighton and Robert Hallam spoke in a shorthand that told of long acquaintance. They had worked closely together for years.

One frenzied, delicious moment in a closet did not change that. Nor would it sidetrack Jennifer Leighton's ambition. And yet Severin could not help but feel, based on the tone of Hallam's voice and his choice of words, that he did not really see Jennifer Leighton clearly as a playwright, because he saw her first as a woman. One with skills he could make use of, to be sure, but defined and limited by her sex.

Hallam's estimate might be true of Jennifer Leighton's body, although Devere's experience with the Merry Widow had taught him that not all women were limited by that—his ribs still ached dully as a reminder—but it was most assuredly not true of the girl's mind.

Severin listened as she suggested clever ideas, dismissed one by one by Hallam, for luring their loyalist audience back to the John Street while keeping the Liberty Boys at bay. Reduced ticket prices, a benefit night for beleaguered Boston, a banquet catered by Mr. Fraunces . . . until finally Jenny gave up and receded into the role Hallam expected of her. He did not want a partner in management for the John Street. He wanted to play Garrick to her Divine Fanny, and he would not—could not—see how ill-suited clever Jennifer Leighton was for the part.

When their voices at last became quieter, then dwindled, and Severin was certain they had left the stage, he slipped out through the door to the boxes and picked his way carefully through the wreckage.

It could have been worse. The chairs were smashed, but these could be replaced. The curtain appeared to be in tatters, but he had seen sailors repair such in a day's time. The Hallams had learned from the riots in '66. The John Street was an altogether more substantial building than the earlier theater on Chapel had been, much harder for a mob to destroy, and from all appearances it had weathered the attack relatively unscathed.

Like Jennifer Leighton.

She had obviously known about his parentage—known, and expressed no distaste, or any distasteful fascination. Not that he wouldn't have taken advantage of that. He'd come to think of it as his due, as recompense for a host of other prejudices and slights.

The aunt, no doubt, must have told her. A part of him had hoped that Jennifer Leighton would reject him for his Indian blood, that he could dismiss her as no better than Burgoyne, and deliver her to him without overmuch regret. Or that she would be entirely drawn to him for the novelty, the spice of exoticism and danger that Englishwomen sought him out for. But instead she had plucked the chicken feathers out of his hair with touching practicality and commiserated with him over the absurd roles they were each forced to play, parodies of their true selves.

He'd acted on impulse, kissing her, and *that* irony was also not lost on him. When they had come back to New York after those years in the wild, he had understood at last the mocking smile that had always stolen over Ashur Rice's face when he talked about the English.

It was the way the English had looked at Severin, and his mother, but not—he'd noted immediately—at his brother. Julian was the eldest and the heir, and advertised to be wholly English, unlike Severin.

The women in particular regarded his mother with a mix of scorn and pity.

For an eleven-year-old boy ripped from his home, the results had been predictable. He'd endured, for weeks, their quiet suspicion and open mistrust, and when his polite, dulcet behavior did nothing to change theirs, he'd lost his patience and taken the license they had granted him to act the savage.

Only Courtney Fairchild—a gangly, direct boy with long arms and a quick smile—had seen through him. It had been Fairchild who had said plainly, and with no intention to wound, "They will change how they look at you when you grow up, because you will be a man, and your brother will have a title. But if you go on like this, they will *never* change how they look at your mother."

It had cut Severin to the bone. Courtney had been right, of course, and on his next visit home from school he had dropped the act and been everything quiet, pleasant, and *English*. They had interpreted that as just another variety of savage, of course—the "noble" sort—but over time he had learned to be more English than the English. This had eased, somewhat, his mother's difficult path, and later paved Severin's.

They had become fast friends at school after that, Severin and the openhearted Fairchild. That tie had been strengthened by a halcyon English summer spent at Fairchild's family home, where Severin had fallen hopelessly in love with the man's sister.

Phippa had cared for him too, in the puppyish way that teenagers did, though it had seemed like so much more at the time. After three weeks of shy glances and afternoons spent riding and fishing, all three of them together, she had arranged to meet him at the garden folly, a ludicrous two-story crenellated Gothic flight of fancy, in the middle of the night. They had shared something awkward and tender and precious there. She had sighed his name as he entered her and clung to him tenderly afterward, but in the morning she had laughed off his proposal of marriage as an impossibility.

Severin's friendship with her brother had endured that turn of events because Fairchild had shrugged his bony shoulders and declared girls inscrutable. They both knew the real reason, and Fairchild had alluded to it once, years later, when he'd said simply, "Phippa always cared too much what others think." She was married now with children, three living, two dead, and a fat roaring country squire of a husband who drank.

When Severin presented himself at the King's Arms and asked to see Fairchild, it took him a moment to apprehend why the publican was giving him queer looks. Then Fairchild came rumbling down the stairs and his eyes widened, and Severin realized he was still wearing the grease paint and feathers. A lapse testifying—to his chagrin—more to how much this business with Jennifer Leighton had distracted him than to the quantity of liquor he'd consumed throughout the day.

"What the devil happened to you?" asked Fairchild. "Family reunion?"

"Most amusing."

"What *did* happen?"

"I went out for a nice little riot. Apparently it's what you do in New York when Vauxhall is closed."

"Have you been drinking?"

"Too much and not enough."

"That is the effect New York has on everyone these

days, my dear Severin. The only solution is to have another drink and hope matters improve," said Fairchild, leading the way up to his rooms. "How does one get that off?" he asked, in reference to the face paint.

"Bear grease works."

"I doubt the publican has any," Courtney said with an air of apology.

"Butter will do."

Devere washed his face and plucked the remaining few chicken feathers out of his hair in the small closet adjoining Fairchild's comfortably appointed room.

He could see why so many of the garrison's exiled officers chose to risk staying discreetly in town rather than retreating with their men to the safety of the *Asia*—especially those officers with staff positions, like Courtney, who were not responsible for discipline or a body of troops. The King's Arms had modern chimneys, large windows, and fully curtained beds. It was warm and dry and did not move underfoot. Severin had never enjoyed sea voyages, but this one, with Burgoyne, promised to be particularly unpleasant, and the King's Arms made him wish he did not have to make it.

Courtney pulled two chairs up to the fire and poured Severin a glass of sweet, dark rum, which he accepted gratefully.

"Tell me, then," said Courtney, "how you came to be in a riot."

Severin told his tale. Or at least he told the part about his dealings in the city, the telltale signs of quiet preparation he had observed along the docks, the gathering at Jasper Drake's, and the attack on the theater. He left out his interlude in the slots with Jennifer

Leighton, because he had not as yet decided what he was going to do about it.

"And Frances?" asked Courtney sharply. "Is she all right? Was she hurt?"

Severin did not miss the familiar usage of her name. "She was not onstage during the riot."

Courtney set down his drink. "I'll just send a message around to John Street," he said, "asking if there is anything they need. On behalf of the garrison in exile," he finished, making light of his obvious concern.

It confirmed suspicions that had been forming in Severin's mind as he collected bits and pieces of gossip during the day. Combined with the rumors that had swirled around the Divine Fanny's departure from the stage and the death of her lover in London, it forced Severin's hand. He watched Courtney write the letter and ring for the publican and pay for the messenger; then he waited until they were both comfortably seated like civilized Englishmen before the hearth with firing glasses in hand and a full bottle on the table before broaching the subject. He only prayed he was wrong.

"Frances Leighton," Severin said softly. "You told me she was too expensive for your purse."

"And so she is," said Fairchild, smiling faintly into his glass. Severin hoped he had not arrived too late.

"We have always been honest with each other, Courtney," prodded Devere.

"But discreet," replied his old friend. "Especially with secrets that are not ours to share."

"It is not such a secret in some circles in London, Courtney. The price for that particular lady's favors is too high, even if she offers them for free."

Fairchild drank his rum off and set the glass on the table. "Have you been following me, Severin?"

"No. I made inquiries."

Fairchild swore.

"It is what I do."

"Not to friends."

"If you were my enemy, I would encourage you to bed her."

"It isn't like that, Severin. I *know*. I know about Harry. Frances and I aren't lovers. She won't take one. Not after Harry. And not with the episodes of confusion she suffers. She knows what is coming."

He moved his empty glass on the table. "We dine and we talk and we read to each other—out of the public eye, lest it hurt her career to be known to be unavailable— and it is . . . enough."

Severin could tell that it wasn't, but it was all they could ever have, unless Fairchild wanted to share her fate.

"You know how it must end," said Severin.

"It will end the way all affairs end, just sooner," Fairchild said quietly. "And I think I should rather have a few happy years than the lifetime of quiet dissatisfaction to which Phippa has consigned herself."

Devere decided against further argument. That such a liaison could result in scandal, and destroy his future marriage prospects if the whole truth were widely known, went without saying. Fairchild might be throwing away the unquestioned social acceptance he had been born into—the security that Severin had never enjoyed because of the rumors clouding his childhood—but it was his friend's decision to make. Courtney Fairchild was not by nature a man who kept secrets. That he had kept his affair with the Divine Fanny secret even from Severin spoke to the strength of the attachment.

He had pried into Fairchild's business, and even if it was for his own good, Courtney was owed a confidence in return. And Severin did not think he could take his dilemma in regards to Jennifer Leighton silently back to the *Boyne* with him. When he closed his eyes he was back in the dark with her, caught up in an attraction he was now certain was mutual.

"Frances Leighton's niece," Severin said. "I promised to arrange a meeting for her with Burgoyne."

"Frances tried to talk her out of it, but she is determined," said Fairchild. "And really, what is there for her here? Riots and theater closings. The girl is willing, and Frances thinks she can fix it so Hallam won't interfere."

"That isn't the problem." It was difficult to articulate. "I made a gentleman's agreement with Burgoyne. He has remained safely aboard the *Boyne* all week in expectation of being brought a night's entertainment."

"I still fail to see the issue."

"She doesn't belong in his bed."

Fairchild pursed his lips. "You don't have what Jennifer Leighton is after, Severin."

He didn't. Not if she planned to use Burgoyne just as he planned to use her, each to their own ends. It still didn't sit right with him.

"But you might be able to get what she wants for her *and* spare her a night with Jack Brag," said Fairchild, with unexpected calculation. "If you had something over Burgoyne, you might be able to convince him to forgo the pleasure of her body, and still obtain for her the introductions she desires. And no doubt the fair Jenny would be suitably grateful to you."

"I had no idea you could be so devious, Courtney."

"I suppose that is Frances brushing off on me," said Fairchild. "She is one of life's natural strategists. And a keen observer of people. She saw how *you* looked at the girl."

It shocked him to think he had been so transparent. "Jennifer Leighton was . . . not what I was expecting."

"I'd no idea she had such a fine figure myself until the other night. It's not what you expect a clever woman to look like under her clothes, exceptions like the Divine Fanny notwithstanding."

"That is not exactly what I meant," said Severin.

"Of course not," agreed Fairchild. "She's pretty enough, but you can find that anywhere. The girl is an original, like her aunt. Frances would see Jenny have her chance in London, but it seems a pity to waste all that . . . *cleverness* . . . on Jack Brag."

"I'm sure I don't know what you mean," said Severin, who did. The idea filled him with pleasurable anticipation. He was already considering what strategy he might use to persuade Burgoyne to forgo the charms of the fair Jenny.

Courtney laughed. "Just so. And naturally I won't wish you success in your endeavor, but I will offer a word of caution. I was going to send a warning to the *Boyne*. My informants in town say that two decided villains have been asking after a man meeting your description. Whatever you did for Howe in Boston—and I really don't want to know—has caught up to you here.

You'd be unwise to walk the streets of the city after nightfall. I would offer to act as bodyguard, but I have obligations to a certain lady."

Severin did not expect Fairchild to play nursemaid. His present quarrel with the Widow was of his own making, and evading her chastisement was entirely his own responsibility. Such enmities were an inevitable product of his calling.

"We hope to sail Saturday," said Severin. "I've bargained for all the supplies the *Boyne* requires. So as long as the merchants deliver, I won't need to be back in town again and you're unlikely to have my untimely death on your conscience, but I thank you for the warning all the same."

Severin accepted responsibility for his predicament, but he was not a fool. He had no further obligations in New York and he was not in any haste to meet his ancestors, so he returned to the *Boyne* directly. He was grateful for the warning and was satisfied—as far as possible—that Courtney knew the perils of becoming too deeply involved with Frances Leighton.

And he had business with John Burgoyne.

Jenny had emerged from the darkness of the slot—and the intense intimacy of Severin Devere's embrace— into the aftermath of a battle. The curtain lay across the stage like a fallen tree, hundreds of yards of dusty velvet in a tangled, immovable heap. The little table they used onstage and two chairs were smashed to flinders, and the Arcadian backdrop that had been Jenny's closest brush with the wilderness was slashed with a dozen cuts from top to bottom.

Bobby looked as though he had put up more of a fight than the scenery. The silver lace was ripped off one side of his blue suit and he had the beginnings of a black eye. The relief on his face when Jenny emerged unhurt was not feigned. She was an actress. She could tell. But when he opened his arms she did not fly into them, and not because of what had just happened with Devere.

"They were shouting Burgoyne's name," she said. "The mob. When they first stormed the pit, they were looking for him."

"His presence in New York is an open secret," replied the man who had nurtured her talent these past two years.

"But his invitation to occupy the royal box was not. Our greenroom is hardly a hotbed of radicalism. Someone tipped off the Liberty Boys."

Bobby sketched a little bow. "I won't deny it, then," he said. "It was supposed to be only a dozen Mohawks or thereabouts. They were going to carry him out of the theater and take him to Connecticut."

"*Why?*" She couldn't believe he would endanger John Street like that.

"To keep the theater open," he said. "The Tories are the ones buying tickets, but the Committee of One Hundred is under pressure from Congress to shut us down."

"Better to be shut down than burned down," she said. "And to reopen when the Liberty Boys have been dealt with."

"Jenny, who do you think is going to *deal* with them? Howe cannot break out of Boston. Parliament is disinclined to spend the money to raise more troops.

And if the Rebels manage to defeat Howe's army at Boston, where do you think Washington will go next?"

Here.

Where at best he would close the playhouse, and at worst he would throw the players—Jenny, Bobby, and Aunt Frances included—in jail.

When Severin reached the *Boyne*, her august passenger was once more working on his plans, a map of New York spread over the table.

"The Leighton girl," Severin said, "is after your patronage."

"Of course she is," replied Burgoyne evenly. "It is one of the not inconsiderable perquisites of writing for the theater: ambitious actresses."

"Your wife might feel differently."

Burgoyne put down his pen. Severin felt the thrill of incipient victory. He had chosen the right tack.

"My wife," said Burgoyne, "is not a well woman, and I would not want her unduly distressed."

"Then perhaps you might offer Jennifer Leighton an introduction to Garrick, but forgo the pleasure of bedding her."

Burgoyne laughed. "Is the girl such a fair flower that your savage heart is stirred, Devere?"

Devere felt his hackles rise. "A Mohawk warrior," he said, "would have little use for a pretty playwright." It was Severin Devere, Englishman and spy, who was beguiled by Jennifer Leighton. "And this one is, if not innocent, then far too inexperienced for this kind of game."

"You don't know actresses, Devere. She needs a

patron, not a white knight. And you're hardly the right color to play that role for her."

"Is that what passes for wit in Drury Lane these days?"

"It is how business is done between gentlemen and actresses in the theater, Devere. We can't all rut our way through the virgins of the minor gentry playing Squanto for them. Or do you woo them as Oroonoko, the noble savage?"

"It would be a pity for you," said Severin, gathering Burgoyne's papers and thrusting them into his pocket to lock away in his cabin, where at least they would be secure, "if the role I play most naturally is Iago."

Seven

Jenny understood why Bobby had gambled with the safety of the playhouse to secure the protection of the Committee. She did not know why *she* had jeopardized her opportunity to meet Burgoyne by kissing—no, it was more than kissing—Severin Devere.

And she did not care to imagine what Devere might think of her. It was what most men thought about actresses—that they were promiscuous. Only she wasn't. And yet she planned to be, although that wasn't really true either. One man would not make her promiscuous. She had avoided entanglements in New Brunswick because she had hoped there was something more for her than a life of domestic duty. At John Street she had found that something, though only through Bobby's patronage. If there was a way for a woman to have a voice—and Jenny knew she would be mute if she could not get her plays performed—without going through a man, no woman to her knowledge had yet discovered it.

She must forget about her folly with Devere. Aunt Frances had lost her head over a man and been cast out of the London theater for it. Jenny would not be so foolish.

The plan was simple enough. They must wait until Friday night. There was no sooner opportunity. If Jenny tried to go during the day, when the wharves were bustling, she would be seen, and the same tradesmen who supplied the docks also provisioned the John Street Theater. Bobby Hallam would be sure to hear that one of his actresses had been rowed out to a naval vessel.

It had to be night.

The company was working around the clock to put the theater to rights, and Bobby had announced the Scottish Play for Friday in the hopes that the radicals would find the murderous king more to their liking than Jenny's *American Prodigal*. This, fortunately, meant that Bobby Hallam and Frances Leighton were indispensible, but Jenny was not. If Jenny took ill, someone could replace her in the minor parts she played, but Bobby's responsibilities and role would not permit him the opportunity to check on her.

Frances had thought it all out: "You must go home after you are seen to be ill and remain there until the play has started, then get to the docks and meet the boat Devere will send for you. Do not return home until the greenroom has emptied and I have placed the lantern in the upstairs parlor window to indicate that Bobby has left for the night."

It was a very sound plan, and it made Jenny wonder

exactly how Aunt Frances had come to be so good at devising such a plot.

Jenny downed the little blue glass vial of ipecac her aunt had given her in the darkness of the wings while Mr. Dearborn was running his rehearsal. Its effect was startling and immediate. She was very, *very* sick, on her hands and knees on the apron staring down at the boards, in unhappy intimacy with every knot in the grain, with Mr. Dearborn bringing her water and Bobby holding her shoulders while she retched.

She had not expected him to want to cancel the night's performance over it.

It was more than that. Bobby was genuinely worried about her. He *carried* her all the way across the street and up the three flights of stairs to her room. She could hear him outside her door pacing on the small landing, insisting that Aunt Frances call the doctor and send for Margaret to act as a nurse—and generally stop the world—so that Jenny Leighton might be cosseted like a princess.

And she had done all this to deceive him.

Her ribs ached from retching. She hadn't expected the ipecac to affect her so powerfully. When she'd asked Fanny why exactly she had a bottle of the stuff, her aunt had said, "In case someone is poisoned." Then she'd added, "Accidentally, of course."

Jenny *did* feel as though she'd been poisoned. Her throat burned and her head ached, and when Aunt Frances brought her a cup of tea thick with honey she drank it gratefully.

Bobby put his head in the door and asked once more if he couldn't call the doctor. Jenny insisted that it was

probably something she had eaten, and finally he relented, but not before he'd gone to his lodgings to fetch
her a convalescent's bolster for the bed and a lap desk
and extra candles—the good spermaceti kind—and ink
and paper and a stack of new plays just delivered from
London and the latest novel from the circulating library.

"Shall I read to you?" he asked, sitting in the chair
by the window and picking up the book.

His concern, his tenderness, the way he set aside
his business—all for her—made Jenny worry that she
was making a mistake, throwing away the reality of
John Street and Bobby's undeniable affection for the
possibility of Drury Lane and Burgoyne's theoretical
patronage.

There was a scratch at the door and Mr. Dearborn
put his head in to ask if Jenny would be performing
that night.

"Absolutely not," said Bobby. "Put Miss Richards in
for Jenny, Matthew, and continue with the rehearsal."

Mr. Dearborn's interruption reminded Jenny of one
of the more persistent reasons she had always hesitated
to hitch her future to Robert Hallam's. The stage manager had long since earned enough money to buy his
freedom, banked with Quakers who had pressed time
and again for his release, but Bobby would not sell.

Aunt Frances had always said that a man who
thought he could own another man would be certain
he owned any woman foolish enough to call herself his
wife. No, Jenny could not stomach the idea of being
any man's *master*, as she would be Mr. Dearborn's—a
man whose skill and experience in the theater exceeded
her own—if she became Bobby's wife.

"If I said I would marry you," she said impulsively, "would you sell Mr. Dearborn his freedom?" *And relieve me of so many difficult choices*, she added to herself.

Bobby looked as surprised as she felt.

"Now you've really worried me, Jenny. Are you so near death's door?" he asked, half in jest and half in genuine concern.

"I feel awful," she confessed. "But I'm certain I'll live. Would you do it?"

They had discussed it once before, when he had casually proposed marriage, sitting in Frances' second-floor parlor after a long night in the greenroom. She had not attended the party. He had been flushed with drink. He had confessed that the patrons had repeated lines from her prologue and her one-act play over and over, to raucous laughter, all night long. That had pleased him. He had proposed, not down on one knee, but sprawled in Frances' comfortable wing chair, saying simply, "We should get married."

She had told him she did not want to become a slave owner. He had waved away her objections, saying that it was really his elder brother, Lewis, who owned Mr. Dearborn, and Bobby was just a steward for the property. But Lewis had been gone two years now, decamped with the rest of the company to the more welcoming shores of Jamaica, and there was no sign they would return anytime soon.

Bobby's objections were much the same now.

"Jenny, if there was another stage manager in America his equal, I would free him, and gladly. But there isn't. And without him, we could not run the John Street. It is not just the bookkeeping and house managing, and his way with the patrons. It is Lewis' infernally complicated stage machinery as well. We could not find a man with the skills to run and maintain it."

"Matthew could manage John Street as an employee, rather than as a piece of the property, like one of the flats."

"He could, but he wouldn't," said Bobby Hallam. "I know *I* wouldn't stay in New York either were I a black man with skills, money, and options. The people here look at a black face and they see a plotter. They remember the fires. If I free Mr. Dearborn, he will take the next ship for London."

"That is not the answer I hoped for," she said. And yet it was what Jenny herself wanted to do.

"It is an honest one. I could have lied. Another truth is that Mr. Dearborn is only mine in name. If I freed him, I'd have to answer to Lewis for it when he returns. If I'm successful enough, it won't matter, but times are just too uncertain right now, Jenny. I'm not saying I won't ever free him, but I can't do it now."

"And how does that square with your republican ideals? When you meet in secret with the printers and the mechanics, do they toast liberty while you stage-whisper an aside excusing slavery?"

"I know you think I am playing the tyrant, but it is not an arbitrary exercise of authority. I am trying to *build* something here, and to do that I must be a realist. A generation ago players could not get a license at all. Now we have permanent theaters in Charleston, Philadelphia, and New York. If I can keep the John Street open—if I can keep *you*, and Mr. Dearborn—we might in time have a theater to rival any in London, and you would not have to look across an ocean for an audience worthy of your talents."

"It is a grandiose ambition," she said.

"Pot, kettle, my love," he said, and kissed her forehead, and adjusted her bolster and lit an extra taper before he left.

She listened to him descend the stairs and take leave of her aunt. Jenny heard the familiar whine and click of the door to the street swinging shut, the latch falling into place, and by then she felt well enough to get up and begin to wash and dress and prepare to meet Burgoyne.

She had decided to embrace the part of the actress this time, because one did not go to meet a successful London playwright dressed as a frump. If her person did not follow fashion, Burgoyne might assume that her plays didn't either.

When they had first arrived in New York, Jenny had possessed a wardrobe more suitable for a New Brunswick burgher's daughter than a famous actress's companion. Jenny had not been able to fit into any of the willowy Fanny's castoffs, so Aunt Frances had used her excellent eye for color, cut, and cloth to buy her a selection of used garments that could be remodeled. It had been an education in taste and style for Jenny, who had been used to the practical garments of the housewife: loose cotton jackets and plain linen petticoats topped with well-washed aprons. She had never before given any thought to how color and proportion might alter her shape or frame her features, but Fanny was expert in all of this.

The Divine Fanny knew that vertical stripes emphasized curves like Jenny's without adding weight, that a girl of five foot and two pence ought not to wear large patterns unless they were simple damasks of a single color. But that she oughtn't to wear those at all because they were a decade out-of-date in London and, though they could be had cheaply secondhand, they were not a good investment. Aunt Frances knew that an older gown could be brought up-to-date by narrowing the pleats at the waist, lengthening the sleeves, and concealing any little defects with accessories.

The gown Jenny chose to impress Burgoyne was the most striking of Fanny's selections, a polonaise in lilac and gray that alternated narrow stripes with slender trellised flowers. It had a petticoat and stomacher in the same fabric, expertly matched to emphasize Jenny's full, round breasts and defined waist. Aunt Frances had bought a white work apron for it so fine that you could see the stripes straight through the gossamer cloth, and there were matching ribbons for hanging a watch—Frances', naturally—from the waist, along with another set to tie around her neck. The cleverly extended sleeves were trimmed with box pleating, and there was a generous hood attached at the back, large enough to be worn over an elegantly piled coiffure, an embellishment that was both stylish and practical, because Jenny did not wish to be recognized.

The hem was short enough to show her ankle, so she chose a pair of clocked stockings and her best black silk shoes with the paste buckles. Her hair she gathered loosely at the back of her head and secured with a comb. Then she used hot tongs to curl the pieces that framed her face and rested on her shoulders, just as she did for Aunt Frances, though with—in her own eyes—noticeably less impressive effect. The color, a coppery brown, had never taken well to powdering. Her first experiment with the stuff had ended with her brothers rolling on the floor in laughter. They had said it looked like a corroded gutter, and she had been forced to agree. Now she wore it plain and hoped it did not make her appear rustic.

When at last she stopped to survey herself in the glass, she was satisfied with the result. Burgoyne would not be disappointed. She was more interested, though, in what Severin Devere would make of the ensemble. He had seemed to like her well enough in her ugly maid's gown. Though the linen shroud had been made for the stage, it was her fashionable polonaise that felt like a costume, her role tonight a character to be acted for another's entertainment.

That, she told herself, was the ipecac talking. Aunt Frances had instructed her to eat something to settle her stomach after the noxious draft, but Jenny wasn't sure she wanted to eat ever again. She left the buttered toast and raspberry jam Margaret had brought her untouched on the plate.

Burgoyne had already read her *American Prodigal*—she had replayed the compliments Devere had relayed over and over in her mind, basking in his praise—but the new play she was working on now would be even better. At least she hoped so. The manuscript was held together in places by pins and was stiff with ink where she had struck out whole passages. A work in progress, to be sure, but she tucked it into her pocket anyway. If she could share some of it with Burgoyne, it might persuade him that she was both talented and prolific.

Jenny watched from the parlor window until she saw the doors of the John Street close to signal that the play had started, and then she slipped out of the house. It was still light enough—just—that she felt safe walking down to the waterfront on her own, the streets still teeming with commerce and the docks bustling with trade.

It was when she reached the end of the wharf where the little boat was waiting, just as Devere's reply had promised, that she hesitated. Devere was not there. The lieutenant in charge of the six-man crew did not smile or bow or greet her. He did not offer her his hand or make any effort to help her into the boat.

She had never felt so small or insignificant, so scorned. It was a taste of the way she would be treated in future, the way Aunt Frances was sometimes treated, by those who thought of actresses as well-dressed whores. It was the very opposite of how she had felt talking with Severin Devere in the greenroom.

She took a step back from the edge of the dock.

The dour lieutenant sighed and put out a hand. "Come now," he said in clipped, impatient tones, "or we will lose the tide."

Her stomach churned. Just the ipecac, she told herself, gathering her petticoats. She placed one foot gingerly in the boat. It rolled and bilge sloshed over her embroidered-silk toe.

She imagined Drury Lane as she had seen it in engravings, thronged with eager theatergoers, not a Mohawk in sight. And she thought of the riot at John Street, and how she had gasped for breath after the vandal had struck her. She must go forward with this, she told herself, settling on the cold, hard bench.

It was colder out on the water. Spray from the oars stippled her gown. She watched the thick forest of masts dwindle behind her and the *Boyne* grow larger as they drew near, the harbor stretching empty all around the warship.

Jenny had never seen a ship of the line up so close. The *Boyne* was massive, with two tall decks bristling with guns. She would not put on a brave appearance during the day. Her paint was too chipped and her sails too stained, but she radiated menace and power tonight, rising tall out of the water, and Jenny wished very much that she had Aunt Frances with her now, because this was part of Fanny's world. London actresses walked the corridors of power shoulder to shoulder with men like Burgoyne. They knew how to resist creatures like Severin Devere. They *belonged*.

Bricklayers' daughters from New Brunswick, no matter how clever their plays, did not.

Some of Jenny's confidence returned when she was hoisted aboard in the little swing—like something from a pastoral engraving—and a young sailor helped her, with detached courtesy, to the deck. The roll of the ship at first threw her gait off, but by the time she had descended the ladder to the deck below she was walking steadily enough.

There was no sign of Devere.

She ought to feel relieved about that, but she did not. A familiar face, even one that belonged to a spy and an assassin whose kiss and caresses had unnerved her, would have been comforting.

There were none such here. If she had been Aunt Frances, she would have been greeted and escorted by the captain, or at the very least some junior officer. She would have been *acknowledged*. Jenny did not even rate a spotty midshipman. Instead she was hurried along by a servant—a surly New Englander in curiously theatrical blue and silver livery—past sailors who schooled their faces not to sneer, but she heard the catcalls, and the barked orders that cut them short.

They passed three closed doors on a short corridor. Then they reached the end and the servant who escorted her scratched once at a handsome panel, waited a breath, and then opened it.

On a pasha's splendor.

Jenny had accompanied her aunt to the great homes of New York, to the mansions of the DeLanceys, the Van Cortlands, the Phillipses, and others. Luxury abounded in Manhattan, but it was a bourgeois sort of opulence, the tasteful paintings, the gleaming silver, the restrained classical ornament all chosen to impress.

Not so Burgoyne's quarters, which were shockingly large after traveling tight passages, and brimming with sensuality. The floor had been painted in a tiled pattern, but little of it was visible. Turkey carpets in a profusion of rich colors were scattered from the door to the wide expanse of sash windows. These were open to the night air and faced out to sea, the breeze fresh and crisp and untainted by the city air. There were furs draped over damask chairs and heaped on guns, and paintings crowded together on the walls. A polished mahogany table was set with china and silver plate and crystal glasses that sparkled in profligate candlelight—more tapers than Jenny allowed herself for a week of writing. Beside the board stood a marble pillar topped with a plaster bust of a Muse.

The richness of textures was almost overwhelming, and such was the jumble of art and furnishings that Jenny almost missed the curtained bed built into the wall behind the table. It was the only practical fixture in the entire cabin, simple carpentry in fresh white paint, but the silk bed hangings were tied open to display plump cushions and a damask coverlet on an overstuffed feather mattress.

The sight stirred butterflies in her stomach. She forced herself to look away from the bed. There was no one waiting for her in the cabin, and the dyspeptic servant departed without a word.

Jenny wasn't certain what to do, whether to sit or stand. Again, Aunt Frances would have known. Jenny felt keenly her lack of sophistication. In the end she crossed to the window to look out because it was the point in the room farthest from the bed and the view was spectacular. Somewhere across that sparkling ocean, under the same moon, was London with her painted theaters and her audiences of thousands.

The door opened and Jenny understood at once why she had been left to wait. Burgoyne had set the stage and now he wished to make an entrance.

It was a good one. He did not strike her as handsome as Severin Devere had done. And he was not young. His eyes were perhaps too closely set, his face a trifle too long, his jaw a bit too heavy for real beauty, but he did project a certain martial splendor and an undeniable vigor. He wore a fine red coat with gold lace trim over a white silk waistcoat with gold embroidery. His hair was black, neatly curled at the sides, and tied in a silk faille ribbon.

With casual elegance, Burgoyne bowed, his gold braid winking in the candlelight. He crossed the room and kissed her hand. She caught a glimpse of Severin Devere scowling in the corridor before the door closed.

"Miss Leighton," the general said, with unfeigned pleasure. "I knew your aunt in London. How is she?"

Going mad. "Very well, thank you. We both read your play *Maid of the Oaks*, and have been petitioning our company's manager to stage it."

She did not add Bobby's remarks on the quality of the play or its likelihood to please an American audience that knew Burgoyne first and foremost for his fatuous and patronizing proclamation of amnesty to Rebels who laid down their arms, which he had authored in General Gage's name.

"The Divine Fanny would make an excellent Bab Lardoon," said Burgoyne graciously. "Better even, perhaps, than Mrs. Abington," he added, naming Fanny's greatest rival, and the actress who had originated the role.

"Were she here, Aunt Frances would express *unqualified* agreement," said Jenny drily.

Burgoyne's heavy-lidded eyes widened and his full lips pursed. She had surprised him. "You take your wit from your aunt, I see. And your ambition, also."

Jenny did not think she took her ambition from anyone but herself, but it was flattering to be compared to the Divine Fanny. "If only success were heritable," she said, "I would follow close in her footsteps."

"Who is to say you won't?" asked Burgoyne.

They dined—or at least he dined—at the polished mahogany table with the plaster Muse looking over their shoulders. Jenny did not eat. She moved her food around on her plate so that Burgoyne would not notice.

It was not the cuisine that put her off, the beef in pastry or the cherries in souse or the fresh green peas with ham. Burgoyne's cook was obviously skilled. It was her stomach that was at fault, still churning from the ipecac, hungry and at the same time completely repulsed by food. The brandy, though, was smooth and went down easily, and kindled a soothing warmth in her belly. She drank rather more of it than she should.

They talked about the state of the theater in America—dismal—and he charmed her with a recitation from the prologue he had written for a performance of *Zara* in Boston.

"'Then sunk the stage quelled by the bigots roar, truth fled with sense, and Shakespeare charmed no more,'" he said, pouring her another glass of brandy. "'Amidst the groans sunk every liberal art that polished life, or humanized the heart.' The Rebels," he added after he had declaimed the whole thing for her from memory, "outlaw theater because it has the power to move hearts and minds. Because they rightly fear that art and finer sentiment might sway a crowd—the *people*—more powerfully than their own ugly brand of demagoguery."

"Then they are fools twice over not to use the theater to their advantage and write their own plays brimming with republican virtue," said Jenny.

"They lack the native wit to compose such, though they churn out sermons at an astonishing rate. Boston is steeped in a particularly Calvinist form of prudery. Silver plate on their tables is all well and good, but they suspect, and suppress, any sort of art or beauty that can be enjoyed by the masses."

"'Dost thou think because thou art virtuous there shall be no more cakes and ale?'" Jenny recited.

"Sir Toby!" said Burgoyne, recognizing the line from *Twelfth Night*—a rebuttal of Malvolio's Puritanism—with obvious pleasure. "I confess that I knew you would be pretty—Devere's kind has an eye for a *fair* beauty—but diverting conversation is seldom found among American women. Your wit is wasted in New York. Pearls before swine. London is the place for an *ambitious* actress."

He was saying things she had longed to hear, and yet she found his praise oddly slighting, and the news that Devere thought her pretty altogether too gratifying. Flattery was *not* what she had come for.

"It is not ambition, but introductions I lack."

"Has your aunt no connections she might call upon, no interest she might bring to bear?"

"My aunt," she confessed, "has burnt her bridges, professional *and* social." Jenny had never gotten the whole story, but it had something to do with the Divine Fanny's defection from her royal lover to her common swain.

"That is unfortunate. I'll warrant you have the looks to make it on the London stage, but your origins *will* count against you. The assumption that an American actress is little better than a barnyard player would be very hard to overcome."

She *had* played barnyards. It was their only recourse when the city fathers closed the theaters, which was all too often. Though she had lamented the provincial circuit herself, Burgoyne's scorn made her feel surprisingly defensive. And it made her recall, with sudden fondness, a barnyard they had played in the Jerseys, where the locals had paid in pies and produce, and the blueberries and peaches had been the very best she had ever tasted. There had been nothing but a painted cloth for scenery and their costumes had been too drenched from a recent rain to wear, but the audience had been rapt. "John Street is not Drury Lane,"

Jenny conceded, "but I have studied closely with my aunt for two years."

"So much is evident from your grace and manner," he said smoothly, picking her hand out of her lap and lifting it to his lips. The gesture brought him to the edge of his chair, his knees sliding between hers and rustling her petticoats. "One might scarcely guess you were a colonial."

His pronouncement flattered and irked her at the same time.

"But—for good or ill—there is more to success in that crowning glory of England, the theater," he added, "than thespian skill."

"I am aware of that." She was aware, mostly, of how his right knee was pressing hers apart and the artfully casual way in which his elbow was balanced on the arm of her chair. How the movement of his hands to illustrate his point brushed his knuckles over the tops of her breasts.

"Mr. Garrick," Burgoyne said, leaning closer, "is not only the finest actor of his generation. He is a demanding—and discerning—manager. It would be my pleasure to introduce you, but I fear that anything less than a detailed tally of your virtues would fail to move the great man, and if I am to deliver such, then we must come to know each other better."

He meant intimately, and there was no way now, with his knees between hers, his arm resting in her lap, his touch grazing her breasts, to refuse gracefully; no way that would not paint her as an unsophisticated rustic.

"'Say then, ye Boston prudes,'" he prompted, speaking a little more of his prologue to *Zara* and giving voice to her fears of inadequacy, "'if prudes there are, is this a task unworthy of the fair? Shall form, decorum, piety, refuse a call on beauty to conduct the muse?'"

She could find no words to reply, so she forced herself to use his, the next stanza from his prologue: "'Perish the narrow thought. The slanderous tongue. Where the heart's right, the action can't be wrong.'"

She hoped it was true.

He took her hand and placed it, palm down, over his fall front. All at once she understood how theory and practice differed. She had heard all about intercourse from her aunt and other sources, but describing copulation was about as useful as describing acting. It was the doing that mattered, and she had absolutely no idea how to go about it.

But this was not a monologue—it was a scene played between two people—and Burgoyne proved more than happy to cue her. When she remained awkwardly in her pose, he unbuttoned his flap and drew her hand down and into his breeches.

Somehow she had not anticipated meeting warm, bare skin. He wrapped her fingers around his hardening shaft, and demonstrated how he wanted to be stroked.

It was far too intimate, far too *personal*, and it was only the beginning. The next step, of course, was putting that—him—into her, and the thought suddenly panicked her. Her hand stilled. "I'm sorry," she said. "I don't think I can do this."

Burgoyne's eyes filled with impatience. "Even the *orange sellers* on Drury Lane can do this."

What a fool she had been, to see herself as men

like this saw her. "Then I fear I am too provincial even for that humble role."

She tried to draw her hand back, but he kept it firmly in his grasp.

"Don't be silly. You do not apprehend all the little traditions of the English stage. I understand that," he said with a horrible condescension that stripped her soul bare. He took her wrist in a firm grip and guided her. "There is nothing so provincial about you that a little practical instruction cannot mend."

She had thought that the patronage of a powerful man would open avenues and expand her opportunities, but now she realized that she was staring down the narrowest path of all. She did not know what to do. He had placed one knee upon the seat of her chair and his body caged her within the confines of the damask-covered wings. It was a silken prison and he loomed over her, now strumming himself with her captured hand.

She could not go through with it, but neither could she bring herself to say the words that would destroy her future. She tried to rise, but he brought his other knee to bear, pinning her skirts to the cushion.

"I ought to be getting home," she said. "My aunt will worry."

"A few moments more, girl," he said, eyes closed, breathing fast.

In a flash he released her hand and grasped handfuls of her petticoats.

She tried to scramble out of the chair but she had nowhere to go, and he would not budge. She reached wildly for some source of leverage, and her knuckles smacked the marble pillar beside the table. Her fingers scraped the plaster bust atop it, scrabbling over the serene face of the resident daughter of Zeus.

If Burgoyne could call upon the Muses, so too could she.

Jenny wrapped her free hand around Melpomene's slender neck and swung.

Eight

She aimed for his shoulder, but the plaster was heavier than she expected. The Muse connected with Burgoyne's head with a crack.

Melpomene's tender cheek fractured, powdering Burgoyne's black hair gray. He grunted, stilled for the moment, and slumped atop her, a dead weight. The bust fell from her fingers and landed on the carpet with a dull thud, then rolled sonorously to the other side of the cabin, leaving a trail of white gypsum.

Jenny tried to move, but Burgoyne's weight pinned her, his head atop her collarbone, his shoulders digging into her stays. She braced her hands against his chest and shoved and twisted until she was able to squirm out from under him and climb over his back to exit the chair. She lost her shoes in the process, the paste buckles snagging on the cushion, and emerged to stand in her stocking feet on the Turkey carpet.

Burgoyne remained slumped over the damask arms, a profane *Pietà*.

He looked dead. She did not want him to be dead. She would have to touch him to find out, and she did not want to touch him.

She forced herself to do it, feeling for a pulse at his neck. His starched collar was rough to the touch, the edge crisp like paper, his cravat tightly knotted. She could not find his pulse, but she could detect his breath, warm and moist, against her fingers.

He was not dead, but he *was* a British general. And she was an American actress and presumably a whore, and she might well swing for striking him. No jury would be sympathetic, not when she had come to meet him like this. Not considering her profession and her aunt's scandalous past.

Her only chance was to run. Or rather walk. Serenely, from the cabin, as though she had come from his bed. If she demanded a boat to return her to shore, she would most likely get one. That was one of the first lessons of the theater: if you carried the stage with you into the street and strutted as though you were part of the scene, most people would go along with the program. If she demanded a boat quickly enough, before Burgoyne was discovered, she might get clean away, and once she was home, Aunt Frances would know what to do.

It would be the most important performance of her life.

It was, fortunately, a part she had studied. She must, for a space, *be* Frances Leighton, regal, witty, wielding her powerful charms to weather the gauntlet of sly looks and catcalls on the way to the rail. She took a breath, as Aunt Frances had taught her, as Bobby always did before beginning a scene, and let the role settle over her like a mantle.

Jenny risked one last look back at Burgoyne. She would not touch him again. She snatched her shoes out from under the chair and backed to the other side of the cabin to shove them onto her feet as best she could, tightening the crumpled lappets. She fluffed her hood around her face and tucked her copper hair—now she regretted the lack of anonymous powder—into the striped folds. Her steps were muffled by the Turkey carpet as she crossed the room, hastily fastened paste buckles sparkling lopsided in the moonlight streaming through the windows.

She opened the door and peered out into the hall.

Severin Devere stood in the second door on the left. He was leaning against the jamb, in shirtsleeves and fawn breeches, his pose deceptively casual, his black eyes anything but.

"Is he dead?" Devere asked. His voice was without inflection. She could not read his expression, but then it occurred to her that she had not seen his face in the darkness of the slot.

He was blocking her only path of escape. She had no choice but to answer.

"He doesn't seem to be."

Devere straightened and prowled toward her. His feet were silent on the deck, a nearly impossible trick on such a creaky tub. He came to stand within inches of her, and she was conscious, more than ever, of their difference in size and stature. He was taller and broader than she, and he moved with a feline grace that suggested coiled strength and dangerous speed.

He was here to protect Burgoyne, the man's body

and reputation. No matter what they had shared in the darkness at John Street, she had injured one and posed a not insignificant threat to the other. They were in the middle of New York Harbor, in December, the waters a frigid waste. Her aunt's warnings were suddenly no longer theoretical. This man could break her neck and tip her body over the side, and no one would ever know what had become of her.

Severin Devere scrutinized her from head to toe, and she was certain his dark eyes missed nothing even in the dim corridor. He would see through her masquerade. He would know the gown had been bought used and remade, suspect the watch belonged to Frances Leighton and the tortoise combs had come from one of her long-ago admirers. He would be able to read the guilt written across Jenny's face, because this was a man who also wore masks and played roles. And because she was not the Divine Fanny, and she was not adequate to this part.

She flinched when he took her hands in his, expecting to be manacled. Instead, he gently lifted her wrists to the lantern and turned them over.

She followed his gaze and noticed for the first time the purple bruises. They circled her wrist like a bracelet of rough-cut amethysts. When she looked up she saw a muscle in Devere's jaw twitch, and she could feel the restrained violence vibrating through his body.

"What happened?" he asked, his face still unreadable.

"We had a misunderstanding," she said.

"That is one way of characterizing it."

Devere lowered her hands deliberately and stepped past her in the hall.

Relief washed over her. Whatever he intended, her immediate demise wasn't part of it. Running, now that he was aware of the situation, would be futile. There was no way she would get off the *Boyne* without his knowledge and permission, so she trailed him into Burgoyne's cabin.

"Shut the door," he said, stalking to the table.

Devere turned Burgoyne over ungently and thrust his body upright in the chair. The general groaned and his head lolled. Devere peeled back one eyelid and checked his pulse. There was something brisk and businesslike about his manner that made Jenny wonder just how often he made such assessments, separating the incapacitated from the dead.

Devere turned from the unconscious man and surveyed the room, his eyes taking in the toppled pillar, the chipped bust, the half-eaten meal on the table, the nearly empty decanter of brandy.

At last he said, "I can fix this, if you will allow me, but we have very little time, so you must choose, quickly."

She didn't see how anyone could *fix* this. "What does that mean, exactly?"

"It means that I can arrange the scene to suit the lies that must be told—if you will embrace a fiction that the relevant parties will find more palatable than fact. It means subverting—and breaking—the law, and giving up all hope of any measure of justice for the indignity and injury you've suffered"—his eyes lighted briefly on her bruised wrists—"but it also means that you will sleep in your own bed tonight."

"And my other choice?"

"I call for Captain Hartwell, and you may relate your version of events. The general, of course, will certainly have his own."

He did not elaborate on what would happen to her if Burgoyne's version of events was believed. He did not have to.

"The fiction, if you please," she said.

Devere looked relieved. He nodded, took up the brandy decanter, and upended it over Burgoyne, the tawny spirits soaking into the scarlet of his coat and infusing the cabin with the atmosphere of a pothouse. He uncorked two more bottles of brandy and poured them out the window. He set one beside Burgoyne on the table and left the other to roll around on the floor. Something about the care with which he set it rolling reminded Jenny of Mr. Dearborn's methodical preparation of the stage, of the thoughtful precision with which he placed the props.

Devere surveyed the room one last time, then turned to Jenny. "Go to my cabin. It is the second door on the left. Bar the door and do not answer or open it to anyone but me, no matter what you hear. Can you do that?"

She wanted to ask him what he was going to do, what would become of her, whether Burgoyne would recover—but more than that she wanted to live, and she recognized that she had slim chance of that without this man for an ally.

"Yes."

"Go now."

It was said quietly with no hint of threat or force, but with the assumption that she would trust him in this.

She went.

The hall was dark and quiet, and she dashed from

Burgoyne's cabin to Devere's and shut the door behind her in a single breath. The bolt was a fragile defense. If Devere did not champion her, the *Boyne*'s captain would have the door down in a trice. She had to trust him.

She did not know him.

She would trust him only so far.

There was barely room to stand beside the bed. A locked chest was tucked in the narrow space between a cannon and the berth. A folding desk built into the wall lay open atop the gun, covered with papers. Some looked like ordinary letters; others were clearly written in a code of some kind.

Of course they were. He was a spy, as Aunt Frances had told her. And neatly stacked on a carefully penciled map was a manuscript in a different hand, one replete with ornate flourishes and peppered with drawings and small, carefully penned diagrams. There was an inkwell lying unstopped on the desk and a half-finished missive spoilt now by a spreading stain where the discarded quill lay.

The scene spoke of an evening's work interrupted. Jenny wondered just when Severin Devere had dropped his pen and decided that his coded letter was less important than the muffled sounds coming from Burgoyne's cabin.

And whether he cared at all, really, about what had happened there, or only about which story was most convenient to tell. *That* was sentiment and foolishness, like her dreams of Drury Lane, and she was never going to be so foolish again.

She had nothing to bargain with and she could not be certain of his intentions, so she did her best to think like Aunt Frances, who kept her love letters and her memoirs in a locked chest because the secrets of powerful men could be wielded like a sword—or a shield.

Jenny took the florid manuscript. She removed the top page, folded the rest of it in thirds, and slipped the liberated pages inside her stays. Then she replaced the absent pages on the desk with her now worthless play and topped it with the original manuscript's ink-stained cover page. No one on Drury Lane would ever read anything she wrote now if Burgoyne had anything to say about it, and her work was just so much paper.

A moment later she heard footsteps and voices in the hall, but they continued past her cabin. Distantly she heard the clank of plate and the ring of crystal, and then, a few minutes after that, she heard a scratch on the panel and Devere's voice saying, "It is Severin."

She lifted the latch and opened the door. Devere filled it. He had donned a leather coat with wide skirts that concealed two pistols, a saber, and a foil with a well-worn handle.

He looked, in a word, *dangerous.*

"Come quickly, now, and do your best to look irritated."

"That should not be too difficult."

He flashed her a brilliant smile then, full of sly joy, and it transformed his face from merely handsome to truly breathtaking.

"I do believe we shall get away with this," he said. Then his smile vanished and was replaced by the same focused intent he had shown in Burgoyne's cabin. Blessedly, he did not glance at his desk before drawing her out into the corridor and locking the cabin door.

She was grateful to have a role to play, even if she did not know her motivation. It was enough to know she must adopt Lady Highstep's offended hauteur, heels clicking deliberately over the deck, shoulders thrown back, arms swinging at her sides.

They were up the ladder before she had a chance to lose her nerve. The moon had risen and it silvered the deck and sails and lit her way to the rail. This time there were no catcalls but there were a few indrawn breaths, and as she waited for the crane and the swing—it would not do to show haste—a little eddy of laughter, discreetly enjoyed behind cupped hands and upturned collars, rippled through the watch.

Then she was in the swing and Devere was climbing down into the boat beside her, and she was surprised to find that it was only her and her unlikely savior alone in the small craft. No sailors, no crew. Devere wordlessly took up the oars and began to row.

She had been right about the body concealed beneath the fine tailoring. He rowed with powerful, even strokes, and neither strained nor slowed. Her fingertips had traced those muscles in the dark, but to see that strength in action was to understand its power. The boat shot smoothly through the choppy water of the harbor, and Devere's broad shoulders shielded Jenny from the better part of the chill spray.

Neither of them spoke until they were out of earshot of the *Boyne*. When there was no sound but the water lapping at their hull and the steady beat of Severin's oars, she broke the quiet.

"What did you tell the steward?"

"I told him that the general had rather too much to drink, and was unable to rise to the occasion for which he had invited you."

"Oh."

Now Devere's actions in the cabin made sense. He had been setting the scene for his story, sousing Burgoyne in his own brandy and emptying those telltale bottles into the sea.

"And the knot on Burgoyne's head?"

"Acquired when he passed out from a surfeit of brandy."

"Will the steward believe it?"

"Of course he will. It confirms all his prejudices about the man. And he will spread the parable amongst the crew, where repetition will polish it to the luster of gospel. What sailor or young officer would *not* want to believe that the rich general—who dines nightly on fresh beef and French brandy in his warm cabin while they freeze on deck and subsist on salt beef and peas porridge and grog—has disgraced himself with a beautiful lady? Particularly when the lieutenants have had to give up their wardroom to enlarge his quarters, and the crew suspect the sabotage that killed two of their number was aimed at Burgoyne."

She'd heard no word of sabotage aboard the *Boyne* in New York, but it explained the ship's sudden arrival and odd behavior. "And was it?" she asked. "Directed at Burgoyne?"

"I believe so. I thought your invitation to the theater might be part of another plot. The second one certainly was."

"I did not send a second invitation." Bobby had, but she would not tell Devere that.

"I knew you were no plotter from our first meeting, but you have proved far more dangerous to Burgoyne than the Rebels."

If all his aid had been a ploy to get her away from the

Boyne and prying eyes, if he meant to do away with her here on the open water, there was little enough to stop him. Aunt Frances always carried a small knife and she owned a muff pistol. Jenny had thought these charming eccentricities. Now she realized they might be sensible precautions for a woman who thought to make her own way in the world. Tomorrow, she would buy a pistol. If she had a tomorrow.

"Are you really going to take me home?"

He stopped rowing. Waves buffeted the still boat. The hair on the back of her neck rose and her heart raced.

"What exactly did your aunt tell you about me?"

Her mouth felt dry. The chill of the night penetrated her thin gown. She must tread carefully here. "That you were here to protect Burgoyne."

"I am. We both know that isn't why you're so afraid."

"She said you are a spy."

"Half of New York is selling information about the Rebels to the officers who are living—not particularly secretly—at the King's Arms. Half of those supposed loyalists are also reporting the movements of those officers to the Rebels. And many of the transactions are taking place in your greenroom. You cannot be oblivious to it all, and so I beg leave to doubt my intelligence work worries you much either."

She wasn't oblivious to it, and he was right. "Aunt Frances said you kill people."

He didn't answer all at once. Then he said, "Is that all that is frightening you right now, about being alone with me in the middle of the harbor? That I . . . work for the government?"

"The customs man *works* for the government. What you do is something else."

For some reason this amused him, and he smiled. "Would it help to know that I don't go around indiscriminately slaughtering innocents?"

"In the present circumstances, I'm not certain that I should feel any safer with a discriminating murderer."

"And yet you felt safe with me in the slot."

"'Safe' is not the word I would use to describe how I felt."

His gaze raked her and she wondered for a moment if he had felt it too. *Caught up in something irresistible.* Then finally he said, "There is hardly time—if there should ever be a time—for a résumé of my career. But any killing I've done has involved direct threats to the safety and security of His Majesty's subjects."

"I thought the *law* was supposed to deal with those who threatened public safety, and—come to that—I brained one of His Majesty's major generals in his private apartments."

"I act when the law cannot work swiftly enough, or when public opinion or misplaced delicacy might prevent justice from taking its course." His voice was measured. "As for Burgoyne—well, he got exactly what he deserved. But we both know how difficult that would be to prove in court."

Because juries thought just like the general. "That still doesn't explain why you are helping me."

"I am helping you," he said, taking up the oars once more, "because I try to take some responsibility for my mistakes. This was my fault. I knew you weren't as worldly as your aunt."

"I understood what Burgoyne wanted," she said quietly.

"The bruises on your wrist argue otherwise."

"I thought I could go through with it, but I couldn't. But it was too late by then. You must think me very naive." She certainly felt so. The footlights at Drury Lane did not burn so bright in her imagination now, and she marveled at how easily she had mistaken the provincial insecurities of New York's merchant elite for sophistication.

"For the most part, there is no such thing as 'too late.' That is an excuse men use for behaving like animals, or as cowards. I think you simply discovered there are limits to your ambition. Better to understand them now than when it may be *truly* too late, and you can no longer change your path."

Like Aunt Frances. "Rousseau would tell you it was inevitable. That a woman who will sell herself in performance to an audience of hundreds must do the same for an audience of one. That she cannot resist the impulse to satisfy the passions she stirs."

"That," said Devere, "suggests a sadly narrow understanding, of both women and passion."

When they reached the dock, he helped her from the boat. It was a marked contrast from her embarkation with the dispassionate lieutenant. For a moment she could still feel the roll and pitch of the water, and Devere grasped her waist to steady her. It was far less intimate than his touch had been in the slots, and yet somehow more so. The gesture was so unexpected that she looked up into his eyes, and found them full of concern—and remorse.

That was when she knew she was safe with him. Or at least safe *from* him.

The city at night could be treacherous. Devere understood that. He had come armed. For her part, she had never been to the docks this late, never seen them so deserted. The moon was up but the tall warehouses, dark and shuttered, cast deep shadows over the quay and the daytime smells of hemp and tar and hot pitch had given way to that of rancid cooking oil and rotted fish and brine.

Devere released her as soon as she stopped swaying. She opened her mouth to thank him, but he motioned for silence and scanned the wharf, listening intently. She checked the timepiece hanging from the ribbon at her waist. Incredibly, it was not yet nine.

"Where do you live?" he asked softly.

"With Aunt Frances. Above the greenroom at the John Street," she said. "But I can't go home yet."

"Why not?"

"Bobby forbade me to meet with Burgoyne. He will toss me out of the company if he discovers I went to the *Boyne*."

Devere raised one black eyebrow. "And just where does he think you are now?"

"Sick in bed."

"*Above* the greenroom, in which no doubt Mr. Hallam is at this very moment entertaining his patrons."

"Yes."

It was possible that her luck had run out. Her troubles with Bobby Hallam were all of her own making and no problem of Severin Devere's. He had gotten her off the *Boyne* and saved her from hanging. He owed her nothing more.

Most men would not think that he had even owed her that. Particularly when she had gone blithely to Burgoyne after what had happened between them in the slots. Devere would be within his rights to leave her here on the wharf at the mercy of the thieves and cutpurses who roamed the New York streets at night. A *lady* might merit an escort to her door, but a provincial actress—a prudish would-be trollop, an overambitious barnyard player—surely did not.

Severin knew that Jennifer Leighton deserved better than to be cast out of her home and her profession for a folly he had engineered, and which *he* should have prevented.

When she had emerged from Burgoyne's cabin, head held high and lips pressed firmly together—if they trembled at all, she'd hid it well—he'd felt pure admiration for her nerve. Then he had seen the bruises on her wrist, and he'd felt something else entirely.

It had been difficult to enter that cabin and handle the unconscious Burgoyne without losing control, but brutalizing Gentleman Johnny would do nothing to help Jennifer Leighton. Quite the contrary.

"How long," he asked, "until it will be possible to smuggle you back into your lodgings?"

She checked the little watch pinned to her petticoat. "Two hours, possibly three. Aunt Frances plays cards late into the wee hours, but Bobby usually goes home by midnight or so."

He considered their options. After Fairchild's warning, it would be foolhardy to show his face in any of the Rebel taverns. "The King's Arms," he decided, arranging her hood to cover her copper bright hair. If he could deliver her that far, Courtney could see her the rest of the way home.

And if something befell him on the way back to the dock, at least Jennifer Leighton would be safely out of the mess he had gotten her into. He'd left strict instructions with Hartwell to sail without him if he did not return. Severin's possessions were to be locked in his trunk and sent ashore to his man of business in New York, a precaution he always took when he knew his life was in danger. And Burgoyne would be safely away, bound for England.

"With any luck," he said, "no one will recognize you, and you can wait out Bobby Hallam in relative comfort."

A long stretch of shuttered warehouses lay between them and the King's Arms. The storehouses of New York's merchant princes were not the treasure vaults of Boston or Philadelphia, stacked to the rafters with tea and silk and spices. They were not patrolled by night watchmen or prowled by guard dogs. They held spars and cordage and rice and pots and pans, and the prosaic manufactured necessities of everyday life that the colonists were required to import from England. Very little was portable or profitable enough to attract thieves. All this made the warehouse district extremely safe for kettles and copper pots, but decidedly less so for a man and a woman on foot.

They had gone less than a block when he began to suspect they were being followed.

Jennifer Leighton noticed as well.

"There are footpads behind us," said the girl.

"I know," he said quietly. "Follow my lead and keep

step with me." He hoped that they were ordinary foot-pads, street thieves with good sense who would give up when it became apparent that Devere and his companion were not easy targets.

They were not street thieves. Twice, Severin sped up and slowed down. Jennifer Leighton kept pace with him both times. And so did the men following them.

That was a bad sign. Jennifer Leighton's skills from the stage, her ability to match her movement opposite other players, enabled her to anticipate and mirror him, as though they were partners in a dance.

Petty thieves opportunistically prowling the docks for a rich purse would not have shown to such advantage. They would not have sped up and slowed down in tandem with Devere. They would not exhibit such canny caution when stalking one man and a small girl. They would not take such care to keep an even, measured distance between themselves and their prey.

They would have pounced. The girl's rich dress, the gold watch pinned to her gown, the silk of her petticoats would have excited their avarice. Real footpads would not risk letting such rich prizes get away.

Which indicated that these men were waiting for something. An ambush, most likely. Severin should be able to handle two armed men, so long as they did not have pistols at the ready. If those men wished to make a nice quiet job of it, they would use clubs or knives. But he did not care for his odds against a greater number. That meant he had to engage these two and dispatch them here in this block, preferably without alerting their confederates.

It would not be easy. If the Widow had hired them, they would be very, very good, and difficult to draw into a fight not of their making. If he had been by himself, his chances of luring them close would have been poor, but he was not alone.

He spared a glance at his companion. Jennifer Leighton had kept her head about her on the *Boyne*, and she appeared to be doing so now. Growing up on the frontier and in the forests of New York, Severin had known women every bit as capable and brave as men, but when he had returned to English society he'd been introduced to a more cosseted notion of femininity. Jennifer Leighton was neither pioneer nor English lady. She might be an asset or a liability in this fight. It was time to discover which.

"They are after me," he said evenly, careful not to speak too loudly or urgently or give any indication that he was aware of their pursuers. "But they will very likely kill you," he said, "to make a clean job of it."

"How do you know that?" she asked. There was no quaver in her voice, just genuine inquiry. That was good.

"Because I am in the same trade. If you will trust me, I can deal with these two before we find ourselves outnumbered."

"You think there are more of them."

"I'm rather sure of it."

"Tell me what to do."

"Giggle, stumble, and then follow my lead."

"Actresses *hate* being given line readings, Mr. Devere," she said, and then giggled, her convincing laughter a counterpoint to her tart retort.

She stumbled, throwing her whole body into it fearlessly, and he felt a rush of genuine admiration for the girl. Indeed, she would have fetched up on the cobbles if he had not caught her. Her performance was as convincing as any spy's imposture.

He steadied her, hands gripping her waist, the stays firm beneath his grasp, and swung her into the shadows of the nearest warehouse door.

"What is my motive in the scene?" she asked quietly.

He had not done this in so very long, worked side by side with someone else. Not since he and his brother had hunted together as boys, tutored by Ashur Rice in the dense forests of New York. They'd shared the thrill of spotting and tracking deer, of bringing home meat for the table.

His hands were still on her. Unnecessary, but gratifying.

"Your motive and aim, Miss Leighton, is that of a mercenary trollop: to distract me with the promise of passion, and then to liberate the gold in my pocket." He backed her against the door, as a man might a cheap harlot he meant to enjoy quickly, and he was shocked when he felt her small, capable hands sliding into the pockets of his waistcoat.

His body responded. To her touch, to the scenario he himself had suggested, and to the threat of danger. He well understood how often violence and passion marched hand in hand. Images flashed through his mind, of Jennifer Leighton, gown unpinned, head thrown back, spine arched, *his*. He swallowed and banished such visions from his thoughts.

And he listened. To booted feet on cobblestone, to the men who had been following them, drawing closer.

He pulled his coat open, exposing the hilt of his foil. From behind it would look as though he was dallying with the girl and vulnerable to attack. "Take the sword," he said quietly to Jenny.

She complied at once, wrapping her hand around its hilt in a practiced grip and drawing the blade silently from its scabbard.

"When I turn and step away," he instructed, "lunge at the man nearest you as you might at Mr. Hallam in a duel onstage, but do *not*—on your life—cheat your blade to the side. Drive it home beneath his ribs. Do not flinch at the consequences—make to drive it *through* his body and clean out the other side."

She nodded wordlessly. He said a silent prayer that he was not about to get her killed, and then the men were upon them and he could not spare her another thought.

Nine

Jenny grasped the foil. Devere's weapon had a comfortably worn leather-wrapped hilt that seemed to mold to her hand. It was a light blade, not unlike the kind she was used to practicing with onstage, and she knew that if she wished to live to see the morning, she must throw herself entirely into the moment—the scene—and think of it as a role. To think of it as murder would stay her hand, and she did not want to die.

Devere moved with elegance and economy, pivoting out of her way to confront one of their attackers.

Which left her facing a tall, sallow man with a long face and cold, glittery eyes. He brandished a heavy cudgel in his hand and wore a stained leather vest that smelled of the slaughterhouse and a knitted cap pulled down to cover his ears. Those cold eyes turned—for an instant—to follow Severin.

She did not think. She lunged. She was aware of

the hard silvery light of the moon on her blade and the round shapes of the cobbles beneath her slippers and the object in front of her that had to be dealt with, and nothing else.

It was like skewering meat, only meat did not howl. Her blade pierced the leather doublet and the man's stomach and kept going. He crumpled with her sword in his belly and his weight pulled her blade—and her—down with it. His cry—ragged, almost plaintive—was loud in her ears.

She flung herself back and her blade slid free with a wet pop. Her shoulders hit the brick wall behind her. The man kneeling on the cobbles continued to whine, his hands clutching his stomach and blood pouring out between his fingers, turning the alley's cool air harsh and metallic. She knew she must do something to quiet him or risk bringing more assassins down upon them, but she could not.

Devere stepped in front of her, blocking her view of the sobbing man. There was a sound like a turkey's wishbone being cracked. Then Devere stepped away, and where once a man had been, there was now only a twitching corpse. And another—she saw now—on the ground, a few feet away, its limbs bent at unnatural angles.

Her blade glistened in the moonlight, slick with blood. Devere took the foil from her hand, wiped the steel clean on the dead man's shirt, and gave it back to her. "You did well."

His praise filled her with unexpected pleasure. It was like receiving applause from the gallery, always the hardest audience to please.

She knew she ought to feel remorse, not satisfaction.

She had taken a life. Or at least she had dealt a man a mortal blow. But the two dead men had been rogues— more, paid killers. Devere had been certain. And innocent men did not fall upon you silently on a dark street.

That wasn't why she felt so sanguine, though.

Then it came to her, why she had been able to do as she had done, why she had not frozen in terror. "Only because I have rehearsed the part," she replied.

Devere nodded, seeming to understand, and then said, "One killing, in self-defense, does not a callous murderer make."

He had protected her from harm, in the theater, on the *Boyne*, and just now, and the two bodies in the street told her she had nothing to fear from him tonight. But his words raised the question: how many killings did it take to become as coldly effective as Severin Devere?

"We should alert the watch," Jenny said, turning away from the bodies.

"Unfortunately, the watch is unlikely to rush to our aid. I'm a British officer, of a sort anyway, and out of uniform—which, in the eyes of the Liberty Boys who control the city, may suggest under the circumstances that I am a spy. And an *actress* will be presumed to be my ardent Tory accomplice."

He was right, though she'd felt her loyalties shifting like sand beneath her feet since she had left Burgoyne's cabin on the *Boyne*.

"It seems I am destined to end this night in shackles," she said.

A whistle sounded behind them and was answered by another from the west, in the direction of the fort. Devere surprised her utterly by smiling—as sly and winning an expression now as before—and putting out his hand. "I promise you that together we are equal to the obstacles in our path and that no one else"—his eyes moved to the bruises on her wrists and she knew that he alluded to what had happened earlier with Burgoyne—"will hurt you tonight."

She believed him. She had lived in New York long enough to know the danger they were in, had seen bodies pulled out of the river and men stabbed in brawls, but she had just seen him deal with two armed men, and because he had made room for her on the stage, she herself had taken no small part in that victory.

She took his hand, and he tugged her gently forward, and they ran.

Their pursuers kept to the south and west of them, cutting off any possible retreat to the boat and the waterfront. The villains were clever about it too, staying between Jenny and Devere and the main thoroughfares, where lights blazed in the houses of the rich. She knew better than to fly to that false safety. The noise she would make pounding on Van Dam's or Van Cortland's door would bring their pursuers down on them before it would bring the Dutchmen's dozing servants.

Instead they were forced up the narrow lanes of the working poor where no one would be foolish enough to open their home to a man and woman fleeing armed attackers in the middle of the night.

Devere led them from stygian archways to darkened alley mouths, testing doors and garden gates, until finally he found one that was unsecured. It was a great batten affair, all broad planks and iron bands, and that must have been why it had survived the fire that had gutted the house. Devere opened it carefully, beckoned Jenny inside, and closed the door as quietly as possible.

The bar on the inside was missing, but the brackets on either side of the door were still there, and Jenny watched as Devere fitted a length of charred timber in its place. It would not hold anyone for long, but it might buy them some time.

They felt their way through the dark house, the charcoal tang of the fire still heavy in the air, to a courtyard littered with household debris, bordered on three sides by a soot-stained brick wall and dominated by a reeking cesspit whose extraordinary breadth suggested equally remarkable depth.

The whistle sounded once more, this time from the street they had just left behind. If their pursuers were clever, they might guess that Devere had gone to ground in the burnt-out structure.

"I'm afraid that your gown must be sacrificed," said Devere, taking hold of the neck of her polonaise and ripping it neatly down the middle so the pins bent, then tore through the fragile dimity.

She was well used to the casual dishabille of the theater, to scampering around backstage between costume changes, but that was at John Street. It surprised her that she felt almost equally unconcerned here and now, but then she realized that it was Devere who made her so. He was brisk and businesslike about the disrobing, the destruction of her gown. Neither his hands nor his eyes lingered. There was nothing salacious about it. In one economical gesture he ruined fifteen yards of very dear sewing and stripped her down to her chemise and petticoat, leaving only a few colorful shreds of the striped fabric pinned down the center of her stays.

The polonaise looked a sad and mangled rag in his hands, but she found she could not mourn a gown she had worn to impress Burgoyne. "It does not exactly hold happy memories," she said.

"Yet I promise you it will shortly fix itself forever in the memory of our pursuers," said Devere, with that sly smile she was coming to recognize.

Jenny had no idea what he planned to do with her gown, but she suspected it involved the foul pit they were so carefully skirting, and she doubted any memories Devere intended to bestow on their pursuers would be pleasant.

She watched him disguise the nauseating pool, working quickly and quietly, listening for any sign of their pursuers from the street. Devere chose purposefully, a board here, a beam there, until the pit looked just like the rest of the yard, strewn with debris, and the shortest distance between the house and the south wall at the back of the garden, where he draped her poor striped polonaise to look as though it had been caught and abandoned during the climb over.

"A dunk in that pit, awful as it might be, probably won't kill anyone," she said.

"Have a few hours in my company turned you so bloodthirsty?"

"Not in *your* company, no."

That was when Jenny heard it, the sound of the batten door being forced.

"Quickly," said Devere. He led her to the west side of the garden and helped her over that wall and into the neighboring yard. She landed in an herb garden, the parsley and basil still struggling on under the frost and giving up their cleansing scent as her slippers crushed their tender leaves. Devere followed a moment later, landing less luckily in the woody rosemary; branches and boughs broke noisily beneath him.

It was no matter. The clamor from the yard they had just left drowned out his arrival. There were shouts when the men spied her gown and the clatter of booted feet over rotted boards. And a snap, a yowl, a squelching, liquid sound—such as the whale might have made when it swallowed Jonah—that made Jenny cringe and forced Devere to bite his fist to hold back laughter.

The cursing that followed was not inventive but it was heartfelt, and Jenny could still hear it faintly when she and Devere emerged into a ramshackle street she recognized.

"'And the children of Israel,'" said Devere, "'even the whole congregation, journeyed from Kadesh, and came unto Mount Hor.'"

"We're in the Holy Ground," she said. They had run farther than she realized. The slum between Saint Peter's and the college was north of John Street, and unlike the quiet streets near the Battery, it was teeming with people at all hours. She had only ever seen it by day, but night did not improve the prospect. The lots were narrow, the wooden houses dilapidated, the streets rutted, and the gutters half choked with rotting food.

"At least you are dressed for it," said Devere drily.

"I fear I am *under*dressed for it," she said.

The women who strolled the disreputable tract and lounged in its narrow doorways were not the stylish, sportive demimondaines who frequented Bobby

Hallam's greenroom. They did not dress to seduce in silk or lace, because everyone knew what wares they peddled, and on what economies of scale. *Practicality* was the watchword here. They dispensed with confining stays and wore loose jackets pinned over petticoats. There was passing little flesh on display. Most, in fact, were wrapped up tightly in warm woolen shawls or long enveloping cloaks, their clothing beneath loose and easy to remove.

The whores, though, didn't frighten her. They were only doing what Burgoyne had expected of Jenny, without the blandishments of French brandy and a feather mattress. Tempting as it might have been to look down on them for it, she knew better now.

It was the men—the men who leaned against the tumbledown buildings, chewing tobacco and drinking from green glass bottles—it was they who made her nervous.

"Are you cold?" asked Devere.

"A little," she admitted.

His leather coat was draped about her shoulders before she could protest.

"You're sensible to be frightened here," he said, putting an arm too over her shoulders and leading her down the center of the street. "We're only a little safer in the middle of this crowd than we were in the empty lanes near the Battery. A stabbing in a press like this is very easy to carry off."

"More government work?" she asked.

"I have never stabbed anyone in a crowd, but I once took a blade for a man I was protecting, and it was a near-run thing."

"Where?" she asked.

"Bristol."

"I meant in what part of your anatomy were you stabbed."

"I know what you meant. Ask me someplace warmer and perhaps I'll show you."

They were moving briskly down the center of the street, hip to hip, like a trollop and her customer on their way to someplace discreet and private.

She did not mind the contact. It was light and impersonal. He rested no weight across her back. To the contrary. His hand hovered over her shoulder. It was rather like the way the reverend used to lead her grandmother into church, two old cronies with a platonic acquaintance of some seventy years. There was a kind of intimacy of spirit in that, but to her surprise Jenny would have welcomed more. She wanted to lean into him, snuggle into the crook of his arm, feel his hip press hers.

It was the stress and danger of the situation, that was all. After an interlude like the one she'd had with Burgoyne, no sane woman would be angling for *that* kind of attention. Certainly not in a place like this, a warren of sorry sporting houses, gambling dens, and unlicensed drinking establishments. But she knew what Aunt Frances would say, because she had asked her, once, why she had left the security of her aristocratic lover's protection for the uncertainty of a future with a man of no fortune. Aunt Frances' response had been pure Fanny: "Because sometimes good sense is overrated."

Fanny's words had closely echoed Jenny's reply to her mother's pleas to stay home in New Brunswick. Her parents had outlined all the reasons that she should *not* go to New York with Fanny: that there was no security in acting, that she would be subject to vile importunities, that no respectable man would marry her after her time on the stage.

She had gone anyway, and her life would not have been worth living if she had stayed home. But the same logic had driven her to Burgoyne's cabin aboard the *Boyne*.

"Where are we going now?" she asked.

"Gethsemane," he said, unhelpfully.

"How appropriate."

They traversed the Holy Ground unmolested and crossed a scrubby open lot, then began to stroll beside a tall hedge that stretched off into the darkness ahead of them—shielding what grand residence from its blighted neighbors, Jenny knew not. Devere kept her on his right and the hedge on his left, which would have been rude in ordinary circumstances, but these were not ordinary circumstances, and in their brief acquaintance she had seen him do nothing without a purpose.

When he paused and released her to examine the hedge more closely, she found she missed his warmth. After a moment he dropped to his knees, thrust his arms into the foliage, and she heard the sound of metal scraping against metal. She bit her tongue. Then he stood and parted the greenery and she saw a batten door in a brick wall hidden behind the yew. Devere pulled hard on a ring handle. The door resisted a moment, then swung open on oiled hinges.

The vista beyond was enchanting. A familiar landscape viewed from a new angle. It took her a moment to place it. Then the raked gravel paths, manicured lawns, and cunningly clipped topiary triggered memory. "Shouldn't that be locked?"

"It was."

"Ah."

Beyond the hedge door lay the pleasance of Vauxhall. She recognized the garden folly in the distance, a two-story crenellated structure that flew silk pennants and sold raspberry shrubs in summer, and the rippling box hedges that bordered the rose garden, and the brick stairs that led down to the leveled enclosure where lawn games were offered.

"For an Englishman, you know New York passing well," she observed.

"My family took me back to England for school, but I was born in America, on the frontier, north of Albany."

"Vauxhall is hardly the frontier. How did you know about this door?" she asked, stepping through and watching Devere lock it behind them.

"Because I collect useful information."

So, of course, did old women and the baker down the street and Aunt Frances—but it was what Severin Devere did with useful information that worried her. Especially after an evening spent in his company, during which she might have been able to resist his physical appeal but could not help coming to like him. Not because he had rescued her, and not because she thought him handsome, but because he had treated her as an equal from the start, the only possible balm for her humiliation with Burgoyne.

Except perhaps for a stroll in a moonlit pleasure garden. Jenny had heard that you could pay to have Vauxhall all to yourself, that rich men rented it to impress their mistresses or fete their business partners or celebrate the weddings of their children. She could see why. She had always found the gardens pleasant. They were probably more impressive in the full bloom of summer, but tonight, deserted like this, the gravel paths carpeted with fallen leaves, the faint scent of wood smoke in the air, they were positively enchanted.

"The kitchens will likely still be warm," said Devere, leading them past the boxes of the open-air theater where Mr. Fraunces offered concerts and lantern shows. The petite enclosures looked naked without their curtains, but the gilded chairs left behind bestowed on them an air of almost theatrical anticipation.

"We played *Midsummer Night's Dream* here in June."

"It must have been magical. I would have liked to see you as Titania."

"Aunt Frances played Titania, of course. I wore breeches and played the little Indian boy."

His eyes slid down her body, hidden for the most part by his soft leather coat. "I might have enjoyed that even more."

"How is it," she said, ignoring the inconvenient flush suffusing her face, "that a frontier-born Mohawk knows so much about the theater?"

"Traveling players?"

"The American Company has never ventured north of Albany."

"Creative missionaries, staging passion plays to convert the heathen tribes?"

"Even more difficult to imagine than Robert Hallam dragging his wardrobe past Albany."

Devere smiled. "But very amusing to picture. The

truth is that I have little claim on the role of the noble savage. I was raised from the age of ten in England, at English schools, and developed a typically English passion for plays and playhouses."

"And lady players?" *Like Burgoyne.* She did not want him to be like Burgoyne.

"It is the plays themselves I come for, the opportunity to visit other times and other places, and to release the emotions in catharsis. I do not mistake playbills for *Harris's List of Covent Garden Ladies.*"

Perhaps he *had* been visited by missionaries.

Beyond the main entertainment space there was a counterfeit wilderness dotted with private dining rooms heated with portable stoves, where one could arrange meals prepared by Mr. Fraunces. The decorative little clapboard houses with their rusticated masonry corners nestled among the trees were cold and shuttered at this time of year, but a misspent youth reading novels from the circulating library imbued them in Jenny's imagination with sublime mystery.

Devere stopped short when they came to the centerpiece of the garden: the grotto. Normally the waxwork tableau of Dido and Aeneas was hidden behind a screen of potted beeches and required adults to pay an extra fee. Someone had removed the togas along with the potted beeches and the scene had lost much of its subtlety.

"She looks quite cold like that, in this weather," observed Jenny.

Severin laughed. "He, on the other hand, appears to be suffering no ill effects."

Jenny blushed. "No. Evidently not."

Beyond the grotto was Scipio's tent. This amused

Devere even more. "What," he asked, "has happened to poor Africanus?"

Scipio had been on display in one form or another since before Jenny had arrived in New York. Originally the lifelike figures in wax had portrayed Africanus, the Roman general who defeated Carthage, in his tent after the Battle of Zama with the spoils of war heaped at his feet. The tableau had opened to great fanfare and had been an instant sensation, but after two seasons ticket sales fell off and the scene was changed.

The diorama had evolved to show the Roman general surrounded by his family, most notably his beautiful daughters, and later the old man had been relegated to a supporting role and his most famous offspring had taken center stage.

"*Cornelia Showing Off Her Jewels* has proved more palatable in the current climate," said Jenny, "than the conquering and magnanimous general of an empire." The poses had been borrowed from a popular engraving sold in coffee shops. Cornelia was draped in silks as many aristocratic women liked to be painted, *à la turque*, and she entered stage left with her jewels—her children, who would grow up to be crusading land reformers—preceding her into a lush atrium of potted plants.

It was a thoroughly republican scene and sentiment.

"Mr. Fraunces would seem intent on cultivating a Whiggish clientele," observed Devere.

"The Tories will come anyway," she said. "For the pastry."

"So Mr. Fraunces has found a way to have his cake and eat his cake."

Her stomach grumbled at the mention of cake. She hoped Devere did not hear it over the rustling leaves and wind.

"More successfully than Bobby, anyway," Jenny agreed.

They pressed on through the grounds, skirted the maze, and came out in front of the pretty brick banqueting house, dentil entablature and sash windows picked out in rich cream paint. Devere didn't stop at the fashionable grain-painted double doors with their glistening coat of fresh varnish. These, Jenny knew, opened on a broad staircase that led to the great hall, more than fifty feet long and lavishly appointed in gold-worsted draperies trimmed with a fortune in green fringe. She had been to a party there once, and the memory of the roasted meats and delicate pastries made her light-headed with hunger.

Instead, they hugged the shadows of the building until they came to a two-story service ell projecting from the back, where the windows were smaller but still exceedingly grand for kitchens. Devere knelt beside a batten door at the end, and now she saw what he had been doing in the hedge earlier: picking the lock. He had a steel ring with several small wicked-looking instruments attached, and it took him less than a minute to select the correct tool and ply his suspect skill.

The batten door swung open, revealing an unlocked paneled door. Devere lifted the latch and opened it, and Jenny walked through.

She almost swooned. She had not eaten since morning, and their ruse with the ipecac had stolen even that small breakfast from her. She had traveled to the *Boyne* and back on an empty stomach across rough water with the temperature dropping and then run nearly a mile with Devere through the chilly streets.

The kitchen was warm and scented with nutmeg and mace and caraway and brandy and citron, and the yeasty, sweet aroma of freshly baked bread. A trestle stretched from the door to the end of the long, narrow wing, more than thirty feet, with towering pyramids of macaroons and pastry covering the entire length.

Devere shut the door and the sudden stillness was profound. Outside the wind had whispered through the trees and rustled through the leaves, and weather vanes had sung as they turned and turned in their iron sockets. Inside was perfect, sugared peace.

Her stomach broke the silence with another awful growl.

Devere raised one well-formed eyebrow and allowed his wicked smile to surface.

"I see we've come to the right place," he said.

"I am not normally a woman of ravenous appetites."

"A pity."

He was trying to flirt with her again. She fought an impulse to flirt back, because she knew she would make a botch of it. No matter how she studied Frances Leighton, she would always be Jenny from New Brunswick, and after her experience with Burgoyne, she was no longer certain that was such a bad thing. "Aunt Frances gave me ipecac so we could convince Bobby that I was truly ill."

Devere's smile faded. "What was Frances Leighton doing with ipecac?"

"She said that she keeps it in case anyone is poisoned."

"With something worse than ipecac, you mean."

"Are there things worse than ipecac?" she asked.

"Yes."

She doubted she wanted to know what those things were.

"Why," asked Devere, "was Robert Hallam so adamant that you not meet with Burgoyne?"

"Because Bobby wants me to go into partnership with him."

"The business or the marital sort?"

"Both."

"One would assume," said Severin Devere, "that marriage to the manager of the company would guarantee you the choicest roles."

"It would," agreed Jenny. "But it would also mean that I could never work for anyone else. Marriage offers actresses security, but security that comes at a price. I wouldn't be able to sign my own contracts with another theater, and Bobby certainly wouldn't allow me to perform or write for anyone else. It is the female thespian's great dilemma. Mrs. Cibber would have owned a part share in Drury Lane, but she could not, as a married woman, act for herself—and Garrick did not want to do business with her husband."

"And Mr. Hallam does not share your ambition to appear on the London stage," guessed Devere.

"Bobby's family *is* the theater in America, Mr. Devere."

"Severin."

"*Severin*, then." She had not realized until then how much she desired the intimacy of his first name. "The Hallams," she explained, "have been playing the colonies for a generation. Here, while his brother is in

Jamaica, Bobby is the most important theatrical man on this side of the Atlantic. In London he would be just another provincial actor."

As she would be just another provincial actress. She had learned that much from Burgoyne tonight.

Devere sighed. "You really are altogether too good for Jack Brag. After speaking with you in the green-room, I had hoped you would not accept his invitation."

"He never read my play, did he?" she asked.

"No."

"So the compliments you paid *The American Prodigal* were not Burgoyne's."

"No. They were mine."

"Were they true?"

"Yes. It is a very good play. Witty and intelligent and well observed. Although the end is perhaps a little too neat, a little too sentimental. The American prodigal returned to the forgiving parental fold strains credulity at present."

"I am not certain I would write it the same way now," she admitted. Her play was suddenly the same contested ground as *Caesar*, and she found herself on the other side, sympathizing with the prodigal, and unrepentant.

"Not that it matters. I doubt I will have much opportunity to write anything at all for the stage in future. I have just brained one of David Garrick's personal friends. Your general did not strike me as a particularly forgiving man."

"Proclamations of amnesty for the Rebels notwithstanding, no," agreed Devere.

"I suspect I would end up on the short list of exceptions, alongside Mr. Hancock and Mr. Adams."

"And perhaps a few of the general's creditors for good measure," said Devere. "Burgoyne would find it difficult to prosecute you for assault now," he continued thoughtfully, "with no witnesses and a very different story already circulating aboard the *Boyne*. But I cannot think of a way to shield you from his petty malice, from whatever stories he might choose to tell his cronies in the theater."

"I shall never tread the boards in London, then, shall I? Nor see my work performed at Drury Lane."

"*The American Prodigal* would never have got past the censors in London."

"But it was an entirely *Tory* play."

"Yes. But it ridiculed the ineffectual Tory governor. Just the sort of thing Walpole passed the Licensing Act to suppress. London may be closed to you, but there is still the American stage, and local authorities here offer you greater freedom to perform what you will."

"That is what Bobby always said, but John Street *was* the American stage. Congress has closed all the other theaters, and now they are pressing the Committee of One Hundred to shut us down as well."

"Is that why Hallam told the Sons of Liberty about Burgoyne?"

"Did you guess that it was Bobby, or do you have proof?" she asked.

"I overheard you talking at John Street."

"Can you blame him?" she asked. "When the Crown will not protect us from the Liberty Boys? He did it to safeguard our livelihood."

"No," said Devere. "He might have told himself that,

but he really did it to protect you from Burgoyne—and *that* I cannot fault him for."

Her heart skipped a beat at the admission, but Devere made no move to touch her as he had in the slots. "He almost got all of us killed," she said. "The theater might have burned."

"That is the difficulty with mobs," said Devere evenly. "They are nearly impossible to control. You cannot bargain with a rabble."

"Is the Rebel Washington truly fond of the theater?" she asked.

"Are you thinking of changing sides?"

"I doubt we shall be given the choice. The Calvinists of Boston have no love for the theater."

"I did omit some facts, but Washington is no Boston Puritan. He is a Virginian. He enjoys dancing, and music, and all manner of pastimes that scandalize the doughty New Englanders he must answer to in Congress."

"But he is an aficionado of *Cato*, you said, and a leveler."

"He does have a weakness for Addison. But he is also—I failed to mention—a devotee of *The Rivals*, so the man must possess some sense of humor. And he is no leveler. He owns a sizable plantation worked by slaves. This war has done something that the late conflict with France could not. It has compelled colonies—and men—with absolutely nothing in common to work together."

And it had thrown her together with Devere, who, by her aunt's account, was a spy and an assassin and, by Jenny's own experience, a killer, but one who was hiding in a bakery in the middle of the night so that *she* should not lose her position with the New American Company. He was a puzzle, one she suddenly wanted very much to solve.

"Why did those men wish to kill you?"

"Because they were being paid."

"By whom?"

He didn't answer. Instead, he strolled the table, examining the dizzying array of sweets that must be intended for a wedding or some grand celebration. In the moonlight streaming through the window they were a fantasy city of pastel towers and pyramids.

"So what takes your fancy?" he asked. "Fruit jellies?" They were lined up on a porcelain platter in a rainbow of delicate tints.

"We'll ruin the display if we take one," she replied.

"Pastry hearts?" he asked.

"The pyramid will crumble," she pointed out. "And I am not interested in sweets." Her stomach grumbled again, making a liar out of her.

"Cake, then," he said, stopping in front of the great iced tower. There were tiny sugar figures dancing around the top. Beneath the hard white icing shell would be a layer of almond paste, and then beneath that the brandy and currants and citron that had met her in a cloud of luxury at the threshold. She could almost taste it.

She had been silent too long. A look of mischief—so youthful and altogether at odds with Devere's cultivated sophistication, the citified elegance of his dress, and the nature of his calling—suffused his face and he appeared positively boyish. A knife, the handle elaborately worked with glossy porcupine quills, materialized in his hand, winking in the moonlight slanting through the windows, and before she could object—or perhaps she never meant to—he sliced through the cake.

He made neat work of it, fast and deft, like the backwoods hunters who had peddled meat at her father's door, carving off choice cuts at her mother's direction. Two strokes, and then Devere was offering her a wedge of the heady stuff, balanced on his blade.

"You are trying to avoid answering my question by distracting me from the subject at hand," she said.

"The *subject* is cake. You want some. I have provided it."

She did want some. The aroma was so potent she could almost taste it.

She took the slice, velvet against her fingertips, and bit into it. The sugar icing melted on her tongue, the thick layer of marchpane, rich with almonds, exploded in her mouth, and the brandy-soaked currants burst between her teeth. She chewed and swallowed, and the candied citron tasted like the last breath of summer and the first chill of autumn, all come to blazing warmth in her tender affronted belly.

She devoured the slice with Devere watching and no shame whatsoever, and she didn't protest when he cut another and handed it over wordlessly. She ate, and truly hunger did make the best sauce because it was the finest cake she had ever tasted, and she didn't care that her lips were sticky with sugar and her petticoat covered in crumbs. It was the purest physical pleasure she could imagine, and she wanted to share it with her unlikely rescuer.

"Here," she said, holding out the last bite. "Have some."

That was when she became aware of how still he was standing, how taut his body had grown while watching her devour the cake, how carefully he had kept a distance between them, cutting and serving her pieces at arm's length.

"You finish it," he said quietly.

She brought the morsel to her lips, aware of his intent gaze. The last bite was as good as the first. Without thinking, she licked her sticky fingers and lips.

"I'll have my taste now," he said, and closed the distance between them.

Ten

All at once his hands were at the small of her back and on the nape of her neck and his palm was cupping her head, and his mouth was on hers. His tongue swiped the fullness of her bottom lip, licked her cupid's bow, then slipped inside her mouth.

It was like being struck by lightning. Just like in the darkness of the slot. She was caught fast by a force she didn't fully understand and she could not let go. Jenny was engulfed by the warmth and scent of him, which was not of kitchens and baking, as heady as those distillations had been, but of crisp autumn night and spiky rosemary and bay rum cologne.

Her hands, trapped between their bodies, came to rest against fine cool cotton over firm heated flesh, his stomach and chest thick with the muscle that had rowed them back from the *Boyne* and made short work of their attackers in the street. When he pressed closer, her hips met the hilt of his saber, the buckle on his sword belt, the smooth wooden stock of his pistol.

It was deliriously wonderful, this fusing of mouths and bodies, richer than the buttery cake, sweeter than the marchpane, more luscious than the candied citron. She wanted it to go on forever, and she wanted more.

He released her and stepped back, and she looked up into his nearly black eyes, which were fixed on her. "I'm not Burgoyne," he said. "You can say no with me, Jenny."

"I know that."

He smiled, an expression of pure delight and so different from the mischievous smirk she had been coming to know. Then his face turned intent once more, and he swept the fruit jellies and the tower of macaroons and the little marchpane flowers from the table to fall to the floor with a crash and lifted her to sit on the trestle.

There was no question in her mind that she wanted this with him. Nothing about it was wrong. This man had no desire to control or contain her. They were not *using* each other. She was not trading herself for influence or security. There was nothing awkward about the way their bodies fit together and he made no demands on her, only offered persuasions.

Here, at last, was the temptation Aunt Frances had spoken of.

He kissed her again, openmouthed and slowly, and then his lips made a trail down her throat and his tongue painted the tops of her breasts and his fingers dipped inside her stays. His hands pushed the leather coat he had lent her off her shoulders and the warmth of the garment was replaced by the warmth of his body. He nipped at her earlobes, stroked up her thighs through the silk of her petticoats, pressed himself hard and ready against her belly.

Her body remembered his coaxing fingers in the darkness of the theater and anticipated his touch, then started at the cold kiss of his blade's hilt.

"Apologies," he said, unbuckling the sword belt and laying his pistol and saber down on the table. Then there was nothing poking or prodding her and only a thin layer of clothing separating them.

She was panting and ready for whatever came next when he stepped back from the table, began untying his neck cloth, and said, "What kind of protection did you bring?"

She was flummoxed that he should ask such a question in the midst of disrobing, but she answered honestly. "Aunt Frances always carries a knife and a muff pistol, but I don't have either."

He bent to nip her ear and laughed, a joyous sound she wanted to hear again. And again. "My company *has* made you bloodthirsty. I meant sheaths."

He meant *that* kind of protection. "Oh." She felt her face flush, knew her skin had turned beet red.

"Please tell me you didn't intend to bed Jack Brag without taking precautions."

"Aunt Frances said Burgoyne would balk at using anything himself, and be put off if I mentioned it. She advised me to wash afterward, in private, so as not to offend him."

"Your aunt seems an admirable woman . . . but that is possibly the *worst* advice I have ever heard. There are men, it is true, who don't like to use French letters if they think the woman is clean and they're paying for her time, whether in coin or favors, but they are taking a stupid risk. And so were you. You could have ended up poxed or pregnant. I hope, for your sake, that you have been more careful in the past."

"There hasn't been a past."

He paused in his disrobing and stood still a moment just looking at her. Then he bent to kiss her, but this time it was a chaste buss on the lips and he was already knotting back up his cravat. "You should have said."

He stepped back and reached for his sword belt.

"What are you doing?"

"Taking you home," he said, buckling the well-worn leather around his narrow waist.

"Because I'm a virgin?" she asked, incredulous.

"Don't sound so aggrieved. I'm doing you a favor."

"There are men who will pay two hundred pounds to bed a virgin," she said.

"How on earth do you know that?" He sounded amused. That made her irrationally angry. He had treated her as an equal up until now, but suddenly he was patronizing her.

"I overheard it in the greenroom." That was not exactly a lie. She had heard the number from Bobby, during one of his more prosaic marriage proposals. He had wanted to save her from all that, he said, the insulting offers she would receive in the greenrooms of London and New York if she took leading roles and was not married to a man of stature. Instead she had wondered how long she could live in London on two hundred pounds and whether it would be long enough to connive an introduction to Garrick.

"Then it is probably true," said Devere. "But at that

price, the man isn't using French letters, and he's very likely paying for a virgin because he has already caught at least one of Venus' curses."

"I wasn't proposing to sell myself to a roué," she said.

"No. You were going to let me have my wicked way with you on a bakery table in a cloud of double refined sugar and orange water."

"Better that than soaked in Burgoyne's brandy," she said, and suddenly she felt the prickle of tears. But there was no catharsis here, only farce. She fought them back.

Devere bent and kissed her again. He licked the tear track from her cheek and said, "Don't cry, Jenny." He lifted her hand and turned it over and kissed the tender bruised underside of her wrist. "I was a fool to touch you after what you experienced earlier. If I had another night in New York, I would *swim* back to the *Boyne* for my French letters and make all of this up to you, and there would be sugar and orange water and marchpane—and a fire and a bed and a feather mattress—but I have only tonight, and a girl as clever and remarkable as you deserves better than that."

Severin Devere surveyed Jennifer Leighton's delicious dishabille and wished he had fewer scruples. Or that he had never promised to fetch her for Burgoyne. Or that he had lied to Jack Brag about her and seduced her himself in front of a warm fire where he could show her the joys of congress—with precautions—between two willing partners. Or that she was less tempting. Jennifer Leighton was more enticing than the cake or the macaroons or the pastry hearts that surrounded her, though the sugar and brandy had tasted truly delicious on her lips.

It wasn't her beauty that beguiled him—though he'd been struck by her artful appearance when she opened Burgoyne's door on the *Boyne*, he'd wanted her just as much in the horrible linen gown. It was her spirit that appealed to him. Jennifer Leighton would never be the diamond her famous aunt had been, but pluck and wit lent her a charm—a surpassing charm—all her own.

She was sitting on the trestle in nothing but her chemise and stays, surrounded by a forest of pastry towers, her remaining petticoat rucked over her knees, clocked stockings tied with black silk ribbons just above her firm calves. He had tried to blackmail Burgoyne to get her for himself and now here she was, sweetly willing, served up, quite literally, on a banquet; and here he was, forgoing the pleasure of having her. If she'd been experienced, he might have done it, tried to erase the memory of Burgoyne's boorish transgressions from her body with his own, but he didn't like to think of himself as the kind of man who would save a virgin from ravishment at the hands of one rake only to debauch her himself.

It was a fine distinction for a spy of dubious heritage who traded in secrets and carried a loaded pistol and a set of lock picks, but it was vital to his amour propre, and he could not do what he did without that.

And he didn't engage with women without French letters. The risks were too great, on *both* sides.

"You're not quite the villain Aunt Frances painted you," she said, almost as though she resented it. And well she might. Thwarted desire was a prickly, restless thing and he felt it just as keenly as she did.

"I am," he said. "That and more. But not in this."

"Why did those men want you dead?"

"Do you really want to know?"

"You said that you were in the same trade as they were. I killed one of them. I'd like to think he was a greater villain than you."

Because she had her own amour propre. Just so. And if together they encountered those men again between Vauxhall and John Street, she might need to kill once more. "Fair enough," he said. "It is because of something I did in Boston."

"What?"

"I attempted to recruit a woman to the government's cause."

"And her husband is trying to kill you?"

"Her husband, if she ever had one, is dead. At least she styles herself a widow. And she is a dangerous provocateur. She stirs up trouble in Ireland and Scotland and on the Continent, and anywhere that Britain has enemies."

"So she's a Rebel."

"She is working for them. Her exact origins have proved difficult to ascertain. Irish, it is suspected, but not sure. There are all kinds of mountebanks flocking to the American cause these days—some from far afield indeed—but she is the prime article. A spy, an assassin, a strategist of the first caliber, adept in the art of disguise, and she cannot be suborned. My orders were to win her to our side, or kill her."

"Surely a *woman* couldn't be as dangerous as all that."

"*This* woman has been funneling French and Spanish gold to the Rebels for over a year. She worked with Adams to stir up the mob in Boston. She made certain that the American side of the story from Concord and Lexington reached London first. She understands the usefulness of propaganda and is as dangerous, capable, and ruthless as any man. I should have remembered that when dealing with her, but I didn't. The Widow cracked my ribs and threw me out a second-story window."

"You sound," said Jennifer Leighton, "as though you admire her."

"I suppose I do." He had, in fact, been attracted to her. That had caused him to think of her first as a woman and second as an adversary, and that had been his greatest mistake. She used her sex to her advantage, and had clearly learned all the ways in which a smaller, lighter opponent might turn the tables on a larger, stronger one. "It would seem that I have a weakness for dangerous women."

Jennifer Leighton smiled and smoothed her petticoats over her knees. "Apparently not a debilitating one." She slid off the table and picked up the salver that had held the fruit jellies, which were now stuck to the floor. "Some poor bride or hostess is going to be affronted tomorrow when she discovers that her buffet is missing several dishes."

"Leave it," said Devere. "It is Mr. Fraunces who will discover the damage, and take fair warning."

"Because Mr. Fraunces courts Whigs with his wax displays as well as Tories with his cakes?" asked Jenny, incredulous.

"Because Black Sam Fraunces has been spying for both sides and must decide, soon, where his loyalties lie."

"Loyalty," said Jennifer Leighton, in wisdom largely acquired, Severin feared, in the last few hours, "is a luxury that not all in New York can afford—and it is fragile as spun sugar."

In the end they did nothing to put Mr. Fraunces' kitchen to rights, though Jenny obviously felt guilty leaving it in such a state. Devere convinced her that there was no point in letting the cake go to waste, and he cut several more slices from the top layer and wrapped them in the banquet hall's best linen napkins for her to tuck in her pockets. She insisted that he take one as well, and he did not tell her the truth: that he had no appetite for cake if it wasn't tasted from her lips.

He made her tuck his knife, the one his father had given him the day they parted, snug in its quilled sheath, into her stays, in case they met with further trouble on the way. By the time he closed the batten door to the kitchen behind them, dawn was not far off, and when they slipped out through the hidden opening in the hedge, it was light enough that the whores had gone to bed. The first fires of the morning were smoking from the chimneys on Nassau Street and servants were stirring, and the water sellers were pushing their laden carts through the tree-shaded lanes.

They were safe enough now. Too many eyes, too many witnesses for murder at such an hour. This was all to the good, because Jennifer Leighton was dozing on her feet and Severin himself was beginning to feel the lack of sleep as they turned onto John Street.

The little blue house next door to the theater had also been awake all night. There were empty firing glasses, their bowls sticky with the last drops of punch,

lined up on the granite porch, and someone's neck
cloth was tied around one of the railings, ends waving
like a pennant in the breeze.

The sight cheered Severin. It was his first signal of
victory in America. He had failed with the Widow, and
it would be a stretch to call his current errand with Burgoyne a success, but he had determined to get Jennifer
Leighton home safe, and short of encountering Robert
Hallam on the stairs, he was bidding fair to do so.

On the porch Jenny produced a shiny brass key
from her pocket, streaming with lilac ribbons that had
once matched her unmourned gown. She aimed it at the
lock but she was clumsy with exhaustion and missed.
Severin took the brass from her cold fingers and let
them into the house. There was an unexpected intimacy
to it that made him wish that this was her home alone,
that he had a pocketbook full of French letters, and that
he was staying for the next several hours.

Both parlors were littered with empty plates and
glasses. The card tables stood open, their green baize
surfaces seeming to stare up, exhausted, at the ceiling.
Gleaming mother-of-pearl counters, carved like flowers and fishes, along with a square set bearing a very
exalted monogram—a trophy, no doubt, of the Divine
Fanny's—were heaped in piles at the corners. The
bones of a whole salmon hung from the chandelier,
and beneath it sat a patient gray cat with a put-upon expression; fortunately, there were no unconscious party-
goers amongst the litter, and there was no sign of Robert
Hallam.

A door opened on the landing above and light
spilled out. Frances Leighton descended the stairs in a

blue silk night robe with her fair hair unbound. She stopped when her eyes lighted on Devere.

She had not expected to see him, which raised the question of who she *had* expected. Burgoyne, no doubt, come to whisk Jenny off to London, playing Caesar to her Cleopatra.

The Divine Fanny surveyed her niece, half dressed in her soot-stained stays with her petticoats frosted in castor sugar. Finally she said, "Comedy or tragedy?"

"A little of both," replied Jennifer Leighton.

Frances nodded at the open shutters in the parlors. "Close them," she said, "and then come up and tell me the whole story."

Devere helped Jenny shutter the windows and followed her up the stairs to a snug little parlor that was a study in contrast with the dissipation on the ground floor. It reminded him of the best room in his childhood home, the furniture worn but comfortable, the painted floors bare but clean. There was an old-fashioned daybed with a yellow silk cushion pulled up to the fire, and opposite that, a set of wing chairs in the same frayed damask and a little tilt-top table where Frances Leighton was pouring two glasses of brandy with her elegant ringed hands.

Jenny kicked off her silk shoes and flung herself on the daybed, petticoats streaked with sugar and soot, and accepted a glass of brandy from her aunt. Devere took the fireside chair opposite Frances, and a noticeably fuller glass of brandy, with gratitude.

Seeing the homey little parlor, he could understand how Jenny might live above the greenroom of a theater but remain, to a remarkable age for a woman of her profession, a virgin. The cozy space more resembled the salon of a Boston or London bluestocking than the private precinct of an expensive courtesan. The scene also lent credence to Fairchild's insistence that his romance with the Divine Fanny abided in chastity.

There were closets on both sides of the fireplace, their lower cabinets fitted with paneled doors, the tops with clear glass to show off the household's treasures, which in this case were not china plates or sparkling crystal but books. There were bound collections of plays and works in Latin and French, and a small selection of novels from the city's most popular circulating library.

Jennifer Leighton proceeded to tell their tale. She turned out to be not only a talented playwright and promising actress, but also a skilled raconteuse. The events of the night were only a few hours old, but she had already begun shaping them into a coherent narrative, shaving off the rougher edges, summarizing the duller passages, and burnishing the hero of the piece.

Severin doubted that he had ever been the hero of anyone's story before. The fact that he had arranged the disastrous assignation to start with was glossed over. Miss Leighton omitted the detail that together they had killed two men in the street, revealing only that he had fought off a pair of footpads. But her description of that action was both evocative and flattering.

She gave no specifics of her encounter with Burgoyne, but said only: "I changed my mind about the value of the general's patronage. He strove manfully to persuade me that it was necessary to my career and future happiness. At some point I brained him with a bust of one of the Muses."

Frances Leighton's plucked brows rose at this, but she made no comment.

There was no mention of moonlit gardens, scented bakeries, trestle tables, or the regrettable want of French letters. When she was done with her recitation, Jennifer Leighton drew her feet up onto the chaise and rested her head against the cushioned arm.

Severin tried not to stare. There was something sensual and uninhibited about her posture that called to him, something decidedly erotic about the sight of his quilled knife hilt peaking above her stays. He had always enjoyed a healthy appetite when it came to the fair sex, but he could not recall a time when it had ever seemed so acutely focused on one girl.

And he had lately surrendered his only real chance to have her. The irony of the situation was not lost on him. He had worked tirelessly for a week to make the *Boyne* ready to sail, partly out of duty and partly out of a well-developed instinct for self-preservation, but also, it had to be admitted, to prevent Jennifer Leighton from meeting with John Burgoyne. And now it was he who was out of time.

The object of his desire stretched and then curled like a cat on the frayed silk cushion and favored Severin with a sleepy smile. He fancied it was the same expression she would have bestowed on him if he'd found them a sturdy bed, initiated her with care, and then when she was awake to the business, tupped her silly, showing her just how much fun a man and a woman could have when they came together as equals.

He discovered, sitting there watching her, that he did not want to leave New York just yet.

His efforts *had* saved the *Boyne* a week's delay. His

powers as outlined in Lord Germain's orders were broad enough that he could forestall Hartwell from sailing for a day. And a night. And under the guise of intelligence gathering he could find a bed and a fire, and perhaps teach Jennifer Leighton how to tie a French letter on him with a firm knot and a jaunty bow.

"It seems we owe Mr. Devere a debt," said Frances Leighton, interrupting Severin's erotic idyll.

"I would never have gotten off the *Boyne* without him," said Jennifer Leighton, capped by a yawn.

She would not have been on the *Boyne* at all without him—or her aunt's connivance—thought Severin, but he was drinking the woman's excellent brandy and enjoying her fire and it would be churlish to remark upon such a thing, so he kept silent. Frances Leighton was probably no one's idea of an ideal chaperone, but she was the girl's aunt, and in any case his mind was running in a different direction entirely, imagining just what forms Jennifer Leighton's touching appreciation might take in bed.

"The difficulty with debts," said Frances Leighton, recalling him once more to the present and the prosaic, "is that a woman who makes her own way in the world accumulates a number of them, and sometimes they conflict. You saved my niece, and for that you have my gratitude, but you also tried to kill a woman who was, at one time, like a sister to me—and she very much wants you *dead*."

It took a minute for her meaning to penetrate. For a fact, his mind was *not* working fast, fuddled with exhaustion and blunted with frustrated desire and set free to wander by good brandy.

She meant the Widow. Also known as Angela Ferrers. The bits and pieces began to fit themselves together in a pattern he should have discerned earlier. It was unusual to keep ipecac in a personal medicine chest. And somewhere in Angela Ferrers' obscure past had to be an acquaintance with the theater, with wigs and costumes and paints and disguises, with accents and voices and distinctive manners of walking and speaking.

"You work for the Widow, then," said Severin.

"I did once," replied Frances Leighton. "I don't work for Angela anymore, but she helped me on an occasion when I very much needed her, and I still count her among my close friends."

Jenny's copper eyebrows knitted. "Your friend in Boston," she said, and tried to rise. She fell back upon the chaise, swaying. "You never write letters," she said, with a puzzled look on her face. The brandy glass fell from her boneless fingers and her eyes fluttered closed. She teetered there, clutching the cushion and trying to stay upright.

Severin's capacity for underestimating women, apparently, was without limits.

"I had a very particular set of talents, you see," said Frances Leighton. Her face had begun to blur in the candlelight.

"Poisons," guessed Severin, though the word was thick in his mouth. Memory teased at him, something to do with Frances Leighton, a piece of information he had picked up somewhere, but he could not seize hold of it in his disordered mind.

"Drugs," she corrected. "My father was an apothecary and he trained me to mix his compounds. I see you are familiar enough with the workings of toxins to know better than to get up."

He did know better. Movement would only speed

whatever bane—nonfatal, he hoped—had been in the brandy that was now coursing through his veins and had already begun to steal his wits. He knew from experience—because he'd had occasion to employ potions himself—that he would just lose consciousness faster that way, and the distance to the floor, when he fell, would only be farther.

Jennifer Leighton lost her struggle with the drugged brandy and slid from the chaise to the ground, quite insensible.

Reflex trumped good sense and training and Devere started toward her. The ceiling lurched and the walls spun. He managed to stand upright, but either the room swayed or he did, and his first step was also his last. The polished surface of the table rushed to meet him. He clutched at it for support. His numb hand knocked the crystal decanter to the floor, where it shattered. He grasped the heavy mahogany pedestal, and knocked it over as he fell.

His shoulder smacked the painted floor. He rolled his head to see Jenny lying beside him, facedown, only inches—that might as well be miles—away. A rivulet of spilled brandy snaked between them and disappeared between the wide pine planks.

He was too deep in the drug's clutches to move now, but with his ear pressed to the floor he could hear Frances Leighton push back her chair and cross the room, her small feet light on the boards, her steps quick and close together. He heard the latch rise, the door swing open, and the threshold creak. Then a different set of feet entered and walked with a more measured pace to within a few inches of his motionless head.

The important thing was to use what little time he

had wisely, to try to gain some control over the situation, to threaten, to bribe, to bargain, with whoever held him in their power. To save himself.

But the words that tumbled from his mouth were *not* for him.

"What did you give her?" he asked thickly. An associate of the Widow might be capable of anything, and he was unable to tell from the floor if Jennifer Leighton was still breathing.

A shadow fell over him. The wooden heel of a shoe bit into his shoulder and pushed him onto his back, and he was staring up not at the Divine Fanny, but at a far more dangerous woman.

"Juice of poppy," said Angela Ferrers smoothly. "It was only opium."

She was as beautiful—in face and form—as he remembered. But her eyes were far, far colder.

"Don't hurt her," he tried to say, but his tongue felt furred, would not wrap itself around the words.

The sense must have been plain enough, though, because Angela Ferrers placed one delicate slippered foot upon his chest, leaned over him, and said, "*Jenny* will wake up in the morning, Mr. Devere. The question is, will you?"

Eleven

Jenny could feel the ropes beneath the mattress digging into her back. It took her a moment to remember why that might be; then she recalled borrowing feathers from her bed to stuff the cushions in the royal box. She had done that for Burgoyne, but Severin Devere had come instead.

Her head ached. She was not prone to migraines like Aunt Frances and she did not usually wake so muddled. She could not immediately recall what day it was, or what play she had acted the night before. There had been the performance on Wednesday . . . that had ended with John Street sacked. And then last night she had gone to Burgoyne.

The events aboard the *Boyne* came back to her in a rush and she did not know how she could have forgotten them even for a few fleeting moments upon waking, but then she recalled a similar morning, long before, at home in New Brunswick. Her hale and hearty Grandmother Ackerman had dropped dead crossing the street, to the shock and surprise of the whole community and to Jenny, her constant companion, most of all. The Ackermans were venerable Dutch stock, absurdly long-lived, pickled in spirits and thorny as the symbol of their tenacious old church.

Jenny had come home from the funeral and discovered that the house sounded different without Grandmother in it. The rhythm of roof and beam had altered irrevocably and would never be the same again. She had served out the funeral breakfast, the pies that Grandmother had been alive just days before to make, and went to bed that night feeling the hollowness and lack to the marrow of her bones.

She had woken up the next morning without a care in the world and thrown off the covers and then she had *remembered*. Grandmother was gone. Everything was different.

This morning felt the same. Only it was her dream that had died.

She opened her eyes on the familiar pale ceiling of her room. In lieu of a tester, she and Aunt Frances had pushed the low bed to one wall and strung blue wool curtains across the side. They were closed now. Jenny reached to part them and let the world in.

The sun was midday bright and the window was open and the bustle and noise of John Street floated in through the casement, reminding Jenny that she was not the only person in New York whose fate had hung in the balance last night.

Severin Devere.

He'd gotten her off the *Boyne* and saved her from

likely imprisonment and hanging. And they'd *almost* . . . and then it had come to an abrupt end, all for want of French letters, which Aunt Frances had said were scorned by the kind of men whose patronage she sought.

She hadn't wanted patronage from Severin. She'd wanted . . . his hands, his mouth, his hard, trained body, his wicked invention, and his dangerous smile, *for herself*. Something pure and untainted by barter or ambition. She'd enjoyed playing opposite him in the street, evading their pursuers, and sparring with him verbally in the empty pleasure garden. After the interlude in the kitchen, though, her memory of the evening was murkier. She could recall passing familiar landmarks on the walk home, the firing glasses lined up on the granite steps, the cold brass heft of the door key in her hand, Severin taking it from her gently and then . . .

The parlor. Aunt Frances. *You saved my niece, and for that you have my gratitude, but you also tried to kill a woman who was, at one time, like a sister to me—and she very much wants you dead.*

Jenny sat up and pulled the bed curtains wide and looked out. The shutters were open and the room was light, but it was not the brightness of midday; it was the wan sun of a December afternoon.

Frances Leighton sat in the chair beside the window looking down into the street. She was rubbing her temples, as she did sometimes during one of her headaches when she thought Jenny wasn't looking.

"Are you all right, Aunt Frances?"

The Divine Fanny dropped her hand and looked up, plastering a serene smile across her face. "Of course, dear. Just tired. We had rather a late night, if you recall."

She did. All too well. "What did you do to Severin?" Jenny asked.

"I drugged his brandy."

"Why?"

"Because I owed a debt to Angela Ferrers."

"The woman he calls the Widow?"

"The same," said Frances Leighton.

"And you wrote to her in Boston. You told her Severin was here in New York. And she sent the killers who attacked us in the street."

Aunt Frances looked away. "I could not have foreseen that you would be in his company."

"But you knew she wanted to kill him."

Aunt Frances looked her direct in the eye. "That is the business they are in."

"That you were in too," said Jenny.

"Not really," said Frances. "Never like that."

"Like what?"

"With such conviction. That is what makes them dangerous, people like Devere, people like Angela. They entertain no doubts. They never hesitate. They just act. And people get killed. Sometimes at their hands, and sometimes at the hands of others, but such distinctions make little difference to those bereft, and none at all to the dead."

Jenny had seen it firsthand. She had helped Severin dispatch two men in the street. He *was* a killer. She could not deny that. But he was also something more. He could have arranged a far nastier accident for their pursuers in the burnt house, or sprung back over the wall to take them unawares after they blundered into the pit. He could have left the mob to its own devices and Jenny to her fate in the riot, because Burgoyne had been safely aboard the *Boyne* at the time. He could have turned her over to Hartwell aboard the ship, or left her to find her own way home at the dock, especially when he must have suspected the danger to himself.

"You are wrong about Devere," said Jenny. "He saved my life."

"Because he wanted you."

Jenny flushed.

"That much," said her aunt with asperity, "was obvious in the greenroom. Men will sometimes act foolishly over a woman they desire, but they rarely make real sacrifices for women like us. Honor is reserved for their wellborn wives and sisters."

"He made Burgoyne look like a fool in order to spirit me off the *Boyne*."

"Yet he did not challenge him to a duel or bring him before a court of law."

"To be fair, Burgoyne was unconscious and there is no court of law in New York at the moment."

"So Devere did what was expedient," said Frances Leighton. "He smoothed over a potentially embarrassing episode with a highly ranked officer and an actress who would have been presumed a whore, and if I did not mistake the way you were mooning at each other last night, he took the opportunity to exploit your gratitude."

"He didn't, actually," said Jenny, "because we had no French letters."

The Divine Fanny's face betrayed her surprise. "Well, there is a point in his favor, but it does not change *what* he is."

"And what is that?" Jenny asked.

"A wolf in sheep's clothing," said Aunt Frances. "He may dress and speak like a gentleman, but he is not."

"This is America, Aunt Frances. Indian blood is not so very uncommon here. And he makes no secret of his origins. He told me he was born on the frontier."

"But not how, or to whom. It is an old scandal, but it was fresh enough still in London when I made my debut on the stage. Devere *was* born on the frontier. His noble father was a second son with an appetite for land and he dragged his wife and their firstborn, Severin's older brother, into the borderlands to get it. Unfortunately the man lacked the temperament for taming a wilderness. He abandoned his family to the care of servants in favor of the lure of town life."

A fair number of the men who frequented the greenroom kept their wives and children on estates in the Hudson Highlands or in the Jerseys. "Husbands like that are not so very uncommon," said Jenny.

Aunt Frances shrugged. "Men are what they are. The Deveres had, I heard, a fine house and many servants and hired men, but no contacts or goodwill among the Indians, something essential to living in their domains. Servants and hired men look to their own when trouble threatens. Accounts vary, probably because they are to no one's credit, but this much is certain. There was a raid on the house. Devere's mother and her son were taken by Indians, and by the time his father came back it was too late to track them. Elizabeth Devere disappeared into the wilderness with one child. Ten years later, with a war brewing, she returned from that wilderness with two. It has always been assumed that Severin Devere is the get of the savage who raped her."

"But he calls himself Devere," said Jenny. And a bastard surely could not.

"His mother claimed, and her husband did not

dispute, that she was pregnant when she disappeared. By the time she came back, the elder Devere had inherited an earldom and wanted an heir. He had been trying for years to get his wife declared dead so he could remarry, but reports of her survival continued to reach Albany, so the courts refused to grant his suit. And indeed, she was very much alive, and she had brought his firstborn back to him. No doubt when husband and wife were reunited they struck some mutually agreeable bargain about her bastard."

"What will happen to him now?" asked Jenny.

"I would worry more about what will happen to you," said a cool voice from the doorway.

The woman on the threshold gave the appearance of being tall, but Jenny knew that height could be an illusion, increased by pattens and heels and enhanced by the color, shape, and cut of an ensemble. The lady—her confidence marked her as such—wore head-to-toe deep blue worsted with a subtle sheen, the gown plain in front, the petticoat sewn from the same fabric. It emphasized her slenderness, the length of her neck, the elegance of her simply dressed hair. This was free of powder, but Jenny could not tell if the color was the woman's own or altered with dyes.

"You're Angela Ferrers," said Jenny.

"That is one of the names I use," said the lady, with a nod of her head.

"You tried to kill Severin."

"He tried to kill me first."

"That is a child's response."

"And you are not playing a children's game," said the lady softly. "*You* are bargaining for the life of a man whom you have just learned is a savage."

Jenny snorted. It was not a pretty sound. "Severin Devere did not kill your assassins with a war whoop and a tomahawk. He skewered one neatly with a sword and broke the other's neck with a very modern wrestler's maneuver, in perfect silence. He refrained from killing the others, even when opportunity presented itself. His job was to protect Burgoyne, as Aunt Frances said, but the general was safely aboard the *Boyne*, and he risked himself to save me from the mob during the riot anyway. An aberration for a spy, but hardly a savage one. Apart from an unfortunate susceptibility to dangerous women, he does what is expected of him. I cannot imagine a man more *English*."

"You are perceptive, Miss Leighton, but you have missed a crucial fact about Severin Devere, the very root of the matter. Grasp that, and you grasp everything. He *is* more English than the English because he *has* to be. When Earl Devere went into the borderlands to retrieve his wife ten years after he misplaced her, he wanted the eldest son, Julian, who he was certain was his heir. The Mohawk Ashur Rice who held Elizabeth Devere handed her and *both* boys over, without a fight. Severin Devere is a man without a country. Neither his Indian nor his English father wanted him. His own half brother barely acknowledges him. Only by acting where others hesitate in the service of the British government has Devere made a life for himself. A man like him will not give up such hard-earned status lightly. He saved you last night, but he would be obliged to throw your aunt to the wolves tomorrow if we freed him—because he knows that through Frances he can get to *me*."

"What do you intend to do with him?" Jenny asked.

"Devere's fate, until I have determined how best to protect you and your aunt, will remain an open question. Let us speak of yours, now that Hallam knows you defied him, and both London and John Street are lost to you."

"Bobby knows?"

"When one wishes to hold an unconscious man prisoner in another's cellar, some explanation is usually required. As you see, everything has its price. Devere is still alive, but it has cost you something. What will you give so that he might keep on breathing?"

Devere woke in total darkness. He was lashed upright to a chair, and the ropes circling his chest made his bruised ribs ache and his breath come short. His hands were bound behind him and his feet together in front of him, and he could not, at first, feel either. When circulation returned to his fingers, he discovered that the knots had been tied expertly. When the blood returned to his feet, he could feel that his shoes and stockings had been taken. The bare skin of his heels rested on cold, damp stone. Not surprising, if the Widow was involved, because she was a professional, and the woman never left anything to chance.

He was not gagged, which indicated he was someplace that no one would hear his shouts . . . or screams. *Never a good sign.*

And even more worrying, he could hear no other breathing, detect no other warmth in the darkness. Jennifer Leighton was not with him. He ought not to find that perversely satisfying withal, but he did. A wave of schoolboy giddiness washed over him. The aunt had drugged her too, which meant the girl was not in sympathy with their plans for Severin.

Which told him that, unlike all of his other affairs since adulthood, everything that had happened between them last night was real and meaningful. And that he had to get out of here.

He tested the ropes first. The ones around his wrists had indeed been tied well. Extricating himself would cost him skin and blood, possibly even a few small broken bones.

It would have to be his left hand, then. He would need his right to pick the lock of whatever door separated him from freedom. And to deal with whoever might be guarding him beyond it. That was provided that his lock picks were still in his pocket. If they had been taken, there was another, smaller set, sewn into the seams of his coat, along with ten gold sovereigns and ten silver shillings, concealed inside the leather-covered buttons.

He was not given enough time. He was still bound helpless to the chair, blood running down his hands from his efforts, when the world erupted into noise and light. A door opened, scraping loudly across the floor, and a lantern blinded him. Too late to shut his eyes against it, he looked away to give his vision a precious moment to adjust. A gust of warm, dry air hit him, and he realized how very cold his prison had been.

He turned back to the light. The nimbus resolved into the graceful shape of a woman carrying a lantern.

"I shan't apologize to you for the quality of the hospitality," said Angela Ferrers, "as it is still better than a coffin."

"To what do I owe your forbearance?" he asked.

Her perfume was different. It had been neroli in Boston. It was gardenias now. He thought neroli might have suited better, but then, he was not certain he really knew her at all.

She smiled. It was an unusual smile, slightly crooked and full of delight—a glimpse, perhaps, of the real woman behind the nested masks. He felt, even now, the pull of her. Like attracts like.

She set the lantern atop a crate so that light shone down on him, and she took his chin in her slender, agile hands and tilted it so that he was forced to look up at her. "Are you vain, Devere? Would you like me to say it is your pretty . . . *face*?"

"You liked it well enough in Boston."

She shrugged. "That was a game we both played."

"You seemed to enjoy it at the time."

"And *that* is a game all women are obliged to play, on occasion. Did you really hope to turn me in your bed?"

He tasted bile. He felt, no doubt, somewhat as Jennifer Leighton had in the hands of John Burgoyne.

She laughed and her hand left his chin. "The noble savage act, I am sorry to inform you, did not entirely move me. Better had you shown me the real Severin Devere, as you did Jennifer Leighton. She *was* moved."

There was a crate opposite his chair. The Widow pushed it, wisely, several feet back before lowering herself onto it, so that if he took the desperate chance of heaving himself, chair and all, at her, his effort would fall short.

She sat, arranging her blue wool skirts, which were every bit as sensual as the cool touch of silk, on a woman who knew how to use them. From her pocket she drew a folded sheaf of papers, written in a familiar hand.

"Where did you get those?" he asked.

"From Jennifer Leighton, as it happens. In exchange for your life."

Burgoyne's plans, which Severin had locked in his cabin for safekeeping. Where he had also put Jennifer Leighton—for safekeeping—while he called the steward and fabricated his tale and left instructions that the *Boyne* was to sail without him if he did not return.

Jenny had stolen them.

Burgoyne's manuscript was a rough outline of the plan he would present to the King in London. King George, of course, knew little of military strategy and had no firsthand experience of America. Severin understood both. The plans were daring—possibly even a work of genius. The colonies were vast, their peoples spread over varied terrain, their cities and towns—the traditional objectives of European wars—unimportant. It was controlling travel, the waterways, the corridors of trade—north to south and east to west—that truly mattered.

Burgoyne's strategy, if successful, would cut New England off from the rest of the colonies and secure Britain's hold on America. Jennifer Leighton was unlikely to grasp all of that, but she was not stupid, and she must have understood the value of the papers she held in her hands. Must have known they could be traded for a measure of security from the Liberty Boys, for herself or for her beloved theater.

She had instead traded them for Severin Devere, to this very dangerous woman.

Foolish, lovely Jenny. He had saved her from

Burgoyne, but that had just been out of the frying pan and into the fire, because the Widow was in many ways a far greater threat.

"Jennifer Leighton is nothing to do with you and me," he said.

"What a very ungracious thing to say. I will admit she surprised me," said Angela Ferrers, to whom he had made vigorous love in a *performance*, he now realized, worthy of the stage, but to whom he had shown nothing of his real self.

"Frances proved a weak reed, but *Jenny* . . . now, Jenny is promising."

He remembered Frances Leighton's admission about Angela Ferrers last night. *She helped me once, when I very much needed her.* That, along with the rumors he had pieced together about the Divine Fanny's former, very dead lover. "Harry's wife accused Frances Leighton of murder," he guessed.

"It was never brought to trial," replied Angela Ferrers.

"But it's true, isn't it? She killed Harry. And you supplied her with the poison."

"I helped her when she needed me. As friends are wont to do."

"I didn't know you had any."

"They are, admittedly, most often a liability in our line of work. An indulgence we can ill afford. They may even lead to rambling conversations in damp basements."

"Harry wasn't political. That makes Frances Leighton a murderess. And poison is a coward's weapon."

"Poison is a *woman's* weapon, you mean. Yet one you and I both use. What a lovely English fiction, to pretend that it is only employed by the fair sex. Frances is not lacking in intelligence or courage. Only in ruthlessness."

"I beg to differ. She sent Jenny into Burgoyne's hands unprotected, exposing her to the same fate."

"Don't be so quick to judge the Divine Fanny. She is what the whims of powerful men have made of her. And she only came to America to see for one last time the lovely Jenny. And Jenny—well, Jenny has proven far more interesting than I anticipated."

"Your quarrel is with me," said Devere. "Leave her out of this."

"You would be dead now if it was not for her," said Angela Ferrers bluntly.

He had not wanted Jennifer Leighton ruined by John Burgoyne, but the Widow posed a threat to more than her virtue and self-regard. "You have embroiled her in treason."

"And *you*, dear sir, offered her up on a platter to John Burgoyne. Who, after all, would care about the honor of an obscure provincial girl of undistinguished birth and no fortune, who fancies herself a playwright and an actress?"

He didn't answer.

"*You* again, Devere. When push came to shove. And *that* is why you are still alive. Because I think it is just possible that you may remember that you are an American yourself."

"Being born in a manger does not make a man an animal."

"Ah, if only your masters were so enlightened. But they are not, are they? You have worked to be more English than the English, these past twenty years, and they barely tolerate you. It soothes their consciences to send a man like you to carry out their injustices, grand and petty, because they can blame the butcher's bill—blame *their* savageries—on *your* heritage."

"Are *you* trying to turn *me* now?" he asked. "Because this chair is considerably less comfortable than the bed I found for us. Though I am sure we could improvise nicely on the crate. Untie me, and I will demonstrate."

"No, thank you," she replied, meeting his eye. "A command performance will not be necessary. I somehow doubt you would show me the genuine passion you demonstrated for Jennifer Leighton, and outside professional demands, I have no tolerance anymore for the counterfeit kind. I cannot, of course, release you. Nor can I keep you tied up in Hallam's basement forever."

Here was the crux of the matter. She could slit his throat now and he would be able to do nothing to stop her. He'd try, of course. His body was already tensed to upset the chair if she approached.

She did not approach. "I have promised the Leightons that I will spare your life, but I must have a care for their safety. You know, or have guessed, too much about Frances. For that sin, I am sending you to the Simsbury Copper Mine."

The prison Fairchild had described in Connecticut, where Isaac Sears and the Liberty Boys and the Committee of One Hundred and Congress and Washington all sent their political prisoners.

"I am not officially in America. If you send me to Simsbury, it will be difficult or impossible for Howe to trade me back," said Severin.

"That," said the Widow, "is rather the point." She

departed in a swirl of soft wool skirts. The scent of gardenias lingered after her for a moment, and was then replaced with the smell of damp and mold.

He had blamed his failure on a weakness for strong, ambitious women, on his attraction to the Widow, and his tenderness for Jennifer Leighton, but his interview with Angela Ferrers had shown him the truth. She was *better* than he was. More ruthless. Less sentimental. He had thought he could go through with it in Boston, garrote her in the very bed they had shared.

He had been making excuses for his failure ever since. That she had felt the cord in his pocket, or under the pillow. That she had felt his body tense before he made his move. All of these things might very well be true—but the real reason he had failed to kill her was because he had hesitated. Because she was a woman, and he had been intimate with her.

She had not hesitated. She had not been sentimental. She had moved like an eel, had snatched the cord and flung it from the window, and in the series of maneuvers that had followed, had bested him, because he had been unwilling to truly hurt her while she had felt no such constraint.

He could not afford such weakness again. He had learned that much at least from her. He was going to get out of this basement, and he was going to get Jennifer Leighton away from Aunt Lucrezia and her chest of poisons—and back to boring New Brunswick, where she could not get herself into any more trouble. And this time he would not forgo the pleasure of bedding her.

He began to work at the ropes once more. It hurt rather a lot, the raw rasp of hemp cutting into his flesh. A final, desperate wrench and he was able to pull his left hand free, leaving strips of skin and a little blood behind in the coarse fiber of the rope.

Rolling his shoulder forward was pure agony. Two fingers were crooked and useless and these he had to bend back into place, quickly so they would not swell and freeze. He was glad no one was there to hear him cry out in the dark.

They had done a very good job of trussing him. His hands were free, but the ropes that crossed his chest and circled the back of the chair made it impossible to bend forward and reach the knots that bound his ankles. And the knots that held him lashed to the chair were, very wisely, also out of reach.

The chair, unfortunately, was sturdy, and would be difficult to break. The back splat was probably the weakest link, and he went to work on this first.

It was not easy. He had to focus all of his strength and concentration on straining against the ropes, first forward, and then back, the coils biting wickedly into muscle and bruising bone. The wood was creaking, very near to giving way, when the door opened.

He thrust his hands behind his back, because he did not want to give away the tiny advantage he had gained.

Oranges.

He breathed in their freshly peeled scent. It registered on his brain before light, before sound, cutting through the dark and his pain.

He was saved.

Twelve

Devere drank in her scent. "Jenny," he said. "Untie me."

"I am so very sorry," said Jennifer Leighton, who did not rush to his aid. "I didn't know about my aunt."

She closed the door quietly behind her and stood there with her back to the panels. She had only a small candle to pierce the gloom, but it sparkled off her dark, perceptive eyes and illuminated the blush on her fine, pale skin like a Dutch painting.

Jennifer Leighton was not costumed for seduction as she had been the night before, nor was she wearing a shroud like that awful linen gown, which had looked and felt like sacking. She was dressed in a little velvet jacket of coral pink, laced in front with a green ribbon over a matching stomacher. Her petticoat was white silk, embroidered with sprigs of flowers, and her copper hair was pinned loosely back from her face to fall in long waves over her shoulders. She still had his knife, tucked into the waist of her petticoat, the quilled hilt glossy in the lantern light.

He was cold and his hands and shoulders ached, and there was something nearly irresistible about the textures of her velvet jacket and silk petticoats that made him desperately want to touch her. That, and the scent of oranges. But the way she hung back at the door urged caution, and he kept his bloody hands hidden behind the chair.

"Jenny, untie me, and I promise, whatever your aunt is mixed up in, I'll see that you aren't hurt. And that no one ever knows you took Burgoyne's plans." He should not promise it. He should not *do* it. But he knew he would. He had a certain measure of discretion in his work, required it in order to cultivate his sources. He could justify shielding her if he so chose. He was very good at justifying things to himself.

She remained standing near the door. "But you can't say the same for my aunt, can you?"

He ought to lie to her. His business was lies. He traded in secrets. His value to the men who paid him lay in his willingness to do unpleasant things, like deceive innocent young women whose lips tasted like brandy and sugar. His job was concealing the weaknesses of powerful men, and he had been doing it for so long that he would surely be able to indulge and conceal his own.

He would have to. Because he found he could not lie to *this* girl. "If you let me go, I promise that I will undertake no initiative against Frances myself. But if I was asked to by the government, I would have little choice."

"Then that is no promise at all."

"Your aunt," he said carefully, "was once part of Angela Ferrers' network. She likely has information material to our success in this war."

"And you would hurt her to get it."

"My superiors could not rely on information she gave up freely."

"You mean you would torture her. I had convinced myself that you wouldn't. That my aunt and her unsettling friend were wrong. I came down here to free you, Severin. *That* does make me naive, doesn't it?"

"I won't apologize to you for what I am," he said. "Were I anything other, I could not have gotten you off the *Boyne*, or past those cutthroats in the street last night."

"That isn't who you are," she said. "It's who you choose to be."

She was right, after a fashion, and wrong, because she had not walked a mile in his shoes. "Not all of us have so very many choices."

"But you chose to save me last night, and that is why I am here now. I want to help you as you helped me, but I cannot do it at the price of my aunt's safety."

"She sent you to Burgoyne like a babe to the slaughter and then drugged you to ensure that you did not interfere with her friend's plans last night. Your aunt keeps ipecac and opium in her medicine chest and uses them with the casualness of a Borgia. Are you certain your loyalty is so well placed?"

"I am certain of far fewer things today than I was yesterday, but my aunt is not one of them. And an evening with Burgoyne has given me a new sympathy for poor Lucrezia. The wants of women are so easily swept aside by the whims of men. You sit here tied hand and foot and still, in so many ways, the advantages remain yours."

He could not deny that. It was truer than she knew. If she came close enough, he would be able to overpower her, even with his ankles and chest still bound to the chair. He did not want to do that. "The world was made unequal, Jenny. That is why most women dare not face it alone. I can't do anything about that, but I am not working against your best interests. Quite the contrary."

"That is what Burgoyne imagined, that he was helping me."

"And that is the line Angela Ferrers will take when she tries to recruit you. That she is acting in your best interest. But in truth she intrigues for the same people who would close the playhouses and banish you and yours to the road. The Rebels have no love of the theater. If they had their way, you and your aunt would starve."

"If the choice was scraps from Burgoyne's table or starving, I think I would choose the latter."

"Then I think that you have never known real hunger." He could recall it even now, the gnawing, agonizing pain. The consuming desperation of it.

"I am not asking you to hand America to the Rebels," said Jenny, "though the governor seems to have done his level best on that score these past months. I am asking you to forget what you know about *one* woman, who is no threat to anyone. Yesterday you did not know she had any connection to Angela Ferrers. You would have sailed home to England none the wiser. Can you not pretend this is yesterday?"

"Can you?"

Jenny did not want things to be this way. She had glimpsed something with Severin Devere last night that made her understand how Aunt Frances could throw away her career. Not for a man, as Jenny had always thought, but for the thrill she had experienced running beside Severin Devere in the streets of New York, for the laughter they had stifled together crouched in the rosemary, for the sheer joy of partnership.

She wanted very much to untie him. And to touch him. To push his hair back from his face and straighten his collar and stroke his cheek. She wanted to recover the intimacy that had grown between them in the garden, and bloomed in the banquet hall kitchen, and somehow survived their frustrated desire to persist on that sleepy walk home, so that when he had taken the brass key from her fingers on the doorstep it had felt like they were lovers, even though they were not. Afterward, he had looked so very right sitting in her aunt's parlor, as though he belonged there with their little family.

Of course, that was before her aunt had drugged him. What he looked at this moment was dangerous, like the brown dog that the brewer kept tied up at the end of the block. Sweet natured when he was free and fed and lying in the shade, but snarling and slavering when tied up without food or water and set to guard the empty premises for hours at a time.

Devere was like the dog now, parched and pent, and she could not release him, but she was running out of options and out of time. Devere had been so practical last night. If only he would be so today. She had to persuade him to see reason.

"In Burgoyne's cabin," she said, "you advised me to embrace a lie and forgo justice. I am asking you to do the same, and the stakes are no less dire. If you give me your word that you will leave my aunt out of your business with the Widow, that you will forget what you have learned about her, I will get you out of here, and Angela Ferrers be damned."

He shook his head and looked at her with those intent, magnetic black eyes. "In the slot during the riot, I advised you to go home to your parents. Why didn't you?"

"Because there is nothing for me in New Brunswick."

"And because at John Street your gifts are recognized. As mine are by our government, by the King and men like Lord Germain and General Howe. No one *wants* to do the kind of things I do, but someone must. And I am valued for it."

"I was wrong," she said. "About the theater. And a lot of other things. You are wrong about this. Promise me you will not tell anyone about my aunt's connection to the Widow. If you don't, I cannot free you, and they are going to send you to a loyalist prison."

"I was educated at an English public school. After Harrow, prison holds no fears for me," he said.

He is more English than the English because he has to be. "This one should. The greenroom is a fine place for ghoulish gossip. It is in a worked-out copper mine in Connecticut. The Rebels have been using it to hold *inconvenient* Tories. They lower the unlucky wretches down to the bottom, more than a hundred feet below the ground, by a windlass. There is no light and there is no air, and it will make this cellar look like the royal box. Most of those immured die within a few months."

"I know of the mine, Jenny. And I know how to survive in such a place. But that your aunt would banish anyone to that kind of hell just to save herself ought to make you question what kind of woman she is."

"My *aunt* begged for your life, Severin, and secured it. It was not Fanny but Angela Ferrers who has proposed this unhappy compromise. You cannot turn me against

Aunt Frances. If it wasn't for her, I would be living a very different life. I would never have seen New York or set foot on a stage, or had my words brought to life there."

"And you wouldn't have ended up on the *Boyne* with your life in peril," replied Devere. "People like the Widow, people like your aunt, people like *me*—we sacrifice lovely young things like you all the time. Angela Ferrers does it for a cause; Frances Leighton out of self-preservation. *I* was prepared to hand you over to Burgoyne to keep the wretch aboard the *Boyne* and out of trouble. For England, you might say. The reasoning makes no difference—none at all—to the victims of our agendas."

"You don't know my aunt. She tried to discourage me from going to Burgoyne. There was nothing she could say to dissuade me."

"That isn't true," said Devere. "She could have told you the truth about her illness."

His words struck her deaf and dumb like a thunderclap, and she was alone in the silence. Devere, the walls, the door—all seemed miles and miles away. Then the world rushed back to her. She could hear a faint dripping somewhere in the distance, feel the chill of the basement through the soles of her shoes, smell the damp, crumbling stone.

At last she found her voice. It sounded small and frightened. "What do you know about my aunt's illness?" she asked.

"Jenny," he said in a gentle voice that made her light-headed with foreboding, "your aunt is dying."

"No."

"You live with her. You know it is not drink," said Devere. "Or late nights, or the natural progress of age."

"You cannot know what is wrong with her," insisted

Jenny. "*She* does not know what is wrong with her. She has not seen a doctor."

"She has no need of one," said Devere. "Neither for diagnosis nor for what passes as 'treatment.' Her father was an apothecary. She would have recognized the *signs* in her lover early on. She must have long known what is coming. She may have thought, at one time, she had been spared, but she must know by now that she has not. The disease is like that. It disfigures some but spares others. It can hide undetected for years. But you have seen the symptoms. The forgetfulness, the headaches, the stiff and sore muscles, the numb fingers and toes."

Jenny shook her head and felt for the latch on the door. Devere was wrong. He knew nothing. She could not go on without Aunt Frances. "That is just age. She can't be dying. I need her," said Jenny baldly.

"Untie me, Jenny, and send for Major Fairchild at the King's Arms. Frances Leighton has abused your trust. She will not be able to keep her secret much longer. Think of how it will tarnish you when it is known. There are those who will say you are her daughter. It will make you a pariah, to be the child of a syphilitic."

It fit. It fit the facts she knew and the rumors she had heard and it answered the questions that Frances Leighton had so deftly sidestepped. "How do you know this?" Jenny asked.

"It's my business to know things. I collect and sift information. I look for patterns, and this one is all too clear, even if the general public has not yet guessed it. She withdrew from the stage and public life to nurse her dying lover, and then fled to America once he was no more. It is a *terrible* way to die, Jenny, and she put you

into the very same peril when she told you to accommo-
date Burgoyne without protection. And when she is
found out—when her condition is known—it will forever change how people think of you. And it will give
credence to the even uglier rumors about her lover's
death that were circulating when Fanny left London."

"What rumors?" Fanny only ever spoke of Harry
in wistful terms.

"That Fanny was not a dutiful nurse. That she
murdered him. Those, at least, were the accusations
that Harry's wife made against Frances. No charges
were ever brought, and it was widely agreed that Harry
and Fanny were devoted to each other—he'd been separated from his shrew of a wife for years—but if Frances learned that Harry had given her the disease, that
she was going to share the same ugly fate, then she
might have a powerful motive for murder indeed."

It was all too much. Jenny did not know if Severin's
narrative was entirely accurate, but she feared that the
terrible burden of it was on the mark. She had not
really felt the effects of her brush with danger the night
before, neither John Burgoyne's assault nor their encounter with the footpads—because Devere's companionship had shielded her and his strength had buoyed
her—but she felt it now.

The impulse to throw herself at him for comfort
was strong, and utterly useless.

She did not feel betrayed, as Devere plainly wished
her to. She felt bereft. Aunt Frances had almost led her
down the selfsame path to destruction the great actress herself had walked, but Jenny could not fault her
for it. She had not *made* the road.

Her lip was quivering. Grief fused with anger. The one was weak, the other strong. She bit down, hard, until the trembling stopped.

"I cannot let you take my aunt, no matter what secrets she has been keeping, no matter how poor her counsel to me. I will never be anything but proud to own her. She may be reckless with her own person, but she saved your life last night from her very dangerous friend, and I will not see her suffer—will not see her *tortured*—for it."

"Then get out," said the man who had saved her from the riot and the *Boyne* and the cutthroats in the street, and who had seemed to understand—as he'd rowed them across New York Harbor—just how limited her options, like her aunt's before her, had been. He said it pleasantly, but with a tired indifference that made her feel sick with shame because she had been stupid enough to think she had shared something important with this man.

She was a stubborn little thing. He quite liked that about her, but it meant that he was going to have to be cruel. He could not give her his word that her aunt would be spared. He wished he could, but there were some lies that even he could not tell. The woman knew how to get to Angela Ferrers. Even if Severin was not himself capable of breaking that formidable agent, there were other men in government—specialists of a sort—who were.

He needed Jennifer Leighton to leave. She wasn't going to release him, which meant he had to release himself, and that was going to require work.

"Get out, Jenny."

"You have earned my help," she insisted. She took a step forward in the dark. If she discovered that his hands were free, he would have to prevent her from raising the alarm. He did not want to do that. With his legs and chest still tied to the chair, there was no way he could reliably subdue her without the risk of doing her a serious injury.

"I don't need the help of a naive little provincial like yourself. You proved too much the rustic to manage John Burgoyne. Don't fancy yourself my equal, or my savior, now."

She blanched at his crudeness. It did not come easily to him, and he could not keep it up for very long, but hopefully he wouldn't have to.

"Why are you doing this?" she asked.

"Because you are of no further use to me."

"I don't believe you," she said. "I'm an actor. I know a performance when I see one."

"No . . . you don't. You were completely taken in last night. You thought I was refraining from fucking you on the bakery table out of tender concern for your innocence. That you were *special*. That is what every opera singer wants to believe. That is how the poxed rake who infected your aunt convinced her to engage with him without protection. I am no different, only more fastidious. I planned to return to John Street tomorrow night with a pocketful of French letters to enjoy the fruits of your touching gratitude."

"I will not get another chance to come back," she warned. "The Widow is out now and Aunt Frances could not stop me, but once the Widow returns I will have no second chance."

Neither would Severin. He heard it a moment before she did, footsteps on the other side of the door, the key scraping in the lock.

Her expressive eyes went wide with fear. She looked

frantically for a place to hide, but the small chamber was bare. She took a deep breath as though preparing to step onto the stage, squared her shoulders, and moved to the center of the room.

The door swung open.

Robert Hallam stopped on the threshold, his lips a little apart, his eyes fixed on Jenny.

"What are you doing here?" asked Hallam.

She edged away from the entrance and Hallam—and a little closer to Severin. Almost within his reach. If she took another step, he would be able to grab her, even tied to the chair. He could threaten to break her neck. Trade her life for his release. It would be a bluff, but Hallam could hardly know that.

"Devere saved my life last night," she said.

"And we have spared his," replied Hallam. The actor's attention, fortunately for Severin, was entirely locked on Jenny.

"The copper mine is a death sentence, and you know it."

"It is that, or cold-blooded murder. If we release him, he, or one of his friends in government, will come for Frances. Isn't that so?" Hallam turned at last to Devere.

And saw the slack ropes hanging loose behind the chair.

The actor moved, fast as a snake, to grasp Jenny by the arm and snatch her back out of Severin's reach.

She gave a shocked cry.

"His hands are untied, Jenny," said Hallam. He stepped in front of the girl, putting himself between her and Severin.

Her eyes settled on the loose hemp hanging from the

back of the chair and her face fell. She knew now how vulnerable she had been with him before Hallam's arrival.

And how safe.

She looked Devere in the eyes and said, "You are indeed a better actor than I gave you credit for."

He regretted the performance now. In the process of saving her last night he had glimpsed a spirit more compatible with his than any he had ever known. They should not part like this, with harsh words and too much left unsaid between them. He felt a flash of insight, bittersweet.

We should not part at all.

"Go upstairs, Jenny," said Hallam. "Mr. Devere and I have matters to discuss."

"What kinds of matters?" Jennifer Leighton, who was nowhere near as naive as he had accused her of being, asked sharply.

Hallam's attire spoke to the business at hand. His hair was not powdered and he wore practical wool breeches and a linen shirt in dark, telling colors that would not show blood. Their tailoring, of course, was impeccable.

"Mr. Dearborn," called Hallam.

The theater's manager appeared in the door with a lantern.

"Escort Miss Leighton upstairs," ordered the man's employer.

Jenny looked helplessly from Hallam to Devere and back again. "You're not going to hurt him."

"Of course not," said Hallam, who was also an excellent actor.

"It will be all right, Jenny," said Devere, though he knew it would not.

Thirteen

Jenny followed Mr. Dearborn out of the basement. Upstairs the chandeliers over the apron were lit and Angela Ferrers was waiting for her, center stage, dressed now in an elegant gray riding habit. The Widow stood the boards as though born to them, but Jenny suspected that the woman did a great many things with seemingly effortless grace, and she knew from long study that nothing in the theater was effortless. All was craft.

"Is my aunt really dying?" She could not hold the question back.

"Did Devere tell you that?"

"He wanted me to release him."

"You understand now why we cannot, I hope."

"I do." Because he would turn Aunt Frances over to the wolves to capture this dangerous creature. "Was he right? Is it syphilis?" Even now, it was difficult to give voice to the word.

"That was not Devere's secret to tell."

"So it is true."

"Yes. It is true." She did not reach out or offer Jenny any kind of comfort. She was not, that Jenny could see, that kind of woman.

"How did she come by it?"

"The same way as anyone else."

"I meant, did she get it working for you?"

"I am no Mother Midnight, Miss Leighton. Seduction is a tool of my trade, not an end in itself. And your aunt never worked for me in *that* way. She was an established actress with a string of lovers already behind her when first we met. I wanted to learn stagecraft to improve my art, and I sought out the best of teachers."

That was not the whole story. "You mean you sought out the best teacher who would be sympathetic to your aims. One who had played Calista from *The Fair Penitent*, both onstage and off. One who knew she was capable of more than domestic devotion, who had been early denied the world's acquaintance, and all the joys of freedom, by virtue of her sex."

"Whereas you have been denied even the opportunities the Divine Fanny had by virtue of being born and bred on the wrong continent. 'Wherefore are we born with high souls,'" quoted Angela Ferrers as she gracefully crossed the stage, "'but to assert our selves, shake off this vile obedience they exact, and claim an equal empire over the world?'"

Aunt Frances had tried to claim hers, through the narrow channels open to a woman of beauty and intelligence without fortune or rank. She had tried to help Jenny gain access to those same narrow channels, because it was the only route she knew.

"Why did she not trust me with the truth?"

"It was not a matter of trust," said the Widow, taking a seat in the wing chair at the edge of the stage. "It was a matter of *time*. She knew that hers, with you, was limited, and she did not want it to be shadowed by the fate that hung over her last years with Harry. It may console you, Miss Leighton, to know that she always spoke of you as the daughter she never had. She visited America, of course, when you were but a child."

"She brought me a box of plays. And a wig," said Jenny.

"She and I were working together at that time," said the Widow. "She came back from her visit with your family and vowed she would return for you, so your promise wouldn't go to waste in New Bumpkin, as she dubbed it. You were, apparently, a prodigy at eleven, reading everything you could get your hands on and spinning the most fantastical stories. She wanted very much to take you with her then—to raise you as hers with Harry, in the little house they kept in London—but your parents thought that sort of upbringing would fit you for nothing but whoring. Their limited experience and ambitions meant your own father and mother could not see you for who you were, for what you might become."

But Aunt Frances had. "Devere said that she killed Harry, for giving her syphilis."

Angela Ferrers raised one plucked eyebrow. "You have lived with your aunt these past two years. Do you really think her capable of murder?"

"No."

"Then you have your answer."

"I do not think that is the whole truth," said Jenny,

who was learning to see through this woman's evasions.

"Then take it up with Frances. Tell her you know about her condition and press her about Harry. Shatter the happiness she has found here with you, and this remarkable swain of hers, who is content to read and drink brandy with her. A rare bird, that one."

Fairchild. Jenny had not known, though she should have guessed. There had been so much she had not understood, so much she had not valued sufficiently. "You want me to lie to Aunt Frances."

"No, not lie. *Act*. Act as though nothing has changed, or you will color the rest of your time together with desperation—with anxiety—she does not now feel or need."

"How long does she have?" Time had been slipping away without her knowledge these past two years.

"That is impossible to say. Harry lasted a decade, with his health waxing and waning. The disease is unpredictable. It disfigured her lover, but it has entirely spared her beauty."

"But it is taking her *mind*, a thing she would gladly have traded her beauty to be valued for."

"Yes. Frances gambled . . . and lost. Or perhaps not. She *is* going to die, badly, but she has lived boldly, and that is not something most women—or men for that matter—can say."

"She is going to die," seethed Jenny, voice breaking, "because her only choice was to cater to the selfish whims of powerful men or to live in obscurity." She loathed showing so much emotion in front of this cold and calculating woman, but she was angry, at the world, at her aunt, at herself.

"We cannot choose the circumstances into which we are born," said the Widow. "Frances made the best of hers. The question you must ask yourself is: are you bold enough to do the same?"

"Devere warned you would try to recruit me."

"Devere was wrong. You don't have the stomach for our work."

Jenny wanted nothing to do with Angela Ferrers, but her dismissal somehow pricked. It was too much like Burgoyne's. "I brought you Jack Brag's invasion plans."

"Is that what they are calling him now? I like that. I do hope it catches on. So much more fitting than 'Gentleman Johnny.' The plans will come in handy, provided he doesn't simply publish them in the *London Times* himself prior to embarking."

"You spared Devere in exchange for them."

"I did not say they had *no* value, but burglary and espionage are different trades. The former can be practiced by anyone with a light step and lighter fingers. The latter can only be practiced—in the long term—by men and women who can purge themselves of sentiment and survive without strong attachments."

"Devere is not devoid of sentiment."

"No," Angela Ferrers admitted, "he is not. That is why he is tied up in a cellar right now and I . . . am not. He should have garroted me—naked and unguarded— in that bed we shared in Boston, but he hesitated. You see where *that* has led him."

Devere had told her he had tried to turn the Widow, and that, failing that, he had tried to assassinate her. It had all sounded so bloodless. He had neglected to mention that they had been lovers.

It set Jenny's teeth on edge to think of Devere in bed with this woman—sharing confidences, endearments, bodies—no matter that he had never met, nor even heard of, Jennifer Leighton when the tryst had taken place. But he had not told her, she was certain, because he *did* have feelings for her. All doubts on that score had fled from her mind when she had seen the slack ropes hanging from the back of the chair.

She had been alone with him in the cellar for a quarter of an hour, and he had not been helpless. He could have overpowered her, even in those final moments—used her to force Bobby to release him. Yet he had not—even when he knew what awaited him in Connecticut. That spoke to a depth of feeling she could not deny. He had arranged her meeting with Burgoyne, but she could not blame him for it, any more than she could blame her aunt for following the only paths and patterns open to her. And in all other ways he had acted nobly toward her.

She had, as Aunt Frances predicted, finally met a man to tempt her, and she was obliged to betray him, because he cherished an illusion about himself that was as flawed as her imagining of Drury Lane.

Devere, she could see, had good reason for keeping his liaison with the Widow secret, but Jenny also understood now that people like Angela Ferrers gave nothing away without a purpose. The casual disclosure of their coupling, the telling detail of her own nakedness—to limn a more indelible image in Jenny's mind—the Widow meant to harden her heart against the man. More than that, as long as Angela Ferrers thought she cared for Devere, it was leverage that the Widow could use to manipulate her—a dangerous attachment.

"I am not holding a tender for Severin Devere," lied Jenny.

"I beg leave to doubt that, Miss Leighton. You are developing nicely as an actress, but you are hardly on the Divine Fanny's level yet. Do not allow Devere's chivalrous gesture and handsome face to sway you. You have the potential to be more than a powerful man's plaything or a poor man's helpmeet, even if I do not think your gifts fit you for *my* business. You move like an actress, which is an asset in any profession. You have some skill with a blade, I'm told, at least onstage, which is useful. But you lack nerve."

"I stabbed a man last night."

"But you did not, I think, do the *killing*. And you didn't have the resolve to see the matter through with Burgoyne, to engage his passion, his trust, his confidence. Such a *small* sacrifice."

She relived it vividly, the taste of the brandy in her mouth, the feeling of his warm flesh in her trapped hand, his knees pinning her petticoats to the chair, his breath coming hot and fast against her temple. All that, but it was his words that raised bile in her throat.

"It was his condescension I could not stomach."

"*That* is a feeling you have in common with the fifteen thousand men camped outside of Boston. They too are tired of condescension, and of being told they should be grateful that all their most important decisions are made for them."

"That is why Aunt Frances let me go to Burgoyne. Against her wishes, and advice. So I could enjoy the privilege of making my own mistakes."

"Was she wrong?" asked Angela Ferrers.

"No." Jenny shook her head. "I would never have learned any other way."

"Fortunately not all Americans are as hardheaded as you Leightons. They do not have to live through injustice and suffer thwarted ambition themselves. They can experience—and triumph over—those things vicariously. And no matter what Congress dictates, they are hungry to do so."

At last, Jenny knew where this was leading. "Through the theater, you mean."

"There is a good reason that Parliament controls the licensing of the playhouses in London. They know that satire is a powerful weapon, that it can sway public opinion and bring governments down. That is why Walpole drafted the Licensing Act in the first place, to ensure that the English theater would be nothing but bread and circuses. Dry bread, saccharine circuses. No man repeats the contents of a proclamation, or a sermon, to his fellows. But give him a tale worth telling about a hero—or a heroine—worth rooting for, and he will declaim the prologue, the play, and the afterpiece for you."

Angela Ferrers was trying to recruit her, but *not* as a spy. And the woman was right. Jenny did not have the stomach for espionage. She did, however, know how to spin a story. The real dilemma was whose story she should tell.

"The great difference," said Jenny, "between me and the Rebels presently besieging Boston is that a change of government might actually win them their rights. Mine will forever be limited by my sex."

"And here I thought you were a bold thinker, Miss Leighton, full of ambition."

"I was. I have become a realist."

"A realist would tell you that an army of farmers and shopkeepers could not keep ten thousand regulars bottled up in Boston. History is not made by men—or women—who see only what is plain before them. It is made by visionaries. Small minds turn inward after an encounter such as you had with Burgoyne—they retreat to safety, and diminish themselves. A greater one may instead look beyond its narrow demesnes, perhaps for the first time, and translate individual misfortune to universal experience."

"That is no small feat."

"I did not say it was easy. Or that you would necessarily succeed if you tried. Many writers have talent, but most are paralyzed by a fear of failure."

"It is not courage I lack. It is opportunity. I would write a response to *The American Prodigal*, this one unrepentant, but I have lost my patron. Bobby Hallam promised to expel me from the company if I went to Burgoyne. I shall be lucky to have a roof over my head tomorrow."

"Hallam may be swayed by an apology, particularly if you play the wounded dove for him. But you do not need a theater to find an audience. The stage, the curtain, the backdrop are all extraneous refinements. Once, we made do with the ground, the sky, and the nearest tree. The only absolute requirement is *words*. Wield them skillfully and others will lay the boards and hang the curtains and imagine the backdrop, in a hundred college refectories, in a thousand parlors, genteel and rustic, from Albany to Charleston. And they will never suspect that the words they speak were penned by the Tory author of *The American Prodigal*—an actress and undoubtedly a loyalist who engaged in all manner of British frivolity and dissipation."

Jenny could imagine it. This was not the dream that had been born in her heart in the wings at John Street, the false idol of Drury Lane. It was not Bobby's dream of profit and prestige—British respect—for the American stage. It allowed her to stop looking for someone to smooth her path. It required her to make her own.

"Is this Virginian who commands the Continentals really a lover of the theater?"

"An ardent one. In Williamsburg he was known to spend as much time in the playhouse as in the House of Burgesses. But he does not court actresses or keep a mistress of any kind. He encourages his officers to stage cabinet productions, just as Howe does in Boston. He is interested in the play, not the players; he understands the power of the theater. And he has access to the only thing you need to reach the multitude: a press."

"I think," said Jenny, "that I should like to meet this Washington."

Fourteen

Severin watched Jenny leave the cellar at John Street, taking the scent of oranges with her. Then Hallam shut the door and said, "I would not have her distressed, but I believe we both know what we are about here."

"It is hardly gentlemanly to beat an unarmed man who is tied to a chair," said Severin.

"I am a provincial player, Mr. Devere, just like Jenny. If she cannot expect to be treated like a lady by a British major general, then why should I be held to the standards of a gentleman when I entertain one of that man's officers? Particularly one who thought nothing of pimping her to an untalented hack whose scribbling saw the light of day only because he married the daughter of a lord."

"I got Jenny off the *Boyne* unmolested."

Hallam was no fool. He knew Devere's hands were

unbound. Warily he circled Devere's chair. "She did not look unmolested when she arrived at John Street."

"That is Frances Leighton's fault. She is the one who told the Widow that I was in New York and set Angela Ferrers' assassins on us."

"Was it Angela Ferrers who tore off her gown, or was that the assassins?" asked Hallam from somewhere in the darkness behind Devere.

Marvelous. "No. That was me."

Hallam kicked Devere's chair over from behind, cracking Severin's slowly healing ribs once more and knocking the air from his lungs. He coughed, mouth agape and flooded with bile, tried desperately to take in breath.

Severin lay helpless, back and ankles tied to the chair, one arm pinned beneath him and the other useless to fend off the blows, which soon came hard and fast. Hallam kicked him viciously, over and over, until there was no fight left in Devere and the actor could approach without hazard. Then he used his fists.

The black man—Mr. Dearborn—returned a little while later. He collected the broken bits of the shattered chair and they tied Severin again, less expertly than Angela Ferrers had, but it didn't matter because he did not have the strength to free himself a second time. He lay on the floor with the cold and the damp seeping into his bones, a taste of what lay ahead for him as a prisoner in the mine.

He had no intention of remaining one for long. Guards could be bribed. The seams of his coat were intact. He had enough hard cash to get messages out. He was the acknowledged—however grudgingly—son of an earl and a favorite of Lord Germain, and even if

Governor Tryon was in no position to ransom him from New York, General Howe would surely do so from Boston. Severin had surveyed the Rebel lines for him at Cambridge, brought back desperately needed intelligence that no other officer was willing to risk hanging to obtain.

Devere passed several hours in the darkness, curled on his side, shivering, trying to conserve body heat, before the door opened again and Angela Ferrers appeared once more, this time in a gray wool riding habit. She was accompanied by Frances Leighton, who blanched when she saw him. A weak reed, as the Widow had said. The Divine Fanny did not have the stomach for their work.

"It hardly seems necessary to drug him," said the former sweetheart of Drury Lane.

"He is as skilled in escape as I am. There is no way to get him securely to Connecticut, Fanny, if he is conscious. And if he breaks free, he will be obliged to tell his masters that you are acquainted with me. You know what will happen then."

"This is poor payment for the service he did my Jenny," said Frances Leighton.

Severin agreed.

"With the beating Hallam gave him, opium will doubtless come as a balm," replied Angela Ferrers, shining the lantern in Severin's face and surveying him. "Won't it, Devere?"

His reply was ungentlemanly.

Hers was dry. "No, thank you. Once was enough. Take *that*, as you like. Now, open your mouth, please, or we shall be forced to dose you like a child."

His pride would not permit him to submit, so Angela Ferrers pinched his nose and Frances Leighton poured her vile draft down his throat. Then both women stood back, looking down at him.

"I won't take the buttons and whatever is sewn into your coat, Devere, because some coins aren't enough for you to bribe your way out," said the woman he should have killed in Boston. "The guards at Simsbury are amenable to inducements, but many of the inmates are rich and the going rates are accordingly steep. If you are wise, you will use what you have to stay alive. Conditions in the mine are not known for their salutary effect, and the prison itself provides only the barest sustenance. But you are a fool and believe yourself *important* to Lord Germain. Waste your gold writing to your superiors, and you'll earn nothing but silence and an empty belly. They will not acknowledge you, and they will not trade you back."

"Of course they will," said Devere through a split lip. "Otherwise they would have to do their dirty work themselves."

She looked almost wistful, not an emotion he associated with the Widow. "They'll simply find someone else, Devere. They always do."

Frances had told her not to watch them carry Severin Devere up from the basement, but Jenny found she could not stay away. She'd almost dropped the lantern when she saw him. He was out cold and his face was purple with bruises. The lips she had kissed the night before were split and bloodied. Bobby and Mr. Dearborn heaved him into a cart behind the theater and pulled a tarp over him.

"He did not deserve to be beaten," she said to

Bobby, who was dressed in a brown wool traveling cloak and shabby work clothes. Mr. Dearborn waited for him atop the box.

"That is a matter of opinion," said Bobby. He bent to buss her cheek. She stepped back. She could not bear the idea of him touching her. Not after what he had done to Severin.

Bobby cocked his head. "Just remember, Jenny," he said, "*none* of this would have happened had you not gone to Burgoyne."

He climbed up onto the seat beside Mr. Dearborn. While his back was turned, she raised the tarp and slipped Devere's knife out of her jacket and into his pocket.

It was a pathetic gesture, really. He'd saved her life and she was repaying him with imprisonment. She had turned it over and over in her mind, but Angela Ferrers was right. They could not allow him to go free. Not when he knew about Aunt Frances.

Bobby flicked the reins and the horses started forward. Jenny winced as Severin's unconscious body thumped against the backboard. She forced herself to remain there, standing in the alley behind the theater, until the cart rumbled out of sight.

Severin had no way of measuring time, but his journey had to have been carried out in stages over several days because he had been forced to drink Frances Leighton's vile tonic at least twice more that he could remember. In between all were blackness and cold and pain and ceaseless jostling, of a carriage, of a cart, of a horse, of a boat, of another, meaner cart.

When he finally struggled to full consciousness, it

was to choking smoke from a charcoal brazier that could not banish the fetid odors of men in close confinement with no recourse to washing water, and of an open latrine.

Lying on his back on a floor slippery with waste, he came to full awareness, and wished he hadn't. Three pinpricks of light from rush lamps pierced the gloom of a chamber perhaps forty feet in diameter, hewn of rock and buttressed by balks of timber. The wretches confined there—fifty at least, how many more he could not tell—huddled around tin stoves that failed to banish the chill.

It was not unusual to make prisons of surplus buildings, to convert warehouses or hospitals or mills into houses of detention. Any great barracks of a place would do as long as it could be secured. Most of the vileness in such an institution came not from the structure or even the guards, but from the inmates themselves: the cutthroats and swindlers and opportunists who traded, even behind bars, in human misery.

The Simsbury Copper Mine prison was different.

It had clearly been conceived to discourage, to intimidate, to kill. There was no means of removing waste, so it pooled and overran the shallow depression built for it and fouled the air, which barely reached them down the shaft that led to the head house. There was another vertical shaft, he later learned, fifty feet or so down a narrow lightless tunnel, but it had no windlass, no ladder, provided no means at all of escape.

Someone had dragged him into a corner and left him, probably for dead, but no one had taken his coat or his boots, and all of his buttons were still there, which meant there was some order at least in the place. He shifted and felt something hard against his thigh. His quilled knife. In his coat pocket. The one he had given Jenny. He remembered it tucked into the waist of her petticoats in the basement at John Street. Somehow she had given it back to him.

He ran his fingers over it in his pocket, bumping over the smooth quills worked into the hilt and over the sheath. A comforting feeling.

He was weak from the beating and from hunger, and it was probably some days since he had eaten. When the bucket of porridge was lowered down and passed through the bars and the bowls were handed round, he got stiffly to his feet and waited his turn. The scanty portions were doled out by the prison's resident bully, a hulking brute who kept the lion's share for himself.

The stuff was rank, but Severin ate it because he knew he must. He was not really feeling the cold, as the others did, had no desire to press close to the tepid stoves, and *that* was a bad sign. He asked the guard in his most cultivated London accent, one that caused not a few of the other inmates to turn and stare, to buy him paper and a pen, and he provided a coin in payment.

When he turned back from the bars, his way was blocked by the bully, a giant of a man in poorly tanned leather who smelled like a sewer and snarled when he spoke. "You from the injun school?" he asked.

The man meant Wheelock's in Lebanon. "No," said Devere politely. He was in no shape to fight anyone. Not now. And very soon he would be worse. He could feel the fever coming on, the kind that came from bad water and damp conditions and a sound beating and that could, if he was unlucky and without friends, be the end of him. "London, by way of New York."

"You look to me like an injun. One of the kind who eyes our women."

No, that was my father.

"My name is Severin Devere and I am an officer of the King, being held here illegally."

He said it loud enough to be overheard by the knot of sometime gentry, in once-fine wool and tattered silk, clustered round the brazier to his left—because discretion bought him nothing in such a place.

"Sounds French," said the big man, who Severin began to doubt was here for his political beliefs. House-breaking or throat cutting seemed likelier.

"It's not. Or at least it hasn't been for a very long time. My father is an earl. That makes me Colonel the Honorable Severin Devere, and not a man to cross."

The brute shrugged his great shoulders and swung; Severin gripped the quilled knife in his pocket and jabbed the bastard in the stomach. He felt the blade go in and warm blood spurt out—and in a place like this with filth and an open latrine a belly wound would al-most certainly prove mortal—but Severin twisted the hilt just to be sure, because he would not get another chance. With a fever-fogged head and cracked ribs, Devere could not afford a real fight.

The huge man fell back, mewling and yammering, and no one rushed to his aid. Severin had guessed cor-rectly. The bully had no friends among the political prisoners being held here. That was good, because he was dizzy and he very much needed to sit down; mo-ments later, an Anglican reverend with a lisp was guid-ing him to their brazier and offering him a drink from his flask, and Severin very much needed *that* as well.

The fever took him that night. The paper and pencil

he'd bargained for came, but he was in no state to use them, could only hope that in his ravings he did not disclose any sensitive information. His illness lasted a week and left him enervated, and he lived only because one of the inmates was a doctor. Of the rare, practical kind that actually knew something of the healing arts.

He wrote to Howe as soon as he was lucid, and awaited a reply for more than a month before sending another letter. When another month passed, he tried Tryon, and then the next month Howe once again. This time he wrote in code, on the presumption that the Widow had been right but for the wrong reasons, and it was simply not politic at present for the government to acknowledge Severin.

His employers might not be able to ransom him, but there was no reason they could not break him out.

In his letter to Howe, he coded a list of the inmates whose presence here warranted government action, men of wealth and position whose unlawful incarceration could serve as a pretext for a general rescue. He coded a description of the mine, its layout, the number of guards and sequences of the watch and most likely candidates for bribery. He went further and tendered his assessment that the mine *could* be taken, and all of the prisoners liberated, in a well-planned strike by a single company of dragoons.

And at the end of the missive he coded what should be an irresistible incentive: he knew now how to get to the Widow.

He prayed his letter reached someone who could decipher it and act with speed. It was impossible in the mine to recover fully, from either the beating or the fever, and with such meager rations he felt himself grow weaker by the day. He used a little of his precious coin to bribe the guards to buy him fresh meat and fruit—and by sharing some of it, he was able to keep most of it—but the reality was that if he did not escape, the next time dysentery or small pox ravaged the prison population, he would surely be among the first to die.

At the end of another month without reply he wrote a final letter to Howe, his funds running short, and prayed his coin was sufficient to carry it all the way to Boston. He learned a week later that Howe was not in Boston at all, that the Americans—that Washington—had mounted cannon on Dorchester Heights and driven the British from the city. Some of his fellow prisoners wept.

Severin did not have enough money left to get a message to Halifax, where Howe was said to be sailing with his army and baggage, as well as large numbers of camp followers, hangers-on, and loyalists. Nor did he have enough to buy decent food and clean water for another month. He *did* have enough to get a letter to Lebanon, forty miles southeast, where there had once been a school and might still be a teacher who had known his parents.

He did not compose this appeal in code, but he wrote it in a language spoken by few and written by still fewer. He included all of the information he had gathered for Howe, with the exception of the intelligence about the Widow, because it would be of no interest to this man. If Harkness still lived, if he had remained in Lebanon or nearby, if he was at all the man Severin's mother had described, he would be capable of reading the letter, using the information contained therein, and engineering an escape. And if not, Severin would very soon be dead.

The Rebels, under the command of the slovenly and eccentric Charles Lee, took control of New York in January. They sent a company of dour New England militia to close John Street, but by then it hardly mattered—most of the theater's wealthy loyalist patrons had fled the city for their estates on the Hudson anyway. Jenny and Frances had no such luxury.

The last remaining officers of the British garrison staying at the King's Arms packed to go aboard the *Asia*, and Courtney Fairchild made his final visit to the robin's egg blue house beside the theater.

Jenny had not meant to intrude. Just as she preferred no one inquire too deeply into the matters of her own heart, which were in turmoil, she certainly didn't mean to pry into anyone else's. But the door to the parlor was open and she could not help but look inside.

Lord Fairchild was kneeling in his scarlet regimentals, his broad back to Jenny, his turned-back wool tails kissing the rug, sword scraping the floor, before Frances Leighton's chair. He held Fanny's hands, which had been painted by Romney and engraved by myriad nameless others in her most famous attitude as Ophelia. *There's rue for you, and here's some for me.*

"We can bring Jenny too. I can take care of you both," Fairchild was saying.

They were so absorbed in each other that neither had noticed Jenny in the door.

"And destroy your own future in the process," said Fanny. "Billy Howe can get away with cosseting Elizabeth Loring, and lavishing preferments on her cuckold husband, because he has won honors enough on the battlefield to be forgiven little indulgences like a flamboyant mistress. And the Sultana, as the papers like to call her, is a society beauty from a fine family. *I* am not."

"I don't care a damn for that," said Fairchild.

"But you will, Courtney. You will someday. Onboard ship or in a small garrison, my condition will be discovered. There will be someone who knew or suspected about Harry, and they will reach all the right conclusions about me. And jump to all of the *wrong* ones about us. Who will believe we have not been intimate?"

"I don't care what anyone believes."

"Not now, perhaps, but you will want to marry someday."

"There can be no one else."

He did not say *after you*, but it hovered unspoken in the air.

"I never thought there could be anyone else after Harry," said Frances Leighton gently. "Then I met you."

The sound that Jenny made was involuntary, a little sob at the back of her throat that was half for Frances and Fairchild, and half for herself and the sick longing she felt for Severin Devere.

"My apologies," Jenny said, swallowing the lump in her throat and backing into the hall.

Fairchild turned to her, his pose now like Atlas holding up the world, and there were open tears on his face. "Tell her," he implored Jenny. "Please tell her she must come with me."

Jenny did not know what to say.

"Tell her," insisted Fairchild. "If we part now, we might never meet again."

"Courtney," said the Divine Fanny softly. "She doesn't know."

But she did. Jenny had kept the secret of Aunt Frances' illness to herself, just as Angela Ferrers had advised her, because she did not want it to color the time they had left, but that was selfishness now.

"I do know," said Jenny.

The Divine Fanny looked up and her gray eyes met Jenny's. A little smile played across the actress's perfectly formed lips. Then she said, "Courtney, might Jenny and I have a moment alone?"

Fairchild made a visible effort to compose himself and rose. "Of course, Fanny." He kissed her hair, this man who was not Frances Leighton's lover and who never could be, and smiled bravely at Jenny as he passed her on the threshold.

When they were alone, Jenny stepped gingerly through the door.

"I take it Angela told you," said Aunt Frances, patting the chair beside her.

Jenny crossed the room and settled on the threadbare cushion. "It was Severin Devere, actually. He also said there were rumors that you murdered your lover."

Fanny sighed. "Severin Devere is the last man on earth who should credit the sort of rumors that swirl around love affairs. Some things, Jenny, are too private, too painful even now to share, but I can tell you this: I did not murder Harry. I loved him. You can ask Angela Ferrers. She was there."

"I did," admitted Jenny. "It was Mrs. Ferrers who told me not to dredge it all up with you, that it would color the time we had left and steal all your happiness."

"Angela has always been the most practical of

women," said Frances Leighton drily. "She has many admirable qualities and a dazzling array of skills. The one thing she is not, Jenny, is an expert on happiness. I didn't keep my illness from you, Jenny, just to preserve our domestic tranquility. I kept it from you because I wanted you to be free to make your own choices. To go to London, if the opportunity presented itself, to go home to New Brunswick if ever this life did not suit you."

Her aunt had given her all that and more, but they had still not said it plainly. "You're right. I would never have considered going to London if I had known you were"—she forced herself to say it—"that you were dying. You have given me opportunities, shown me a life I could not have dreamt of in New Brunswick, and I am grateful for it. But I don't understand why you didn't tell me before I went to John Burgoyne. If I had lain with him, the same thing might have happened to me."

Frances Leighton looked Jenny squarely in the eye. "Just because a thing is dangerous doesn't mean it isn't worth the risk. Sons follow their fathers into the army every day. If you had known that I had syphilis, it would have distorted the danger in your mind, from a very remote possibility to a very immediate reality. We discussed the precautions you could take, and I knew that Johnny had always been . . . fastidious in his choices. Rich men can afford to be."

"But we poor players cannot," said Jenny. The injustice of it stung.

"I have no regrets, Jenny. I played the hand that was dealt to me and I have had more than my fair share of joy and triumph."

"And what about Major Fairchild? Has he had his share?"

Fanny smiled and glanced away a moment before answering. "Courtney Fairchild is the very best of men, and he deserves the full measure of love, which is something I cannot give him."

"I do not think he minds."

"No. He doesn't. Except on occasion. But there are things he would mind. He has a very personal sense of honor, and discovering that his beloved is an associate of Angela Ferrers would likely tax his finer sentiments. Not to mention the fact that we handed his childhood best friend over to the Rebels."

A fact that was never far from Jenny's mind. "Now that we are safely behind the American lines, why can't Devere be freed?"

"I know that you regret the part you played in his capture, Jenny, but you must take solace in this: Devere is alive only because of you. Angela Ferrers is nothing if not thorough."

It was cold comfort for Jenny. "And what about us? Was she right? Should I have kept my knowledge about your illness to myself?"

"No. Not unless you plan to go weeping wanly about the place like some Restoration Tragedy heroine."

Jenny wasn't sure whether to laugh or to cry. "I don't even know how long you have left," she said, trying very hard not to be weepy.

"Neither do any of us, my dear. If there is any lesson to be found in my life, it is that one: make the most of the time that we have."

Rescue for Devere did not come in the form of a company of dragoons storming the mine. The prisoners could not tell day from night in their airless vault below the ground. The building at the top cut off all light from the laddered shaft down which their food and jailors came. Only a faint glow sometimes at the end of the tunnel, beyond the bars that sealed them off from the rest of the works, told of the rising and setting of the sun.

Severin had already picked the lock and ventured beyond that gate, quietly when most of his fellow prisoners were sleeping, while the doctor who had nursed him through his recurrent fevers kept watch. He discovered that there was no way to stage a mass escape by that route. The walls of the shaft were sheer. A rope, secured from above, would be required to scale them. Severin was strong enough, just, to make the climb unaided, but few of his fellow prisoners were in any shape to do so. They would have to be hauled up by strong men. If the shaft had been farther away, out of sight of the guardhouse's walls or hidden by trees, it might have been possible, but it wasn't.

According to the bespectacled doctor, the opening was on a flat plain with no cover. Any escape by that route would have to be accomplished with speed, in the darkness, which was no one's favorite way of making a fifty-foot climb up a sheer rock face.

"*Karekohe!*"

A name out of memory, one he had not been called by in twenty years. He heard it whispered through the bars and thought for a moment that he was in the grip of another fever. Then, when it was followed by a second word in Mohawk, this one not at all polite, he knew he was not.

"Here," Severin replied in the same language. His

fellow prisoners were sleeping, including the Tory doctor. It would be safer not to wake any of them, but Severin's conscience would not allow that. He would have died if not for the physician's care. He placed a hand over the doctor's mouth and gingerly squeezed the man's shoulder until his eyes opened, then motioned for silence.

Although far from a man of action, the doctor, at least, should be up to making the climb. Severin was not certain that he could do it himself. The cold and the damp, and the subsistence diet of gruel, had done their work on a body already taxed by Hallam's beating. The bruises and small fractures along his arms and legs, and, most important, the cracks in his ribs, had still not healed—and never would without light and air and proper nourishment. If he did not make the climb, he would die down here, but better to die from the fall than from shivering in a pool of filth.

He crossed as quietly as possible to the iron bars, the doctor following him without question. In the gloom he could make out two faces on the other sides of the bars, both familiar, though he had never laid eyes on them before. The boys were young, barely out of their teens. They were dressed like Englishmen. Indeed, despite their dark complexions, they could probably *pass* for English the way Severin could, but their features bore the unmistakable stamp of their common Mohawk ancestor.

He picked the lock, the metal scraping on metal sounding loud as church bells in the silence of the echoing vault, but no one stirred. The gate swung open. Devere and the doctor passed through, and then he locked it again behind him. Cruel perhaps, but necessary, because if he allowed it to remain open, as soon as the other prisoners woke there would be a stampede to the shaft and the guards would take notice. Locking the gate bought the doctor and himself, and their rescuers, time to make good their escape, and he owed as much to those who were risking their lives to save him.

It was dark in the tunnel, and they moved cautiously, hands in front of them and feeling above their heads for low-hanging rock and beams. Then finally there was no more ceiling and they were standing in an open space. It was a thing they could not at first see, but only sense. The moonless canopy of night overhead was important for making their escape from an open field. It was not ideal for climbing.

There were two ropes, dimly visible, hanging just short of the floor.

"The boys first," said Severin, this time in English and for the doctor's benefit, as he examined the walls of the shaft as best he could. At the top was a circle of paler black.

"If you are seen," he told the boys, "run, and forget about us. We will take our chances."

"Mother says we're to bring you back with us," said the taller of the two.

"Then go first," said Devere, "in case I can't make the climb and you have to haul my sorry carcass up."

The boy shrugged and nodded at the same time, a gesture Severin recognized: a family tic, he supposed. The familiarity of it made his eyes water for a moment, but sentiment would not get him to the surface.

He watched the dark shapes of the boys scurry up the rope, seeming light as birds, fast as squirrels, and wondered if his own body would ever answer that way again. Already chills were racking him, the tunnel here colder even than their prison had been, his clothing rags, and his constitution spent.

The ropes stopped dancing. Their rescuers were aboveground. Severin and the doctor began their ascent.

It was the stuff of nightmares, to be dangling in the dark over a fifty-foot drop, struggling ever upward, inch by inch, and when he reached the top Severin knew he had come to the very end of his endurance. The boys had to take his arms and haul him onto the stiff dead grass. They half carried, half dragged him over the scrubby plain to the sheltering line of trees.

After that there was a path through the wood, then a road, and then a cart. And air. Fresh, clean air. He drank it in like liquor, like there would never be enough. He lay in the plank bed of the cart, too exhausted and fevered to move, and content just to feel the emptiness of the moonless sky above him.

They drove on for hours, Severin lapsing in and out of consciousness, and then stopped. Light splashed across Devere's face. *A door opening.* That was what it was. They had doors in the world aboveground. He had almost forgotten about those. From his rough bed in the cart, Severin heard the cries of a woman, some sobbing. Then his companion the doctor was bending over him, and there was arguing.

The doctor wanted to bring Severin inside. Severin was probably dying. That was good to know. The doctor wanted him to die comfortably. That seemed very considerate of him. A woman climbed onto the cart and tipped something fiery down his throat. Very raw, very homemade whiskey. *Ambrosia.* She mopped his brow with a cool cloth and he tried to thank her but his tongue felt thick and heavy.

The boys consulted together in Mohawk and came to a decision, one of which Severin approved. They were taking him the rest of the way home to their mother. He liked that idea. It meant he did not have to move from the cart.

The doctor said something to Severin. Most likely thanking him. That was gracious. Severin would have liked to say something in reply. Perhaps he had. It was all so very jumbled. The cart jerked forward. The light dwindled. And the night swallowed him whole.

Fifteen

April 1776

Jenny woke to shouts in the street. When she looked out the window, she saw Continental dragoons in bright blue coats below, hammering on the doors to the theater, their leader demanding entry.

Appearing as if on cue, Robert Hallam came running from the opposite direction—his cravat loose about his neck, shirt untied, hair falling free over his shoulders—and a fierce argument ensued. Bobby demanded the dragoons leave. Their major slid from his horse with an economical movement and presented an order from the Committee of Safety decreeing that John Street was to be commandeered as a hospital for American soldiers, several thousand of whom had been struck down by typhus.

Bobby tore up the decree. The officer of dragoons watched impassively as the pieces fluttered to the ground, then ordered his men to take up axes and break down the doors.

A crowd gathered, then parted, as Frances Leighton emerged running from their robin's egg blue house: skirts caught up in her hands, dressed from head to toe in gray silk, with her hair piled on top of her head and an ostrich feather adding height to her petite frame. She stopped in front of the theater doors, looked breathlessly at the armed men intent on gaining access to the playhouse, put a pale, beautiful hand to her pale, beautiful forehead, and swooned—directly into the arms of the dragoon major.

All work stopped while the Divine Fanny was carried back across the street to the house. Jenny donned her robe and played her part with burnt feathers and smelling salts. And a strong drink for the major, who had laid Fanny tenderly on the daybed in the upstairs parlor and promptly subsided into a parlor chair himself, entirely overwhelmed by this display of feminine sensitivity.

Bobby took the opportunity to saddle his horse and ride hard for Black Sam Fraunces' tavern, where the Committee of Safety was supposed to be meeting.

They would not admit him. He returned to John Street to discover that Fanny's performance had bought him a day's reprieve, and spent the afternoon calling on favors and promising all manner of future largesse if only the theater might be spared.

It was not. The major did not return the next day, but another officer, less impressionable and more hardhearted, did—with a train of thirty wagons and six hundred patients for the newly christened John Street Hospital.

Bobby penned a strongly worded letter to the

Committee, full of high-minded rhetoric about liberty and the sanctity of private property, and of thinly veiled threats to savage and ridicule them in his next production. For his pains, he received only a summons in reply, from a different committee, the one Washington had asked the Provincial Congress to form in order to try suspected Tories.

"I have been an ardent, if covert, Son of Liberty for years," fumed Bobby, pacing the little upstairs parlor.

I have not, thought Jenny. But so many things had changed since her night with Burgoyne. Before that, she had identified with the loyalists whose patronage had kept John Street open. She had mimicked their scorn for all things provincial. On the *Boyne* she had experienced just what that scorn led to. Her loyalties were no longer fixed.

An identical summons from this new "Committee of Seven" arrived an hour later addressed to Jenny. And she too was ordered to present herself at Black Sam's tavern at eleven o'clock the following morning.

"Shall I faint, as you did?" Jenny asked her aunt.

"Only if you are reasonably certain a gentleman stands ready to catch you, dear," replied Aunt Frances.

Bobby made a show of harnessing the matched bays to the coach that had sat little used in the shed next to John Street since Lewis Hallam's departure, and Mr. Dearborn drove them the half mile to Mr. Fraunces' tavern.

The four-story brick mansion that housed Black Sam's premises, where Jenny liked to drink her chocolate and read her mother's letters, had been built for the DeLancy family fifty years earlier, on a scale and with an elegance that fitted it for use as a public building even five decades after its completion. The place had long been the haunt of the Sons of Liberty and the Committee of Safety, and more lately of General Washington, who was said to be so partial to Mr. Fraunces' cooking that he'd begun ordering his meals sent from the tavern all the way to his headquarters at Richmond Hill, two miles north of the city.

Bobby had dressed in republican homespun and sober leather kneebands.

"I did not know we were staging *The Siege of Boston*," said Jenny, surveying his costume. "Who are you playing? Sam Adams?"

"I would go in sackcloth if I thought it would save John Street," replied Bobby.

Jenny would not. If she was going to be accused of grand intrigue, she was going to face such accusations as Aunt Frances or Angela Ferrers might: in silk and lace and with a feather in her hair. The latter detail gave her pause to think of Severin's meager chicken feather "headdress," and that bittersweet, eventful night they'd shared, an age ago, it seemed.

The tavern was already bustling when they drew up. A servant greeted them at the door and Bobby was shown at once into a ground-floor receiving room, leaving Jenny adrift and stranded in the hall.

She retreated to a bench beside the door. Aunt Frances would not have done so. Aunt Frances would have struck an attitude on the first riser of the grand staircase, leaning gracefully upon the newel post. Improvisation, though, was not one of Jenny's gifts, and she realized sitting here that she had no desire to be the center of attention.

What she wanted was to observe, and there was

probably no better place for that in all of New York right now. The sheer number of people coming and going, some elated, some dejected, and some playing their cards very close to their vests, was staggering, and she realized that the city had not felt so alive in months.

There were patterns in the chaos too. Men came and went from the door Bobby had disappeared through; some of them were trailed by families and not a few wives carrying babes, intended no doubt to incline the Committee toward mercy.

On the landing above was a door just to the left of the stairs with two remarkably tall Continentals stationed to either side, looking smart in dark blue wool, their bayonets polished to an extraordinary shine. Only a single servant came and went through that door, ferrying silver and fine china and sparkling crystal inside.

At last the parade of tableware stopped and the landing door opened wide. A young man in Continental blue emerged and came down the stairs, descending the risers two at a time and scanning the hall until his eyes lighted on Jenny. He was dark haired and compactly built, and he took Jenny utterly by surprise when he stopped in front of her and bowed deeply.

"Miss Leighton," he said, with an Irish lilt that charmed her utterly. He offered her his hand. "I am Captain Moylan, the general's secretary. Please forgive the delay. The kitchens are overtaxed, but lunch is served at last, and His Excellency is delighted to have your company."

She had absolutely no idea what to say, but she accepted the hand offered, and he placed hers over his arm and led her up the stairs to the guarded portal at the top.

The room beyond was neither large nor grand, but

it was carpeted and there was a good fire. The chimney drew well and the windows were large, so it had that seasonally rare advantage of being warm and bright *without* being clouded with smoke.

There were two tables: one covered with green baize and papers and inkwells and ledgers and maps, where two men sat scrutinizing a broadside; the other laid for a meal for four with white linen and china plates and silver dishes.

The taller of the two men stood and Jenny was forced, as so often happened, to gaze up at her host. Captain Moylan conducted her into the room and said, "Miss Jennifer Leighton, may I present His Excellency, General Washington."

Washington himself was an imposing figure, and not entirely because of his height. He was neatly dressed in a blue uniform and his hair was carefully tied back and powdered. He had a sober air about his person, but something about his mouth suggested that he had once been quick to smile.

The other, unnamed gentleman rose also. He was several inches shorter than the general, with a long, dour face at odds with his smiling eyes, and wore a very fine white wig with the curls pinned just behind his ears to soften his features. His suit was sober black silk, but his waistcoat was sumptuous red velvet with gold wire embroidery, and a gold watch chain peaked from one embellished pocket.

"This," said Captain Moylan, indicating the man in the red waistcoat, "is—"

"A most ardent supporter of the cause," supplied the man.

"I am so very sorry about your theater, Miss

Leighton," said Washington, cutting off further discussion of his companion's identity. He led Jenny, Moylan, and his nameless friend to the table laid for their meal. The general took up a seat opposite Jenny, while the Irish captain sat down beside her, and the unidentified dandy flanked His Excellency. "But I must bow to civil authority in this. Congress has decreed that the playhouses be closed."

"Even if Mr. Hallam promises to perform nothing but *Cato* three nights a week?"

"Even so."

"And yet you allow your officers to stage productions in camp, I am told."

The Irishman beside her paused in buttering his roll.

Washington pursed his lips. "My officers are *my* responsibility, and under my command. Civilians are not. That is the distinction. If I overreach in this, Congress will say, 'He was very loath to lay his fingers off it.'"

"You mean they will accuse you of playing Caesar."

"The parallels will be impossible for those learned gentlemen to resist."

She had not considered that, but his troubles were not hers. "Your officers are paid. If the John Street closes, I will lose my livelihood."

"For that, I am also very sorry, but there may be a remedy. Someone has recently pressed into my hand a most excellent composition. It purports to be a new translation of the *Miles Gloriosus* for American audiences, and it is anything but. Do you read Latin, Miss Leighton?"

She did not. The title and the frontispiece of the play were a conceit. She had added them as an afterthought, before posting it via Mr. Fraunces to a false address maintained by Angela Ferrers. And now she knew where it had traveled since.

"No."

"Neither do I," he said, perhaps a little wistfully. "I was educated for a career as a surveyor, where Latin is deemed of little use, and later I went into His Majesty's army, where French would have served me better. But in truth nothing would have served me well at all there, except had I been born someplace *else*. Had I stayed in royal service, I would always have been passed over, time and again, because I am a colonial. Your 'translation' of *The Braggart Soldier* leads me to believe you understand something of this."

"Yes." She had been so glib with Burgoyne, and now she found herself monosyllabic in the presence of a man who had actually read her work.

And for Jenny, like the "learned gentlemen" in Congress, certain parallels were impossible to resist. Once again she was being entertained by a general, a man she hoped might become her patron, supping off china dishes and silver plates and being offered good Madeira wine.

In all other ways the circumstances could not be more different. This was no uncomfortable tête-à-tête: her play was not a pretext or a prelude to seduction. Washington made no effort to impress her with his person, or with the difference in their stations. He did not flatter and he did not ply her with drink—and he did not, during the meal, manufacture any excuse to touch her at all.

And yet he was no plaster saint. He was a slave-holder, like Bobby.

"My friend here," and now Washington indicated the dour-faced man in red and black, presently engaged in chasing peas across his plate, "has also read your play."

"Witty and spirited," said the man, spearing a last runaway sphere.

Washington smiled. It confirmed her suspicion. This had once been a man with a wry sense of humor. She could see it now as he struggled to hide his amusement over his companion's resolute pursuit of his vegetables.

Then he turned to Jenny, all mirth banished again, and nodded at her plate. "You have barely eaten. If it is feminine delicacy that restrains you, abandon it. Men who admire such coquetries are seldom worth sitting down with at table. If it is the meal that is at fault, though, let us ask the steward to bring you something else."

Jenny had no doubt the food was very good, and she was in fact partial to roast chicken, but she had been too focused on their conversation to eat any of it. "I breakfasted before coming and did not anticipate being given lunch," she said. "I had in fact anticipated being given a trial and possibly a sentence."

Even now Bobby might be receiving such, at less than impartial hands. Of course, Severin never even had that privilege before his abduction and imprisonment at Simsbury.

"I apologize for the deception, but it seemed a sensible precaution. The Committee of Seven exists precisely because there *are* Tory plotters in the city, some of whom would rather see New York burned to the ground than in Rebel hands. Desperate men, who are loath to surrender the privileges they have 'earned' from a lifetime of toad-eating. The fortunes of war being as they are, better that you remain unknown and insignificant to such men."

When the luncheon dishes were cleared and the

steward had retreated, the general's friend produced her manuscript, a little dog-eared, and placed it on the table. The cover page with her title and name was slightly water-stained. "It will sell well in the city, on cheap paper, with no binding, to keep the price down. I suggest you publish anonymously, of course."

"Anonymously?" Her heart sank.

"To avoid . . . *difficulties*," said the Irishman, the way the pastor back in New Brunswick used to say "sin."

She ought to be flattered by their concern for her reputation, but it seemed absurd. "I am an actress, sir, not a lady. If I cared for my good name, I would have chosen another profession, one that would not cause so many gentlemen to mistake me for a whore."

The room was utterly silent for a moment. Ladies did not utter such words in polite company. Jenny knew it sounded coarse to this audience coming from her mouth, but she no longer wanted to trade in fantasy offstage.

"The assumptions of such gentlemen," said Washington, breaking the quiet, "are much like the assumptions Parliament has made about Americans: in greater part based on wishful thinking and self-interest. I aim to change them. I would have you join me, but in the event that I fail, I would not see a woman hang for it."

"They are but plays, sir, not a hanging matter."

Washington would have answered, but there was a scratch at the door. The steward entered carrying a silver tray and bringing with it the rich scent of almonds, the perfume of citron, the essence of brandy. Longing swept her. There was a small pyramid of macaroons at the center, flanked by a row of pastry hearts and an iced cake, white and glistening.

"The power of words," said the general, when the servant had gone and left this poignant reminder of her night with Devere upon the table, "of drama, can beggar the force of powder."

"Which is a fine thing," said the young officer in his Irish lilt, "because we're damnably short of the latter commodity."

"So we are," agreed Washington, reaching for a macaroon. "And while we have men aplenty for the moment, they are summer soldiers, and their enlistments will shortly expire. An apt phrase, though, a stirring scene or a cutting satire, can fire the passions. Disseminated, it can turn and resolve a thousand minds. Words and ideas, Miss Leighton, may well decide this present conflict."

And, apparently, could get her hanged. She ought to be frightened by the prospect, but then again she ought to have stayed home in New Brunswick. "The theater has never been a safe occupation in America," she said.

"It is your background as an actress that I fear puts you at particular risk," said Washington. "There is a writer in Boston who dared to put pen to paper in a farce mocking the blockade. The author had never trod the boards and, as a consequence, the play lacks a certain dramatic force. It was never, to my knowledge, performed, but the pamphlet came to the attention of John Burgoyne, and he vows to see this patriot hang from the Liberty Tree. The play was published anonymously, yet Howe's spies were able to trace the author through an opportunistic printer, forcing the writer to flee. A more effective piece of satire, we must assume, could elicit an even more intemperate response."

"You need have no fear of discovery through me,

however," interjected the dour man in red and black. "I am discretion itself."

That, as far as she could tell, rang true, considering she did not even know his name. Now at least she knew he was a printer.

He plucked a pastry heart off the top of the platter.

"Would you like one, Miss Leighton?" asked His Excellency, observing her.

"No, thank you." They had not eaten the macaroons or the pastry hearts that night, she and Devere. "I would have a piece of cake," she said.

The general sliced. He did it very neatly, but he did not do it with a quilled knife from his pocket, and he did not offer it to her point first balanced on his blade. When the little plate was set before her, she breathed in the perfume of the almonds and the brandy and the currants and the citron, and knew she could not eat it. Not when Devere was suffering at the bottom of a mine because he had risked himself to save her.

"Surely," she reasoned, "a British hanging list"—and a free Severin Devere—"is only a danger if they take Manhattan, yet you hold Boston and New York both."

"For the moment," said Washington, looking her in the eye.

The intensity of his gaze unnerved her. "You have twenty thousand men," she said quietly, feeling the measure of security that she had known since General Lee had entered the city slipping away.

"I have twenty thousand men. Some of them are militia, well armed and disciplined. Most of them are not. Fully a quarter of them are suffering like those in the John Street Theater, from typhus and dysentery, and it will be a miracle if it isn't smallpox too by the end of the month. Twenty thousand men, raised to answer an emergency in Boston, who have now marched to New York, leaving their farms and businesses and families to fend for themselves. When their enlistments expire at the end of this year, I may well have nothing, while Howe will still have twenty-five thousand professional soldiers with a fleet to take them wherever he chooses to strike."

"That," said the printer, "is why you must publish anonymously, my dear, with a *reliable* printer. If you choose to publish at all."

"I wish," said Washington, "that I was offering you the opportunity to be the dramatist of a nation, but the truth is that I am asking you to put your life in danger for a precarious endeavor. Anonymity may at least shield you, and those you care for, if it comes to the worst."

She had desired the opportunities and freedoms so often denied her sex. If she was to seize them, she must also accept the risks.

"I will do it."

He nodded but did not smile, because it was no small thing she had decided. He lifted the cover page from her manuscript and passed it to the young Irish officer, who stood, walked to the hearth, and fed it with care to the fire.

"History will remember us, Miss Leighton," said Washington, "if we carry the day."

"I understand, and agree with, the need for discretion," she said, watching her name burn away to ash. "But I would ask two things in return."

Washington nodded, listening.

"There is a man being held at Simsbury. His name is Severin Devere. I want him released and returned to his people."

Washington looked to the Irishman, who said, "Simsbury is under the authority of the Connecticut General Assembly and the Committee of Safety. We can't order this man's release, but we can *request* it. They are unlikely to refuse."

"Then do so today, Captain Moylan," said Washington. He turned to Jenny. "And your second condition?"

"I will not write entirely anonymously. I wish to be known, as a distinct voice at least, beyond the confines of this room. I will use a pen name."

"An excellent idea," said the printer. "Particularly if you mean to write a number of works. They will sell better. May I suggest something patriotic, such as Columbia?"

"No."

"Cincinnatus?" asked Washington.

"No," said Jenny, pushing aside the plate of cake. For a moment, with the scent of almonds and brandy and citron she was in Vauxhall Gardens and it was night and she was with Devere in front of the grotto, and she knew a heartsick hunger that food would never satisfy.

"I would be known as Cornelia."

Sixteen

It was a very pleasant place to die. The house was old. Devere could tell that from the small batten doors and wide yawning fireplaces, but someone had cased the beams in paneling, and painted them in gay colors, and papered the walls in the sort of cheery English florals his mother had favored. They spun when he looked too hard at them, so he gave up trying. Fever was like that.

Someone was cutting his hair. He could hear the blades chirping like crickets on his pillow. He opened his eyes again and a face swam into focus—like his father's, but decidedly prettier. She was wielding a pair of iron scissors with care, and it was like looking into a mirror because her features were also so like his own.

She continued to shear him, carefully, and he tried to make sense of what was happening in his disordered mind. "Are we going to war?" he asked, the only explanation he could think of.

"Yes. A war on lice."

"But what if I lose all my strength, like Samson?"

Then she was lost to the darkness again and it occurred to him only as he was slipping into blackness that she had been speaking Mohawk.

He woke again sometime later—hours or days he could not tell—and felt nearly lucid. He was lying in a great tester bed on a feather mattress, surrounded by wool curtains pulled closed on all sides but the one open to the window. There were flowers blooming outside the casement, and the sun was bright in the sky. May, at the very least. Possibly June.

Severin felt weak and wasted, but he was clean and warm and he was alive.

No thanks to General Howe or Lord Germain, who had left him to rot at the bottom of the mine. Who would have expressed mild distaste if he had handed Frances Leighton over to them, then clapped her in irons and made such use of her as they had always intended.

He had dirtied his hands, time and again, so they could keep theirs clean, and they had not come for him. He recalled, with a sense of shame, how he had so often acted on all that they left unsaid, done the unpleasant things no gentleman could put into words but that were *necessary*.

How he had forfeited his opportunity to remain with Jennifer Leighton out of misplaced loyalty.

The door opened and a man entered. He was tall and lean and graying, but he walked with an easy stride and bowed his head beneath the lintel and the center beam as if from long habit.

Severin struggled to sit up. Good God, he was weak as a newborn kitten. "I owe you a debt, sir," he said, trying to find some dignity while swaddled in blankets and wearing someone else's nightshirt.

"There is no debt where family is concerned." The man offered him a pained half smile and pulled a chair up to sit beside the bed.

"Your sons could have been captured, or shot." *Coward.* He ought to own them, after what they had done for him. It occurred to him now that he had not really believed they would come. "It was a risky undertaking, for you and yours."

"Your cousins knew what they were about," said the man, who was his uncle by marriage and whom Severin had never laid eyes on before today, but who had risked his all to save him. He had the patient air of a schoolmaster—a profession he had once followed— with bad news to impart.

"But I won't lie to you about your situation. We brought you here at night, in the dark, but you've been at death's door for eight weeks now, and it was impossible to keep your presence a secret from the Committee of Safety. They have their headquarters here in Lebanon, not six miles from this house, and they meet every day, sometimes more than once. Their business is requisitioning supplies for Washington's army and ferreting out and trying suspected Tories. They know they have an invalided British officer on their very doorstep. The only real question before them is what use they can make of him."

July. He could remember only bits and pieces of the last eight weeks. No wonder he felt so enervated, and his mind was working so slowly. But not *that* slowly. "You know a great deal about the workings of this committee."

"That is because I am a member."

So his uncle was a Rebel. It should not have surprised him. The Indian School that had educated Severin's father had been a place of advanced, if often misguided, ideas. That Solomon Harkness—who had defied the school's founder to marry one of the Mohawk students, and set up his own rival institution—should have caught republican fever was of a piece with the little Severin had heard about the man.

"Yet you still came for me," said Severin.

"You're Molly's brother's boy, and the son of the best friend I ever had."

The son he so blithely gave away, Severin thought, but did not say.

"We would have walked through hell to get you out of that place," continued Harkness, "but with the condition you were in when the boys brought you out, we didn't have a whole lot of choices. You have even fewer now."

"Are you advising me to switch sides?"

"You don't *have* a side. Not anymore. The men who left you to die in that hole made you a free agent. I can't judge you for whatever you've done to get where you are, Severin, because you and your mother weren't given any choices, but you have some today. This is your opportunity to decide what kind of man you want to be."

I think it is just possible that you may remember that you are an American yourself.

"You must know your side employs people like me, every bit as ruthless," said Severin.

That isn't who you are. It's who you choose to be.

"I know it," said Solomon Harkness. "Doesn't mean *you* have to be one of them."

It didn't. But he had obligations, debts from that life, and they had to be paid before he could build a new one.

"I am prepared to give them everything they want," said Severin. "I'm even prepared to put myself at their disposal, though it's high time to draw some lines. I'll gather intelligence and write reports, but I will not start riots or blackmail or kill for them." He would leave that to Angela Ferrers. "And there is something I want in return."

"I can put your condition before the Committee, if it's within reason."

"There was a girl, in New York. She risked a great deal to save my life. A very great deal. The British could hang her, twice over, for the things she has done, and I believe that one of your side's less scrupulous agents is trying to get hooks into her. I want her out of New York. I want her back with her family in New Jersey, where she'll be safe." And where perhaps, when he was recovered, he might see her again. His mind kept returning, over and over, to the sense of promise he had experienced standing beside her on the steps of the little blue house beside the theater, fitting the key to the lock.

"You could ask for more," said Harkness.

"I expect so. But that's all I want."

The Committee visited the next day. Eight men, including the governor, who Severin knew had refused

General Gage's call for aid after the debacle at Lexington, siding early and decisively with the Rebels. That had been one of the many tasks Severin had carried out for his government: compiling dossiers on the royal governors and tendering his opinion as to which would remain loyal to the Crown, for how long, and with what provisos. He had been right about John Trumbull, and his close study of the man allowed Severin to put all of his considerable gifts on display.

The committeemen took up chairs around the bed and listened to what Severin had to tell them. He did not give them everything, but he gave them enough to buy his life and Jennifer Leighton's safety and whet their appetites for more. He had been with Sir William Howe in Boston sufficiently long to provide them a very detailed assessment of the Crown's forces there, and he had studied the general carefully enough to offer them a finely limned portrait of their adversary. "He will not press his advantage in any fight that he stands even the slightest chance of losing. Bunker Hill was too bloody for his liking, and he still believes some form of reconciliation—that *peace*—is possible."

"He and his brother," said Trumbull, meaning Billy Howe and Black Dick, the admiral who had been angling for months to be part of the peace commission, "wish to negotiate, but they are not empowered to treat with an independent America. What are the terms they have been instructed to offer?"

Severin had been in the meeting with Lord Germain where the terms were discussed. "Entirely one-sided," said Devere, frankly. "You will lay down your arms in exchange for not having your cities burned, and sixty of you will hang, publicly, in each colony, as a lesson to future generations and a demonstration of imperial power." He had attempted to explain, patiently and more than once, the stupidity of this to superiors who had never set foot in America, who believed that mass executions would cow the populace.

These men were not cowed.

"General Howe is not your true enemy," Severin continued. "John Burgoyne is the real danger. He is anything but sentimental about America. He is not obsessed with capturing her cities. He is pleasure-loving and self-indulgent, but it is London that calls to him—not Philadelphia or New York—and he will not go to winter quarters or set up court like the provincial administrators you are used to. He is a hard campaigner. He knows that the best way to break the rebellion is to control the Hudson and cut New England off from the rest of the colonies."

It went on like that for some time. They asked astute questions and Severin gave them frank answers, and at length they thanked him and took their leave, all save Severin's uncle, who remained behind after the door closed.

"Are you sure that's all you want? This girl out of New York?" he asked.

"Yes."

"What about money?"

"I have money."

"If you mean Devere money, you must know that's lost to you."

"I have my own money." He had funds in good hands in Boston and New York. And in France and Portugal and Italy. It was a sensible precaution for a man in his line of work. "And I'm not without skills."

"No. That much was obvious today. You've got your father's head for politics and strategy. It can't have been easy for you, rising through the army with Ashur causing trouble on the frontier these past twenty years."

"It is surprising what powerful men will overlook when it is convenient for them," said Severin. "And what infamies they will claim as their prerogatives. I want Jenny safe."

"What do you intend to do about the girl, once she is out of New York?"

"I'm in no position to do anything at all about *any* girl until I can get myself out of this bed." That was something he was determined to do. He had seen prisoners in France who had been broken by their confinement, their health never recovered. He had been injured often enough in the past to know that it was possible to claw his way back from this, but it would not be quick or easy.

"When you're mended, then," said Harkness, doggedly.

"She may have no desire to see me. Or she may be attached to another." Or she too might want to take up where they left off in the kitchens at Vauxhall, once he procured some French letters. The stirring he felt at the thought did a good deal to reassure him that he would indeed recover.

"Washington holds New York," Harkness said. "It should be an easy enough thing to get her out. I'll make enquiries. In the meantime, write to her. I'll see that the letter goes by private channels and that prying eyes don't intrude on your sentiments. If she'll see you, I'll take you to New Jersey myself, when you're well enough. If not, think about what else you might ask from the Committee. If you break ties with England, you'll have to make a new life for yourself here. There are great opportunities for men with ambition and vision."

Severin believed that, and he tried to take his uncle's advice to heart. He considered his options as he began his slow recovery, using two chairs at first to cross small distances in the room, from the bed to the bureau, from the bureau to the washstand. Even sitting upright in a chair was exhausting in those first few weeks, but he persisted. He wrote to Jenny, and he made his first foray outside his room, and after a month he managed to get down the stairs, and finally to move from the kitchen to the keeping room to the best room with the assistance of his young cousins—who, it turned out, were part of the local militia protecting the stores gathered by the war office.

No matter how far his mind ranged, though, it always returned, a bird to the nest, to Jennifer Leighton.

Jenny did not tell Bobby about her interview with Washington. The fewer people who knew what she was doing, the better, or so the young Irish officer— Moylan by name, a former neighbor of Washington's in Virginia—had told her after their lunch as he counted gold coins into a purse for her.

"I did not think Congress had coin to spare," she said, watching the gold glimmer in the sunlight of a little office adjacent to the room where she had met the general.

"It doesn't come from Congress," said Moylan. "His Excellency serves without pay. He asks Congress to reimburse his expenses, but he takes a Roman view of patronage of the arts. This gold, and the coin to buy paper and ink to print your play, comes from his own purse. It is his hope that you will send him more of your work in future, and that he may continue to support your endeavors."

The gesture struck her dumb for a moment, but then she recovered her wits and said, "Then I will do my best to see that it is not all bread and circuses."

Bobby's interview with the Committee had been less to his profit. They had threatened him. He could volunteer the use of the John Street for the good of his country and to alleviate the sufferings of his fellow Americans, or his property would be forfeit, and he himself would be sent to Simsbury.

Jenny lied and said her interview had been much the same, and Bobby did not question her. She decided, with as much regret as satisfaction, that she was *indeed* developing as an actress.

She did tell Aunt Frances, because she trusted her, and it was necessary to speak of money, and she did not want to lie about where her funds had come from. They agreed to tell Bobby that their support came from Courtney Fairchild, even though Frances had refused his money.

With the theater closed, they decided that Jenny ought to make a visit to her parents in New Brunswick. She was writing a new work, a one-act pamphlet piece for Washington, and she reasoned that she should be able to write as well at home as in New York.

In this she was proved wrong. After three weeks in the little brick house where she had grown up, Jenny managed to write a grand total of two pages. At home there was no escaping the domestic duty Aunt Frances despaired of. It took all morning, starting before dawn, to keep a household even of that modest size fed, swept, and laundered. In the afternoons there was a parade of suitors arranged by her mother.

The house, Jenny discovered, was smaller and more crowded than she remembered. Two of her four brothers had recently married and brought their new wives to live with them. Jenny's father had added a wing—in brick, naturally—to the back of the house for the new couples, but her sisters-in-law, Ida and Letty, were obliged to make do sharing the old summer kitchen, and their arguments could be heard throughout the house.

When Jenny finally returned to John Street, she had a new appreciation for the working conditions Aunt Frances provided. In three days she managed to finish the play and work in two characters inspired by Ida and Letty and their epic dispute over the bread oven.

While Jenny had been away, Aunt Frances had put her knowledge of medicines to use nursing the sick Continentals at John Street. Jenny soon joined her, measuring out tinctures from Aunt Frances' collection of blue glass bottles. In the evenings they took up their pens and wrote, and by some unspoken but mutual agreement they avoided talk of Courtney Fairchild and Severin Devere.

When the letter arrived, Jenny did not share it with anyone. It was unsigned, but she had no doubt from whom it had come.

My dr Jenny

I hope that I do not give offense by using your Christian name on such familiar terms. It is a liberty I granted myself in the privacy of my imagination, and I hope you will grant it me in truth when next we meet. I wish you to know that I am grateful for the sacrifice you made on my behalf and only sorry that I did not comprehend at the time how very right you were, and how very wrong I was, about the business I was engaged in.

I cannot come to you at present, and the knowledge that others will doubtless read this letter before it reaches you constrains me, but I wish you to know that I am free and resolved to quit my former life and give up the business that separated us. I promise that you and the people you care for, and even the person whose machinations parted us, are all safe from me.

It is possible that you will wish nothing more to do with me. I have undertaken to see that you are repaid for the kindness you did me, and I wish you to know that I expect no consideration in return for that aid. If, however, I remain in your thoughts as you have remained in mine, then I hope we might meet again and take up the matter that lies un-resolved between us. A reply to a gentleman *by way of the usual channels will reach me. If not, I only ask that you do not share this missive with a certain mutual acquaintance. An able intelligencer could with a little effort trace me by it, and the people who delivered me out of Egypt should not be made to suffer in the desert for their pains.*

I do not wish to put you in any further danger by this correspondence, but I am, and have been since that night, and would be in future if you permit it, yours.

As love letters went, it would not make the poets weep, but it did move Jenny. She read it alone in her bedroom beneath the stuffy eaves, and let the longing and the loneliness she had known since her encounter with Devere consume her. What she felt for him was undoubtedly physical. She ached whenever she thought of what had almost happened in the slot at John Street and then again in the kitchens at Vauxhall. But it was more than that. Much more. It was the way she had come alive running beside him through the darkness, and then later wandering the garden, and even closing up the shutters at John Street. She had felt light and free and believed when she was with him that she was capable of *anything*—even as her dreams had been crumbling all around her.

Men—husbands and marriage—had always represented obligations and burdens to Jenny. That had been an unavoidable conclusion growing up in New Brunswick. The wives and mothers she had known acted as servants or, if they were wealthy enough, managed complicated households, directing the activities of servants. They did not write books or plays or paint portraits or any of the thrilling things that Jenny had heard women could aspire to in London and Paris.

That a man might ever be a source of delight, or partnership and pleasure, had never truly occurred to her. Before now. Aunt Frances had represented her affair with Harry in that way, but it had come at a terrible cost. Devere, though, had described how they might have passion and pleasure without risk, and if he had truly given up his ambition to eliminate Angela Ferrers and any designs upon Aunt Frances, Jenny could see no reason why she *shouldn't* share those things with him.

She composed, in her mind, while at work in the hospital the next morning, a reply that *would* make the poets weep. An outpouring of feeling and a confession of physical longing, but when she sat down to put pen to paper the result sounded rather like a prologue for the stage, and she remembered too that anything she wrote in these difficult times was likely to pass through many hands and be scanned by many eyes. So, in the end, she trusted in Devere to anticipate her as he had in the street by the docks and replied with a single word.

Yes.

Devere tried not to be impatient, but when a month had passed he asked his uncle directly for news of Jennifer Leighton.

"There are difficulties," his uncle said.

"What kind of 'difficulties'?"

"Trumbull put his request to remove the girl from the city directly to General Washington, and it was refused."

Angela Ferrers. He knew it had to be her thwarting him. "I shall go myself, then," said Severin.

"You can scarcely walk more than a few yards unaided and you're in no condition to sit a horse."

Solomon Harkness was right, but it galled Severin.

"As soon as I am able, then."

Had he not been worried about Jennifer Leighton, it would have been an almost Arcadian convalescence. The Harknesses were like so many American smallholders. They did a little farming, a little dairying, and their days were ruled by the progress of the sun and rhythm of the seasons. There were blackberries and peaches and fresh corn and there was very good meat. It was like a second childhood for Severin—enfeebled as he was by starvation and sickness and injury—the boyhood he might have had if things had gone differently for his parents, if they had been left to carve out a life for themselves as Harkness had.

By August he was out of bed and making slow circuits of his room, but Howe was also in Long Island and Jenny was not yet out of New York. Severin's letter to her, which had traveled by private channels, was finally answered. Jacob brought it with him on his return from a trip to Long Island, the purpose of which neither Severin's cousin nor his uncle would divulge. They had saved him and they cared for him but they did not yet trust him, and this filled him with a great sense of relief. These were perilous times, and he was glad that the Harknesses were so cautious. Severin would not see this island of familial happiness destroyed.

He opened the letter in private in the best room, where his aunt Molly had put on display all of the homemaking skills she had learned at the Reverend Wheelock's Indian School—the ones that were supposed to fit her for a life as a missionary's wife. There were swag curtains here, neatly sewn from bright red worsted, and an embroidered chair back with a classic English scene, a man and woman fishing by a lake beneath a willow. It was not a room much used except by Harkness himself, but it was exceedingly comfortable, and his aunt had set a table and chair by the window for Severin's use.

It was impossible to sit in this room and anticipate opening a letter from Jennifer Leighton without thinking on his parents. Molly and the other girls at the Indian School had been educated to be helpmeets for ministers. Eleazar Wheelock's vision had been a peculiar marriage of New England thrift and New Awakening devotion. Sending missionaries into Indian country was costly and dangerous. Training Indians themselves to spread the Word could be done at half the price with—to a European way of thinking at least—none of the risk.

Molly had not married an Indian missionary. Instead she had married one of the teachers, Harkness, which had raised few eyebrows. On the frontier it was not unheard of for Englishmen to take Indian wives. It was when her brother—Severin's father—who was also studying at the school, proposed to an English girl that all the trouble started.

So much trouble.

If Severin was honest with himself, he would admit that he had avoided falling in love with Phippa after that summer at Courtney Fairchild's home, when his heart was still an unruly thing, because he had seen grand passion—that of his parents—up close, and it had blighted all their lives. He had never dared to imagine that he could shape a different fate for himself.

Jenny had sent him permission to try: *Yes.*

Elation gripped him. A sense of promise, the kind Englishmen felt when they looked at the wilderness, the kind that Severin had learned to reject in the forests of New York, but that could be true for him with Jenny: *I can build something here. A life.*

By September he could get about the house himself ably enough, but he was still too weak to wield a blade or sit a horse or jolting cart, and New York was once more in British hands, and *then* she was in flames. They learned of the fire in October; nearly a quarter of the city had burned and accusations were flying over who had done it: the fleeing Americans, the arriving British, a cabal of real estate speculators, or perhaps the slaves again.

Harkness could get no word at all of Jennifer Leighton, and Severin determined that if his uncle could not spirit her out of New York, then he would have to do it himself, under the nose of the army he had lately betrayed. For that, he would *need* to be his old self.

His early attempts to ride were slow and clumsy, but his uncle Solomon was generous with his time. One day, when Severin was mounted on an elderly pony that was more used to drawing carts than carrying people, his uncle said, "We never blamed her. Your mother. For marrying Devere. She didn't know what he'd done to Ashur. She thought your father had abandoned her."

"You didn't have to blame her," said Severin. "She blamed herself." He blamed her too, for lacking faith in his father, for lacking the courage to find out what had happened to Ashur Rice, for making choices she couldn't live with, that he'd had to live with.

The early frost made Severin's first game efforts to spar with his cousins more difficult, but he was determined to sit a horse properly by the new year.

He managed the feat by Christmas: a modest celebration by English standards, marked with a dinner and prayers. They cooked and ate as a family, with Uncle Solomon winding the clock jack that Molly considered to be an English idiocy, but that gave her mechanically minded husband enormous pleasure. They argued— no, they bantered—about it in Mohawk, and Severin felt something tighten in his chest to be around such easy companionship.

When the clock jack was finally wound and the meat rotating on the spit, his aunt turned from the fire and said, "Your father taught Solomon to speak my language, to woo me."

"The bastard," said Harkness with fondness, "sabotaged me. The first set of phrases he taught me would like as not have gotten me scalped if Molly did not already like me."

"What did he teach you to say?"

Harkness repeated it—verbatim, Severin could tell, because Molly mouthed the words as well—and when he was done Severin burst out laughing, and it occurred to him that it was the first time he had really laughed since he had spent the night with Jennifer Leighton. And thankfully, his ribs no longer ached.

That was when he realized how much he wanted a life like this, with someone like Jenny. Someone he could laugh with. Someone who would tolerate his foibles and have ones of her own.

His strength returned slowly. His speed and swordplay were not yet what they ought to be—not for a trip into a city occupied by an army he had so lately deserted— but he was a veteran of many such dangerous undertakings, and never before had he been better motivated: by his own desires. He kept Jenny's precious, laconic letter in his waistcoat pocket.

The raid on the Harkness farm occurred in the dead of night, when everyone was sleeping. At first he thought the dull roar was thunder in the distance, but when it grew steadily louder he knew it had to be cavalry. Muffled spurs, he realized, with a sinking heart, but at least thirty horse. Severin knew better than to reach for his pistols. He could not risk an armed confrontation with his aunt in the house. *That* was how civilians got killed.

He tied his shirt closed and went into the darkened hall. It was a moonless night, but he could see the riders, splashes of red in the night, from the window over the stair. His uncle was up too now and carrying a musket, but Severin took it from his hands and shook his head.

"There are too many of them, and your resistance will only provide them an excuse for brutality."

Joshua and Jacob emerged from their rooms, knives in hand.

"Put them away," said Harkness, who had fought in the last war and knew Severin was right.

His aunt, for her part, was steely eyed, pinning her bed jacket closed and putting her hand in her husband's with absolute trust.

Everything happened quickly after that, and Severin had to admit that it was very well done. The door crashed open. Harkness led the way down the stairs, Molly's hand still in his, Severin and the two boys following. The dragoons at the bottom herded them into the kitchen at the points of their bayonets, and Severin made sure to put himself between his family and the steel blade of the wild-eyed young cornet barking the orders.

Severin marked the man, in case things turned violent. Body language and bearing distinguished the young officer as a real threat—his bite, likely, as bad as his bark.

He supposed there was some justice in what was happening. Severin had planned raids like this for General Howe, with these very men: Harcourt's 16th Light Dragoons, created two decades earlier by Gentleman Johnny to fight the French in Spain and Portugal. Burgoyne's hand in their origins showed in their decidedly theatrical uniforms: scarlet coats with striking blue wool facings, gold lace, leather helmets sporting leopard-fur turbans and bearskin crests. Light horse units were an innovation borrowed from European cavalry—light, as their name indicated, fast, and damnably effective. The sort of swift, nimble, *tactical* unit he had advised Howe to use to break him out of Simsbury.

His uncle stepped forward and addressed the cornet. "It's me you want."

Severin very much doubted it. Kidnapping high-ranking Rebels was one of Howe's favorite tactics, but Solomon Harkness did not rate the risk of sending a troop of horse deep into enemy territory. They were here for him.

"And who are you, exactly?" asked a voice from the hall, cultured, melodious.

The speaker was no dragoon. Severin did not know him. He wore the uniform of a captain in the 26th, that much-depleted regiment that had come to deal with the Stamp Riots in '67 and never left. His coat was scarlet with a yellow collar, turndowns, and cuffs; silver buttons; and a silver gilt epaulet on one shoulder. His coal black hair was neatly clubbed, and his gold-flecked hazel eyes were quick and alert, taking stock of the room and its occupants, before coming to rest on Harkness.

Severin had devoutly wished to leave his former life, but he knew he must take up its trappings again now if he was to have any hope of saving his family.

"He's no one," said Severin, in the disaffected drawl he had perfected in London clubs and gambling halls. "A local functionary receiving a stipend for my keep. It is me you are here for, I presume."

The reasons didn't matter. There were only so many possibilities, none of them good. It was possible that the Lebanon Committee of Safety had a spy in their midst, someone who had told Howe that Severin had turned coat, informed the general that one of his spies was in the hands of the Americans with a head full of valuable secrets. Or it was possible that this was some machination orchestrated by Angela Ferrers, to remove him from the playing field once and for all. Or most remotely, perhaps the post had been exceedingly slow and Howe had only lately opened his mail.

Would-be saviors or no, on balance, Severin's chances of getting out of this seemed rather poor. The important thing was protecting the people who *had* saved him, who had delivered him from hell, given him a place to recover, reflect, and find his way. A lump rose in his throat at the thought of anything happening to his family. He vowed that he would not allow it.

The handsome captain bowed to Devere, his formal manner at odds with the rustic simplicity of the kitchen, and said, "My apologies, Colonel. My name is André, and I would have come sooner, but your letter languished at headquarters due to certain deficiencies on the general's staff. By the time I arrived and read it, you were no longer at Simsbury. You are, in fact, a damnably difficult fellow to find."

"Surely not as difficult as all that," said Severin.

"No," admitted Captain André. "You are quite right, sir. There was gross incompetence involved as well." His eyes flickered over the Harkness family. "Is there someplace we might talk in private?"

"There's a parlor," said Severin.

"Excellent," interjected the young cornet who had ordered the door knocked down, as though he was an invited guest. "Perhaps there might be some refreshment for the men?" He looked at Molly meaningfully, and Severin's aunt nodded, her face perfectly blank as she stepped cautiously toward the cupboard.

"Shall we?" said André, gesturing for Severin to lead the way. The cornet showed no inclination to follow, appearing more than happy to leave his superiors to whatever clandestine business they were about.

Severin guided the glittering captain through the darkened keeping room to the parlor, where his aunt's curtains and embroidery were on display—where Severin very much wished he might use some of his hard-won skills to kill this elegant intruder—but that would help no one at all. Severin was not quite prepared to believe that this young man represented the rescue he had once longed for, and no longer wanted. He must know more.

When they were seated at the little table, and his aunt had made up the fire and left them two glasses and a bottle of her very worst local whiskey, André waited until the door closed before speaking.

"I won't make excuses for the abominable treatment you have received, because we both know quite well there aren't any," said André, pouring. "I spent the last year in captivity myself, though my circumstances"—he gestured to indicate the room—"were not so pleasant."

"As it happens, Simsbury," replied Severin, "was not nearly as homely."

"No," agreed André. "I am certain it was not. What did you give the Americans to extricate yourself?"

Severin shrugged. "Fictions mostly, and a few truths they already knew, to make the whole convincing."

"There are those who will say that such a long captivity would tax any man's powers of invention."

Severin knew what the man was hinting at: that he had turned, and of course he had, but hopefully he was good enough to convince this fellow otherwise. "I would reply that I had extraordinary leisure in which to exercise my creativity."

"Just so." André nodded. "And I am deeply sorry for it. Had I been with General Howe when you were taken, I would have acted, but his adjutant general is Gage's brother-in-law, Stephen Kemble, whose chief qualification for the job is that everyone wants to fuck his sister."

It was crude talk after spending so many months in a household where a man and a woman lived companionably with each other, where Severin had fallen asleep more than once to the soft sound of the bed ropes sighing in the room next door and had envied that kind of deep and lasting happiness.

"I met Kemble in Boston," said Severin. "If he had other qualifications, they escaped me. He prefers running and relying on spies to cultivating informants, and hasn't a clue how to turn disaffected Rebels into useful allies."

"Such was my assessment as well. Unfortunately, I lack the connections to rise to such high office with so little acumen, so I must advance by hard work alone. I have studied your career, and I hope you will not take it amiss if I confess that certain of my own ambitions have been shaped by your failures. I mean to replace Kemble as adjutant general in North America, and I intend to do it by capturing the Rebel agent known as the Widow."

So Severin had been right to doubt his government's belated recognition of his service. This man had not been *sent* at all: he had come because Severin could be useful to him. It explained the midnight ride into enemy territory.

"You want my help," said Severin.

"I would value your guidance," flattered André. "I understand you bedded her in Boston."

Severin was no longer sure who had bedded whom, but he *was* certain that he had been discreet and that his tryst with the Widow was not an easy piece of intelligence to come by. This Captain André was a very dangerous young man, decided Severin. "I do not suggest that particular method for getting close to the woman."

"But you did get close to her. What was she like?"

He had asked about the Widow, but despite the fact that Severin had bedded her—with some brio, in fact—she herself had somehow become indistinct in his memory. It was Jenny whom he could recall with crystal clarity: the copper of her hair, the music of her voice, the lithe curves of her body.

"Ruthless," answered Severin at last.

"Do you sketch, Colonel?"

"No."

The young man looked slightly surprised. "It is a useful skill for men in our profession."

"My chief expertise lies in handwriting," replied Severin.

André smiled. "I had heard that. It may yet be useful. Perhaps, though, for the moment you could describe her to me. A portrait in words."

"Tall," said Severin, though he was not sure that was exactly true. She had given the appearance of height, but so did Frances Leighton, her mentor in the theater, and the Divine Fanny was almost as petite as her niece.

"Pale and beautiful, in face and form." Though, again, artifice might enhance or conceal those features with relative ease.

"Fair haired." That much he was certain of, unless she dyed *all* of her hair.

"*Athletic*. She has forged herself into a formidable opponent. Underestimate her at your peril."

"And yet, she has weaknesses. Liabilities. *Connections* in New York. Or so your letter indicated."

The letter he had written when he still thought that he mattered to William Howe, to Lord Germain, to the system he had devoted his life to maintaining and that had left him to die in the cold and dark. He had no intention of giving Frances Leighton to this ambitious, calculating man. To the government's latest willing agent.

"Why now?" asked Severin. "Howe has had twelve months to find and deal with the Widow, and while we may flatter ourselves that his capacity for intelligence work was much diminished by our respective captivities and absences, surely there are fresher leads than my year-old encounter with the woman."

"Trenton," said André. "She was all but invisible for the last year. There was talk of her being in Cambridge and in Salem, but then nothing, until Trenton. One thousand Hessians captured, the Jerseys lost to us, on what should have been the morning of our victory in America. Our 'Merry' Widow turned up in Mount Holly and ensorcelled one rather sentimental Jaeger colonel into tarrying there for three crucial days, with all of his forces. But for her, we would not have lost Trenton."

Oh, Angela, thought Devere. *And I imagined we had something special.* He hoped the poor German bastard had gotten away with his ribs intact. Jenny had been right: he did admire the woman. He hated her a little too, but he definitely admired her.

"You were resourceful enough to find me," observed Severin. "Surely you have been able to identify at least some members of her network."

"I have," said André. "Unfortunately, they are so well placed that they are currently untouchable. I need new leads. You tracked her in Boston and managed to meet with her. She attempted to have you killed in New York. She *succeeded* in getting you immured in Simsbury. That means you had contact with at least one of her disciples."

"Such encounters do not usually compass a polite exchange of introductions."

"But you no doubt have your suspicions as to whom she might have used."

"Suspicions that are a year old, and wholly unconfirmed," said Severin.

"And naturally you wish to pursue them yourself, to allay any doubt as to where your loyalties lie after so long a captivity. I understand. That is why I have brought this."

He drew a pamphlet from his pocket and placed it on the table. "In Boston, I believe, you discovered the true identity of the writer of *The Blockheads* and recommended the Warren woman's arrest, but Howe moved too slowly and she slipped our grasp."

"I did." It was one of the many things he had done for Howe, who had not repaid his loyalty.

"This," said André, tapping the pamphlet, "is very much of a piece with that business—though, unfortunately, it is an altogether more effective, and popular, bit of propaganda."

He slid the booklet across the table and Severin glanced at the cover. It was an unbound play printed on cheap paper: *The Miles Gloriosus in a New Translation for American Audiences.* Severin affected disinterest while his heart pounded in his chest with sick anticipation.

"The damnable thing is *everywhere,*" said André with some asperity. "We have confiscated thousands of copies in the coffeehouses, but it is impossible to suppress. Students perform it and wags quote from it and scenes are recited in parlors from Williamsburg to Albany. Copies and reprints have even reached London."

The captain sat back, steepling his fingers. "The

title character is a very thinly veiled version of John Burgoyne, who is incensed and has vowed to hang the author. General Howe and he both blame it for the poor turnout in loyalist support, although I do not entirely credit their assessment of that situation. Americans are, as a people, not much given to loyalty."

"It is a play, for heaven's sake," said Devere, ignoring the jibe. "An entertainment, like a Punch-and-Judy show. If Burgoyne ignored it, the thing would fade into obscurity. Vowing to hang the scribbler is like printing a thousand handbills. It inflames public curiosity. Cry 'sedition' and every fashionable young buck in America will decide he *needs* a copy."

"Quite so. No doubt Burgoyne's advisers told him as much, but wiser heads did not prevail. And the thing has struck an uncomfortable chord. Read the bit where Jack Brag recruits the savages to plunder the frontier."

Severin flipped through the play, trying to ignore the feelings stirred by the familiarities of phrase and style. *Oh, Jenny.* Let this be coincidence only: my mind reading too much into these printed words.

He found it easily enough, a speech before a crowd, a bit of bombast that was a very good imitation of Gentleman Johnny's oratory, in which he exhorts the Indians to chastise the wicked Rebels. And, reading it, hope died. Severin knew all too well where the author had gotten the idea: from the plans she—*Jenny*—had stolen from his cabin and given to Angela Ferrers.

"Much of this strikes me less as sedition and more as perspicacious *observation*," said Severin, casually, tapping the very passage with one finger. "It is no secret that Burgoyne wishes to employ natives in his campaign. And it is not sedition to call that what it is: a terrible idea."

"But one approved, I understand, by the King," said André.

"Who has never been to America. Burgoyne sees the Indians as an instrument he can use to terrorize the colonists. He imagines that they are childlike in their simplicity and will look to a white man for leadership. He thinks they will fight for him. They will not. They will fight for themselves, for their own aims, to drive settlers out of the borderlands. They will not discriminate between loyalists and Rebels, and as soon as some overeager brave scalps one English child, Sam Adams and his rabble-rousers in Massachusetts will paper the country with broadsides and engravings and it will be the Boston Massacre all over again."

"Burgoyne sometimes has difficulty distinguishing between the playhouse and the battlefield," agreed André, "but the damage is already done."

"Then why come to me?"

"Because I want Angela Ferrers. You had your chance at her, sir, and you failed. I want your informant, this associate of the Widow, and I am prepared to give you this playwright fellow in exchange. It is a good bargain. Angela Ferrers will never come to trial, but her capture and execution, behind closed doors, will make my career. This seditious scribbler, though, Burgoyne will hang publicly. *He* is not enough to advance me to the rank I desire, but delivering him up to the general is ideal for proving your loyalty."

Severin schooled himself not to betray any emotion as he reached for the play. "What you are giving me," he said, "is nothing." He held up the booklet. "It is written under a pseudonym."

André regarded him coolly. "You are an expert at

handwriting, Colonel, and were, until your imprisonment, scrutinizing an extraordinary breadth of North American correspondence, including the private writings of hundreds, if not thousands, of Rebels and suspected Rebels." He drew another set of papers from his pocket and pushed it across the table.

It was the manuscript text of the play, written in an all too familiar hand.

"Do you recognize it?" asked the captain.

He hesitated a moment too long.

"You do, don't you?" pressed André.

He did. It was mate to that first fateful letter addressed to Burgoyne, to the single-word missive in his breast pocket. *Oh, dear God, Jenny, what have you done?*

"It is possible that I have seen the hand before," he said.

André smiled. "I think we understand each other, then."

"My memory will doubtless improve when I am once more in New York," said Severin. Where he was going to find Jennifer Leighton, and get her and her impossible aunt the hell out of the city—away from Howe, away from André, and beyond the reach of British cavalry and the hangman's noose forever.

Seventeen

Manhattan
January 1777

The fire had destroyed Trinity Church but spared
John Street, which, as Bobby had remarked, ought to
settle once and for all the question of whose side the
Almighty favored: the pulpit or the playhouse.

Jenny reserved judgment.

The British reopened the theater, but they did not
return it to the stewardship of Robert Hallam. Instead,
they informed him that the interior had been so wrecked
by its use as a hospital that repairs were going to cost a
fortune, and the considerable expense of refitting it after the American occupation must be underwritten in
some fashion. All profits from the newly rechristened
"Theatre Royal" were to go into the pocket of Howe's
Strolling Players—the amateur association that had
fronted the repair money—with the exception of those

nights held as benefits for widows, orphans, and deserving performers in the cast.

Deaf to Bobby Hallam's protests, they fixed a notice to the theater door that read:

> The Theatre in this city, having been some time in preparation, is intended to be opened in a few days for the charitable purpose of relieving the Widows and Orphans of Sailors and Soldiers who have fallen in support of the Constitutional Rights of Great Britain in America. It is requested that such Gentlemen of the Army and Navy whose talents and inclinations induce them to assist in so laudable an undertaking be pleased to send their names (directed to T. C.) to the Printer of this Paper before Thursday night next.

The players were made up largely of army officers and their mistresses. The soldiers appointed a physician named Beaumont, their surgeon general, manager of the company, and the only deal Bobby was able to strike with New York's latest high-handed occupiers was that he should be paid a pistole a week for Mr. Dearborn's services.

Bobby seethed quietly and Jenny kept out of his way, particularly after the too charming Captain André from the 26th engaged her to play certain parts that seemed to require a professional thespian, being "a bit beyond the repertoire" of the officers or their mistresses. Jenny agreed at once. As Angela Ferrers had said, no one would suspect a loyalist actress who had lost her livelihood to the Rebels of being the infamous Cornelia, whose plays were now being quoted in coffeehouses and acted in parlors and refectories up and down the coast.

Both of Lewis Hallam's sets of fine London painted scenery had been destroyed, the first in the riot, the second during the theater's use as a hospital. Captain André himself volunteered to create a new backdrop, and Jenny watched, fascinated, as a new Arcadia took shape before her eyes.

"You draw beautifully," she said to André in quiet tones. They were standing upstage, and he was roughing in the design with charcoal, while Lieutenant Pennfeather rehearsed his role in *The Beaux' Stratagem* opposite Captain Bradden's mistress. Captain Bradden, for his part, sat in the pit and looked on with displeasure.

"But I can't *paint* worth a damn," said André. "Bayard Caide is a far better colorist than I, but he's off terrorizing the Jerseys, so it will have to be Captain DeLancey who daubs it in for you."

"It doesn't look like our last Arcadia," she observed. "It's missing all the pointy trees."

André laughed out loud. "That is because I am not painting *Italy*. This is New York, around Fort Ti. It seemed absurd to import someone else's wilderness here, when you have your own so close to hand."

Jenny had never thought of it that way before. Scenery had always been something to be brought from England. She had assumed that anything painted in America would be inferior, and she had never even considered the idea of using American scenery for an American stage.

"It is every bit as wild and beautiful as Italy," she decided.

"It is every bit as beautiful as Tuscany," agreed André. "Though far more likely to kill you, in my experience."

Later that week Courtney Fairchild returned, now attached to Howe as a staff officer and thoroughly sick of ships and sailing. He announced that he was moving into John Street with Frances, and that he would entertain no arguments to the contrary. Jenny supposed she ought to be scandalized, but in truth she was relieved. Fanny had declined to appear in the British productions at the "Theatre Royal," no matter how much Beaumont or John André had implored her, saying it was high time she retired and allowed the younger generation to have its turn. Jenny suspected that her aunt wished to make the most of her days with Fairchild, and she could not fault her for it. Not when Jenny herself carried Devere's unsigned letter in her pocket and read it to herself daily.

Opening night at the John Street Royal was, appropriately enough, *Tom Thumb*, with Jenny taking the role of Princess Huncamunca. Fairchild, who had taken over the rent for Frances and Jenny and leased the rest of the building, ground floor included, had declined to allow the garrison's company to use the parlor for their greenroom. And so the late-night postshow suppers took place at the King's Arms, with the players and the general's party—Howe, Howe's favored coterie of officers, Howe's gorgeous mistress and *her* husband—all conveyed to the tavern in sleighs.

Where once Jenny had avoided these "entertain-ments after the entertainment," now she embraced them as a continuation of the play. As long as she acted the part of the loyalist, she could remain here in New York, near her aunt—and near her mysterious printer, who corresponded with her through a dead drop at Mr. Fraunces' and had begun paying her a percent of his respectable profits from her work.

So too, no matter how tempted she might be to retire to her rooms after rehearsal, she instead lin-gered, for a time at least, in the theater with the ama-teur players. They treated John Street like a private club: ordering catering from Mr. Lenzi and leaving bottles lined up on the gallery railings, and trysting when the mood took them, in the slots where she had almost succumbed to Devere.

The play ran a week, and on Friday after their final performance Jenny emerged from the theater to find snow falling gently and three sleighs waiting to carry the players to supper. Jenny traveled in the first with the mistresses of the garrison, their conveyance piled high with furs and strung with brass bells. The next carried the gentlemen in their heavy wool cloaks, bells jingling a note above the ladies. John André and young Hulett, the almost painfully handsome son of the danc-ing master of the disbanded American Players, followed in a brightly painted two-seater, their bells providing the third note in a wintry chord.

The ground floor of the King's Arms was a sea of scarlet coats, and Jenny moved through them unchal-lenged. It was assumed, she learned from André, who was not only charming but also a bit of a gossip, that because she lived with Aunt Frances and Fairchild, the major was keeping her as well. She had opened her mouth to protest, but André had laughed and forestalled her by speaking first.

"It is an absolutely delicious rumor and even if there isn't a grain of truth in it, you should encourage it. *Especially* if there isn't any truth in it. Such febrile gossip merely increases your fame as an actress and, from a purely mercenary perspective, your allure to audiences. The seats can hardly fill themselves, my dear."

He was right, though *in truth*, of course, she didn't want to be known for her supposed lovers, or even for her acting. She wanted to be known for her writing. It filled her with secret pleasure to hear her *Miles Gloriosus* talked about, but it chafed to hear General Beaumont declaim her prologues and afterpieces on the apron, and to see him receive praise for them afterward. She supposed he had appropriated the scripts from Bobby's office in the same way that the British had expropriated the whole theater.

Howe had ordered a turtle dinner upstairs for the players, but Jenny had no taste for the dish, and she crossed the hall to the long room fitted up for dancing.

That was when she saw him. It took a moment for understanding to follow recognition, because she could not comprehend his appearance here. Her hand slipped into her pocket, searching for his letter, as though somehow she could grasp and hold on to the real Severin Devere. Because *this* was not the man she had met in the greenroom at John Street, who had kissed her in the slots, who had gotten her off the *Boyne*, who had almost made love to her in a cloud of double-refined sugar and orange water.

She felt alternately flushed and then icy cold. He had

not yet seen her. He was standing beside Howe, speaking in his ear. His hair was as glossy black as she remembered, shining darkly in the candlelight. His face was as angular and finely wrought, but his cheekbones, always sharp, were bladelike now, and his whole graceful frame appeared slighter, more cleanly limned. It was as though the sculptor had returned to refine his work, chiseling away everything that was not essential to Severin Devere.

All this she would have welcomed as her spirit had longed to welcome him for these months. All this, save the scarlet coat with blue turnouts and cuffs. She did not recognize the facings and lace as belonging to any particular regiment, and she deduced that, like Courtney Fairchild, he must now be a staff officer of some kind. He wore no sash or gorget, which made sense since he was not on duty, but a battered blade hung from his belt beneath his coat, and he had a pistol tucked beside it as well.

She knew the moment he sensed her presence, not because he did anything so blatant as to turn and look at her, but because he inclined his head in silent acknowledgment while still speaking to Howe, the way the John Street cat cocked his ears when he knew you were there but had not chosen, just yet, to recognize you.

When he turned, it was a performance, as convincing as any she had seen onstage, but a performance nonetheless. He anticipated it a little, pivoting his body before he turned his head, saying something crude that elicited a sly smile from Howe and allowing his gaze to light on her and sweep her body from head to toe.

Howe nodded, filled his punch glass quickly, and led Devere across the room. Jenny felt like a sailor who could see the fin in the water, heading straight for her.

And then Howe was standing in front of her and

Devere was at his side and the general was making the same introduction Courtney Fairchild had once made, only this time Jenny had not been hoping for the arrival of another man. Except, of course, that she *had*.

Devere took her hand and pressed it to his lips. She felt the contact through her whole body and tried hard not to show it. Howe bowed and left them in relative privacy, and finally, after a year, she was standing again face-to-face with Severin Devere.

He hated the way she was looking at him, as though he had somehow disappointed her. Perhaps he had.

She had changed. So had he, of course, but the regimentals, which Captain André had rightly insisted he wear, loudly proclaimed that he had not. He wished to God there had been some other—*any* other—way to meet her again without endangering her. John André had men watching him. That would have been a sensible precaution with an officer one suspected but dared not yet accuse of turning coat. It was an absolute necessity with one you believed held the key to your professional advancement.

"Jenny," he said.

"A very familiar use, considering we have just met."

He had liked her tart and clever in her ugly linen smock. Tart and clever, he liked her as much or more in marigold silk turned iridescent by the candlelight. It outlined her admirable curves and set off her copper hair, which, unpowdered, was piled high on her head in a luxurious tangle of curls. A glossy plume of them hung down her back. She wore sparkling paste around the throat he wanted to lick and the wrists he longed to kiss.

"The introduction," he explained, "was a necessary fiction."

"Yes," she said, the disappointment plain now in her voice. "You have always been very good at doing whatever was necessary."

He had worn the uniforms of many regiments and many nations, but never felt such a fraud as at this moment, in his own. "It is a costume, Jenny," he assured her. "Nothing more. Everything I wrote to you in that letter is true, and more."

"Then how do you come to be speaking so intimately in the general's ear?" she asked.

"You are smiling now," he said, "for the benefit of others, because they cannot hear our words but they can read our expressions. We are giving them the scene they all know, the one Burgoyne wished to play with you. The one in which the officer with a reputation for bedding beauties seduces the pretty niece of an infamous actress. You play your part well. Pray give me credit, then, for a little skill in mine."

"Your performance with Howe was very convincing," she said.

"And so it has to be. If our host suspected how I really felt about him, believe me, he would fear for his life. He left me to die at the bottom of that mine."

A little of the color left her face and threw her cosmetics into relief. She looked fragile, her skin porcelain with painted roses.

"And my aunt and I sent you there."

"The Widow sent me there, and I hold no grudges. She was doing her job. I was doing mine. But Sir William Howe was supposed to be my ally, a brother officer, a *gentleman*. He did not rescue me. Indeed, he did not stir himself at all on my account. Nor, it seems, did anyone on his staff spare a thought for me."

"How did you escape?"

"With help from my family—the American family whom I was too English and too proud to own before. They got me out of the mine and nursed me back to health. And they risked everything they had to do it, because their farm is deep in Rebel territory and rescuing me could have cost them their land, their fortune, and their lives. As it is, they had to endure a visit from a troop of dragoons in the middle of the night—although if you were to ask my aunt, she would likely tell you the King's soldiers caused a fair bit less damage to hearth and home than did I in the grip of my fever."

Jenny swallowed, the muscles in her slender neck working, and said, "What happened to you at Simsbury?"

"The usual sort of thing that happens in prisons compounded by Mr. Hallam's superbly vicious enmity and the inhuman conditions of the mine."

"I am sorry," she said, "for all of it. I did not know what else to do. I could see no other course."

"Necessity is a harsh mistress, as I have cause to know. But you didn't do it for yourself. You did it for your aunt. I know that. In your position, I like to think I would have done the same, but I'm not certain of it. I was misguided then. I *would* do the same now. I *am* doing the same now. Or at least I am trying, because I am a little wiser at least than I was a year ago. Howe ignored my letters, my entreaties for aid. Three times he denied me, and I am no saint."

"Then you are here for revenge."

"No. Though the instinct glows hot, like a muse of fire. I am done with them. I'm here for you."

"Then why not come to me in private, where we could . . . be ourselves?"

Oh, how he hated the uniform then. "Because I am being watched, and because I know what you have been about, *Cornelia*."

All the color drained from her face now, but she hid it with a flourish of her fan and asked, "Who else knows?"

"No one, yet. That is why I came back. To ensure no one else finds out."

"What does that mean?"

"It means that I must put the gifts of my calling to use one last time to make sure you are safe, and then I can take off this uniform—this costume—for good, and you and I can begin again."

"No," she said.

"No, what?"

"I won't have you kill for me."

"You did not scruple over it in the street that night."

"That was different. You were defending our lives. What you are planning now is cold-blooded murder."

Her mask was slipping, her smile fading, her voice rising. He could not risk discovery here.

"We must talk in private," he said. "Meet me in the gardens tomorrow night."

"Vauxhall is closed."

"I'll leave the hedge door unlocked. You know where the private boxes are. Come to me there, and I will explain everything."

He had come back for her, and he was prepared to do murder for her. It would make a very good play.

It was not how she wanted to live her life. Entrapped in such a dark drama. It was not how she wanted him to lead his. He said he had changed, but if he intended to do this thing, he had not. He had only changed costume.

General Washington had warned her that she would hang if she was discovered. She had heard the talk, read about Burgoyne's oath to execute the seditious scribbler and about Howe's generous reward for the man's capture. She had felt safe, because everyone assumed the writer had to be a man.

She was not safe at all.

Devere had not told her to make sure she was not seen—perhaps he hadn't felt it necessary to belabor the obvious. She knew that their meeting must be secret.

It was easy now to understand why Angela Ferrers had sought out the Divine Fanny's tutelage. Anyone could buy a wig or don a costume, but the art of impersonation relied on carriage and gesture and gait. Jenny entered her room Saturday afternoon as herself and emerged from it as Margaret, their part-time maid, in a brown linen gown with a white kerchief tucked into her neckline, a plain muslin apron, and her distinctive copper hair hidden by a black wig and tucked into the ugliest cap she could find. With a thin wool cloak that both entirely failed to keep out the cold and became quickly drenched with melting snow, she not only looked but *felt* the part.

She took the precaution of carrying a basket of washing with her as well, and set out on the long walk through the falling snow to Vauxhall. Huddled into her miserable excuse for a cloak and stooped against the wind, she received a second glance from no one.

When she reached the hedge that bordered the pleasure gardens, she panicked, because it was thickly covered in snow and she could not see the door, but she thrust her hands through in the place where she thought it had been. Her fingers met cold brick. She moved a little farther along the wall and tried again, and her fingers at last met cold iron and smooth wood, found the ring, and pulled.

Beyond was a fairyland covered in pristine snow, the paths deeper depressions in the blanket of white. She retraced their steps from the year before, stopping when she reached the manicured grove where the little private dining rooms were nestled in the snow-frosted trees. They were all identical: single-story garden follies with large windows, painted green doors, and rusticated masonry corners with Chinese fretwork galleries running around the top. The little structures were closed for winter but footprints in the snow, coming from the direction of the banqueting house, guided her to the right one.

She pressed her thumb to the latch and pushed the door open on surprising warmth. The room was heated by four small brass foot stoves, the Dutch kind, with coals glowing red and throwing splashes of light on the paneling. The furnishings were pushed to the walls, a table along one, four chairs along another, a caned chaise topped with a cushion tucked into a corner.

Devere sat in the window seat, one foot up on the bench, looking out at the snow. When she entered, he turned to look at her. He was not wearing his regimentals tonight and in the moonlight his face was full of relief and something else.

Joy.

"I was worried you would not come," he admitted.

"Who can refuse a private invitation to Vauxhall?" she asked, setting down her basket of washing.

He smiled. "I wish that I could lay a banquet before you this time."

She thought of the cake and his mouth on hers, and suddenly the little room felt very warm. She untied her cloak. He rushed to take it, but he was careful not to touch her. He draped it over the chaise and retreated to the window, his tall frame leaning against the embrasure.

"A banquet of sweets is not necessary, but I am grateful you have provided heat," she admitted.

"I find I've grown less tolerant of cold places," he said.

Like the mine, which had been her fault. "I am sorry for what you have suffered, Severin, but it's all the more reason I don't want you to embrace your former profession—not on my account."

"I have never killed lightly—or for better reason. The man who threatens you bids fair to replace me, and he is, as far as I have been able to ascertain, like Angela Ferrers: ruthless, with few if any weaknesses."

"But he does not yet know my name," said Jenny. "Which would make killing him murder. An assassination."

"He does not *yet* know your name," agreed Devere. "He doesn't even want Cornelia. He offered her to me, in a bargain. He wants the Widow's New York contact. He wants your aunt, Jenny, so that he can discover everything she knows about Angela Ferrers."

"Why?"

"Ambition. Something you and I can both understand. I chose this work because it promised quick advancement for men who can get results. I chose it because it is one of the only ways for a man to succeed on his abilities alone, without the advantages of wealth or powerful friends. So has he."

Devere continued softly. "Howe's current adjutant general is *not* an able intelligencer. Stephen Kemble came by the job through interest and family connections. Kemble's appointment was pure cronyism—made at a time when this was only a rebellion in Boston, and the fate of America did not hang in the balance—but he is General Gage's brother-in-law, and so not easily displaced. André has already made the first move. He has supplanted me as indispensable during my absence—in the space of a few months. Now he wants to rise higher, to take Kemble's place. It will be nearly impossible to deny him the job if he can capture the Widow."

"*André?* Captain John André?"

"Yes."

"Captain André paints scenery at the John Street and sometimes speaks the prologue, rather badly. He hardly seems an assassin."

"No. He isn't the sort to do his own killing, at least by preference. But he is a spy. A very skilled and very ambitious one. And he already has half the evidence he needs to hang you." Devere drew a crumpled sheaf of papers from his pocket and placed it on the table.

She could just make out the words in the moonlight. "That is my manuscript," she said. "How did he come by that?"

"Does it matter? It is in your hand. All John André needs is a sample to match it against. Your writing is distinctive. You must have had a very thorough tutor. You form your loops the same way, without fail, line after line. You dot your *i*'s and cross your *t*'s with neat, short marks. I could attempt to make the case that this is a forgery, of course, but it will be a weak argument. Not something to hazard your safety on."

"The last time I saw this manuscript, it was in the hands of my printer. A man trusted by Washington."

"Who?"

"I never learned his name."

"Describe him."

She did.

"Rivington," said Devere, decisively.

"No. That can't be," said Jenny. "Rivington used to print the Tory *Gazetteer*."

"He is a double agent. He sells information to both sides, and each believes he is loyal to them while playing the other."

"So he is a traitor."

Devere shrugged. "Perhaps. And perhaps *not*. He has to give Howe something real from time to time. Cornelia's manuscript is real, but useless, unless you have a suspect, handwriting samples to compare, and an expert to assess them. Until I returned a few days ago, Howe had no such expert readily to hand."

Relief washed over her. "So as long as I do not put pen to paper and allow any samples of my writing to cross Howe's desk, I am safe."

"No," said Devere. "You aren't safe—certainly not until we discover who has my possessions. I ordered them sent ashore if I did not return to the *Boyne*. They should have gone to the King's Arms and been held there for my return, but the trunk disappeared. Your letter to Burgoyne was in it."

Her heart sank. "Did your things include all the movables in your cabin?" she asked.

"Yes."

"Then the trunk will contain more than just my letter. When I took Burgoyne's plans, I replaced them with a manuscript—a play I was working on—and disguised the substitution by placing the general's cover page on top."

"It is no matter. The letter alone is damning enough. More handwriting would not make the case any more persuasively."

"It is not the handwriting. It is the content. The manuscript I left in your cabin has a decidedly Tory flavor, and the *Miles Gloriosus* is anything but that. Unfortunately, many of the jokes are the same. It seemed a shame to waste them."

"I might have been able to cast doubt on the authenticity of the handwriting. Chancy, but possible. But if the content matches, Jenny, we have no hope of saving you that way."

"Who might have your possessions now?"

"I don't know. Possibly my man of business, who is—unfortunately and rather worryingly—missing. Possibly an agent of Angela Ferrers. Possibly no one of any importance at all. During the period since they were removed from the *Boyne*—and we can only assume that Hartwell followed my instructions in their entirety—the city has changed hands, twice, there has been a fire, and the staff at the King's Arms has had to make many compromises to keep the place open."

"*Compromises*," she said. "Like Bobby. He was a covert Son of Liberty before the Americans turned the theater into a hospital and threatened to arrest him for entertaining loyalists, and now the army has treated him no better. He is not being paid for the use of the theater, only a weekly pittance for Mr. Dearborn's services while Howe's 'players' make free of the theater like it is a public house and tryst in the slots with their mistresses."

Devere smiled and looked her up and down. "If they're half as pretty as you, then I cannot blame them."

"Some are far prettier. And all are better dressed. I borrowed this from our maid."

"Was the smock from *The American Prodigal* not available?"

"*That* is a costume, and would look like one on the street. *This*, on the other hand, is making a game attempt to flatter with its *cut* and failing mournfully in its *cloth*. This is what a real maid looks like."

"You're a very good observer of people. If you hadn't been an actress, you would have made an able spy. Although you are mistaken about the gown. It does most definitely flatter. It makes me wish I could find my missing impedimenta and with it those elusive French letters. I think it might be worth shaking down every fence and vendue master in New York to get hold of them."

"There's no need to go to quite so much trouble because on this occasion I've brought my own."

Eighteen

It should not have surprised him at all: that this woman who had taken her future into her own hands time and time again would take *this* into her own hands. But it did.

And, God help him, he was eager as a boy for her to take *him* into her own hand and other softer places, but an unwelcome thought intruded. "And what, or *who*, in my absence, inspired you to go shopping for French letters?"

"Aunt Frances," she said, matter-of-factly. "I told her that I'd decided that no man who wouldn't consent to wearing one was worth bedding, and she said that if I truly felt that way I ought to have my own. She also opined they would only gather lint in my pocketbook."

"Was she right?" he asked.

"Yes. For all the wrong reasons, of course. Are they really so awful to use?"

"I suppose that depends. If you are a man and intent solely upon your own pleasure, then they are a nuisance, particularly if you have . . . difficulties maintaining your . . . intention."

"But your *intention*," she said lightly, "your intention is unwavering, I should hope." Flirting, as he had not been able to induce her to do in the kitchen that previous night.

"I would show you my intention," he said, warming to the smile that kissed the corners of her lips, as he was about to do, "but first I would see these French letters."

"They are of the highest quality, and new," Jenny said, reaching under her skirt and pulling forth a little pocketbook, flame-stitched and tied closed with an embroidered ribbon. "Aunt Frances helped me select them."

"Christ," said Devere. "No wonder your parents didn't want you to go off with her. Where did you procure them?"

"From an establishment in the Holy Ground run by an old friend of Fanny's."

"By 'establishment' you mean 'brothel.'"

"I believe they also served suppers. I am by no means a lawyer, but if they have a victualing license, then that probably makes them a tavern."

She unrolled the pocketbook and drew out a carefully folded onionskin. Inside were four sheaths, lying flat across the paper, all of the very thinnest lamb gut. They were finished with pink silk ribbons and decorated on the side with an illustration.

"Aunt Fanny advised you to choose illustrated ones, did she?"

"Yes. She said the fresh ink meant they were new.

And in any case, the plain ones had cheaper ribbons. I worried that they would tangle and knot. I supposed the pictures serve to reinforce the gentleman's *intention*, should it waver."

"My intention has been fixed for some time now. It's my turn to see to yours."

Her eyes widened and he leaned in to kiss her, first at the corners of her mouth, then full on the lips, then teasing her tongue out to play.

"My intention is fixed as well," she said, coming up for air. "It has been since you served me cake on the end of your blade. And I *do* realize how that sounds."

He laughed and caught her up in his arms. "I very much doubt your intention is sufficiently fixed," he said, taking her fingers and running them over the sheaths. "These are papery and dry. For this to work, they have to be slick and wet. *We* have to be slick and wet. Starting with you."

She had been told that the slender membrane she intended to put between them would dull his interest and her ardor, but that was not proving to be the case.

He backed her to the cushioned chaise and drew her down on it to lie within his arms. He kissed her, his tongue wet, like he promised her she would be, his hands unpinning, untying, unlacing in all the right places until she was wearing nothing but her chemise and her stays were loose and pushed down to expose her breasts. He folded her chemise back from these and lavished attention on her nipples, first with his palms, then with his thumbs, next with his mouth, suckling— until his teeth scraped lightly at them and her spine was arching and her upper back coming up and off the chaise.

He shifted then to kneel at her side and reach between her legs: no preamble here, but a quick, successful search for her softness and slickness. She groaned when he found her and she thought that they were ready. "Now?" she asked, her hands groping toward the table and the pocketbook.

He grasped both her wrists in one hand and pinned them above her head. "Not yet," he chided, using his other hand to spread the lips of her core and trace circles around her center.

"Yes, yes. Now, *now*," she pleaded.

"No. But soon."

He slid a finger into her and she sobbed.

"How soon?"

"You waited a year for me to come back. Now you cannot wait another minute longer?"

"For *this*, Severin? No."

He reached for the buttons on his breeches. He'd fantasized about teaching her to tie a French letter on him. Now he didn't feel like teaching her anything except how to repeat his name in a dozen different tones of wanting.

Her hands traveled down his chest. They were lying close together on the narrow chaise, and he placed one foot on the ground to brace and steady himself. Her fingers stole over his, fidgeting busily at his buttons. He took her hand and put it where *he* wanted it.

She smiled, then took his free hand and placed it back between her own parted thighs.

He could not question her judgment in this matter. It seemed to him most excellent. Warm and wet and most excellent in every way, and even more so when she took a tentative grip on his shaft and thumbed the head.

The word that came out of his mouth belonged in alleys and whorehouses, and the very happiest of bedrooms. He groaned with the pleasure of her stroking thumb and fingered her in time, a game he could play only for so long.

"The sheaths," he said at last, groping along the table beside the chaise until he found one and rolled onto his back, faced with a rampant erection and a suit of unfamiliar armor.

He had not checked them. They were not his own, though they were undoubtedly clean, new, and from the very best London maker. But they had voyaged across an ocean and passed through many hands. He brought the first up to his mouth and blew into it.

It filled like a balloon. "Oh, thank God," he said.

Jenny, who was perched on her knees on the chaise now, was eyeing him as though he had gone mad.

"If they inflate, they are sound."

"Fascinating," she said with an impatient scowl. "Now are you going to put it on?"

"No," he said, smiling now that that daydream, that fantasy was at long last becoming reality. "*You* are."

She was flushed and breathless with wanting, and very much done with waiting, and the impossible man was lying there, shirt askew, breeches pushed down, member twitching, and *now* he wanted to give her lessons in furbelows.

"Aren't you afraid that if I learn how to put them on, I might consort with other men? I'm a terribly quick study, you know."

"No," he answered, slipping his hand between her legs once more and sliding his fingers over her slick cleft, seeking out her nub—rubbing hard enough that it burned a little and kept her from tipping over the edge. "You won't want anyone else. Not after I'm done with you."

"Careful, or my next play will be *The Braggart Lover.*"

"It isn't a boast if I make good on it." He wrapped his hand around the base of his member and tilted it toward her.

She'd enjoyed touching him tonight, watching the play of reactions across his face, the way his breath hitched when her thumb circled the head, how his back arched and muscles flexed.

"Why are you so insistent that I do this?"

"Because you ought to know how, not least in the unlikely circumstance that you are disappointed in me tonight and compelled to seek another lover. If you don't know how to use a sheath, all the more excuse for him to plead inconvenience and refuse. But quite apart from that, I want to feel you put it on me."

He handed her the French letter. It fluttered, papery, ribbons streaming between her fingers, and she parted the open end and fitted it to the head of him. Then she grasped hold of the ribbons where they were sewn to the hem and drew them down his shaft, the delicate membrane sliding behind to ensheathe him. He groaned, very gratifyingly, and then used a number of choice words as she gathered up the ribbons, the ends dancing over his scrotum, and tried to tie a knot.

"A bow is best," he said. "So it is easy to remove. But a knotted bow is better, to ensure it doesn't slip off."

His flesh was so different from any part of her body, so transformed, so obviously needy and sensitive that she hesitated to tie the bow tightly.

"That will slip free," he said. "Don't be afraid to cinch it."

She started over, taking him at his word, tightening the ribbons until he said, "Just there. With the bow resting beneath. You'll like the ribbons better there, I promise."

He was as good as his word. He flipped their positions until she was lying on the chaise and he was kneeling over her. His sheathed member was pressing against her, sliding in her wetness, becoming slick and supple, teasing her nub and her entrance, one, then the other, until her hips lifted off the cushion, again and again, trying to capture him.

And then he was in with a wet pop, and she cried out in surprise. It was wonderful and incredible and too much and then suddenly quite painful.

"Sorry," he said. "I was hoping you wouldn't have any pain."

She scowled up at him. "As was *I*." All of the wonderful and incredible had fled and she was left with a cold wet intrusion and could feel the folds of the sheath scratching her tender flesh. Now she could well understand why some people chose not to use them.

"Patience," he said, sitting back on his heels while remaining still inside her. His hands settled over her knees, warm and caressing, then began to slide up her thighs, massaging the tight muscles there, and relaxing those where they were joined. Surprisingly—almost miraculously—it began to feel good again, slick and warm once more, and when his fingers peeled back her lips around his cock and painted delicate circles around her button, she started to climb again toward climax.

He didn't tease or prolong her ascent, just went directly for that goal she knew how to pursue on her own but had never experienced in company. She could feel the little ribbons fluttering between them, sticky with their joining, kissing the sensitive, stretched flesh of her entrance. When completion was inevitable, she wrapped her legs around his back and dug her heels into his buttocks and came, a little ahead of him, so she was holding him, and holding on to him, when he began to thrust frantically and the chaise leapt and skipped across the floor beneath them until at last he groaned and stilled.

In the sudden quiet she could hear his heart pounding in his chest. His hair had come loose from its ribbon and sweaty tendrils of it were plastered over her face.

New Brunswick Jenny would have asked for promises: marriage or at the very least financial support. But she had a purse full of gold coins, still growing, from her work as Cornelia, and freedom to love whom she might, so she simply allowed herself to lie there and feel close to him, to enjoy his warmth and the beauty of his finely made body.

While he was still hard inside her he grasped his sheathed cock at the base and withdrew, removing the French letter carefully and laying it on the table. He kissed her one more time, then got up from the chaise, took one of the little pottery bowls stacked on the table, and knelt in the window seat and opened the sash.

"What on earth are you doing?" she asked, as the cold air blew over her.

"Practicalities," he said, scooping up a bowl of snow and closing the window. He set it atop one of the stoves and it melted instantly. He dropped the condom into the water and returned to the chaise. "They are difficult to wash if you allow them to dry," he explained.

She hadn't thought of that, but it wasn't the only practicality they had to consider.

"What are we going to do about André?" she asked.

Devere returned to the chaise and lay down beside her.

"This seemed more commodious earlier," he remarked of the narrow cushion.

"That is because you are easily distracted. I am not. Tell me about André. How close is he to finding out about Aunt Frances and me?"

"That is difficult to say. Like me, he has spent the last year in captivity. He is only just arrived in New York. I am the best lead he has for catching her, but he will certainly be pursuing others. The footpads sent to kill us that night, the men who watched the docks and reported on my movements, the ones who helped the Widow to smuggle me out of the city—all are liabilities so long as André lives. And somewhere out there are your letters and your manuscript, enough to damn you."

"But he has left Cornelia to you. So it is only Aunt Frances we need worry about."

"Would she consider leaving New York?" asked Severin.

Jenny thought about their little household on John

Street. "You were right, of course, about her illness. She is dying. But she is happy here. Fairchild is living with us."

Devere's expression clouded. "Would that I had been here to prevent that. I fear I have failed my oldest friend."

"They don't share a bed," said Jenny. "Fairchild had a trundle built for her room." Her chest felt tight thinking about it. "I can hear them, reading to each other and talking late into the night. I think your friend is the very best of men."

"You'll find no disagreement from me," said Devere. "He acted the part of brother to me at school when my own flesh and blood did not. Julian made it clear to the other boys that I was a by-blow and that made me fair game for abuse."

"I am sorry," said Jenny. "I have four brothers. I can imagine your plight all too well."

Devere smiled wryly. "English public school conditions might beggar even your imagination. Courtney put a stop to it. And he invited me home at the holidays, gave me a family to replace my unhappy one."

"He comes home at midday to share his meal with Frances," said Jenny. "They are devoted to each other. Fairchild is why I cannot ask her to leave."

Devere sighed. "Fairchild *is* the best of men, though right this moment I wish he was not half so good, because it means I must *deal* with John André."

"André has no reason to suspect Aunt Frances right now, does he?"

"No."

"And no reason to suspect me either."

"He will if my trunk turns up."

"Then we must find it first," said Jenny, sitting up. "And my aunt and I are safe for the moment, although I suppose I must have someone else copy out my next manuscript before I transmit it to the duplicitous Mr. Rivington." The little braziers were no longer glowing and the room was starting to cool.

"Jenny, there can be no more manuscripts from Cornelia. It is too dangerous."

"They can only hang me once, and I am already on their list with Adams and Hancock and the like. It is an honor I would choose over ranking first on Garrick's *Critical Balance of the Performers at Drury Lane*. I would be a fool to stop now."

"Are you mad? I didn't come back to see you hang," he said with sudden vehemence. "Not for words on paper."

"It's more than that now," she said. "And less, in one sense, because the paper no longer matters. Rivington could never print another copy, and the play will still exist in people's minds. When all I wanted was my plays performed on the London stage, the best I could hope for was the patronage of an important man and the laughter of a multitude. Now British generals want to hang me, armies march to ditties cribbed from my prologues, and recruiting sergeants quote me to drum up enlistments."

"But I love you, damn it."

"And I love you, Severin, but I have seen love up close now, and I will not settle for the kind that limits and diminishes me. You are capable of more than killing. I am capable of more than domestic devotion. I do not wish the kind of love that reduces over time who we each are. I want the kind that makes the whole of us greater than the sum of our parts."

Severin let Jenny out the little hedge door without convincing her to give up Cornelia. They both knew that it was too dangerous to meet again until the threat André posed could be neutralized. Severin had, in a desperate moment, gone to his knees and proposed marriage. They had both burst out laughing.

"It is a better performance than Bobby gave," she'd admitted. "But poor stuff all the same. Ask me again when it is not just a means to a specific end."

It left Devere in an impossible position. He did not know how to protect her. He could not predict André's next move, could not find or even determine if his dangerous box full of possessions still existed, and she would not let him fix this for her as he had fixed the problems of powerful men, by deceit and murder.

A month passed in which he no more than glimpsed her across a room or from the boxes in the John Street Theater. And after four weeks of careful investigation Devere was no closer to finding his damned trunk and its damning contents, but he had discovered a great deal more about André, none of it good. He had begun his discreet inquiries with the staff and former staff he could locate at the King's Arms, and—as his quest had taken him from the vendue masters of the coffeehouses to the fences who dealt stolen goods in the canvas town that had sprung up in the wake of the fire—he had also gathered information on his dapper adversary.

As Jenny had said, John André was a talented artist

with a passion for the theater. As he had revealed to Severin, the man had been a prisoner of war for nearly a year himself, an experience that had left him with little love for American Whigs. More important, he spoke fluent French and German and had made himself useful to Howe by translating for the commanders of the Hessian mercenaries now flooding into New York. He drew excellent maps and likenesses of people, and had compiled an encyclopedia of valuable intelligence on Rebel possessions while he was in their power.

His past commissions in the army were murky. He had traveled far too widely in the early stages of the war, and with far too much autonomy, for a simple lieutenant, and he had likely been grooming himself—or someone had been grooming him—for a career in espionage for a very long time.

André was also reputed to be an excellent shot and a formidable swordsman. Even a passable boxer.

March and April of 1777 brought first a thawing and then rain and finally spring in the first grass-scented week of May. Vauxhall and Ranelagh opened, and Devere could not keep away because he knew that Jenny strolled the gardens on concert nights with her aunt and Courtney Fairchild.

He encountered her at Ranelagh twice, and the second time his self-control failed him. "Meet me," he said out of the hearing of her companions.

"Have you discovered something?" she asked.

"Yes. That I cannot live another day without you."

A wry smile quirked the corners of her mouth. Her smile, he realized, was charmingly lopsided. He wanted to discover something new about her every day.

"You should be careful what you say to a writer," she warned, "or it will end up in a play."

"The words I plan to use shortly would not make it past even the liberal censors of New York." He leaned forward and spoke them in her ear, and her face flushed and her skin heated, and he could feel the very air warming between them. "Behind the greenhouse," he said.

"It is too public. We could be seen."

"There is a cart selling masks at the entrance to the maze. Buy one, and find me when the music starts."

The concerts were given on a lawn bordered by box hedges and furnished with little gilded chairs. Courtney Fairchild found one for Frances, but Jenny said she preferred to stand and her aunt made no protest. Nor did she or Fairchild appear to notice when Jenny slipped out of the green enclosure and away.

She knew she should not go to him. It was dangerous. They might be observed together. But her desire was as strong as his, and all their care wouldn't mean a damn if Devere's possessions turned up in the wrong hands: because then she would hang. Facing such a prospect, she was resolved at least to die with no regrets.

Jenny found the cart at the end of the path and bought a simple *moretta* mask, the kind shaped like an egg, in black silk velvet, with a little cord attached to the mouth and a paste jewel meant to be held between the teeth like a bit. It would give her an excuse for not stopping to speak with anyone on her way to the fountain, and unlike the fanciful cat and peacock masks, it should attract little attention.

She heard the musicians strike up as the pretty brick greenhouse came into view, and she realized that the structure lay just on the other side of the concert lawn, separated only by a tall line of beeches. Miss Wainryte's voice, familiar to Jenny because she had been employed often to sing at the John Street before the British commandeered the theater, floated through the trees, one of Haydn's Scottish songs.

O Sandy, why leav'st thou thy Nelly to mourn?
Thy presence could ease me,
When naething can please me:
Now dowie I sigh on the bank of the burn,
Or thro' the wood, laddie, until thou return.

There were fires still burning in the greenhouse even at this time of year to keep the orange and lemon trees warm, their leaves waxy green in the flickering light, their fragrance drifting over the lawn.

Tho' woods now are bonny, and mornings are clear,
While lav'rocks are singing,
And primroses springing;
Yet nane of them pleases my eye or my ear
When thro' the wood, laddie, ye dinna appear.

Devere was waiting for her around the back, leaning against the brick wall, where empty clay pots were stacked in neat rows and benches too weathered to use in the garden were stored. She could still hear the music, which meant that they could be heard, so she tried to pick her way silently across the gravel, but that proved impossible.

He looked up when he heard her approach, and his eyes widened and gleamed black in the reflected light when he caught sight of her mask.

She lifted a hand to remove it, but he stepped quickly to forestall her, capturing her wrist and holding it away from her face. "No," he said, speaking softly. "Leave it on. It will help us . . . focus on discretion."

That I am forsaken, some spare not to tell:
I'm fash'd wi' their scorning,
Baith ev'ning and morning;
Their jeering gaes aft to my heart wi' a knell,
When thro' the wood, laddie, I wander mysel.

Inside they might be overheard, might already have been seen. The windows were large and the fires bright, and the whole of the orangery interior one open space dotted with trees. Devere drew her into the shadows of the little walled enclosure, her shoes crunching over bits of broken pottery, and he bade her lean back against the brick.

She wanted to kiss him. She was conscious of the jeweled bit between her teeth, its contours smooth against her tongue, keeping her mouth slightly open but making speech impossible. He surprised her by dropping to his knees in front of her and lifting her hem. Up and up it went like a stage curtain until it met her hands. "Take it," he said, pressing bunches of silk into her palms. She grasped the stuff in handfuls, gown and petticoats and chemise all together, cool air swirling around her ankles, calves, and knees.

He placed his hands on her thighs. "Higher," he said.

Then stay, my dear Sandy, nae langer away,
But quick as an arrow,
Hast here to thy marrow,
Wha's living in languor till that happy day,
When thro' the wood, laddie, we'll dance, sing, and play.

She drew the curtain up, up, up until the edges of her stays were visible and so was everything else: her own coppery curls, his thumbs parting them, her pink flesh, and his pinker tongue swiping her center.

The strangled sounds in her throat died behind the closed mouth of the velvet mask, the jeweled bit and the silken cord stilling her tongue.

He was not silent. He laughed a little, then licked her again, then described for her in perfect detail what it was like to do this to her, how much he enjoyed this little game.

It did not last long. *She* did not last long. When her climax took hold of her, she lost her concentration and her mouth opened. The jewel fell out. The mask dropped from her face. Devere caught it deftly. He sat back on his heels and looked up at her with a hint of smug satisfaction.

"I would kiss you," he said, "but then you would carry the scent with you all night, instead of being able to hide it here." He touched the part of her that was still trembling, and she convulsed again. Then he stood and tugged her skirts out of her hands, which were curled like claws around the silk. He smoothed her gown until she looked almost presentable. She stepped away from the wall on unsteady legs.

"I must leave," he said, "or it will be obvious what I have been about . . . But I hope you will think of me as you stroll through the garden."

She would, of course. Her thighs were slick with what they had just concluded. When she took her seat next to her aunt and the man who shared her aunt's life but not her bed, she felt a pang of longing. She knew from their example that love could survive without passion, but she wondered how long passion could abide without intimacy.

Devere left Ranelagh savoring his encounter with Jennifer Leighton. It occurred to him only in the street afterward that tonight he had not said he loved her. An appalling omission. He must see her again and tell her. It could be arranged. They had managed it tonight.

His optimism faded as he walked home past the defenses that Howe was building to keep possession of Manhattan, and looked out over the water where on the opposite shore Rebel fires still burned. By the time he reached his lodgings at the King's Arms, he was wondering how long this idyll could last.

He got his answer the next day, when John André joined him at his evening meal in the taproom.

"I hope," said André, drinking ale and making himself entirely at home at Severin's table, "that your return to civilization has improved your memory in regards to the Merry Widow's associate."

"I seem to recall that you promised me Cornelia in exchange," hazarded Devere. "Until I can lay hands on the playwright, I don't see why I should give you the Widow's conspirator."

John André inclined his head. "Just so. That is why, Colonel, I shall exert myself to deliver you Cornelia tonight. And tomorrow you will give me the Widow's compatriot."

Fear twisted in his guts. "Do you have a piece of writing for me to compare?"

"Nothing so tenuous," replied André smoothly. "I have received information that our man 'Cornelia' will attend a clandestine performance of his *Miles Gloriosus* tonight. There is a group of students from King's who play it twice monthly in a burnt-out building in canvas town. We have been allowing this gathering to grow—and it has now become a large net we can draw closed around a significant school of traitors. I'm told the play now attracts a crowd of five hundred at each performance—many of them almost regular attendees—including the rebellious sons of some very wealthy loyalists. Men Howe believes will feel obliged to put their money behind raising soldiers for the Crown, if their heirs are threatened with a spell on the *Jersey*."

The British prison hulk was reputed to be as bad as the Rebel-run mine, with the commissioner of prisoners starving the wretches confined there and lining his pockets with the money meant to purchase their victuals. And Simsbury served as a justification for it.

"That tactic will turn known allies into secret enemies and potential plotters," said Severin, with the bitter wisdom of experience.

"No doubt," said André, unconcerned. "But that is Howe's business. I am not terribly interested in the scions of a pack of dour Dutch patroons. The general may do as he pleases with them. Cornelia is our objective, and we'll take him tonight. If you wish to be in on the capture, be at the Battery by seven."

Devere affected indifference and shrugged. "Surely you have oxen to yoke to this plow."

"I do. I have Sir Bayard Caide's notoriously brutal dragoons. Howe is worried the colonel's raids on the Jerseys will turn Bergen County against us, but Caide's men wreak almost equal havoc when we keep them bottled up in New York. A night cracking heads will provide a fine outlet for them. And there is a very useful fellow who follows Caide called Dyson. Something of a prodigy. I mean to use him on the Merry Widow's associate, but you may borrow him tonight for Cornelia."

Severin's dinner threatened to rise. He knew Caide's dragoons, and they were nothing like the light horse troop that had "rescued" him from Connecticut. The colonel and his men were ruthless and brutal, and like Severin—or the man Severin had once been—they were tolerated by leaders like Howe who wished to avoid bloodshed on a mass scale and would countenance private murder and torture to see it done. His lieutenant, Dyson, was the worst of a bad lot: a sadist with a talent for torture.

"That is very generous," said Devere. His mind ran to killing Captain André here and now, of standing up quickly, offering him his hand, and pulling him close and stabbing him. Devere would swing for it, and gladly, if he thought he had any certainty of succeeding. But there was every indicator that André might be just as good as he was, and more ruthless. The man already knew Severin was at least a rival, and possibly an enemy, and he would be on his guard.

"Will we see you, sir?" asked André.

"Perhaps. If nothing else tempts me."

Severin watched André exit the taproom. He signaled for the potboy whom he had been paying ever since his arrival. Though his man of business was still missing, his wife was keeping his books and had advanced Severin funds.

"Make sure that the captain has left," he said, putting a coin in the boy's hand. "Follow him for at least four blocks—more if he does anything interesting. Then run straight back here to me."

It took all of Severin's self-control to wait for the boy's return. His impulse was to hasten directly to John Street and to Jenny. To save her and possibly to throttle her because he had never been so angry—or so terrified—in his life. Not even when the soldiers had come for his mother. He loved Jennifer Leighton, but right at that moment he hated her too. Hated her for putting herself in danger and himself . . . through *this*.

The boy returned to Severin's table.

"I followed him to the Golden Ball. He came out with Butcher Caide and another big man, and they went to the Battery. They didn't come out."

He had a little time. Enough, he hoped, to intercept her. He paid the boy off and collected his sword and the two pistols he had bought at a vendue sale, along with his lock picks and his knives, and he set out for John Street.

Dusk was coming on by the time he arrived, and he found the house much changed. No firing glasses lined the stoop; no discarded clothing fluttered in the breeze. The door was opened by a servant—the maid whose appearance had served as Jenny's model for her disguise the night she had met him at Vauxhall and they had made love for the first time.

The ground-floor parlors were no longer outfitted for late-night parties. The card tables were demurely shut and pushed up under pier glasses, the damask chairs fitted with ticking covers, one whole side of the great double parlor dominated by a simple table with two chairs and two distinct work spaces.

He observed all this in passing, because once he gave his name, the maid showed him up to the little parlor where, months earlier, he had not so happily been reunited with Angela Ferrers. This evening found Frances Leighton in the same chair the Widow had occupied on that occasion. Devere did not wait upon formalities.

"Where is Jenny?" he asked without preamble.

"Not at home," she replied brightly. "Shall I tell her you called?"

"I need to find her, Frances. She's in danger. You both are. Captain André wants the Merry Widow's accomplice. He wants *you*. And he wishes to trade me Cornelia for your name. He knows she will be at this blasted play tonight, and he has Caide's dragoons ready to storm the place and take her."

Frances Leighton paled. "She has already left."

"Where precisely does this performance take place?"

"In canvas town. There used to be a Dutch church on Lumber Street. They play in the ruins."

Devere cursed. He knew the church, knew the street. It had been a poor but respectable enough enclave before the fire. Now it was a rabbit warren of tipple shops and makeshift brothels, with dirty sails stretched across the rotting carcasses of the burnt houses where once secure families now struggled to eke out a living amongst the squalor. Caide's dragoons would not care. They would decimate the place if ordered to it, and gladly.

"I am going to get her out of there, Frances. I am going to bring her here, and then you are both going to pack your belongings and come with me."

"Where can we possibly go, Devere?" asked Frances Leighton. "New Brunswick isn't safe for us. Howe plans to drive down into the Jerseys next month."

"I have family in Connecticut," he said.

She raised a plucked eyebrow. "Do you, now?"

"Don't pretend to understand me or my family, Fanny. You have no idea how few choices we had. It is not always so very easy to do what is right."

She gave him a sad little smile. "It is never easy," she said. "Go and get Jenny. I will pack."

"You mustn't tell Fairchild where you are going," he said. "It would place him in an impossible position."

"No, it won't," said Frances Leighton. "He has scant regard for what others think of him. Private honor is more important to him than public reputation."

And, like that, Severin knew how this woman understood his old friend. Courtney was nothing like his sister, Phippa, or indeed like others of his class and country. God grant that Courtney's uncommon nature might bring him more happiness than had Phippa's conventional turn of mind.

"For what it's worth, I'm sorry."

She acknowledged him with a regal nod of her

head. He left her to pack her things and slipped out the back door, just in case anyone had followed him.

The old Dutch church on Lumber Street had been built of local stone, but that had not saved it from the ferocity of the fire. The curved eaves were gone, burned away along with the gambrel roof and the cupola, so that only a low box of charred stone remained. The gothic window arches were covered in sail canvas that glowed warmly from the lights within, and the curving nave was roofed in more of the same.

If he had not known this was New York, he might have guessed he was on the outskirts of Rome or Naples, such was the ruined atmosphere of the place. Until he saw a flash of movement, the glint of steel at the end of the street—Caide's dragoons, keeping out of sight until André was certain their prey was inside the trap.

If Jenny was here, he was going to have a hell of a time getting her out.

For all of the squalor, the old church was unmistakably a theater tonight, marked as such by the presence of the orange sellers and whores—some of them far, far too young—plying their wares to men and women dressed in silk and lace. A brewer's cart was parked in the alley alongside, kegs tapped and beer flowing, while across the street at a plank-bench-fronted stall, a tot of throat-burning rum could be had at half the price with twice the effect.

Inside the church was an empty shell, benches, pulpit, and sounding board all burned away, only black soot to mark where they had once stood. Someone had piled bricks and laid timbers across them to make seating for the pit, and scaffolding to create a primitive gallery, and at the nave end palettes were stacked on barrels to form a stage. Candles had been set into crevices in the stone with mad abandon, but any hazard of fire was of little moment because there was almost nothing left to burn.

Severin pulled his cloak close about him—he doubted his scarlet regimentals would be welcome here—and scanned the crowd in the uncertain light. He could not fault André's intelligence. There were at least five hundred people jammed into the ruined church, and half a dozen recognizable faces: sons of prominent Tories, some of them stupid enough to bring ladies with them. The players were mostly students, which was to be expected. Professional theater had always faced opposition in America, but college theatricals were tolerated, and at some institutions encouraged as excellent rhetorical training for the pulpit and public life. Scholars, of course, were naturally inclined to radicalism, forever in bed with that engine of sedition, the press. And because there were so many students here, there was open recruiting for the Continentals going on in one corner, while elsewhere pretty young demireps shimmied their way through the rows, pretending to look for seats, and finding them in the laps of gentlemen with coin.

Severin had chosen an end seat so as to be able to make a quick exit with Jenny as soon as he spied her. He turned toward the aisle to avoid a prostitute making her way toward him, but the determined little tart anticipated his move, pretended to trip so she could land in his lap.

He caught her and before he could set the harlot on her feet, irritation turned to shock, because the handful of *doxy* in his grasp proved to be no doxy at all, but Jennifer Leighton. And she was playing her part to perfection. Her gown—very nicely fitted to bosom and backside—was threadbare silk in a huge plum damask pattern twenty years out-of-date, pinned over a gaudy pearl-crusted stomacher of an even older vintage. She was wearing paint, expertly applied, lips ruby red and cheeks blooming roses, and her hair was powdered gray to complement the gown. If he had not wanted to kill her right at this moment, he would have found the impersonation both amusing and impressive . . . and not a little stirring.

She grasped his shoulders for balance—when she had never truly lost hers—and whispered in his ear like a harlot promising pleasures. Even though her words were anything but seductive, his body responded to the press of her curves against his flesh.

"What are you doing here, Devere?"

"Taking *you* home," he said.

"I can't leave yet." She tried to slide out of his arms, but he held her fast and spoke quietly in her ear.

"André knows that 'Cornelia' is here tonight. He has a troop of dragoons closing in even now to capture him. And a torturer named Dyson standing by to interrogate him—to interrogate *you*—before you hang in the morning."

Nineteen

Severin Devere was not a man given to exaggeration. Jenny knew that. The fact that he was here, tense and coiled with fear—fear *for her*—meant that the danger was very real. But that did not make it any easier to leave.

The actor declaiming the prologue already had the greater part of the audience in his spell. In another moment Jenny would hear the opening lines of the first act spoken aloud, see her clandestine work brought to life.

"A few minutes more," Jenny said. "Just one scene. It may be my only chance to see it staged."

"There will be other nights, other plays," said Devere. "To which we will not be inviting dragoons."

Devere rose and urged her toward the entrance. Jenny took one last look at the stage, heard the final line of her prologue, and felt the applause wash over her. It, and her own short brush with triumph, were cut short by a scream, followed hard by a shout.

The crowd surged around them. Dragoons in scarlet burst through the door. The spectators in the scaffolding panicked, and the structure swayed left, then right, and then with dreamlike slowness began to collapse.

"This way," said Severin, turning her roughly around and forcing a path through the crush of people.

She heard the roar of the scaffolding folding in on itself behind them. "There's no way out behind the stage," she said.

He ignored her, dragging her past the makeshift platform and drawing his sword. He slashed at the canvas covering the nave window, two quick cuts, and then he had leapt onto the sooty stone sill and was reaching for her. She hitched her skirts to follow, their escape hidden by the barrels and the palettes and painted sail that had been hung to serve as a backdrop.

They emerged in a sad little walled cemetery: tents pitched now over worn tombstones, a woman sleeping with her infant curled to her breast and her head atop a child's burial marker. There was only one way out, a garden gate that opened on a fetid alley. Devere led her out through the graves, all the while looking back at the church for signs of pursuit. Nothing behind them, for the moment, but sound and fury.

The alleyway was long and dark and stretched ahead of them unbroken for fifty feet, the charred brick walls of roofless warehouses rising two jagged stories on both sides. At the end where the alley met another passage, a man was standing with his head pressed to the wall. Moonlight glinted off his silver buttons and frosted his fine wig and the lace on his coat. As they drew near Jenny could hear him moaning, and for a second she thought he might be injured—until she saw the shape kneeling at his feet: a woman, shoulders and head pressed to the brick, servicing him with her mouth.

Devere maneuvered them around the harlot and her patron, and Jenny saw that the alley led in only one direction: back to Lumber Street, where chaos reigned. Dragoons were lining up the students—with brutal efficiency—forcing them to kneel at bayonet point.

"We must go back," said Devere, "and try to hide in the cemetery, or scale the opposite wall."

The wall had not looked scalable. Shouting erupted from that direction and Jenny heard boots flying over cobbles and the unmistakable jangle of bayonets and cartridge boxes.

Devere heard it too. He spared a quick glance at the couple in the alley and then turned to survey the violence in Lumber Street. They could not possibly escape in that direction, and now there was no retreat.

"Trust me," he said, grabbing her hand and dragging her *toward* the chaos. He stopped abruptly ten yards short of the alley opening. He threw back his cloak to expose his scarlet regimentals, pushed Jenny up roughly against the wall, bricks biting into her back. He tossed up her petticoats. The sooty hem smacked her face. Coarse wool scraped her bare knees, and then—without overture or preliminaries—he entered her.

She was too shocked to cry out at the sudden invasion. It pinched and chafed and her eyes watered and she was caught there, mouth open, gasping like a fish on a hook. The dragoons crashed around the corner, and the harlot on her knees gagged and cried out, and the man snarled. Jenny tried—uselessly—to push Devere away, but he had her fast in his grip.

"Who goes there?" came a young voice, barely broken but surly with new authority.

Torchlight burned away the darkness, and Jenny could see Devere's face, a mask of boredom and callous indifference. His eyes were cold, his lips curled into a smirk, his body held away from her so that they only joined where it served his pleasure.

A performance. She knew it, but her body's reaction to him was all too real. It warmed to him, to *this*, with a liquid loosening that, in truth, shocked her even more than his initial penetration.

Devere felt it too, she felt certain—growling huskily as she slid down the length of him until she was well and truly impaled. When he turned his face to the boy in the bearskin helmet, she did not know if Devere's anger was feigned or real, but his voice dripped disdain and promised retribution. "I am a little busy, just at present, for introductions, *cornet*."

The young officer's eyes found the epaulet on Devere's shoulder, heavy with bullion, and took in the fine gold lacings on his coat.

"I am very sorry, sir," he said. He took a step back, then stopped and looked at Jenny.

Her heart pounded in her ears. The slickness between their bodies increased, and she was exquisitely conscious of Devere's member, thick and stirring, within her. Fear, apparently, worked its own devices on the body.

"I regret the interruption," said the cornet, screwing up his courage, "but I must ask. That is, General Howe has been quite explicit. We are not to *interfere* with the locals. That is, I am obliged to ask if the lady is willing."

"If there were a *lady* in this alley, perhaps you would be obliged to ask, but there is not," said Devere.

The young officer was very near to giving up, but he persisted. "Madam," he said, at the risk, no doubt, if Devere was what he seemed, of his career, "are you quite well?"

"I am. Yes," she managed to gasp out, not certain if she was anything of the kind.

The ensign's expression was dubious, but he was in no position to do anything gallant, so he said, "Very well, then. Good night, sir."

He retreated back up the alleyway toward the church, and she was alone with Severin Devere.

He pressed his forehead to hers. "We must wait until they are gone." He was standing absolutely still now, his whole body trembling with the effort of it. She took his face in her hands and lifted it, brushed her lips against his.

"Don't," he said.

His hips flexed involuntarily. She licked his mouth, her tongue tasting salt. His hips moved again. His eyes met hers. "Jenny," he warned.

"Don't stop," she said.

He didn't.

Devere obliged her. They ended in a tangle of limbs and garments, of silk and cotton and wool snagged on the brick of the alley and snarled in the pearls crusted on her stomacher and bunched around the weapons that hung at his waist.

They stood like that, foreheads pressed together,

hearts still racing, for a long moment, and then he realized what they had done.

"I am sorry," he said, sounding louder than he'd intended. Quiet had fallen all around them, only a few drunks moaning and, here and there, a woman sobbing in the aftermath of the raid.

"You have nothing to apologize for. I wanted that. Insisted upon it, if I recall correctly."

"I was imprudent," said Severin. "We used no sheaths. There could be consequences."

"They seem remote at the moment," said Jenny. The flush on her cheeks and the dazed smile on her lips appealed deeply to his masculine pride, but there was more at stake here.

"You are safe from Venus' curses with me," he said. "I have always been careful. This, in truth, is my first lapse. If you fell pregnant, we would marry." It sounded grudging. He had not intended it to. He tried again. "I mean to say we ought to marry, generally, and be done with potting sheds and dank alleys."

"I rather enjoyed the potting shed," she said, the smile still playing around her lips.

"So did I. All the more reason we should marry. We are well matched, Jenny, in so many ways. And there is nothing to stop us making a life together, one of our choosing, if we leave tonight, and quickly. Frances understands. She is already packing."

"I wish," said Jenny, "that I could say it did not require a troop of dragoons to convince me, but evidently it did. You are right, and I am ready to go."

He felt a wave—almost physical—of relief. They had cheated the dragoons and John André, and they were going to escape. In two days' time, they would be in Lebanon, safe, with his family.

They picked their way cautiously back to John Street, hand in hand, though Devere kept his other at his sword hilt the whole way. When they reached the house, Jenny looked up at the lighted windows and said, "Do you imagine we will ever be able to come back?"

"Of course," he lied.

"Where will we go now?"

"I have family in Connecticut. They will welcome you."

"And Aunt Frances?"

"Will be more than welcome as well. And you may write to your heart's content there."

Inside they found Frances burning papers.

"I have laid a choice of things out for you on your bed," said the Divine Fanny, with the practicality of a Roman matron. "Along with a satchel. I believe Mr. Devere would tell you to pack only what you think you can carry and burn anything that might be incriminating in the event we should be caught."

"Though I'm meant to have offered it myself, that is very sound advice," remarked Devere. "Where is Fairchild?"

"He was called away to the Battery," said Fanny. "For the best, I think. He might have tried to stop me, or been mad enough to want to come with us. I have written him a farewell. We should make haste to leave before he receives it and comes charging back here."

She didn't tell him she was leaving. The news, lightly spoken, somehow made Severin as sad as it did relieved.

"I will get my things," said Jenny.

Devere followed her up the stairs. The last time he had visited the house he had not ventured above the second floor. Indeed, he'd been given opium, a tour of the John Street basement, and the beating of his life, but he could not fault Frances Leighton for loyalty to her friends—or Jenny for loyalty to this woman who had rescued her from a life of domestic business, shut away from the world's acquaintance.

The woman he loved wasted no time gathering her belongings. She pried up a board in the floor and removed a sheaf of papers.

"Works in progress," she explained. "I shall put them on the fire downstairs."

"Give them to me. I will carry them," he said, "and destroy them if needs must."

"No," she said. "I won't endanger you or Aunt Frances by traveling with these. I will start afresh in Connecticut."

There was no vanity in her either. The clothes she packed were practical and suitable for traveling. He had only a few minutes to take in the narrow room that was so intimately hers—a circumstance he regretted, but there would be other rooms. Rooms that they would make their own together.

The tiny garret's windows were open to the night air, and a street away he could hear booted feet on cobbles and the jingle of spurs, moving fast. It was the habit of a lifetime to keep careful track of his surroundings, to be always alive to opportunities and alert to danger. In a moment the sounds would fade into the distance, or boots and spurs would clash louder with approach, and arrival. Breath held, he listened and—breaking another habit of mind—allowed himself a silent prayer.

It went unheard, or perhaps this was its answer. The footfalls grew louder; the spurs were joined by raised voices; there were shouts in the street and the sound, unmistakable, of the door being broken down.

It was louder than a stage effect, the thunderclap of the door exploding below, the thud of feet on the stairs, and yet it all felt curiously like a bit of theater to Jenny when Aunt Frances' voice drifted up the stairs: musical and aristocratic, as though she had been expecting a troop of dragoons, and was simply delighted to see them.

Devere looked calm. That reassured her. Somewhat.

"The papers," he said.

He was right. She dropped to her knees and stuffed them back beneath the floorboards.

"Everything will be all right, Jenny," he said. She didn't believe him, but she nodded and smoothed the little woven rug and then her skirts back into place.

Just in time. A bearskin hat came into view on the stairs, and then the dragoon who wore it—a tall, raw-boned man who had to hunch his shoulders on the narrow landing—offered Severin a cursory salute and led them downstairs.

The little parlor door was open. The furnishings seemed small with so many men crowded into the room. Two dragoons flanked each window, and John André stood just inside the threshold.

Jenny had not been able to see it before—the ruthless intelligencer behind the charming dilettante—but she could see it now. André had abandoned his martial finery, all the bullion and silver lace, for a field uniform of rugged wool and tough linen, but it was more than a matter of dress. It was the way he held himself, like an actor who has just come offstage and only a moment before shed the part he had been playing.

Aunt Frances was seated in her frayed easy chair, draped in blue silk turquerie and striking the attitude for which she was so famous: the Divine Fanny as Tragic Muse. Astonishingly, she looked smug. As though the troop of dragoons investing her home did not worry her in the least. Jenny did not think that her aunt could divert Captain André as she had the young Continental at the John Street doors—by fainting—but a slender hope took root in her heart that Aunt Frances had some trick up her sleeve.

John André appeared surprised by Fanny's poise. "In truth," he said, "I did not expect such a gracious welcome from a friend of the Widow."

"That is because you are so very young," replied Frances Leighton, "and can only imagine a limited number of outcomes for this interview. How old are you? Twenty-three?"

"Twenty-five," he said, scrutinizing her. The condescension chafed him. Jenny could see that much.

"Get out, André," said Severin Devere. "And take your damned dragoons with you. There's no proof that Frances Leighton is even acquainted with the Widow."

"No," said André smoothly. "There is no compelling proof. What of it? That is why men like you and I exist. To act where the evidence would never hold up in a court of law. Former royal mistresses, of course, are a delicate matter, though, and I could not rely on Mr. Hallam's information alone."

"Bobby wants the John Street back," said Jenny. "He would say anything to secure it."

"Indeed," replied André, looking at Jenny and taking in her dishabille, the ancient pearl-crusted stomacher, the brick-stained silk of her petticoats. His smirk told her that he knew exactly what she had been doing an hour ago. "That is why I could not act on his testimony. I needed additional confirmation, and Colonel Devere provided it tonight, when he raced *here* after our dinner." He turned to Aunt Fanny. "If it is any consolation in what is about to happen, I am a great admirer of your gifts."

She raised an eyebrow, but did not stir from her chair. Fanny wore the calm smile of a medieval effigy. Jenny wondered at—and took heart from—her immaculate composure. "I am sorry to disappoint you, Captain," drawled Frances Leighton, "but there is nothing you can do now that will induce me to speak of my friend. I am quite beyond your reach."

Jenny felt Devere stiffen beside her, but she did not know why.

André's expression darkened. He crossed the room and stood in front of Aunt Frances' little card table. There was a blue glass vial on the polished surface that Jenny had not noticed before. The captain reached for it, then stopped himself. He plucked a handkerchief from his pocket and wrapped it twice around his hand before gingerly picking up the tiny bottle. He sniffed it cautiously, then set it back on the table, staring at Frances Leighton with a mixture of profound disappointment and admiration.

"And now we understand each other," said the

Divine Fanny to the splendid young man, a triumphant smile transforming her handsome face.

It was the performance of a lifetime, and every player's favorite part: the death scene. Jenny's chest constricted. She coveted the cautious hopefulness, the blissful ignorance she had known just moments before. She wanted to go back. She wanted the possibilities, the future, that had been alive the last time they had stood in this room. She wanted to deny what was plain before her, but the expression on André's face, the little bottle on the table, the pressure of Devere's hand upon her shoulder, all confirmed all her fears.

John André nodded and the world turned upside down for Jenny. It was more than an acknowledgment. It was a gesture of defeat. Aunt Frances had outmatched him. Jenny knew where the little bottle had come from: Fanny's chest of "medicines."

The Sweetheart of Drury Lane had taken poison.

"No," said Jenny. "Not now. Not this way."

"I am sorry, my dear," said the woman, who had freed her from a life of domestic devotion and brought her to New York to make the world's acquaintance, "but we have had a very good run here together, you and I. That is all any player asks, Jenny, and more than I dared hope for when I took ship for America."

"No." Jenny would not accept it. "There is ipecac in your medicine chest. You said you kept it in case anyone was poisoned." She made for the box in the corner where Fanny kept her cures.

André stepped in front of her, blocking her path, his expression sober. He shook his head. "Ipecac will not answer, Miss Leighton. This particular tincture cannot be readily expelled, or counteracted." He turned to face Frances and said quite softly, "It is very rare."

"It is," Fanny agreed, as though they were discussing a bottle of Madeira. "I was saving it for a special occasion."

"I am honored, then," said André.

"Angela procured it for me," she explained, "for Harry, when the pain became too much for him. We were going to take it together, and go out like Romeo and Juliet, but there was Jenny to think of. He never met you, my dear," said Frances, looking straight ahead, her eyes too dilated to see. "But you were our daughter in spirit, if not in flesh, and we decided together that I should remain in the world a little longer to see that you had the opportunities you deserved."

Jenny choked on a sob. She looked up at John André, still blocking her path.

"Get out of her way, John," said Devere, behind her, in a voice that threatened violence.

André did not move immediately. He glanced around the room, as though confirming guards and exits, calculating. "It makes no matter now," he said, finally, and stepped lightly aside.

But, impediment removed, Jenny did not know what to do. Frances was sitting so stiffly, staring so blindly, that she was almost afraid to touch her. Jenny knelt before her aunt's chair and took the slender hands in hers. They were cold and trembling now, white as paper, chill as snow.

There was so little time, and so much to say. "I am glad you returned for me," said Jenny, stifling her urge to sob. "If you had not come, I would still be in New Bumpkin." The familiar nickname, their shared joke, the thought of the dull gray life she might have had there broke her resolve, and the tears came, splashing over Fanny's cold ringed fingers.

"What the devil is going on?"

Fairchild had entered unannounced, unnoticed by anyone other than the watchful dragoons. Jenny looked at him through eyes blurred with tears. He was disheveled from hard riding and glared at André with something close to murder in his eyes. "What are you doing in my house?"

"My job, Major," said André, without inflection.

"On whose authority?"

Their voices dwindled like buzzing flies, small and unimportant. Fanny's cold hands went boneless, her chest ceased to respire, and the quiet she left behind became deafening.

Frances Leighton, who had crossed an ocean to free the words in Jenny, had slipped silent from the world.

Devere could not grieve for Frances Leighton, but he did grieve for Jenny and Fairchild, who stood stranded in the middle of the room, gaping at his dead lover.

"Leave the body," said André. "Search the house. Now. And take the girl to Dyson."

Two dragoons grasped Jenny by the arms and hauled her to her feet. Her face was tear streaked. She looked bewildered. "Severin?" she said, her voice desolate and full of confusion.

Devere stepped forward. "What is the meaning of this, *Captain*?"

"Come, now, Colonel. We had a bargain, you and I. I

was willing to let you have 'Cornelia' if you gave me Frances Leighton. Now Frances Leighton is dead, and I have only the little playwright. And I must have *something*."

"What makes you imagine Jenny is Cornelia?"

André produced a sheaf of papers from his pocket. With sinking heart, Devere recognized them for what they were: the contents of his missing chest.

"I have had this in my possession since December. Proof enough to hang her publicly," said André. "But Howe will prefer to do it quietly, out of sight, aboard the *Jersey*. And she must be questioned before she goes to the noose. It is possible she will divulge what her aunt did not. I am not heartless, Devere. I know you've been fucking her. Dyson will handle any . . . *unpleasantness*. You need not see any of it."

"You will not touch her." He could feel Jenny behind him, her hand in his, trembling.

"Take her," said André to the dragoons. "And restrain the colonel if he tries to stop you."

Severin knew that he could not be in two places at once. He needed to speak to Howe, but he could not let them take Jenny to Dyson.

"*Courtney*," said Severin. "You must go with her."

Fairchild looked up, his face a mask of grief, his wits disordered.

Devere spoke slowly and clearly. "You must go to the Middle Dutch Church with Jenny, old friend. See that Caide's people do not lay a hand on her until I can speak with General Howe."

Courtney looked at John André and the dragoons and then Jenny, then back to André. "You killed her," he said coldly, his mind still fixed on Frances Leighton.

"Please, Major," said Jenny, the panic rising in her

voice. "I very much fear what will happen if you do not come with us."

Courtney blinked, seeming finally to see her—to recognize her. Then he nodded and stood up. He took his coat off and wrapped it around Jenny, then looked at Severin and said, "What will become of my Frances?"

"I will make sure that she is cared for," said Devere. He turned to Jenny. "Don't be afraid. No one is going to hurt you."

"You are only making this harder for everyone, Colonel Devere," said André when Courtney and the dragoons and Jenny had gone. "Better to get the business over with quickly so the girl suffers as little as possible."

Devere didn't answer him. He lifted the body of Jenny's aunt from the chair and laid her carefully on the chaise opposite, closing her sightless eyes and covering her face with the silk robe that was hung on the back of the door. He did not think the Widow whom Frances had died to protect was worth the sacrifice, but there was no denying that the Divine Fanny had lived boldly and loved fearlessly, and up to the very last had made her own choices.

The meeting with General Sir William Howe took place in the wee hours of the morning because Devere knew that Jenny's life hung in the balance. Gerardus Beekman's mansion overlooking Turtle Bay and the East River had been built less than twenty years earlier in a consciously old-fashioned Dutch style. It sported the distinctive hipped roof and curled eaves found now only on the most antique buildings in New Amsterdam. The manse was as ludicrous an affectation as Ben

Franklin raising money at the Court of Versailles in his coonskin cap, and it did not strike Devere as charming or "eccentric" at all.

The carriage he shared in strained silence with John André traveled through an elaborate garden, past a greenhouse, and under the tree where Howe had hung an American spy last September—a spy whose people had at least *tried* to trade him back, unlike Devere's. Neither he nor André remarked upon it.

Inside the manse all trace of rustic simplicity vanished. The staircase was wide enough for four to walk abreast, the banisters elaborately carved in three variations. The parlors were proportioned on a grand scale and fitted up with French pastoral wallpapers—all winsome beauties on swings and riverbanks, being courted by ardent swains. Devere could not look at them without thinking of Jenny in the custody of Caide's dragoons with only Fairchild to protect her, while he stood here, beneath molded plaster ceilings in a room appointed with marble columns and Dutch-tiled fireplaces, waiting to bargain for her life.

And he had nothing—absolutely nothing—to trade.

Sir William Howe entered wearing a cotton banyan and a sleeping cap, his reluctance to take this interview plain on his face. Severin had never been able to see it before, but the general did not like dealing with men like him, or men like André. Devere supposed he'd prefer—really—that men like them didn't exist at all. Billy Howe thought of himself as on the whole honorable. A conscientious member of Parliament, a loving brother, a devoted husband—at least according to his own lights.

There was a noise in the hall. Devere did not need

to look up to know to whom the gentle tread upon the stairs belonged: Elizabeth Loring—the Sultana of Boston, Howe's mistress—reputed to be the most beautiful woman in North America, known equally well for her extravagance in dress as her passion for the gaming table. Her husband had been appointed to the lucrative post of commissioner of prisoners by Howe, evidently for his ability to sleep soundly through the night. The heart-shaped face made an appearance in the doorway, still bearing traces of fine cosmetics. She exchanged a sleepy smile with her lover, but when her eyes lighted on Captain André, her expression turned frosty and she retreated up the stairs.

The general spared a wistful glance at her departing form, its curves arresting in a light fitted banyan of her own. He returned to the business at hand without enthusiasm.

"The girl is guilty. Devere cannot dispute that," said André, laying his evidence—Jenny's letters and manuscripts—on the table before the general.

"I don't dispute it," said Devere smoothly. "I have known as much for months."

"And done nothing," said André, "because you were fucking her."

"And done nothing," said Devere, "because she was Burgoyne's mistress."

It was the second time that night that John André had been caught off his guard. He recovered nicely on this occasion. "And you were just keeping her warm for the general, were you?"

Devere shrugged. "I may have acted imprudently, but she was so very angry at General Burgoyne for not summoning her north, it seemed a shame to forgo the pleasure. Regardless, surely that is between myself and John Burgoyne. Let us not confuse the matter. The point is that you cannot interrogate and hang a general's mistress."

He saw Captain André's smile fade. Devere did not need to elaborate. He had been doing this longer than André and he was better at it. His calling was more than the collection of secrets and the peddling of lies. It was the weighing of men—and women. The careful analysis of character. It allowed a skillful practitioner to make guesses that came very close to divination.

Howe knew, as did Lord Germain at home and most of Parliament as well, that there was no love lost between the three commanders serving now in North America. He, Burgoyne, and Clinton disliked one another intensely. They disagreed on every point of strategy, and each thought he should have been appointed above the other two—or, in the case of Howe, whose seniority was not in question, that he should have been given the resources squandered on Burgoyne's bold scheme to take Albany.

And all three men now gathered in the ludicrously rich room, with its wool carpets and damask chairs and soaring ceilings, knew also that Howe had no intention of supporting Burgoyne this summer, of marching north into the forests of New York to capture what he firmly believed were worthless outposts in the trackless wilderness. Not with Philadelphia, and the Rebel government, within reach.

It was one thing, though, to disagree with a fellow commander, to make a tactical decision not to reinforce him and instead march your army south to capture the capital, arrest Congress, and end the war in one fell swoop. It was another to do so after hanging the man's mistress.

"I disagree," said André. "You cannot interrogate and hang a general's mistress *publicly*. Done quietly, no one will be the wiser, not even Burgoyne."

"If nothing else," said Severin Devere, with a pointed look at the door where the beautiful Elizabeth Loring had stood only moments before, "that would set a terrible precedent."

Howe looked Devere in the eyes, but it was John André to whom he spoke. "I thank you for your diligence, Captain," he said. "But Colonel Devere is the more experienced in these matters, and I believe his judgment to be correct."

It meant that Severin had guessed right. André had told him that he had identified one of the Widow's associates, a person—a woman, as it turned out—who was too well placed to touch. Howe could not hang Burgoyne's mistress lest someone press to hang his own. And he was too sentimental, too honorable, to shoulder that risk. Now the trick was getting Jenny well away before Burgoyne disclaimed her.

"Only," said André, unwilling to surrender the field, "if she *really is* General Burgoyne's mistress, and not just the colonel's doxy. You can hardly keep her pent up in the Sugar House for months until we find out."

"What do you propose?" Howe asked.

"General Burgoyne has asked for field pieces and men to replace those he has lost. Send the girl north with a small detachment and a few guns. A single understrength company should suffice. The gesture will defray any criticism that you have failed to support Burgoyne's Albany campaign, and if the girl is indeed his mistress, he can decide what to do with her. And if she is *not* . . . then Burgoyne can hang Cornelia out of sight of Tory society in New York, where her status as a popular actress would cast you in the part of the villain."

Now it was André who had struck a chord with Howe, who was already concerned for his reputation with the Americans, a people who had so loved his older brother they had paid for a monument to him in Westminster Abbey after his heroism in the French and Indian War. A people in which he himself found much to admire—beyond Sultana's obvious charms.

"Make the arrangements," said Howe.

"That means a three-hundred-mile journey over half-made roads for a girl who has been bred to town life," said Devere. And he could not rescue her from an entire company himself, understrength or not.

"If her safety concerns you, Colonel," said André, "then I suggest you go with her."

That would suit André, who was clearing the board for his own advancement. First Devere, then the inadequate but well-connected Stephen Kemble.

"And what will Burgoyne say when she turns up missing her fingernails?"

"What is this?" asked Howe sharply.

"André has given her to Caide's dragoons to play with in case she can tell them something useful, like the name of her printer. It's Rivington, by the way. There are easier ways to get a woman to talk than abusing her."

"Where is she now?" demanded Howe.

"At the Middle Dutch Church, where Caide has stabled his horses," said Devere, adding, "Lord Fairchild is with her. You may remember that he was a close friend of her aunt, who has just passed away, Frances Leighton."

André was wise enough to allow this to pass without comment. The general loved the theater, and his fondness for the Divine Fanny was well-known.

"That is sad news. My condolences to the major, and the girl. But she is to be sent to the Sugar House," said Howe. "And thence north. Captain André will make the arrangements. You are free to make the journey as well, Devere."

It was a reprieve, but it would only be death deferred if Devere could not think of something. Because once they reached Albany, Burgoyne would surely hang her.

Twenty

Jenny knew that the pain in her chest was grief, but it felt just like having the air knocked out of her lungs during the riot at John Street. Aunt Frances was gone.

Courtney Fairchild would let no one near her on the walk to the Middle Dutch Church, which smelled like a stable. Caide's dragoons were using it as both a barracks *and* a riding school. Because Fairchild would not leave Jenny's side—and since he was a lord and an officer on Howe's staff, they could not lock him in what amounted to a paddock—they instead locked them both in the vestry. But not before Jenny and Fairchild encountered a hulking junior officer with hooded eyes and a vicious smile. Dyson.

"What kind of a name is that?" Lieutenant Dyson asked, sounding altogether too interested. "Jennifer." He rolled it around on his tongue and Jenny felt icicles down her spine. "Is that Cornish?"

"It is *Miss Leighton* to you," said Courtney Fairchild.

"Just as you say," agreed Dyson. "*Milord.*"

Jenny did not like the way this man moved. Not clumsy or lumbering, as his size might warrant, but like a hunting cat stalking its prey. He circled Jenny and Fairchild, seemingly intimidated by neither her protector's rank nor title.

"Pretty hair too," he observed, his heavy-lidded regard unsettling. "What color would you say that was, Miss Leighton? Red, I'd say, or reddish." Dyson might have made a fine stage villain, or villain's lackey, but Jenny knew with sinking dread that this man had no range; he had in fact *become* the part.

He reached out to touch a lock of her hair. Jenny shrank back and Fairchild's hand shot out.

"Enough, Dyson." The officer who had entered the wrecked church was tall, fair haired with blue eyes, and remarkably handsome in a disheveled, louche sort of way—but Jenny did not like the look of him either. He now nodded to acknowledge Fairchild. "Courtney."

"Call your dog off, Caide," Courtney responded. "The girl is my mistress's niece, and I'll kill any man who lays a hand on her."

"Fair enough," said Colonel Sir Bayard Caide, although he did not seem to care very much one way or another. "*Understood.* I have no interest in the girl myself. André asked to borrow my barracks *and* my man Dyson, and I was happy to oblige. But I'm not partisan enough to meet anyone at dawn in a dispute over the details."

That was when Caide offered them the vestry and locked them in.

When they were alone, Jenny said, "I am so very

sorry for all of this. It is my fault. If I had never written to Burgoyne, she would still be here."

Fairchild's face, always so boyish, looked drawn, haunted. "Never apologize for your choices, or your ambition, Jenny. It is a quality you take from Frances. If you had not been talented and ambitious, she would never have come back to America for you, and she and I would never have met."

"What will you do now?" she asked.

"First, I will see you free of this place and settled as Frances would have wanted."

"Major Fairchild, I am guilty. I *am* Cornelia. André has irrefutable proof. I do not see how there is a way out for me."

"Severin Devere is resourceful. You've no idea. He will think of something."

It was a pleasant fantasy. She would pretend to believe it for now. "And then what will you do?" she asked.

"I shall call John André out, and I will kill him."

Devere did not return until morning, and although he put a brave face on it, she knew that her situation was dire. He accompanied a small detachment of redcoats sent to transfer her to more suitable accommodations. The man known as Butcher Caide was entirely indifferent to their departure, but she could feel Dyson's narrowed eyes on her back as she was marched out of the church, and she could hear him saying something crude about clarifying the "real" color of her hair.

They took her to the Sugar House, which had been fitted up as a Rebel prison, and here Devere counted out more guineas than Jenny had ever seen all in one place so that she might have a private cell, and that Fairchild might remain with her. Severin also promised to send Margaret to her.

"General Howe," he explained, "wants to send you north to Burgoyne."

"Why the devil would he do that?" asked Fairchild.

"Because he thinks she is his mistress."

"Why does he imagine that?" Jenny asked.

"Because *I* persuaded him of it. It is a necessary fiction. As long as Howe believes it, he dare not hang you. But I very much fear that Burgoyne *will*. We must make our escape en route. It will not be easy. They are sending us north with reinforcements for Jack Brag's Albany campaign. We will bide our time and seize the best opportunity that presents itself."

Devere saw her settled in the Sugar House. He wished he could stay longer, comfort her for the loss of her aunt, but time was short now.

Fairchild agreed to put off calling out John André to remain with Jenny. Severin knew he would have to take some more permanent measure to prevent that duel from ever happening—he did not like his friend's odds in such a contest—but he had a few calls to pay first.

Severin saw the wife of his man of business first, because money would be needed. Then he went to call upon James Rivington.

Two years earlier Isaac Sears and the Liberty Boys had stolen all of his type and run Rivington out of town. Severin had never ascertained whether the attack had been genuine—and Rivington a true Tory at the time— or a blind engineered by Washington to give credence to his printer's cover as a loyalist, but Rivington had come back and reopened his coffee shop as soon as Howe had entered the city, and was even now advertising that his new press would be available to print all manner of hand-bills, advertisements, and of course newspapers soon. He had not advertised that he was printing Rebel propa-ganda on a secret press in his basement.

The hour was early and the coffeehouse not yet open for business, but the door was unlocked and Sev-erin found the man himself behind the counter grind-ing beans.

"I have come to inquire about the printing of a pamphlet," said Severin.

"My new press has not yet arrived from England," said the dapper Rivington pleasantly. "I will begin tak-ing orders as soon as it is delivered."

"It is not your new press I am interested in," said Severin. "It's the one you used to print Jennifer Leigh-ton's *Braggart Soldier*."

Rivington's hand on the grinder stopped moving. He looked at Severin's scarlet regimentals and lied smoothly. "I'm afraid you must have me confused with another printer."

"I do not, sir. You are a double agent. You have been selling information to both sides for so long that few know, or particularly care, where your true allegiances lie. But I have been the purchaser, at second hand, of your wares in the past, and I will see you swing alongside Miss Jennifer Leighton if you do not do precisely as I ask."

Rivington considered and took off his apron. "What, *precisely*, do you want?"

"Information and aid. The girl has been arrested. She will be sent north to Burgoyne, who will hang her.

Your people got her into this mess. I want you to help me get her out."

"She knew the risks," said Rivington coldly. "And she was recompensed for them."

"Not nearly so generously as you were, though," said Devere. "What did Miss Leighton receive for her play? A penny on every pound you made? I wonder how much Washington *believes* she has been paid, and how much she really had of you. It can be a very profitable thing to have friends on both sides of a war, but a very dangerous one to have none at all."

"Your point is taken," said Rivington. "I will do what I can."

"I am glad we understand each other. You will find out everything about this expedition that there is to know. The number of men, the size and number of guns we will be carrying, the names of the officers and their financial circumstances, the route to be taken. And after you have reported to me, you will relay the same information to General Washington."

It took Rivington three days to gather the intelligence that Severin wanted, much of it gleaned from talk overheard in his coffeehouse.

"Howe," said the printer, "wants to be seen to be supporting General Burgoyne without actually diminishing his own resources for his drive into Philadelphia. He has scavenged five guns from his brother's ships, and if the navy did not want them you can be sure that they are not fit to fire. Neither does he want to part with a company of his soldiers—not even a company of Hessians—so he has thrown together a half-strength one of stragglers: men whose units were shattered at Bunker Hill and are too depleted to be re-formed. By sending these to Burgoyne, he saves the expense of their passage home. And he has taken the opportunity to empty his prisons as well. You will likely have thirty or forty men, a dozen of whom were set to be hanged for pillaging the inhabitants of New York. Thieves, murderers, and rapists."

"And the officers?"

"There is an engineer going north with the guns, but he drinks and is not fit to command a digging party. John André has handpicked a lieutenant who knows the terrain to lead your expedition. David Jones. A loyalist from Fort Edward. He was hounded from his home by Rebels and has lost all his property so will have no sympathy whatsoever for the girl. Jones walked all the way to Montreal to join up with a loyalist regiment. He desires a place on Burgoyne's staff, but he has a fiancée waiting for him in Fort Edward and, unfortunately, *she* has a brother who is an officer with the Continentals. So Jones has thus far found his path to advancement blocked. The girl, I'm told, is lively and from an honest family, and adjudged a great beauty in those parts on account of her uncommonly fine red hair."

Like Jenny's copper locks. They would be shorn before they hanged her so the hair did not foul the rope. The thought nearly made Severin ill, and also angry.

"I have drawn a map of what I surmise will be the route," continued Rivington. "The guns will slow you down and Jones will have to keep tight discipline with so many likely deserters in his company. His troubles will only increase once you leave the settled areas. The scrapings of Howe's army are all too likely to decamp into the wilderness. That will be your best opportunity."

"Copy it out and send it to Washington, and tell

him that we will be ready to take advantage of any aid he can furnish."

"And if no aid is forthcoming?"

"I suggest you be exceptionally persuasive," said Devere. "If Miss Leighton hangs, sir, I promise you one thing: that you will follow her to the gibbet shortly thereafter."

Jenny had never spent a whole week locked in one room. It took that long for the artillery and a company of foot to be organized. During the day Courtney remained with her in the Sugar House. At night Severin came and slept beside her on the bed in her cell. At all times there were six dragoons posted outside her door, courtesy of John André.

"Do you trust Rivington to deliver your message?" she asked.

"No. Not entirely. That is why I sent one to my uncle as well."

She did not ask how likely he thought it that Washington would exert himself, and expend his scant powder, to save her.

At the end of the week Lieutenant Jones called on them. He was much as Rivington had described: tall, dark haired, and humorless, a stolid frontiersman with shockingly weathered skin for his age. He was reluctant to meet Jenny's eyes, and there was a wary prickliness about him, the kind that picked-on children acquire, that assumes every whispered word to be a slight. It was difficult to imagine him engaged to some frontier beauty with titian hair, but Jenny supposed that the qualities valued in the forests of New York were different from those prized in the quiet lanes of New Brunswick.

Jones wore the uniform of a loyalist regiment unfamiliar to Jenny, ill-fitting and travel-stained cream and yellow wool. She knew from Devere that Jones had been loosely attached to Burgoyne's staff and had carried the general's dispatches south, and had been ordered to return with men and guns.

An outright refusal from Howe might not have reflected poorly on Jones. Returning with a half dozen rotting naval cannon—which would probably kill their crews when fired—and a small band of criminals and demoralized men who had lost most of their friends at Bunker Hill, most certainly would. In short, Lieutenant Jones was not a happy man, and Jenny's presence made him only more unhappy.

On the morning of their departure she was led out to the carts under guard and Jones ordered her shackled to one of the cannon.

Devere protested.

"I am not under your authority, Colonel," said Jones, without even a hint of sympathy. He pocketed the key to Jenny's irons. "I have been given a regrettable task and, frankly, dealt a very bad hand." He looked at the men, who appeared orderly enough for the moment, but sullen, and certainly no credit to the British army. "But I know my duty, sir. And my orders are plain. The girl will be chained to the guns at all times. And if she runs, she'll be shot."

Thirty-five men, three carts, a dozen horses, Jenny, and Devere started north on a bright June morning. Devere stayed close, walking alongside her cart, talking to her of the passing country, of trivial, pleasant things—speaking to her in lower tones whenever he was certain they would not be overheard.

At the Sugar House he had brought her new clothes

for the journey, two heavy linen petticoats and a jacket in dark brown cotton. "The colors will blend into the forest when we make our escape. There is scrip sewn into your jacket, coins spaced inside the hem of your skirt. I will carry weapons enough for the pair of us, once we have broken free. Keep a little food in your pockets at all times—in case we have to take our chances and leave our packs behind."

He was indeed carrying weapons enough for the two of them, but they were different from what he had armed himself with aboard the *Boyne* or what he had carried the night the dragoons had stormed the old Dutch church. He wore the regimental coat she despised, but this was over buckskin leggings and a simple linen shirt. He carried a single pistol, a long rifle, and two knives, including the quilled blade she had tucked in his pocket in the basement at John Street. But no sword: in its place hung a steel-and-hickory tomahawk.

In the Sugar House, lying in Severin's arms at night, feeling the strength of his body and his resolve, she had begun to believe they would be able to do it—to simply bide a while with their escort and then slip free. But then Lieutenant Jones had shackled her to the guns.

"It is a simple lock to pick," Devere had assured her in quiet tones when no one else could hear. "Jones will be on his guard at first, and the men will act disciplined enough for a time, but that will not last."

The first night they were able to break their march at an inn and Jones ordered Jenny chained in the cellar and set six men to guard her. Two of her keepers smirked at the prospect and Jenny felt sick with fear, but Devere brought her bedding from his pack and slept beside her through the night.

This proved a wise precaution. The second night they stopped at a farm, where Jones was forced to pay the farmer damages after two of his soldiers broke into the man's chicken coop and stole a hen and some eggs. The third night the company slept in a drafty barn, and there was nothing to steal. But on the fourth, they stopped at another inn, and there was almost a shooting— four of the redcoats intercepted the innkeeper's daughter on her way back from the necessary and her father had to cow the villains with a leveled fowling piece.

After that Devere rarely left Jenny's side, and made it very clear to the men who guarded her that any importunity would be answered. One ill-shaven, bandy-legged soldier nursed a sore jaw for days . . .

Lieutenant Jones, who could scarcely afford to pay off every inn keep and farmer between New York and Albany, did his best to maintain order, but as Devere had anticipated, he quickly gave up trying to prevent the petty thievery that was second nature to a full third of his men.

They were three weeks on the road, and Jenny knew that if help did not arrive soon, it would not be coming at all. Devere had been honest with her about that. They had discussed it, and they were resolved. If no aid came, he would have to take his chances over-powering Jenny's guards at night.

Six men were very bad odds. Jenny would need to distract them, and that meant taking desperate measures. If she lured two of them close, he might handle the rest, but she was shackled and would be able to do little if anything to defend herself when the duped men realized what she and Severin were about.

Neither of them was eager to put the plan into action, but it must be soon. A few days at most.

They were crossing a ford when rescue arrived, the water only knee-deep but the streambed slick and treacherous. Lieutenant Jones was wise enough to have the horses led across—indeed, was himself leading the pair of the gun cart Jenny rode—but the middle of a rocky stream was an impossible position to defend. Which was why, of course, the Rebels had chosen this spot for their attack.

Bullets struck the water, splashing like skipping stones all around her. The report of nearby rifles was almost deafening. Jenny put her head down, but, shackled to one of the guns, she could not scramble behind a cart for cover as the soldiers did.

Jones cried out, shot through the hand, blood pouring between his fingers. The horses reared and tore the reins from him. They whinnied and plunged toward the bank. The gun cart surged ahead, throwing Jenny against the running board. The vehicle struck a stone and she was hurled back onto the two guns laid side by side in the cart bed. The wheel broke and the bed tilted dangerously. The guns rolled, winding Jenny's chain like a capstan, and the heavy cannon burst through the side rail and plunged into the water, taking her with them.

She scrabbled to stay on top of the rolling guns lest her arms or legs be crushed between the barrels, but her gown became soaked instantly and weighed her down. She tried to raise her hands, but they were anchored to the cannon, and it was a struggle to keep her head above even the shallow water.

Then Devere was at her side, holding her up, searching frantically for the fastening of her shackles, lock picks in his hands.

"It is wedged between the guns," she said, taking deep breaths of air while she yet could. This was their chance. This was their rescue . . . and they were not going to make it.

"No," he said through clenched teeth. "There must be a way."

Ahead of them in the streambed Jones was barking orders and the company was regaining some order of discipline. His men lined up behind the carts and began to return fire. The shots from the tree line slowed, then stopped, and the attack was over.

Severin was still in the water at Jenny's side, struggling to get her free, when silence fell. Lieutenant Jones splashed through the stream—mouth set in a grim line and stricken hand a bloody mess—to regard Jenny and the guns with stony resignation.

In the chaos of the fight, four men had been killed, three injured, and six gone missing—deserted, no doubt. And more would have been lost if Jones had not been an experienced frontiersman, used to fighting over rough terrain and accustomed to ambushes. It took a dozen of the remaining soldiers to shift the guns and free Jenny. The additional weight on the two intact carts slowed their progress to a crawl, but Jones insisted that they press on through the moonlit night to the next hamlet marked on his map. He ordered one of his injured men to ride in the cart with Jenny and announced quite loudly that, if they were attacked again, she was to be shot.

The men's faces—illuminated in the shifting light of the moon and guttering torches or half shrouded in shadow—were taut and wary. But no further attack came.

It was dawn when they reached the inn, if it could be called that, a roadhouse with a few outbuildings. Jones ordered Jenny locked in a shed under guard. She was soaked and exhausted. Devere wanted her in a room with a bed and a hot meal because they must take their chances and break out tonight or never, but Jones would not stand for it.

The loyalist lieutenant had Severin marched into the inn at gunpoint and shown into a tiny chamber with barely space for the breakfast table. He took the seat opposite the grim-faced officer. He heard two soldiers taking up a guard position just on the other side of the door.

"I am not a fool, Colonel," said Jones. "I lost ten men and two horses out there, and the other two carts were practically shot to pieces, but there was not so much as a scratch on Miss Leighton's vehicle. The Rebels were here for her."

Severin did not deny it. "General Burgoyne sent you south for guns and men. You have them. The girl jeopardizes your real mission. You started with more than thirty men. Now you have barely twenty. If the Rebels attack again, you will lose more men and quite possibly the guns. Is one girl really worth all that?"

"The Rebels seem to think so," observed Jones.

"Perhaps because they don't like the idea of seeing an innocent young woman hanged."

The other man shrugged. "My understanding is that *you* contend she is Burgoyne's mistress. If that's true, sir, he's hardly likely to hang her. Your worries seem to be misplaced. Assuming she is something *else*, then I am content to let justice take its course."

"This is not justice, Lieutenant Jones. It is the injured pride of powerful men. The same sort who block your path to promotion because they despise Americans. Your Rebel fiancée is merely a convenient excuse for their prejudice."

"Prejudice that will be overcome, Colonel, when I prove myself a loyal subject. An officer who knows his *duty*."

"And what of your duty to the young woman you plan to marry? I understand your Rebel neighbors have confiscated your family's land, and a lieutenant's pay is hardly sufficient to keep a wife."

"I am insulted that you would think to bribe me."

"Do not speak to me of honor, sir, when you are about to deliver to the hangman a woman whose only crime was *writing a play*, and all this just to serve your own ambition."

"I did not ask for this assignment," said Jones, shoulders slumping slightly. "I would have you know it is exceedingly distasteful to me. My fiancée's name is also Jenny. Her hair is redder than Miss Leighton's, but they are of an age and in all other respects might be taken for sisters. If I had any other choice, I would set her free, but Captain André foresaw that the Rebels might try to rescue her, and his instructions—General Howe's instructions—in that eventuality were quite explicit. I am very sorry."

It was the way he said it, and the presence of the guards just beyond the door. And, now, the guilty tick in Jones' left eye.

"*What* have you done?"

Jones' hand edged toward his pistol. "I did what was necessary."

"Where is she?"

"It is too late, Colonel Devere. Two men took her

to the stream. They will bury her there, and it will be said that she took ill on the march. That she succumbed to a fever."

Severin bowed his head.

"I *am* sorry," repeated Jones.

Severin wasn't sorry. He wasn't angry either. He was cold inside. *Never* had anything been more necessary than this. Jones was on his guard, but Severin had the advantage of initiative, and of having spent half a lifetime killing not just animals but men. He grasped the barrel of his pistol, lunged across the table, and punched Jones in the throat with the heavy wooden stock, crushing the man's windpipe. The lieutenant fell back in his chair, gasping desperately for air. Severin did not care if the man lived or died, only that he did not call for help.

Severin flung open the door and stepped through, tomahawk in one hand and quilled knife in the other.

The man standing guard on the left died with Severin's tomahawk in his neck. A short, savage horizontal chop. He had no time to make any sound at all. The one on the right managed a short, strangled cry before Severin stabbed him in the throat. The inn keep came running, but Devere put a bloody finger to his lips; the old man took in the carnage, paling, then nodded and retreated into his kitchen.

It had been done in less than a minute with little sound but the table scraping along the floor: one man incapacitated or dying and two dead. But Severin could not deal so with a dozen or more. So he walked—heart in his throat, bloody hands thrust in his pockets—out of the inn and in the direction of the stream.

As soon as he was out of sight, he took a long draft of the cool morning air . . . and began to run.

Twenty-one

Jenny knew something was wrong when the two guards beckoned her out of the shed. Something off in the way the larger of the pair looked at her, and in the way his wiry, pockmarked companion avoided her eyes altogether.

"I'm not going anywhere without Colonel Devere," she said.

The big man clamped a rough hand over her mouth and the poxy one grabbed her feet; then they carried her, struggling, down the hill and out of sight of the inn. She bit and she kicked and elbowed and punched—until they struck her a blow to the gut and she could scarcely speak or think for the pain.

When they set her down, she fell to her knees and struggled to rise, but one of them—the bigger man?—placed a boot across her back to keep her there. The other pulled her ankles out from under her. She tried to scream, but the owner of the boot grabbed her hair and pressed her face into the dirt.

Her vision swam; the ground in front of her face blurred.

Then the boot was gone and the hand was lifted, and she scrabbled madly like a dog, clawing over the earth to get away. Harsh and metallic, the sound of a ramrod sliding down a barrel made her turn.

Her two red-coated tormentors were looking up the hill now, frantically trying to load their muskets. The wiry man had dropped his cartridge and was searching through the carpet of pine needles for it, but a moment later his bigger comrade was raising his gun to fire.

At Severin.

He was running, his eyes fixed on the man with the primed musket. Her lover did not have a gun. But there was a gory tomahawk in his right hand and a bloodied knife in his left. He was moving so fast that before his adversary had a chance to sight along his barrel, Severin had closed a few more yards, and his tomahawk whirred a steel crescent through the air. The heavy blade buried itself in the big man's chest, and then Severin was atop the kneeling, pockmarked redcoat. His knife rose and fell twice, and then no more.

If it were done when 'tis done, then 'twere well it were done quickly.

Jenny took a tentative step toward Devere. He had blood on his face and spattered across his shirt; his cuffs were red with it.

He seemed not to notice. "Are you hurt?" he asked.

"No."

He retrieved the grisly tomahawk and hung it at his waist, and produced his lock picks. His hands were slippery; he stopped to wipe them on the ground, then used his tools to free her. And for the first time in a month, it was daylight and she was not shackled.

"We must go—now," he said as the hated irons dropped to the ground. Her wrists were red and raw.

"We must run, as long and as far as we are able, put distance between ourselves and Jones. He does not have the men to pursue us into the woods and guard the cannon at the same time. If we travel far and fast now, we will make it."

"Where to?"

"We strike out for Fort Ticonderoga," he said, leading her away from the hillside. "Fort Ti is held by the Americans and nigh impregnable. Even if Jones reaches Burgoyne's camp and the general sends a party after us, we should be safe behind the walls."

They ran. She did not look back at the carnage he had wreaked on her behalf, because he had saved her from a very ugly death and she was grateful for it. All she wanted in the world was to repay him by playing her own part now, by keeping pace.

She could not think of a time since childhood when she had run such a distance. Every time she thought she could not go on, Severin encouraged her and she found reserves of energy to continue.

They traveled like that for hours, slowing to a walk every so often and then picking up speed once again, until the sun was no longer overhead in the sky and Devere judged that they were no longer in danger of imminent capture.

"Do you know where we are?" she asked.

"Somewhere south of Fort Ti," he said. "I'm not sure how far. Most of the inhabitants in these parts are

Rebels, so we should be able to find someone willing to sell us food and shelter and, with any luck, horses."

They stopped to drink from a stream, and Devere left her to wash off the blood and attend the call of nature. When he returned, he brought her blackberries wrapped in a handkerchief. She ate them, reminded of the barn the theater troupe had played outside of Albany years before where the audience had paid in produce. All she had seen of the wilderness on that tour had been glimpsed through carriage windows. Too exhausted to appreciate the wonders around them, the New American Company had each night hung their painted traveling backdrop with its pointy Italian trees and played before it. And Jenny had hardly had time to appreciate the scenery on the road with Jones and his men.

Only now was she truly in Arcadia.

She had never known anything like it. The breeze was fresh and cool, scented with pine, so different from the thick cloying scent of the city. The ground beneath her feet was a soft carpet of decaying leaves. The forest stretched empty all around them save for the occasional flutter of wings or the furtive quick movement of some small creature.

"It is the landscape André painted for John Street," she said, marveling at the hemlock, spruce, and fir. "It is beautiful."

Severin produced a stone from his pocket and began to sharpen his knife thoughtfully. "I had much the same reaction the first time my mother took me to the theater. It was a world of wonders. The forest is beautiful, but, growing up, I didn't see it through the eyes of a painter. I saw it as a resource. A landscape of ever changing dangers and opportunities. My father"—Jenny noticed how he left a little air around the word, as though he was not quite sure he had used it correctly—"taught Julian and me to hunt and to fish and to fashion weapons out of the wilderness. I hated the tame emptiness of the English countryside when I got there, but there was no going back, and I soon learned that it held other dangers. And other opportunities."

She had seen him assessing those dangers and opportunities, both in the streets of New York and more recently on the trail. He was always alert to his surroundings, always alive to the possibilities unfolding around him, reading the cues the way actors read one another onstage. It was why he was so very good at what he did, and why they worked so well together, she realized.

"How does it feel to return?" she asked.

He gave her a little smile. "Probably a lot like your visit to New Brunswick." Jenny had told him about Ida and Letty and the battle for the bake oven. "There is something gratifying about the familiarity, but it is possible to be of a place, to be shaped by it, and yet no longer be part of it."

"I think it is possible," said Jenny, remembering how happy she had been in the little blue house with Aunt Frances, "to make a place for yourself in the world with another person, a little country of two." And then she remembered what Aunt Frances had said about Harry wanting to raise her. "Or three. Even if you are out of step with the world."

"We will make such a place, Jenny," he said, gathering her into his arms. "I promise you."

When Jenny was rested, they ran on, and as evening was falling they emerged in a cleared field where corn was growing. There was a farmhouse at the edge. Devere had Jenny wait hidden amongst the stalks.

She watched him approach the house, and then saw him stop, put his hands in the air, and back away. That was when she made out the man with the gun standing on the porch. She was too far away to pick up what they were saying, but after a short exchange Severin pointed to the field where she was hidden. Then he nodded and beckoned Jenny to come out. When she emerged from the cornfield, the man on the porch lowered his rifle and nodded back.

The damage had not been visible from the field. The little farmhouse was pockmarked with musket balls and someone had clearly tried—and failed—to hack the door to pieces.

"Burgoyne's Indian scouts," explained Devere. "The good news is that we are close to Fort Ti. The bad news is that so is John Burgoyne. We must get ahead of his army and reach the fort before he does."

The farmer and his family were kinder than Jenny could ever have imagined—especially to two bloody strangers who had appeared out of nowhere—and she was grateful for water to wash in and a clean shirt for Severin.

Devere did not refuse the meal that was offered them. But she noticed that he did not bow his head when the farmer said grace, and the wide-eyed children still stared at Severin even in his new shirt with all the blood cleaned away.

They lay down after the meal in the keeping room on blankets spread over the floor, and Jenny fell into a deep, dreamless sleep from which Devere woke her when it was not yet light. Her feet ached and her legs were stiff and sore, but she knew they must go on. He used his knife to slice a coin from the hem of her petticoat and left it on the table.

They walked for two days. Once, they heard distant shouting and Devere changed direction and led them off the trail for a time, but by late afternoon on the second day they encountered the first pickets guarding the fort. Not obviously, to Jenny's eye, soldiers, but weathered, rifle-bearing men in leather hunting smocks.

They did not like the look of Devere's red coat, even turned inside out, and they took his tomahawk and his pistol, leaving him only his quilled knife, and led them to the fort under guard. They were hard, determined men, but their tension and anxiety were plain. War was coming—indeed, was already there.

"*Tekontaró:ken*," said Severin when they reached the gates. "The place where two waters meet."

It was an imposing structure, far bigger than the Battery in New York or any building Jenny had ever seen. She could understand now why it was called the Gibraltar of the North. Sun sparkled off the stone and the lake beyond, and she felt safe for the first time in more than a month.

It was not to last. Inside, all was urgent preparation and mounting uncertainty. They were handed over to a harassed lieutenant, who placed them under guard in a ground-floor room in the barracks: ten double bunks lined up between the windows, the beds so new that they still smelled of pine. Jenny was grateful for the chance to sit down, even on someone else's straw tick. With the sun streaming in through the panes and the fresh air off the lake, she found sleep irresistible.

When she woke it was dark.

"Shouldn't someone want this bed?" she asked Severin, who was standing by the window looking out, just as he had been when she fell asleep.

"Yes," he said. "Jenny, I do not know what is happening, but something is amiss."

"The fort is impregnable," she said. "You said so yourself."

"I did, didn't I? But I suppose I am no siege engineer . . ."

A very young captain, in a blue uniform coat that had seen better days, came to question them an hour later. They told him who they were and how they had escaped from a British column. Severin told the man that he was known to someone named Harkness and someone named Trumbull, and that Jenny was known, personally, to Washington. When Devere named her as Cornelia, the young man brightened and recited a speech from her *Miles Gloriosus*, and that made Devere smile, despite himself.

Admirer or not, the captain would not tell them what was happening. A little later he did, however, bring back three young men who—as it happened—had all been students at King's before the war and seen Jenny on the stage at John Street. Two of them asked about conditions in the city and how particular streets had fared after the fire and whether particular buildings were still standing. She answered them to the best of her knowledge. One of them returned an hour later and brought them apples and cheese and a little jug of rum.

Jenny and Devere were left in the barracks overnight. No one claimed the beds, so Devere pushed two bunks close together and they slept next to each other until the sun woke them in the morning.

At midday they were called to General St. Clair's office, where fires were burning despite the heat of the day, and clerks were feeding papers to the flames.

"Burgoyne's a canny foe, for all his bluster," said St. Clair. The general—a British regular officer during the last war, Severin had said—looked both suitably professional and troublingly grim.

"He's managed to bring cannon up Mount Defiance, a bit of engineering that was thought to be impossible, else we would have long since leveled that blasted rock. When he has them in position, he will be able to fire down on us. Our position is indefensible."

He handed one of his clerks a sheaf of papers, food for the flames. "Miss Leighton, I have verified, is who she says she is. I have dispatches from Washington that attest to her identity as Cornelia and confirm her arrest in New York. They instruct me to do whatever is within my power to aid her.

"You, sir," he said to Devere, "I have no knowledge of, and you wear the uniform of an enemy officer. Tonight I must spirit more than two thousand souls from out of this garrison without alerting the enemy. I cannot afford to take prisoners on this march. Miss Leighton will depart with the families who took refuge in the fort and the garrison's women and children. You, sir, will remain locked in the fort—until your countrymen take possession of Ticonderoga and discover you."

"No," said Jenny. "You can't leave him, General. The British will hang him. If not for desertion, then for murder. He killed two men so that we could get away."

"Then I am heartily sorry," said St. Clair, "but I have the safety of *two thousand* men—of an entire army and its followers—to think of, and I cannot risk it."

"Then I will stay as well." She was not going to be parted from him.

"No," said Severin. "You must go with them, Jenny. If I'm lucky, Jones won't have caught up with Burgoyne, and no one will yet know of our escape. The British will free me, and I'll slip away to join you."

"And if you aren't lucky?"

"May we speak privately?" Severin asked St. Clair. "Before Miss Leighton departs?"

The general agreed, and they were returned to the barracks, where she rounded on the man she loved.

"I am not going without you."

"If you stay, you will likely hang, even if Lieutenant Jones has not rendezvoused with Burgoyne. I do not doubt that André has written Jack Brag about you and told him of my ploy to save you. Burgoyne is unlikely to hang *me* unless Jones turns up, but he will string you up without hesitation. I fear we both know the measure of the man."

"What you are proposing is suicide," she said, blinking back the beginning of tears. "I have not endured all this to lose you."

"Never fear, my Mistress Firebrand," he said. "We are not writing a tragedy, you and I, and I am not the type to contemplate self-slaughter. It puts me quite out of countenance. *That* is why I want you to go with St. Clair. We are not very far from the Indian village where I lived as a child. I want you to go there, and find a man for me."

"Who?"

"*My father.*"

Devere did not like the idea of Jenny striking off through the wilderness on her own, but at least this way they both had a fighting chance. If she stayed with him, they had little to none.

"How do I find him?" she asked. He was proud, but by now unsurprised, to see how quickly she turned from anxiety and grief to purpose and practicalities.

He gave her instructions, as precise as he could remember, though much might have changed in twenty years.

"How can you be sure that he—this man who kidnapped your mother—will come for you?" she asked.

"Because, Jenny, my mother was not kidnapped at all. She ran away with Ashur Rice—Kanonsase, as he is sometimes known. They loved each other."

"I don't understand."

"They met at Wheelock's Indian School in Connecticut, though my father was not truly there to learn how to be a Christian missionary. He was there to study the English, the better to devise how to push them out of the borderlands. My mother was a local girl from a good family. When her parents discovered the affair, they put an end to it and convinced her to marry their choice. A young man who had also come to the school for his own purposes: to study the natives, the better to acquire their land."

"Thomas Devere," guessed Jenny.

"Devere," agreed Severin, who had learned to use the name of the man who had ruined his mother's life. "The other side to my father's coin, with his own 'unchristian' motives—and greater ruthlessness, perhaps, in pursuit of his goals. Thomas Devere paid to have my father beaten—almost to death—and driven out of town. But he didn't know my mother was already pregnant. He married my mother, and when she bore Kanonsase's son believed it his own."

"Julian is your true brother, then," said Jenny.

Severin shrugged. "What makes a man a brother? Fairchild was a better brother to me, in England, than Julian ever was. If Thomas Devere had just married my mother and gone home to England, had been content to inherit his earldom, all would probably have been well—or at least if not well, then tolerable—but he didn't. He took his young family north, intent on carving out an American 'domain' that would put his English patrimony to shame. And there my mother saw her Kanonsase again. She thought he had abandoned her. When she learned that Devere had forced him off, she regretted her own lack of constancy, of fortitude. She again became his lover, and finally she ran away with him. Devere was too humiliated to tell anyone that his pretty young wife preferred a Mohawk to an English lord."

"He tried to get her declared dead," Jenny said.

"And failed, because everyone living in the borderlands knew she was alive and had borne another son. Me. My parents were happy together for ten years. But perhaps it could not last. When the last war broke out, Devere used it as an excuse to retrieve his wife and the child he presumed, wrongly, to be flesh and blood, his heir, Julian. He got me into the bargain as well."

"Your mother should have ignored her parents, listened to her heart," said Jenny.

The sympathy in her eyes, the sense and sensibility of this woman—whom he loved—left him breathless for a moment. "She did not have an example like your aunt Frances to follow," he said at last. "And she was not as brave as you are."

"I do not feel so very brave now. In fact, I am terrified that I will never see you again."

"And I have no such fear." He made himself believe it.

He taught her a phrase to say in Mohawk. "But only to Ashur Rice. It will not be well received by anyone else."

"What does it mean?"

He told her. Despite the horror of their situation, she laughed aloud, and cried a little too, but he was grateful to hear her laughter, wanted to remember her exactly this way if it was the last time he saw her.

"My father taught my uncle Solomon to say that to woo my aunt. He will remember that and know that no one but a member of the family would have repeated such a thing. Say that and give him this."

He handed her the little knife, its quillwork burnished by long use, the one that his father had given him so long ago.

"I cannot take this," she said. "You will be defenseless."

"A blade will do me little good in a cell, and Ashur Rice will recognize it. He gave it to me when I was a boy."

She nodded and accepted the knife. Severin taught her to say his name—his Mohawk name—as well, and he kissed her before the guard took her away to join the women and children. A long kiss, yet far, far too short.

They moved him to a cell within the walls, apart from the other British prisoners, in deference to his presumed rank. The sounds of constant activity went on through the night until finally, in the morning, all was silence. Then there was the bark of orders being given above, and the prisoners took up shouting until someone came to rescue them. The Americans had not left keys to the cells, which caused some delay, as no doubt they had intended. Once Severin and the others were released, they were herded into the yard so that a harried-looking young British captain could decide who among them were genuine prisoners of war, and who were likely deserters, and to which regiments they all belonged.

They hanged four men before the afternoon was over, but no one knew what to do with Severin, who was obviously an officer and a gentleman and also, confusingly, an Indian, but had no one who could vouch for him and so might also be an American spy.

The British officers did not yet believe their good fortune. Somehow, they had taken the mighty Fort Ticonderoga without a shot fired. They were wary, and with good reason, but soon they would relax their guard. Then Severin would volunteer for some odious duty, and they would accept his labor gratefully. And he would be able to make his escape.

It was not to be. Lieutenant Jones and his motley, much reduced party rolled through the gates while Devere was under guard. The wounded officer spotted him and exchanged a word with the colonel in charge of the captured Americans they had rounded up: St. Clair's pathetic excuse for a rearguard, who had been left behind to spike the guns but instead had broached a cask of Madeira and had drunk themselves insensible.

The colonel ordered Devere arrested and put back in a cell. That night, Jones—wheezing through his crushed windpipe, his voice a ghastly husk—came to confirm his identity. Jones urged the matter brought to Burgoyne's immediate attention, but the busy colonel did not oblige him.

Over the next week the other cells filled with American prisoners of war, some of whom had been with St. Clair's rear echelons on the initial retreat. Severin learned that there had been a sharpish fight at Hubbardton, but that the main van of the American general's army had slipped away toward the Hudson River. And, he hoped, Jenny with them.

Severin passed two weeks in his cell before he was marched to what remained of Fort Ann, which the Rebels had burned on their retreat and was now a charred ruin surrounded by the turned earth of fresh graves.

Severin and his captors arrived at dusk. In the very center of the blackened fortification—beneath a silk tent with red-tasseled hangings, the ground spread with Turkey carpets—was a long banquet table covered in damask linen and set with china and glittering crystal, lit by spermaceti tapers in silver holders. It was a scene straight from Jenny's *Braggart Soldier*.

Devere had been eating cold porridge with the other prisoners for a fortnight. How unreal now to smell the roasted game and the buttered onions, the pungent, vinegary sauces and the wine perfuming the warm July night, mingling with the rosewater and sandalwood worn by John Burgoyne and the officers and their ladies who dined with him. Though one of the "ladies," Devere knew from the talk in the camp, was no lady at all but the general's latest mistress: a commissary's wife with dyed blond hair and a button nose.

The party beneath the silk awning went on while Severin was chained to a post in the middle of the ruined yard, like an animal. He listened to the tinkle of glasses and the trilling of laughter and heard, distinct amidst the revelry, a voice he knew too well.

An hour passed before Burgoyne stirred himself to rise, wineglass in hand, and stroll over to where Severin was chained.

"I could have overlooked your mischief on the *Boyne*," said Jack Brag, standing over Severin, "but telling Howe that the Leighton slut was my mistress? That is too much even for you, Devere. I'll see you both hang. Her first, so you can watch."

It had been more than a year since Severin had seen John Burgoyne, but the general was little changed. Despite the rigors of the trail, he was flawlessly turned out in a silk waistcoat dripping with gold braid and lace.

Severin hated him.

"That may prove difficult," said Devere, "as Jenny has decamped with St. Clair and his army. *Tomorrow to fresh woods, and pastures new.*"

"St. Clair's 'army' is a shambles." Burgoyne sneered. "Scattered to the four winds. And Miss Leighton is most conspicuous by her hair. My Indian scouts will find her. It's in their blood—as you should know. I have five hundred warriors from the Six Nations out chastising the Rebels . . . and looking for the girl."

Severin could have told Burgoyne that the Indians were not *his*, that they were here for their own interests, as his father had been at Wheelock's school. Their ultimate aim was to drive the outland settlers from their territories, their homes—and they would not trouble overmuch to distinguish Tory from Rebel. Burgoyne had ignored his advisers on this point and he would certainly never listen to Severin now, but it was true all the same. He only hoped Jenny had found his father, before someone *like* his father found her.

Twenty-two

Jenny left the fort ahead of the main retreat with the women and children. There were perhaps a hundred stragglers in all and they had no carts or horses. There was a civilian blacksmith with a portable forge who traveled with them for a few miles and allowed one of the nursing mothers and a pregnant woman to sit on the back of his vehicle, but everyone else, even the smallest children, were weighed down by the pots and pans and blankets and necessities of life they had been forced to carry into the wilderness.

They walked for a solid day, pressing on through the dusk. When night fell, they laid down to camp at the side of the road. Jenny curled herself into a blanket and realized that it was the first time she had slept apart from Severin in more than a month. She thought about the life he had promised they would build together, and the fantasy kept her warm in the scratchy and threadbare wool.

St. Clair's army passed them on the road the next morning. Hundreds of men, most of them on foot, only a few of the officers mounted. They did have carts, but they weren't carrying away guns. They had sacks of flour and barrels of apples and wheels of cheese. Jenny cut some of the scrip from her jacket with Severin's knife and bargained with a young quartermaster for a sack of apples, some dried beef, and a wedge of cheese. She shared a little of her bounty with the nine-year-old boy who had attached himself to her as pint-sized protector, and saved the rest for when she must strike out on her own.

One of the young officers who had visited her in the barracks rode by on a horse and Jenny knew real covetousness, the kind that preachers warned about, for the first time. She wanted that horse. A mount. A donkey, even. Anything that would carry her faster to find Severin's father.

An hour later a party of redcoats thundered past them, fast in pursuit of the retreating Americans. The women and children watched them disappear up the road with trepidation. When they reached a turning in the road, Jenny announced that she would be taking it, reasoning that there would be only fighting ahead of them and that the road had to lead somewhere. If she could find a farmer like the one who had sheltered her and Severin on their flight, she might be able to get directions and even buy a mount.

The women were determined to follow the army. Jenny gave a wedge of the cheese and an apple to the little boy, who did not think that she should go. She traded some of the beef to keep one of the blankets, and then she started walking.

The road narrowed and became a path, barely wide enough for two to walk abreast. The solitariness of it struck her all at once. She had not been truly alone for months, and never this alone in her whole life. Panic gripped her when she looked up the long trail and it appeared to be without end, but she remembered Severin's words and tried to think of the forest as a resource, alive with possibilities. Many of which probably wanted to kill and eat her.

Not a helpful thought. She wondered if there were bears. Another less than helpful thought. She could not afford unhelpful thoughts. She had to save Severin. The path had to lead somewhere.

That became her mantra. Sleeping was the true challenge, alone in the empty wild with only a blanket for protection. She lay on the ground the first night, her heart racing, starting at every sound, until an owl began to hoot somewhere nearby and the sound, somehow, comforted her. She woke groggily from a dreamless sleep the next morning and plodded on, almost missing the farmhouse in the field of corn in her daze.

The farmer was warier than the family that had succored Jenny and Severin after their escape from Jones, but he listened to Jenny's story and noted her mention of Ashur Rice, and took an age-darkened framed map down from the wall. He knew, he thought, the village she was searching for. He would not sell her a mount but he would walk her to the crossroads and from there, if she followed his directions, she should be able to reach Rice's farm by the end of the week.

The farmer was as good as his word. He sold Jenny a sack of biscuits and led her to the crossroads and from there she began walking once more.

The feeling crept up on her gradually, just as it had in the streets of New York when she and Severin had been trying to reach the King's Arms. She was being followed. She could see no one in the trees on either side of the road, but she knew they were there all the same. Jenny did her best to emulate Severin's behavior that night and give no indication that she knew she was being followed. But there were no alley mouths or doorways to shelter in here, and nothing to do when the warriors emerged from the tree line, heads shaved, faces painted, gruesome trophies and sharp axes hanging from their waists. There was not a chicken feather in sight as they descended upon the road with their fierce cries and their raised blades.

Devere spent the night in the open, chained to the post where Burgoyne had left him. Burgoyne's mistress, who appeared to be a sly piece of trouble, snuck him water in the morning. By afternoon Burgoyne's supposed Indian allies began to come in with their prisoners.

The warriors wanted, naturally, to be paid ransoms for every captive they brought. Burgoyne had asked for an Englishwoman, and they had brought him Englishwomen. Dozens of them, young and old, some of them badly beaten, all of them dirty and terrified. A few even had red, or reddish, hair, but most of them did not.

A party of Wyandot, in breechcloths and leggings, arrived in the late afternoon. They had a howling old woman in tow who claimed to be a relation of General Fraser. From one of the warriors' belts hung a fresh scalp. He brandished it in the air, demanding payment. The grisly trophy was distinctive, most definitely taken from a woman—with long copper hair.

Jenny.

The bloody tresses danced in the breeze and Severin could smell their metallic tang on the wind. His gorge rose. The sounds around him dwindled. He watched as Burgoyne was summoned to inspect his grim prize, and could not contain his disgust. He ordered one of his officers to pay "the fellow" and dispose of it, but no one stepped forward.

The Wyandot brave, who called himself Panther, began shouting his outrage. He demanded his bounty. The yard was filling now, the spectacle attracting ever more attention, and still no one stepped forward to claim the scalp or pay the scout.

Panther began to pace in an ever widening circle, laying out, in his own language, his case for payment, logical as any barrister before the bench. When he passed close to Severin, he was holding the grim trophy at his side, copper locks dangling to the ground and trailing through the ashes and dirt.

No. Not copper. Red. Redder than Jenny's hair, and longer. He could see that now, up close. Almost too much to dare to hope. The hair was not hers.

Panther was still circling the yard when Lieutenant Jones entered the fort.

It took him a moment to make sense of the bizarre scene: the outraged warrior, the silent onlookers, the bedraggled and bloody scalp with the long red hair.

Her hair is redder than Miss Leighton's, but they are of an age and in all other respects might be taken for sisters.

Jones fell to his knees when he recognized the

scalp and his wails of grief drowned out even the monologue of the outraged Panther.

A company of loyalists from Pennsylvania decamped that night. By the time the girl's body was found in the woods and brought into camp the next day, several hundred more American loyalists had deserted. Severin, still chained to his post, did not doubt that a good number of them had gone over to the Continentals. It was the sort of story that did not need an engraving by Revere or a pamphlet by Paine to carry it, and it would attract more Rebel enlistments than any recruiting broadside.

Severin felt a little relief to know that Jenny was still free somewhere, and more when he overheard Burgoyne's junior officers insisting that he recall his Indian scouts and put an end to the search for the girl. His advisers urged him, in hushed, worried voices, to hang Panther, swiftly, or risk further desertions.

It was good advice, all of it, but Burgoyne refused to punish one of his "children" who had simply misunderstood his instructions. Severin could have told them that it didn't matter anyway. The real damage was already done. The discontent and disillusionment percolating through the camp would travel, along with the story of the murder of Jane McCrea.

Jenny did not know whether she was a prisoner or a guest of the party of Mohawks who had captured her until they reached the village where Severin had grown up, where she was given food and water and was fussed over as though she were in her mother's parlor in New Brunswick.

The neatly tended fields and imposing longhouses were filled entirely with women and children and the very elderly, who wanted her to eat and drink and were happy to give her Kanonsase's direction if she was really going to bring him news of Kanonsase's son.

The man sometimes called Ashur Rice, who had lived among the English and adopted some of their ways—indeed, as had the village women who cooked in English pots and wore English cloth and sewed English beads onto their hides—lived in an English-style house of two stories with glass windows just beyond the village.

Jenny walked a last mile on shoes Severin had filled with leaves for her when the soles began to wear through, trailed by smiling Mohawk children who dropped back when she reached the very English picket fence. She felt a sense of unreality when she saw the neat little house—in its sun-dappled glade, like something from a fairy tale, where a witch or an ogre might live—but she lifted her hand to knock upon the batten door and her heart rose into her throat when it was opened.

The man was the very picture of Severin, as he might look in twenty years. He was dressed much as her lover had been when last she saw him—in buckskin breeches and a simple cotton shirt—but most of his scalp had been plucked clean and only a single hank of glossy black hair, woven with beads, remained. No one would mistake Ashur Rice for an Englishman.

He looked at her curiously and she had not seen a mirror in weeks but she could guess at her appearance. His eyes were as dark, as magnetic as those of his offspring.

"*Karekohe*," she said. "Your son. Severin Devere. I have a message from him."

The man waited expressionlessly for her to go on, and suddenly she wondered if he remembered his English from his time at the Indian School—but that was nonsense because half the village had been able to speak her language well enough to be understood while she had none of theirs.

"He told me to repeat this phrase, that you would know it came from your sister and your brother-in-law." As she spoke the words, the man's dark brows rose, and then his lips pursed, and then he burst out laughing.

"And where is this son of mine, that has come back to his father, after all this time?" asked Ashur Rice, in accents every bit as cultivated as Severin's and entirely at odds with his appearance.

"He was imprisoned by the Americans at Ticonderoga before the fort fell, and I believe that he is now being held by the British and that they are going to hang him."

The man's smile faded, like the sun behind a storm cloud.

He nodded and held the door wide for her to enter. And she stood for the first time in weeks in something like the home she had known in New York, comfortably appointed and furnished by someone, at some time in the past, who had cared about it, though the curtains were faded and the cushions had long since lost their plumpness.

"Tell me what has befallen my son," said this man, after putting food and water in front of Jenny, rummaging through a trunk, and returning with a soft bundle of moose hide that turned out to be a pair of moccasins—brightly sewn with beads and trimmed in velvet and silk—to replace her ruined shoes.

And so she told him. He listened patiently and asked only a few questions. Then he rose and reached for his long rifle. "I will be back," he said.

"With Severin?"

"With my son," he agreed.

There was no place for her where he was going. She saw that. She was the reason Severin was in British hands to begin with, and her presence would only jeopardize his safety further. She knew that. But she could not resist a question that had been on her mind since Fort Ti, that she had dared not ask Severin when they were about to be separated, possibly forever.

"Why did you let Thomas Devere take them? Why did you let him take your wife and your sons?"

For a moment, Ashur Rice made no answer. "Perhaps because she was his wife, under English law," he said at last, "and that he had the disposal of a troop of dragoons to enforce that foreign authority."

So had John André when he had taken Jenny, but Severin had not let that stand. He had followed her into the wilderness to win her freedom.

"Why didn't you go after them?"

"Thomas Devere wanted Julian, my eldest boy, because he thought that Julian was his, but he took Severin too, as *leverage*. Understand, he did not *want* him. But he took him, and promised to kill him if I followed. There was much killing then, as now, on the border. The death of one little half-Indian boy would have gone unremarked among all the butchery. To Thomas Devere, Severin was nothing. To the English, he was nothing. But that boy was *my* son. Better that he should live among the English than die among the Mohawk."

Ashur Rice had given up his son so that Severin would have a chance, at least, to live. Sent him away as Severin had sent Jenny away from Ticonderoga. "It has to be different this time," she said.

Ashur Rice flashed her a sly smile, much like his son's. "The thing about leverage in the borderlands is that it is always changing hands. That day, it belonged to Thomas Devere and the English. Today, at least, it belongs to Burgoyne's Indian allies, including the Mohawk. I will bring my son home."

She did not doubt him. The American prodigal indeed.

They returned the next morning: in a large party of men of fierce appearance with paint on their faces, armed for war. A small child came to fetch Jenny to the village to see this wonder, the return of Kanonsase's son.

Severin looked thin, but he was smiling. And, she realized, being mocked in a language he spoke mostly fluently but with occasional halting pauses while he searched for a word or phrase he no longer remembered.

It seemed the Mohawks did not much like his hair. It made him look like a woman. Other than that Ashur Rice's son was entirely what everyone expected Ashur Rice's son to be. There was no time for them to speak privately, but Severin kissed her and assured her that everything was going to be all right—and *this time* she could rely on that.

"Jack Brag cannot afford to alienate his Indian

allies, and my father convinced a fair few warriors to desert his cause if he did not free me. And Gentleman Johnny has other, greater problems now."

Severin and his father and his father's friends talked and ate, and Jenny gathered that much of their discussion was about the war and the English. By nightfall most of their guests had left the village. Jenny and Severin retired to Ashur Rice's house, where there was an unused bedroom, dusty but serviceable, and they washed and tumbled into bed together, free at last.

He told her about Lieutenant Jones and poor, murdered Jane McCrea, and Burgoyne's splendid table in the wilderness. Vignettes of fairy-tale fancy, and all too real horror.

"What will happen to us?" she asked. "If General Burgoyne takes Albany?"

"Taking Albany is one thing. Holding the wild places, like this, is another. We are safe enough here for now, and I am content to eat and sleep and love you, while Jack Brag tries to hold water in his open hand."

Jenny was content too. For a week she rested and ate and relished the company of the man she loved, who insisted they be married. "If my parents had married, Thomas Devere would not have been able to twist the law to separate them, to take her away," he said.

"If we marry, I will never be able to sign a contract without your permission."

"Then I must always give it," he said without hesitation.

"And if you don't like the terms or the theater, or the theater manager?"

"Then we will discuss my objections and try to come to a decision together. As we should do everything. But in the end, you will choose your course, Jenny. *Always.*"

He would not take no for an answer, and she found she did not want him to. She relented in the first week of September, though it took two more weeks to find a preacher to perform the ceremony. Jenny only wished Aunt Frances could have been there.

By that time news had reached them that General Burgoyne was on the point of surrender at a place called Saratoga. Among other things, lurid accounts of Indian atrocities—the horrible, damning story of Jane McCrea—had robbed Jack Brag of a good deal of his expected Tory support and bolstered Rebel enlistments.

"It means we can go south," said Severin.

"To where?"

"Boston."

"There are no playhouses in Boston."

"No, but there are presses, and you have been scribbling away for months now. Unless you expect me to write out a thousand copies of this masterwork by hand, we should go to Boston."

They traveled south and spent the winter in Boston, which Jenny did not much like, but where she put her newest work to press. By then General Howe had been driven from Philadelphia, and they continued on to the City of Brotherly Love, where there were not only presses but also a *theater*.

A letter reached her there, addressed to "Miss Leighton" but intended, she quickly realized on breaking the seal, for her aunt.

"It is gibberish," said Jenny, passing it to her husband, who was by now used to being given vast texts and tracts to read, sometimes in the middle of the night, and expected to offer considered opinions and constructive comments.

"It is a book cipher," Severin explained, unable to conceal his interest. "A code keyed to a work both sender and recipient own a copy of, or know by heart. Can you think of any text your aunt always carried with her?"

It took a week to track down a copy of Rowe's *Fair Penitent* in Philadelphia, and another day for Severin to work the code and decipher the letter.

"Angela Ferrers is dead," he said.

"How?" asked Jenny, surprised to find herself grieving for her aunt's remarkable, dangerous friend.

"André," replied her husband. "At Howe's bidding." Severin wished John André joy serving his old masters. The Widow had been an original. They would not see her like again. "He tracked her down in Philadelphia. The writer has taken up her network, but is obviously unaware of your aunt's fate. From the hand, I judge your correspondent to be a woman. From the questions she asks, I surmise she has assumed the Widow's mantle. It is up to you whether we reply."

Jenny considered for a day and then decided to respond. She could not bring Aunt Frances back, but she could honor her memory by taking her place in the Widow's network. Severin—reasonably or not—felt he owed something to the American cause, to his countrymen, and perhaps this was a way to do his part, without the old "necessities" of skulduggery and violence.

And so she dictated a brief account of her aunt's death, and Severin added intelligence from their travels and then put the message into cipher. After that, a new letter came every other week, and as Jenny had resumed her profession, so Severin resumed his, in the service of the country of his birth. With the freedom now to determine his own limits as to the shape that service might take.

They discovered that Courtney Fairchild had been sent home by Howe to prevent his dueling with Captain André. And that Bobby Hallam had fled New York for Jamaica when Fairchild learned of his part in Frances Leighton's death.

When the Southwark Theater in Philadelphia reopened, Severin expressed no objections to Jenny's performing. And when New York was liberated at last, and for good and all, they returned there and bought a very fine house near the Battery. For many years a carriage called at that address three nights a week to take the John Street's leading lady, Mrs. Devere, an actress and playwright who was a great favorite of President Washington, to the theater. She shared the carriage with her husband: a darkly handsome man, even in later life, who—it was subsequently remembered— never missed a single performance.

AUTHOR'S NOTE

Jennifer Leighton is a creature of fiction, but the American writer Mercy Otis Warren did earn herself a place on a British hanging list with her pamphlet plays *The Blockheads* and *The Adulateur*. The obstacles faced by ambitious Georgian actresses and women of letters in the period were formidable, and the theater was a politically charged arena on both sides of the Atlantic. Frances Leighton is modeled on early feminist actress, playwright, novelist, and poet Mary Robinson, a onetime royal mistress who later became Colonel Banastre Tarleton's paramour when he returned home after the war.

The Georgian theater played a leading role in the American Revolution that today has largely been forgotten. Playhouses thrived before the war in Philadelphia, New York, and Williamsburg, college students staged amateur theatricals in their dormitories, and British and American forces acted plays in their camps throughout the conflict. The rhetoric of patriots like Patrick Henry and Nathan Hale owed much to Addison's

Cato the Censor—reportedly one of Washington's favorite plays, which his officers performed at Valley Forge despite Congress's ban on the theater.

John Burgoyne is not recorded to have been in New York in 1775–1776, but apart from the fictive diversion of the *Boyne*, the timeline in all other ways follows his path to defeat at Saratoga.

RECOMMENDED READING

Bailyn, Bernard. *Faces of Revolution: Personalities and Themes in the Struggle for American Independence.* New York: Vintage, 2011.

Bakeless, John. *Turncoats, Traitors & Heroes.* New York: Da Capo Press, 1998.

Ballaster, Ros. "Rivals for the Repertory: Theatre and Novel in Georgian London," *Restoration and Eighteenth-Century Theatre Research* 27, no. 1 (Summer 2012): 5–24.

Berkin, Carol. *Revolutionary Mothers: Women in the Struggle for America's Independence.* New York: Knopf, 2005.

Brown, Jared. *The Theatre in America During the Revolution.* New York: Cambridge University Press, 1995.

Byrne, Paula. *Perdita: The Literary, Theatrical, Scandalous Life of Mary Robinson.* New York: Random House, 2005.

Countryman, Edward. *A People in Revolution: The American Revolution and Political Society in New York, 1760–1790.* New York: Norton, 1989.

Recommended Reading

Hatch, Robert McConnell. *Major John André: A Gallant in Spy's Clothing*. Boston: Houghton Mifflin Harcourt, 1986.

Hibbert, Christopher. *Redcoats and Rebels: The American Revolution Through British Eyes*. New York: Norton, 2002.

Ireland, Joseph N. *Records of the New York Stage, from 1750 to 1860*. New York: T. H. Morrell, 1866.

Johnson, Odai. *Absence and Memory in Colonial American Theatre*. New York: Palgrave Macmillan, 2006.

Johnson, Odai. *The Colonial American Stage, 1665–1774: A Documentary Calendar*. Madison, NJ: Fairleigh Dickinson University Press, 2002.

Ketchum, Richard M. *Divided Loyalties: How the American Revolution Came to New York*. New York: Henry Holt, 2002.

Ketchum, Richard M. *Saratoga: Turning Point of America's Revolutionary War*. New York: Henry Holt, 1997.

Nathans, Heather S. *Early American Theatre from the Revolution to Thomas Jefferson*. Cambridge: Cambridge University Press, 2003.

O'Shaughnessy, Andrew. *The Men Who Lost America: British Leadership, the American Revolution, and the Fate of the Empire*. New Haven: Yale University Press, 2013.

Russell, Gillian. *Women, Sociability, and Theatre in Georgian London*. Cambridge: Cambridge University Press, 2007.

Schecter, Barnet. *The Battle for New York*. London: Pimlico, 2002.

Recommended Reading

Shaffer, Jason. *Performing Patriotism: National Identity in the Colonial and Revolutionary American Theater.* Philadelphia: University of Pennsylvania Press, 2007.

Stuart, Nancy Rubin. *The Muse of the Revolution: The Secret Pen of Mercy Otis Warren and the Founding of a Nation.* Boston: Beacon Press, 2008.

Swindells, Julia. *The Oxford Handbook of the Georgian Theatre, 1737–1832.* Oxford: Oxford University Press, 2014.

Taylor, Alan. *The Divided Ground: Indians, Settlers, and the Northern Borderland of the American Revolution.* New York: Knopf, 2006.

Wheelock, Eleazar. *A Plain and Faithful Narrative of the Original Design, Rise, Progress and Present State of the Indian Charity-School at Lebanon, in Connecticut.* 1763.

Mistress Firebrand

RENEGADES OF THE AMERICAN REVOLUTION

DONNA THORLAND

A CONVERSATION WITH DONNA THORLAND

Readers who haven't finished the book might want to avoid the Readers Guide for the time being—spoilers ahead!

Q. Mistress Firebrand *is the third book in the Renegades of the American Revolution series, yet it opens in December 1775, before the action in the first book,* The Turncoat, *and after the action in the second book,* The Rebel Pirate. *Why did you decide to write the series out of sequence?*

A. Each book is meant to stand alone, so readers don't have to worry about approaching the series in order. I write stories inspired by real women of the period, but because my books are fiction, I have the luxury of placing my heroines at the center of the action during turning points in the conflict. For Quaker spy Kate Gray, inspired by real-life heroine Lydia Barrington Darragh, this meant occupied Philadelphia in 1777. For Sarah Ward, a composite of historical Salem women whose stories I encountered while working at the Peabody Essex Museum, that meant setting her tale during the struggle for the materiel of war played out in the waters off Cape Ann in 1775. For my latest heroine, Jennifer Leighton, inspired by Rebel playwright Mercy Otis Warren, and Jenny's aunt, the Divine Fanny, inspired by early feminist and Georgian actress Mary Randall, that meant the New York stage in the mid 1770s.

Q. *In your view of the American Revolution, power and loyalties are constantly shifting among your major characters according to their unique situation and self-interest. It's a very different picture from what most of us were taught in school and makes our country's origins, and the beliefs for which our forefathers fought, seem more like tarnished realities than shiny ideals. Why is it important to you to present this more realistic picture?*

A. My favorite works of historical fiction, like George MacDonald Fraser's Flashman books and Dorothy Dunnett's Lymond series, blend action with complex political intrigue. Even walk-on characters have their own goals and agendas, which are never as straightforward or as simple as national allegiances. They're the kind of books that make you want to look up all the historical characters and events and learn more about them. I really wanted to write something that would make readers feel the same way about the American Revolution.

Q. I had the impression from my vaguely recalled school lessons that New York remained under British control during most of the American Revolution. But in Mistress Firebrand *control switches back and forth between the British and the Rebels, often with neither side sure of their position. How challenging it must have been to live in the city during this time! What was it like for ordinary citizens?*

A. The British occupied New York for most of the war, but in the early days of the conflict, when it seemed possible that the trouble could be confined to Boston, it was difficult to say who really governed Manhattan—the Rebels, who ruled the streets, or the Governor, who had nominal control of the garrison but dared not set foot on the island.

Ordinary New Yorkers had to contend with food shortages and inflation, and depending on who was in charge at the moment, a shifting political landscape that could put them in jail if they were caught selling goods to the enemy—whoever that might be at any particular moment. The rich fled to their estates in the Hudson Highlands. The poor had fewer choices.

Q. I enjoyed your depiction of early American theater through Jenny Leighton and her aunt. What inspired your portrait of them?

A. Mercy Otis Warren was the inspiration for Jenny's character. Warren corresponded and shared political ideas with Thomas Jefferson, George Washington, John Hancock, Patrick Henry, Samuel Adams, and John Adams. Her satirical pamphlet plays, published anonymously, earned her a place on a British hanging list. After the war she wrote one of the earliest histories of the Revolution, but her portrait of prickly John Adams caused a falling-out between them and inspired him to opine that "History is not the province of the ladies."

Frances Leighton is loosely based on Mary Robinson, also known as Mary Randall, an early feminist, novelist, poet, actress, royal mistress, and longtime paramour of British cavalry officer Banastre Tarleton, who makes a discreet cameo while very young in *Mistress Firebrand*.

The Douglasses and the Hallams, America's first families of the stage, built the John Street Theater after the violence surrounding the Stamp Act destroyed their playhouse on Chapel Street in 1766. The riot in *Mistress Firebrand*, and the formation of a shadow company in the absence of the regular troupe, was inspired by incidents that took place in the 1760s. The Douglass-Hallam company spent most of the war in the relative safety of the West Indies.

Q. Severin Devere's background as the son of a Mohawk Indian and the wife of a British earl seems so unique. Is he also based on a historical figure?

A. Devere's origins were inspired by the life of Mohawk leader Joseph Brant, who was educated at Wheelock's Indian school, where he formed a lifelong friendship with Sir William Johnson, the British superintendent of Indian affairs. Brant's sister, Molly, became Johnson's consort, and had eight children with him. The Brants were raised in an environment that mixed Mohawk and English culture, and were influential figures in both worlds before and after the war.

Q. I love the way you contrast the two men: General John Burgoyne and General George Washington. You suggest that each epitomized the character of the men produced under the British monarchy versus the Colonial republic, and you make clear that Washington is by far the superior man. Can you elaborate?

A. Both men came from privileged backgrounds and both loved the theater, but Washington was cautious about money and devoted to Martha and her children. Burgoyne, though, tended to live beyond his means, and between campaigns in North America, he was seen in Bath with his future mistress, actress Susan Caulfield—while his wife lay dying at home.

Burgoyne himself died insolvent in 1792, leaving Caulfield and their four illegitimate children penniless, remarking characteristically in his will: "During a life too frequently blemished by the indulgence of one predominant passion, it has been a comfort to me to hope that my sensualities have never injured, nor interrupted the peace of, others." One doubts Susan Caulfield, whom he never married and who lost custody of her children to Burgoyne's family, would have agreed.

Q. Aside from George Washington, Angela Ferrers is the only other character who appears in all three books in the series. By now, I've come to admire her, fear her, pity her, and scorn her. Most of all, I find her fascinating. Please say that she'll appear once again in the next book, and that you'll begin to reveal the secret of her origins.

A. I promise that Angela Ferrers will be back in the next book, and we'll learn a little bit more about her in each installment.

Q. Can you tell us more about the Simsbury Copper Mine, where Severin is incarcerated? I grew up in Connecticut but had never heard of it, and was shocked to learn how inhumanely the Rebels treated their prisoners of war.

A. Simsbury was as bad as the infamous British prison hulk anchored in the Hudson, the *Jersey*, and predated it by three years. The first inmate at Simsbury was a burglar sentenced in 1773, but the mine quickly became a convenient place to incarcerate Tories during the war. It resumed being used, as a state prison, after independence and remained in operation until 1827.

Q. Was the murder of Jane McCrea an actual historical event?

A. Yes. It occurred roughly as related in *Mistress Firebrand*. McCrea was engaged to Jones, a loyalist, and was traveling to meet him and be married when she was captured by a party of Burgoyne's native allies. Exactly how she died— whether she was accidentally shot by her own people while being carried off, or was killed by Panther or another Wyandot in a dispute over who was to collect the bounty on her—has never been conclusively determined, but her death was a boon for Rebel propagandists, and the story has resounded through American art and literature ever since, most widely known from Fenimore Cooper's *The Last of the Mohicans*.

I first heard Jane's story in high school. She was a sidebar in an American history textbook, with John Vanderlyn's dramatic painting *The Death of Jane Mc-Crea* accompanying the text. It was the only image of a woman from the American Revolution that I can recall encountering before college.

Q. In addition to writing books and for TV shows, you're also a big reader. Are there historical novels that you've especially enjoyed recently? Or books that readers of your series might enjoy?

A. I find that my readers enjoy a lot of the same authors I do, and I only wish I could come up with a term to describe the qualities that they all have in common. I love a book with a strong female protagonist, a hint of romance, and a historic setting with the occasional dash of the gothic or supernatural. My favorite contemporary authors include Susannah Kearsley, Lauren Willig, Simone St. James, and Diana Gabaldon, and one of my favorite authors while growing up was Mary Stewart.

Q. Can you tell us a little about the next book in the Renegades of the American Revolution series?

A. The next book features a schoolteacher heroine and highwayman hero and takes us to the near-feudal manors of the Dutch patroons in the Hudson Highlands, who ruled their domains as effective lords of the manor during the seventeenth and eighteenth centuries.

QUESTIONS
FOR DISCUSSION

1. What did you most enjoy about *Mistress Firebrand*? Do you find the action or the characters more entertaining?

2. In *Mistress Firebrand*, loyalties to the British and Rebel causes are constantly shifting, and many in the populace play both sides. Many of those fighting for the Rebels are as ruthless as those fighting for the British. Compare this picture of the American Revolution with the one you were given in school. Has the book changed your perception of the war, and of our country's origins?

3. Discuss the life choices that Jenny and Severin have made before they meet each other. How do their choices change once they fall in love? Who changes more?

4. Were you surprised to learn how unstable New York's city government was during this period? Talk about the challenges that ordinary people might have faced living there. Have you ever lived in a place with an unsettling political instability?

5. Donna Thorland contrasts two men in positions of power—General John Burgoyne and George Washington. She clearly considers Washington to be the superior man. Do you agree? How do these men stack up against Severin Devere, Courtney Fairchild, and John André?

6. Knowing that her illness would shorten her life, Frances Leighton deliberately returned to the Colonies from England to "rescue" Jenny from her hometown and bring her to New York, where her talent for acting and writing might flourish. But she also agrees to send Jenny to John Burgoyne, knowing that Burgoyne will expect sexual favors in return for his patronage. Why is Frances willing to let Jenny sacrifice herself? Do you approve of her decision? And what do you think of Frances' choices in her own life?

7. Severin has mixed feelings for Angela Ferrers. Discuss how those feelings seem to shift during the novel. What does he think about her in the end? What do you think about her?

8. Discuss the role of Native Americans in the novel. Did anything about Donna Thorland's depiction of them, and especially of Severin's family, surprise you?

9. Washington believes that Jenny's seditious plays can play an important role in rallying the populace to the Rebel cause. Do you think the written word, whether in a play, a newspaper, or online, has the power to change public opinion today? Why or why not?

10. Does reading *Mistress Firebrand* make you curious to learn more about the American Revolution, or to read the other books in the series? How does the novel compare to other books, TV shows, or movies about the American Revolution that you've read or seen?

11. At the end, Jenny and Severin find a new way to contribute to the American cause. Do you have causes that you believe in? How have you chosen to contribute to them? What sacrifices are you willing to make?

12. If you lived in New York during the time of the novel, whose side would you be on—the Rebel or the British?

Look for Donna Thorland's next novel
in the Renegades of the American Revolution series.

In 1780, in the Hudson River Valley,
where wealthy Dutch patroons have long
held the land, a desirable young beauty with a
complicated past and a secret mission is waylaid
and taken captive by the son of an old enemy
who has become a dangerous revolutionary
and an outlaw highwayman. . . .

Photo by Peter Podgursky

After graduating from Yale with a degree in classics and art history, **Donna Thorland** managed architecture and interpretation at the Peabody Essex Museum in Salem for several years. She then earned an MFA in film production from the University of Southern California School of Cinematic Arts. She has been a Disney/ABC Television Writing Fellow and a WGA Writer Access Project Honoree, and has written for the TV shows *Cupid* and *Tron: Uprising*. She is the director of several award-winning short films, with her most recent project having aired on WNET Channel 13. Her fiction has appeared in *Alfred Hitchcock's Mystery Magazine*. Donna is married, has one cat, and splits her time between Los Angeles and Salem, Massachusetts.